# FIRE
# SPELL

# FIRE SPELL

OR
SPLENDOURS AND GLOOMS

## Laura Amy Schlitz

LONDON  NEW DELHI  NEW YORK  SYDNEY

Bloomsbury Publishing, London, New Delhi, New York and Sydney

First published in Great Britain in September 2012 by
Bloomsbury Publishing Plc, 50 Bedford Square, London, WC1B 3DP

First published in the USA in August 2012 by
Candlewick Press, 99 Dover Street, Somerville, Massachusetts 02144

A CIP catalogue record for this book is available from the British Library

ISBN 978 1 4088 2621 8

Printed in Great Britain by Clays Ltd, St Ives Plc, Bungay, Suffolk

1 3 5 7 9 10 8 6 4 2

www.bloomsbury.com

*And others came . . . Desires and Adorations,*

*Wingèd Persuasions, and veiled Destinies,*

*Splendours and Glooms, and glimmering Incarnations*

*Of hopes and fears, and twilight Phantasies;*

*And Sorrow, with her family of Sighs,*

*And Pleasure, blind with tears, led by the gleam*

*Of her own dying smile instead of eyes,*

*Came in slow pomp; – the moving pomp might seem*

*Like pageantry of mist on an autumnal stream.*

(Percy Bysshe Shelley, *Adonais*, canto 13)

# Prologue

# Fire

The witch burned. She tossed in a sea of blankets, dizzy with heat. It was fever, not fire, that tormented her, fever and the nightmares that came with it.

She opened her eyes, breathing hard. There was no smell of smoke, no crackle of flame. Her doom had not yet come.

A brass monkey with a hideous face hung on a cord above her head. She curled her fingers around the monkey's body and jerked. The bed curtains opened. Outside them, the candles in the wall brackets burned steadily. Cassandra was glad of that. Now that she had reached the end of her life, she was a child again and feared the dark.

She heaved herself out of bed and stumbled to the wash-stand. She splashed herself with cold water, drenching the front of her nightdress. Her fingers went to the filigree locket and the gold chain around her neck. She wished she could take the locket off and cool it in the water.

But the clasp of the chain was tiny and her fingers were

swollen. Cassandra heaved a great sigh and sank on to the stool beside her dressing table.

It was the stone within the locket that burned her. She kept it caged inside the gold filigree: a fire opal the size of a crow's egg, blood red, veined with ribbons of changing colour. For seventy years she had cherished it. Now it fed upon her, burning her and sapping her strength.

*In former times, it was called the phoenix-stone –*

Cassandra's head jerked up. The room was empty, but the words were as clear as if the speaker stood at her elbow. It was the voice of Gaspare Grisini, her fellow magician.

*You have no idea how dangerous it is. You possess it now, but in time it will possess you. It will burn you alive. In former times, it was called the phoenix-stone –*

Cassandra dragged her fingers through her matted hair. Grisini had been in her dream; that was why she seemed to hear his voice. She had dreamed of a dark city, a labyrinth of steep houses half drowned in fog: London, she supposed. Grisini had been there, smiling at her through the gloom.

The strange thing was that he had not been alone. There were two – or were there three? – shadowy figures by his side. Small shadows ... children? Why should there be children? Once again, she seemed to hear Grisini speak: *Like the phoenix-bird, it erupts in flames. I have studied its lore and found out its secret history. Its fire will consume you unless –*

Unless. He had spoken the warning nearly forty years ago, in Venice, but Cassandra recalled every word of their quarrel. She had spun round to face him, shouting, 'If the stone is accursed, why did you try to steal it from me? Gran Dio, but I will punish you –'

She had punished him. He had studied the Black Arts, and she had not, but she was at the height of her power and her magic was stronger than his. By the time she was through with him, the floors of the palazzo were sullied with his blood. Late though the hour was, she had rung for the servants and ordered them to remove all traces of it, but to no avail; Grisini's blood seeped into the pale marble and left a stain. She had sold the palazzo the following month.

*Its fire will consume you unless –*

Cassandra sighed. She wished now that she had let him finish his sentence. In her mind's eye, she seemed to see him as he looked then. Thirty-seven years ago – dear God, but he had been young! She had been forty-six and he had been twenty-three, maddeningly handsome, with his keen hawk's eyes and teasing smile . . . Her frown deepened. Grisini had not been young in her dream. He had looked every day of sixty: a ruined, seedy scarecrow of a man.

What if her dream was a true seeing? What if she had seen him as he was and where he was, in London? If her dream was to be trusted, she might send for him, and he would have no choice but to come to her. She could force him to tell her what he knew about the phoenix-stone. At the thought of seeing him again, her heartbeat quickened and she felt a tug in her belly that she recognised as hunger – not hunger for food but for something far more shameful and dangerous: love.

She recoiled at the thought. Love Grisini? She hated him. She had cursed him, and she was glad of it. Rather than ask for his help, she would burn alive. Better to let the fire opal consume her –

Unless she could destroy it.

A wild hope seized her. Perhaps tonight she might do what she had never succeeded in doing before. Her fingers shook as she pried open the filigree cage and set the jewel on the dressing table.

She looked around for an object with which to smash the

stone. Her eyes fastened on the silver hand mirror. It was heavy and the back was adorned with raised flowers: small, tight rosettes and pointed leaves. The tips of the rosebuds looked sharp enough to puncture the stone.

With one movement, she swept the dressing table clear of everything but the fire opal. A thin glass bottle broke, filling the air with the scent of roses. Cassandra snatched a handkerchief out of the drawer. She crumpled it, making a nest for the opal, so that it could not roll away. The gem seemed to dilate and pulse, like a beating heart.

The witch got to her feet. She set her left hand flat on the dressing table, bracing herself to strike the blow. With her right hand she grabbed the mirror, raising it high over her head.

Her muscles locked. For almost a minute, she stood frozen. Once the stone was destroyed, she would be powerless. She was old, and soon she would die. She knew she would die alone.

But not by fire. And she would die without asking for help from Grisini. That one humiliation she would be spared.

Cassandra clenched her teeth. Her arm cut through the air, slamming the mirror downwards.

But the muscles of her arm betrayed her. The silver mirror changed direction. It struck Cassandra's left hand with such violence that the mirror glass cracked. Four bones shattered and the back of her hand began to ooze blood from a dozen cuts.

Cassandra dropped the mirror. The pain was so great she could not breathe. She curled inwards, rocking, unable to utter a sound.

The fire opal flashed like the eye of a phoenix.

# PART ONE

# FOG

LONDON
Autumn 1860

# Chapter One

# Clara

Clara came awake in an instant. She sat up in bed, tingling with the knowledge that it was her birthday. On this very day, the puppet master Grisini would perform at her birthday party. If all went well, she would have tea with Grisini's children.

The room was dim. The curtains were drawn tight against the November chill. Clara gazed at them intently. If it was very foggy, Professor Grisini might not come. Everything would be ruined; her twelfth birthday would be like all the others, with a trip to Kensal Green in the morning and presents in the afternoon. Clara loved presents, but she dreaded the ceremony of opening them. It was ill-bred to show too much excitement, but if she wasn't grateful enough, she ran the risk of hurting her mother's feelings. Clara thrust the thought aside. This year she would do everything exactly right.

She flung back the coverlet and tiptoed across the nursery floor, noiseless as a thief. If anyone came in, she would be scolded for walking barefoot.

She reached the window and slipped her hand between the curtains. There were two sets between herself and the outside world: claret-coloured velvet on top, frilled muslin next to the glass. The muslin was sooty from the London fogs; though the windows fit tightly, the fog always found its way in. Clara leaned forward and peered through the peephole she had made. Her face lit up.

The view that greeted her was dismal enough. The trees in the square had shed their leaves, and the city was dark with grime. But the sky was white, not grey; there was even a wisp of blue sky between two clouds. It was a rare clear day. Professor Grisini would surely come.

Clara let the curtains fall back together and turned her back to the window. She padded past her sisters' dollhouse and her brother's rocking horse, which she was not supposed to touch. Close to the toy cupboard hung her birthday dress. It was covered with an old sheet so that it would stay clean, but she could see the shape of it, with its puffed sleeves and billowing skirt. It was a beautiful dress but childish; next year, when she was thirteen, she would wear longer skirts and a whalebone corset. Clara wasn't looking forward to that. Her present clothes were constrictive enough.

Footsteps were coming up the back stairs. It was Agnes, the housemaid. In an instant Clara was back in bed. She hoisted the blankets to her shoulder and shut her eyes.

The door opened. Agnes set a pitcher of hot water on the washstand and went to stir the fire. 'Wake up, Miss Clara.'

Clara sat up, blinking. She could not have said why she felt she needed to hide the fact that she was awake. Her secrecy was chronic and instinctive. She put her hand over her mouth as if to stifle a yawn. 'Good morning, Agnes.'

4

'Good morning, miss.'

'Agnes, I'm twelve.' The words came out in a joyful rush. 'I'm twelve years old today.'

Agnes knew it. No one in the Wintermute household had been allowed to forget that November the sixth was Clara's birthday. The servants had cleaned the house from top to bottom and decorated the dining room with white ribbons and evergreen boughs. Seventeen children had been invited to Clara's party, and their mothers would come with them. There was to be a lavish tea: sandwiches and ices and a four-layer cake.

'Many happy returns, miss.' Agnes twitched the corner of the counterpane. 'Now, get up. None of this lying about in bed.'

Clara had no intention of lying about. She wanted the day to begin. She drew back the covers as Agnes knelt by the bed and held out her slippers. Clara slid her feet into them and lifted her arms so that Agnes could put on her dressing gown. As the maid started to make the bed, Clara went to the washstand. She washed her face carefully, brushed her teeth and checked her fingernails to make sure they hadn't turned grimy overnight. 'Is it fine today, Agnes?'

Agnes left the bed to draw the curtains. 'Fine enough to have your party. Your Mr What's-his-name'll come with his puppets.'

'Grisini,' Clara said obligingly. 'The Phenomenal Professor Grisini and His Venetian *Fantoccini*.' She had memorised his handbill three weeks ago, the day she first saw him.

Agnes made a noise like *mffmp*. She had once been nursery maid to the Wintermute children, and she felt it gave her certain privileges – among them, the right to make noises when she felt Clara was being spoiled.

'I don't see what you want with foreign puppets, Miss Clara. English Punch and Judy is good enough for most children.'

Clara looked meek, but she objected. 'The *fantoccini* are different from Punch and Judy, Agnes. You'll see when Professor Grisini gives the show. They work with strings – only you don't see the strings. They're like fairies.'

Agnes gave the curtains a final twitch. Clara held out her comb, appealing for help. Clara's hair was as wild as Clara was sedate, and only Agnes could subdue it. Armed with skill and patience, Agnes could turn Clara's thatch of dark curls into twenty ringlets, ten on either side of a centre parting.

Agnes accepted the comb and went to work. Clara took her prayer book from the dressing table and opened to the section for morning prayers. She locked her knees and held her head still as Agnes dragged at the knots in her hair. Clara had once heard her mother's maid say, "There's many a grown-up lady that doesn't hold still like Miss Clara. Miss Clara's as steady as a rock."

Clara liked that. Most of the time when she eavesdropped, she heard about how spoiled she was. She supposed it was true. She made extra work for the servants, and her parents cosseted her, worrying endlessly about her health. Her father inspected the nursery weekly, using his pocket handkerchief to check for draughts, and the nursery fire was kept burning even in summer. Clara's birthday frock had been made by the finest dressmaker in London, and she knew her presents would be many and expensive.

What she hadn't expected was that her father would allow Professor Grisini to perform at the party. Since the moment Clara first saw the puppet caravan – and the children who worked the puppets – she had thought of little else. She had come upon the puppet stage in Hyde Park. It was a tedious afternoon, grey and chill, with patches of heavy fog. Her governess, Miss Cameron, had stopped to talk to a nursemaid from the other side of the square. The two women gossiped for half an hour. Their conversation was so dull that Clara gave up trying to follow it. She waited stoically, trying not to fidget. Then she glimpsed the caravan, shining scarlet though the fog.

She asked Miss Cameron if she could watch the puppet show and gained permission. She hurried down to the miniature stage, only to realise that she was watching the show from the wrong side.

It was even more interesting than watching from the front. She was seeing what no one was meant to see. She noted the two racks set up behind the stage, each hung with puppets, and the black curtain that covered the puppet workers' heads. At intervals, the puppet master would reach back without looking and nip a new puppet off the rack. The master's apprentice was so small that he stood on a wooden box. He was skinny and his trousers were ragged, but he was as deft as his master. Even from the wrong side of the stage, Clara could sense how skilful he was.

The third member of the party was a girl in her early teens. She was the only member of the company whose face Clara could see, and it was an interesting face: pale, pointed and wistful. The girl had long red hair and carried herself with the grace of a dancer. She provided the music for the show, switching back and forth between a flute, a tambourine and a small violin. From time to time she glided up to the backdrop and handled one of the manikins. The three puppet workers worked together seamlessly. Clara was fascinated. She wondered what it would be like to spend her days in the streets and parks of London, instead of learning lessons in a schoolroom.

She watched until the show came to an end. The audience applauded. The red-haired girl picked up a brightly painted box and went to collect the coins from the crowd. Clara fumbled in her purse until she found a half crown. She wished it was a sovereign. The red-haired girl accepted it with a little curtsy. She met Clara's eyes and smiled.

It was an extraordinarily friendly smile. Clara was struck to the heart. Improbable as it might seem, this girl – who was graceful and clever and older than she – liked her. Of the seventeen children who were coming to her birthday party, there was not one, Clara felt, who really liked her. They were the children of her parents' friends, who lived in Chester Square. Clara thought them dull, and she suspected that they pitied her and thought her queer. But the red-haired girl liked her. Of that Clara was sure.

She had scarcely had time to tell the girl how much she had enjoyed the show before the puppet master sidled over. He bowed before Clara, a florid showman's bow: knee bent, wrists cocked, toe flexed. A dirty handbill materialised between his fingertips. He stayed frozen in his jester's position until Clara ventured forward and took the handbill. There was something unnerving about the fixed grin on his face. Clara felt that in drawing near to him, she was being a little bit brave.

That night, she gave the handbill to her father and begged to have the puppets at her birthday party.

Dr Wintermute refused. Professor Grisini was a foreigner; foreigners were invariably dirty and often ill. Clara pleaded. Dr Wintermute said that the whole thing was out of the question. Clara, accepting defeat, did not argue, but she wept. That settled matters. Spoiled or not, Clara did not cry often. When she did, she generally got her way.

Thinking about the children coming made Clara forget to be as steady as a rock. She twitched, shifting her weight to the balls of her feet.

8

'Hold still, Miss Clara!' snapped Agnes.

Clara stiffened. She lowered her lashes and raised the corners of her mouth, so that she didn't look sullen. Neither Agnes nor her governess had any patience with sulking. Clara had, in fact, practised her present expression in the mirror. It was a neutral expression, a coy mask of a smile. Over the years, it had served her well.

'Your mother wants you dressed and ready to go by nine o'clock,' Agnes said after completing another ringlet. 'She said you should wear the blue cashmere and your sealskins. It'll be cold at Kensal Green.'

'Thank you, Agnes,' said Clara. The expression on her face was sweetly placid. No one must ever guess how much she hated going to Kensal Green.

'Cook's been busy all morning, decorating your birthday cake' – Agnes brushed another ringlet around her finger – 'and your mother had so many presents to wrap, she asked the maids to help her. I don't know what a little girl can want with so many presents.'

Clara hesitated. 'Agnes, do you know–?'

The words hung fire. Agnes gave one shoulder a shove. 'Out with it.'

'If she bought presents for the Others?'

Agnes took in her breath and let it out again. 'If you mean your brothers and sisters, yes, she did, Miss Clara, and there's no point in you staring down at the floor and pouting.'

'I'm not pouting,' Clara protested softly. She lifted her chin and resumed her doll-like smile. Her cheeks burned. She didn't want the Others to be part of her birthday. She was ashamed, but she couldn't help herself.

'You know how your mother is, Miss Clara,' Agnes said

9

firmly. 'It's like that going to Kensal Green. It don't change, and it won't change.'

Clara lowered her eyes to the prayer book. For a moment or two, she was silent, apparently reading. Then she raised her head. 'Agnes,' she said tremulously, 'there's something I want you to help me with. Something I want dreadfully.'

Agnes exchanged the comb for the brush. 'I'm sure I don't know what it could be, miss. I don't suppose Princess Victoria had as many frocks as you have, nor such toys, neither.'

Clara's stomach tightened. Once Agnes got started on how lucky she was, she was likely to go on a long time. There wasn't time to waste. She spun around. 'Please,' she begged, 'please –'

Agnes dropped the brush. Clara dived for it and held it out to her.

'What is it?' demanded Agnes.

'I want to give tea to the children,' Clara answered. 'Professor Grisini's children. You see, Agnes, that's why I wanted the puppet show so much – because of the children. There's a girl and a boy. The boy works the *fantoccini*, and the girl can play the flute and the fiddle. She was ever so nice.' She caught hold of Agnes's hands. 'I want to talk to them – just them – with no one else about; no grown-ups. They're so clever – they must know so many things I don't. Think of it, Agnes. They earn their own living!'

Agnes's mouth twisted. At Clara's age, Agnes had been a scullery maid. She saw no romance in earning a living. 'You know that's wrong, miss. Your mother wouldn't like it a bit. And what would your little friends think, having to take tea with common children like those Greaseenies?'

Clara shook her head. 'Oh, I don't mean that! Of course it wouldn't do to have them with the other children! But we could

10

have tea before the party, if you'll help. You see, Professor Grisini will be here to set up the stage at two, and the guests won't come till three. I thought perhaps – if the professor was given a hot drink in the kitchen, I could have a tray for the children.' She tugged at Agnes's hands. 'Please, Agnes! Just toast – and tea – and jam. And then, I've made them both a little parcel to take home – oranges and sweets. Please, Agnes!'

Agnes jerked her hands out of Clara's. 'I don't know what you'll take a fancy for next, Miss Clara. Taking tea with dirty foreigners?'

Clara sidestepped the question. 'They're not dirty,' she pleaded, which wasn't true; the girl had looked clean, but the man and the boy were very dirty. 'And they're not foreigners. The professor is, but the girl is as English as I am, and she talks like a lady. *Please*, Agnes.'

'Miss Cameron won't allow it,' Agnes said. She expected this argument to clinch the matter – there was no chance that Clara's governess would approve of Clara's mingling with common children – but Clara was ready for her.

'Mamma gave Miss Cameron a half day,' she answered. 'She's going to visit her sister in Islington and won't be back until three.'

Agnes tried another tack. 'You know how your father feels about people tracking dirt into the nursery –'

Clara interrupted her. 'They needn't come up to the nursery. We could take tea in the drawing room, where they set up the stage. I could watch them set up. Oh, please, Agnes!'

Agnes snorted. 'You're stagestruck, that's what you are.'

Clara switched tactics. 'If you're too busy,' she said daringly, 'I could carry the tea tray myself. I could put my pinafore over my birthday frock and creep down the back staircase and ask Cook –'

'You, miss!' exclaimed Agnes. 'Carrying trays! I'd like to see you, going up them steep steps with your hands full! Why, you'd drop the tray – and ruin your dress – and tumble downstairs!'

'I shouldn't mind if I did,' Clara said recklessly. 'I shouldn't – not one bit – if I could have tea with the children. Oh, Agnes, please help me!' She caught the maidservant's hands in hers. 'It's the thing I want most in all the world! And it's my birthday!'

Agnes pulled her hands free.

'Now, that's enough, Miss Clara. I suppose I can manage a tray around quarter after two – only it'll be for you, mind you, not for them. If you choose to share your tea with 'em, that's none of my business – and you're not to say more than you have to, if anybody should ask.' She put her hands on Clara's shoulders, barring Clara's embrace. 'I said, that's enough. You know your mother wouldn't like you hugging and kissing the servants.'

Clara didn't answer. Her ears had caught the sound of footsteps on the front stairs. The nursery door opened. 'Clara, dearest!'

Clara went to her mother. Mrs Wintermute was tall, shapely and dressed in black. Her face was youthful, though her light-brown hair was turning white. Clara embraced her tenderly, careful not to crush her mother's dress.

'Clara, dear, aren't you dressed yet?'

'No, Mamma. It's my fault, Mamma. Agnes told me to hold still so she could arrange my hair, but I wouldn't.'

Mrs Wintermute smiled forgivingly. 'I expect you're excited.' A faint crease appeared on her brow. 'You're rather flushed, dear.' She placed the backs of her fingers against Clara's cheek and then her forehead.

'I'm very well, Mamma.'

'It's the excitement, madam,' added Agnes.

Mrs Wintermute relaxed. 'Of course. Clara, dear, your papa was called out this morning, but he hopes to be home in time for the party. I hope you're not disappointed. We planned to give you your special present at breakfast.'

'I don't mind waiting, Mamma,' Clara said earnestly.

Mrs Wintermute held up her right hand. In it was a velvet box. 'Papa said we needn't wait – that I might give it to you now. We thought you might want to wear it to the party.'

Clara raised her eyes to her mother's face, received a nod of permission and took the box into her hands. It was round and soft, a desirable object in its own right. Carefully she slid her fingernails under the lid and opened it. 'Oh!'

Inside was a locket: a golden oval with a band of deep-blue enamel, a circle of seed pearls and a sapphire in the centre. Clara gasped with wonder. She tilted the locket and watched the sapphire flash; it was a deep, mysterious blue, almost black.

Mrs Wintermute smiled with her eyes full of tears. 'Open it.'

# Chapter Two

# Lizzie Rose

Lizzie Rose was hungry. As she pushed the puppet stage through the street, her nostrils drew in savoury odours from the street vendors: roasted chestnuts, baked potatoes and coffee. Her stomach growled, complaining that she had eaten nothing since breakfast. At noontime, Grisini had bought his usual sausage roll – she could smell the garlic on his breath – but he hadn't brought anything home. That was Grisini. Some days he came home with sausage rolls or meat pies and announced a feast, kissing his fingertips in praise of his own generosity. Other days, he crept off like a cat and slunk back satisfied, never bothering as to whether Parsefall or Lizzie Rose had anything to eat.

Lizzie Rose sniffed. Parsefall had eaten too. Underneath his dirty-little-boy smell, she caught a whiff of cabbage and fat bacon, spoils from their landlady's kitchen. He must have cadged something to eat from Mrs Pinchbeck. Lizzie Rose was glad for him – it worried her that Parsefall was so thin – but she couldn't help thinking that he was as bad as Grisini. He didn't share. If she had begged food from Mrs Pinchbeck, she would have given some to him.

The wheel of the puppet theatre caught on the kerb. Grisini, at the front of the caravan, waited for Lizzie Rose to lift it free. Lizzie Rose grasped the underside of the cart and jerked upwards. For the thousandth time she read the legend on the back: THE PHENOMENAL PROFESSOR GRISINI AND HIS VENETIAN FANTOCCINI. The letters were jet-black, adorned with gold curlicues. Lizzie Rose had watched Grisini repaint them a week ago. Grisini painted with his eyes half shut and his brush looping crazily: first the letters and then a canal scene of Venice, with winged lions and gondolas and a dancer in a black mask. The colours were weirdly bright and the letters almost too fancy to read, but the effect could not have been bettered. That, too, was Grisini: a bad guardian, a bad man perhaps, but a matchless artist.

'Foxy-Loxy,' hissed Parsefall, 'it's my turn to push.'

Lizzie Rose ignored him. She knew she looked like a fox, with her reddish hair and narrow face, but she wasn't going to put up with being called Foxy-Loxy. Her father had named her for a queen and her mother had named her for a flower. She tossed her hair over her shoulders, lips prim.

'Ain't you tired?' persisted Parsefall.

'Don't say "ain't,"' Lizzie Rose corrected him. She went on pushing the puppet theatre. The little caravan was top-heavy and the wheels were worn. Even with Grisini pulling it, it wasn't easy to manoeuvre. The two children generally took turns at the back end, but Lizzie Rose tried to make sure she had the lion's share of the pushing. Parsefall wasn't much younger than she, but he was considerably smaller, and to Lizzie Rose he looked frail.

Lizzie Rose worried about Parsefall. She had lived with

15

Grisini less than two years, and Parsefall was still a mystery to her. Five years ago, Grisini had taken him from the workhouse to serve as apprentice; before that, the boy seemed to have no past. He was skilful with the puppets and practised ferociously, almost if he was trying to get back at someone who had wronged him. Sometimes Lizzie Rose came upon him working the puppets with his legs crossed and a look of anguish on his face; he was so caught up with his work that he had forgotten to empty his bladder.

Except for his industry, he had few good qualities. He was selfish and rude, and his personal habits were disgusting. Nevertheless, Lizzie Rose loved him, as she might have loved a small wild animal she was trying to tame. She had a chivalrous tenderness for anyone weaker than herself and she knew Parsefall was often afraid. Lizzie Rose's sense of smell was extraordinarily acute, and the stench of fear was unmistakable. Parsefall reeked of it, especially when Grisini was in his darker moods. The boy had nightmares; sometimes such bad nightmares that he wet the bed.

'Come on,' Parsefall urged her obstinately. ''S'my turn.' He turned his back to her so that she could drag the canvas sack off his shoulders and ease it on to her own. He took the back handle of the puppet stage and began to steer it through the streets.

Lizzie Rose gave in. It was a relief to be able to walk without banging her knees against the caravan. She patted Parsefall's shoulder by way of a thank you. She knew that he disliked being touched, but she didn't care. She needed to pet someone, and nobody could pet Grisini.

They passed a tea stall. Lizzie Rose's stomach growled again. She felt in her pocket and found threepence. On the way home, the buns would be marked down to two a penny. Parsefall adored

16

buns. *It would serve him right if I didn't share,* thought Lizzie Rose, but she knew she would share. She would even keep a morsel of bread in her pocket for Ruby, Mrs Pinchbeck's spaniel.

She sighed. The takings from the puppet theatre had been poor lately. Grisini was surly, and she dared not ask him for money, but she and Parsefall needed many things that Grisini never bothered to provide. Parsefall's boots were riddled with holes, and his cleanest shirt was dark with grime. Lizzie Rose was tall for her age and growing rapidly; her frocks were much too small. The late Mrs Fawr had lavished love and skill on her daughter's clothes. They had been made of the best cloth she could afford, with tucks to let out and hems to let down. Now, a year and a half after her mother's death, Lizzie Rose had opened the last of the tucks and pressed the hem flat. The skirt was still too short.

Lizzie Rose thought wistfully of the days when she worked with her parents in the theatre. There had been times when there was little money, but her mother had always managed it so that she didn't look shabby. Lizzie Rose was a striking child, with her bright hair and transparent complexion. Her parents had taught her to carry herself well and to speak clearly. The Fawrs had not been rich, but they had been loving and comfortable. It had been a happy life.

''S'there.' Parsefall pointed. 'That's the way. Shortcut. Down that alley, and we'll come to Chester Square.'

Grisini jerked the wagon forward. Neither he nor Lizzie Rose questioned the boy's knowledge of the streets. Parsefall's sense of direction was unerring. He could find his way even through fog.

The little procession passed through an alley and came out into the square. There was a large garden, surrounded on four sides by tall houses. The garden, with its bare flower beds and iron fencing, was dreary enough on a wet November day, but Lizzie Rose could imagine how pretty it might be in the springtime.

She craned her neck to look up at the houses. They were tall and stately, with columns on either side of the door. The windows were heavily draped, but the rooms beyond them looked warm and bright. Whoever lived here had money enough for fires in every room and an army of housemaids to stoke them. Lizzie Rose tried to imagine what it would be like to live year-round in a house like this one, with ample coal in winter and a garden in the spring.

'Shall we knock at the front door?' Grisini flung out one arm as if about to declaim poetry. 'Shall we ring and present ourselves to the butler? Shall we say to him, "The children of joy have come!"?' Grisini spread his fingers like the sticks of a fan and touched his middle finger to his breast. 'Never forget that we, with our puppets and tambourines, are the children of joy! Let us go forth and bring laughter to the children of woe!'

Lizzie Rose and Parsefall exchanged looks of pure irritation. They knew very well that they would be turned away from the front door. Parsefall jerked his head towards the tradesmen's entrance, a half flight of stairs below the pavement. Lizzie Rose gave the wagon a shove, and Parsefall darted forward so that the two of them could wrestle it down the stairs.

# Chapter Three

# Parsefall

Never, thought Parsefall, surveying the Wintermute drawing room, had he seen a house better stocked with things to steal.

It had not been easy, getting the puppet theatre up to the drawing room. There was an outcry when it was discovered that the caravan was too wide to go through the tradesmen's entrance, and another when the housemaids saw that the wheels were caked with filth from the London streets. Hot water and brushes were fetched so that Lizzie Rose and Parsefall could scrub the caravan clean. While the children scrubbed, Grisini paid his respects to the Wintermute servants, fawning and coaxing by turns. By the time the miniature theatre was parked at one end of the drawing room, Grisini was quite at home, and the butler invited him to take tea in the servants' hall.

Parsefall knew what that meant. *Tea* meant gin and hot water; he and Lizzie Rose would have to set up the theatre by themselves. He shrugged off his jacket and turned to Lizzie

Rose. She was gazing round the drawing room as if it was fairy-land. 'It's very grand,' she said, almost whispering, 'ain't it?'

Parsefall eyed her askance. 'You said I mustn't say "ain't."'

'So I did.' Lizzie Rose smiled at him. ''Tain't elegant.'

Parsefall gave a sniff of disgust and turned away. One of the things that bothered him about Lizzie Rose was the way she was kind to him when he was doing his best to irritate her. He found it unnerving. Parsefall liked things to be fair: eye for eye and tooth for tooth.

The children began to set up the theatre. The front of the caravan pulled down, covering the wheels, and the sides unfolded like shutters, adding width to the miniature stage. Lizzie Rose unrolled the canvas that hid the puppet workers from the audience. Parsefall set up the puppet rack and hung the puppets on it. Lizzie Rose unpacked the contents of the canvas sack: a set of glass chimes, a tambourine, a tin sheet for making thunder and a small violin called a kit.

Parsefall eyed the clock on the mantel. There was plenty of time before the show. He would be able to set up perfectly – Parsefall was finicky about setting up – and still have time to steal something. He cast a furtive glance at Lizzie Rose. She had no idea what a skilful thief he was. Grisini wanted her kept in the dark.

The door opened, and a little girl came into the room. She stood aside as a maidservant in a black uniform entered with a tea tray. 'Thank you, Agnes,' said the girl, and the maidservant set the tray on the table and left the room.

Parsefall stared at the little girl. He didn't bother much about girls – it was well known that they weren't as good as boys – but this was the prettiest girl he had ever seen. She looked like a puppet of the very finest quality. Her eyes shone like blue glass, matching the colour of her sash. Her ringlets were as neat as quills of black paper, and her skin was as smooth as wax. And her dress! To Parsefall, who lived in perpetual dinginess, it was blindingly, impossibly white: a frothy confection that showed plump shoulders at one end and embroidered stockings at the other. But though Miss Wintermute was beautiful, she was not graceful. She held herself stiffly and moved as if by clockwork.

She made a slight, imperious gesture towards the tea tray. 'Good afternoon. How do you do?'

Parsefall jammed his hands in his pockets. Lizzie Rose spoke for them both. 'We're very well, miss. Thank you, miss.'

The little girl clasped her hands behind her back. 'I'm very glad to see you. I hoped you might have tea with me.' She sounded suddenly shy. 'We met in Hyde Park three weeks ago – I don't suppose you remember?' She paused as if she hoped they would answer. 'My name is Clara Wintermute.'

'I think I remember you,' Lizzie Rose said unconvincingly. Lizzie Rose was a poor liar. She didn't get much practice.

Parsefall looked impatiently at the tea tray. There were three cups and a dish with a folded napkin in it. He wondered what was inside the napkin. Something buttery, he hoped: crumpets or muffins.

'Do you?' fluttered Clara. 'I'm very glad. I admire you both so much – I wanted you to come for my birthday.' She gestured towards the table again. 'Do sit down. There's hot buttered toast in the dish – and strawberry jam.'

'We'd love tea, thank you,' Lizzie Rose said happily. 'Wouldn't we, Parsefall?'

Parsefall pulled out a chair and slumped into it. The two girls became irritatingly ladylike, murmuring courtesies about sugar and milk. Parsefall rested his elbows on the table and gnawed his toast. He knew better – Lizzie Rose was attempting to teach him table manners – but something about little Miss Wintermute made him want to be rude on a larger scale than usual. He slathered his toast with jam and sucked his fingers.

'This is ever so kind, miss.' Lizzie Rose set her teacup in the saucer. 'A cup of tea is always a treat, especially on a cold day.'

Clara spoke impetuously. 'Oh, please –! Won't you call me Clara? I know I seem –' She waved a hand, indicating the ornate room around them. Her cheeks reddened.

Lizzie Rose helped her out. 'My name is Elizabeth Rose Fawr. This is my brother, Parsefall.'

''M'not her bruvver,' Parsefall corrected her around a mouthful of toast. 'Me last name's Hooke.'

'He isn't my brother by birth,' Lizzie Rose explained, 'but we have the same guardian, so I call him my brother.' Her eyes went to one of the paintings on the wall. 'Are those your brothers and sisters?'

Parsefall looked at the painting. He had not examined it before, since it was much too large to steal. Now that he looked at it, it struck him as queer and therefore interesting. It was huge, with a gold frame full of swirls and little holes. Five life-size children stood together in a tangle of garden. The light suggested that it was early evening, and they had been gathering flowers. There were two girls with long golden hair. The taller of the two leaned against a broken column; the other held a small child on her lap and crowned him with a daisy chain. A boy with curly hair and laughing eyes stood next to a dark-haired girl with ringlets. It was evidently Clara Wintermute, but she looked younger in the picture, and as though she didn't quite belong. The other children stood like deer poised for flight; the air around their

22

bodies was faintly luminous, like mist or pale fire. Beside them, Clara looked dense and stiff: a wooden statue.

A little gasp came from Lizzie Rose. Parsefall looked back at the two girls. Something had passed between them. Lizzie Rose reached across the table to press Clara's hand.

'I'm so sorry,' Lizzie Rose whispered.

Clara shook her head violently.

Parsefall gaped at them, feeling as if a joke had been told and he'd missed the punch line. 'Wot is it?' he demanded.

'They're –' Lizzie Rose lowered her voice. 'They're in heaven, aren't they? I'm so sorry.'

'Wot?' repeated Parsefall.

Clara spoke brusquely. 'My brothers and sisters are dead.'

Parsefall considered this. His eyes went back to the painting. 'All of 'em?' he said incredulously.

Lizzie Rose hissed. 'Parsefall!'

'There was cholera.' Clara spoke hurriedly, as if eager to get the explanation over with. 'Quentin was just a baby. That's Selina by the column – she was the eldest. She was seven, and Adelaide was six, and Charles Augustus and I were five. He was my twin.' She hesitated a moment and plunged on. 'Papa thinks the contagion was in the watercress. I was naughty that day. I've never liked eating green things and I wouldn't eat the watercress at tea. So I wasn't ill, but the others died.' She bent her head and brought up one hand as if to cover her face. 'Of course, it was dreadful for Mamma. For Papa, too, but Mamma nearly died of grief.' She cleared her throat. 'It was seven years ago. I'm twelve years old today.'

Parsefall looked back at the picture. 'You're five years old in that?' he asked, jerking his thumb at the canvas.

'Not in that picture,' Clara told him. 'That was painted four years ago. Mamma had an artist come to the house – she wanted a picture of the way they might have looked, if only they'd lived. Of course we have photographs – and their death masks.' She indicated four white casts over the piano. 'Mamma says we must keep them alive by thinking of them all the time. We must never forget them or stop loving them.'

Parsefall stared at the death masks on the wall. 'Wot's a death mask?'

Lizzie Rose kicked him under the table.

'They take plaster,' Clara said very calmly, 'and press it over the – the dear one's face. And then later take more plaster and make a mask. That way –' She stopped and covered her mouth with her hand. She did not seem grief stricken so much as embarrassed.

Parsefall's eyes went back to the four white casts. 'That's nasty,' he said. 'Stickin' plaster on somebody's face wot's dead. It's 'orrible.'

Lizzie Rose kicked him a second time, harder. But Clara's blue eyes met Parsefall's. Something flashed between them. It was almost as if she said, *I think so too.*

'It's good to remember the dead,' said Lizzie Rose. 'My mother and father died of diphtheria a year and a half ago. It makes me sorrowful to remember them, but it's good too. I think of my father when I practise my music, because he taught me to play. And I sleep with my mother's Bible under my pillow. I have her ice skates and a pair of coral earrings set in gold. Of course, I'm too young to pierce my ears, so Mr Grisini is taking care of them for me. But he'll let me have them when I'm sixteen.'

Parsefall snorted. He had a very good idea how Grisini had

taken care of Lizzie Rose's earrings. He'd seen the ticket from the pawnshop. He pointed to the teapot, and Clara reached for it. 'Would you like another cup of tea?'

Both children accepted. Parsefall saw one piece of toast remaining, broke it in half, and gave part to Lizzie Rose. Lizzie Rose rolled her eyes at him to signal that this was bad manners, but Parsefall didn't care.

Clara took her last sip of tea – she hadn't had any toast, Parsefall noticed. Her eyes strayed to the puppet theatre.

'Would you like to see the puppets?' Lizzie Rose asked, and Clara's face lit up. 'Come and see.'

The children left the table – Parsefall with a piece of toast between his fingers. 'We carry them in bags to keep them clean,' Lizzie Rose explained proudly; the calico bags had been her own invention. 'The fog makes everything dirty. Before the show, we unwrap them and hang them on the rack –'

'The gallows,' Parsefall corrected her. He grinned ghoulishly at Clara. 'It's called the gallows. We 'ang 'em on the gallows, just like men.' But Clara was too intrigued to be squeamish.

'We have to set them up just so, because it's dark under the curtain,' said Lizzie Rose. 'I make their costumes – Grisini can sew as well as I can, but he doesn't like to. I just made a new frock for Little Red Riding Hood – isn't she pretty?'

Clara admired the puppet with her hands behind her back. She looked as if she was used to being told not to touch things. Lizzie Rose had an inspiration. 'Would you like to work Little Red? You hold her by the crutch – that's the wooden bit at the end – and pull the strings.'

Clara dangled the puppet. Timidly she jerked a string. One wooden leg kicked.

'The hardest thing is making them walk,' Lizzie Rose told

25

her. 'It's easy to make the *fantoccini* dance, but hard to make them walk – isn't that funny? I still float them sometimes – that's what we call it when their feet don't touch the floor. That's a sign of a bad worker. Let Parsefall show you.'

Parsefall took the Devil from the gallows and made him saunter towards Clara. The manikin had joints at the ankles; he walked with a swagger, but his wooden feet brushed the carpet with every step. Clara squeaked with delight and clapped her hands.

'Grisini and Parsefall do the figure working,' Lizzie Rose explained. 'I play the music. I'm not good enough to work the *fantoccini*, unless Grisini and Parsefall have their hands full. But Parsefall's good.' She laid a hand on Parsefall's shoulder. 'Parsefall has magic in his fingers.'

Clara looked at Parsefall's hands. She gave a faint start.

Parsefall understood why. His fingers were clever enough, but there were only nine of them. The little finger on his right hand was missing. There was no scar, nothing ugly to see. It was just that the little finger was not there. Parsefall didn't know what had become of it. He was almost certain he had once had ten fingers, and it tormented him that he couldn't remember what had become of the one he lost.

'You're so clever,' Clara said admiringly. 'Both of you. You know how to make the wagon into a stage and play music, and work the puppets.' She sighed. 'I wish I could do things.'

'I'm sure you can, miss,' Lizzie Rose soothed her, but Clara shook her head.

'No. I embroider, of course, and I can play the piano, but there isn't any use in it. Mamma doesn't like music, because it makes her head ache, and we have too many cushions already.' She swept the room with a glance that was almost contemptuous. It

26

reminded Parsefall of what he had intended earlier – to rid this room of one of the objects that crowded it.

'Would you like to help me take the rest of the *fantoccini* out of the bags?' Lizzie Rose asked, and Clara brightened at once.

'Oh, yes, please! May I?'

Parsefall hung the Devil puppet back on the gallows and turned his back. The two girls went on talking. The chirping, purring sounds in their voices seemed to indicate that they were becoming friends, but Parsefall paid no attention to their words. He was searching the room for something to steal.

What should he take? The room was stocked with valuables, many of them small enough to be portable. Parsefall knew what he wanted: something that would fit in his pocket without making a telltale bulge, something valuable but not so precious that its absence would be noticed immediately. He surveyed a table full of knick-knacks: a mosaic box, a wreath of wax flowers under glass, three china babies with gilded wings and an assortment of photographs in silver frames. Another table held a porcelain bowl full of dead rose petals, a prayer book with mother-of-pearl covers and more photographs.

One of the smallest photographs had a round frame with tiny pearls going around the edge. Parsefall eyed it speculatively. Pearls were worth money, and the silver was probably real. There were half a dozen other photographs on the table. That was good; the absence of one might go undetected for some time. He glanced at Clara and Lizzie Rose, saw that they were occupied with the puppets, and his hand shot out. Another moment, and the photograph was in his pocket.

# Chapter Four

# The *Fantoccini*

At half past four in the afternoon, Clara led her guests upstairs to the drawing room and invited them to seat themselves before the stage. The youngest children sat on the floor with Clara. Older children chose footstools, and their mothers sat on chairs assembled from all over the house. Clara's governess, Miss Cameron, shared a sofa with Mrs Wintermute. The servants in the back of the room watched standing.

Agnes dimmed the lamps, leaving most of the room in semi-darkness. The little theatre stood in a pool of light. One of the footmen coughed. The door opened, and Clara's father stole inside. Clara was glad. She had been afraid that Dr Wintermute would be too busy to see the show.

There was a rattle from Parsefall's tambourine, and Lizzie Rose played a weird little melody on the flute. The miniature curtains lifted and parted, revealing a painted forest and a wolf in a green satin frock coat.

The wolf tilted his head and began to speak. Gesticulating with one paw, he told the audience how hungry he was and how he longed for a little child to eat. He spoke so plaintively that Clara fully sympathised with him. Then Red Riding Hood took the stage. The little puppet in her red cloak was dainty and innocent; it seemed cruel that she should be the wolf's prey. Clara locked her fingers together, caught between warring desires. Around her, the audience was held in thrall. The children in the front row no longer saw the strings that worked the puppets. The miniature actors appeared to swell in size; their painted features looked as if they smiled and frowned.

Red Riding Hood was tricked, devoured and reborn by the axe of the hunter. The front curtain dropped, while Lizzie Rose played the kit and Parsefall changed the backdrop. The curtain lifted to reveal a Venetian street scene, complete with humpbacked bridges and moving gondolas. A handsome young puppet lamented his lack of money. A stranger with a plumed hat overheard his complaint and offered to sell him a magic bottle with a demon inside it. The Bottle Imp, he explained, would grant him all the gold in the world – only he must sell it before he died or risk the fires of hell. Ten minutes later, the hero lay at death's door, and the demon leaped out of his bottle with a clap of thunder. He was sea green, with horns sprouting from his temples and bat wings instead of arms. His countenance was so frightful that one little girl left her seat on the floor and plunged into her mother's lap.

But the play was not yet over. A maiden with golden curls nursed the hero back to health. In the end, the stranger with the plumed hat was tricked into buying back the bottle, and the hero married his golden-haired sweetheart. The children clapped lustily. Before their hands had stopped

29

smarting, the curtain rose again, and Lizzie Rose's fiddle played a lilting air.

A tiny ballerina tiptoed on to the stage. She was so light on her pointes, so perfectly balanced, that she might have been a fairy. Clara leaned forward, enraptured. She wished she could dance like that. Sometimes when she was supposed to be in bed, she danced in the dark nursery, twirling on half pointe and holding out the skirts of her nightdress. She wished that she could be a ballet dancer. She saw herself in pink gauze, with rosebuds in her hair, gliding like a swallow, leaping, fluttering, soaring ... Then her conscience rebuked her. Dancing wasn't proper, and it was her duty to stay home and be a comfort to her parents. Clara's breath left her in a sigh.

The dancer was replaced by a juggler, who tossed three balls into the air: green, lavender and silver. After the juggler came a tightrope walker – and by now even the grown-ups had forgotten that they were watching *fantoccini* and worried lest the manikin should fall and break his neck.

The final act was the strangest of all. The curtains parted to reveal a churchyard and a skeleton puppet. As Lizzie Rose played the kit, the skeleton jogged along happily, raising its knobbly knees and grinning. Then, with a trill from the fiddle, the legs parted company with the spine and sprinted to the opposite side of the stage.

The children gasped. Several tittered. Clara knelt upright, forgetting the children behind her. Both halves of the skeleton were dancing – and now the skeleton shattered a second time. The skull rose in the air, floating high over the arms and rib cage. It landed centre stage, the upper jaw jerking in rhythm with the tambourine. Clara pressed her fingers against her lips. She was shocked – and entranced – and tickled.

The children giggled. The music grew softer. With another trill from the kit, the skeleton's arms collapsed, making a pyramid of white bones. The legs buckled. Now it was only the skull that moved, clacking open and shut in a fiendish laugh. The white teeth gleamed. The spectacle was grotesque. It was –

Clara heard a strange sound: a cry of laughter that was almost a shriek. It took her a split second to realise that the sound came from her own throat. Her fingers tightened; she covered her mouth with all ten fingers, but it was no use. If she didn't laugh, she would choke to death. She opened her mouth for air. Another whoop escaped her. The children around her had stopped giggling. They were no longer watching the skeleton. They were watching Clara.

There was a rustle from the back of the room. Clara turned. Her mother was on her feet, making her way to the door. Dr Wintermute hastened after her. Horror stricken, Clara clamped her hands over her mouth. But the laughter within her was explosive, and knowing that she should stop – *must* stop – only made matters worse. Peal after peal escaped her. Tears blinded her, first warm and then cold upon her cheeks.

The children shifted restlessly. The skeleton onstage was reassembling itself: rib cage on top of pelvis, head on top of spine. Clara whimpered, bent double. Her sides ached.

The kit trilled its final note. In the silence that followed, the skeleton took a bow. The curtain fell. A few of the children clapped half-heartedly. Even the smallest child knew that Clara Wintermute had disgraced herself.

Miss Cameron stood up. She went to stand in front of the miniature stage, facing the audience. Her face was stern. 'I hope,' she said, 'that you have enjoyed the entertainment.'

There was a timid ripple of applause.

'Clara,' said Miss Cameron, 'you must thank your little friends for coming to the party.'

Clara took a deep breath and got to her feet. Her cheeks were wet and scarlet. 'Thank you,' she said hoarsely. She could think of nothing else to say.

Several of the children said thank you in return. Miss Cameron nodded towards the door and began to herd the guests downstairs to the dining room. A few soft thuds and rustles came from backstage. Parsefall and Lizzie Rose must be packing up the puppets. Clara followed her governess downstairs.

The servants rallied around Miss Cameron. Coats were fetched. Gloves were sorted out, slices of cake wrapped up, paper cones filled with sweets for the children to take home. In the midst of the leave-taking, two footmen helped Grisini bring the caravan down the stairs. Lizzie Rose and Parsefall trailed after it. Clara would have liked to wave to them, but she forced herself to speak only to her guests. She stayed close to Miss Cameron, uttering stock phrases of hospitality. She knew that the other children would talk about her as soon as they were out the door.

It was more than half an hour before the last guest left the house. Then Miss Cameron turned on Clara. 'What on earth possessed you? How could you laugh in such an unladylike manner?'

'I don't know,' said Clara.

Miss Cameron's frown deepened. 'Skeletons and cemeteries –! And in a house of mourning! Nothing could be in worse taste! You know how tender your mother's feelings are, Clara! Did you know that – that vulgar skeleton – was going to be part of the programme?'

Clara lifted her chin, glad that there was one point on which

32

she might defend herself. 'No, I didn't! Truly! That day in the park, I saw the show from behind. I didn't know –'

'Even so,' Miss Cameron interrupted, 'you laughed. And the way in which you laughed was improper. Aren't you ashamed of yourself?'

'Yes,' said Clara. Her cheeks burned.

'You had better go to bed. There will be no more festivities today. I will tell Cook you will not require dinner.'

Clara nodded. She had not been sent supperless to bed for many years. To have such a babyish punishment on her birthday was a double disgrace, but she supposed she deserved it. 'Yes, Miss Cameron. Only, please – before I go up to bed – oughtn't I to see Mamma?'

The governess hesitated. When she answered, the sharpness had gone from her voice. 'She may not wish to see you.'

Clara waited. After a moment, Miss Cameron inclined her head.

'You are right to want to apologise. Very well. You may go to your mother's room. After you have spoken to her, you must go to the nursery and get ready for bed.'

'Yes, Miss Cameron,' said Clara. She turned from her governess and began to mount the stairs.

# Chapter Five

# Grisini

Something glistened on the stair landing. Clara caught sight of it as she climbed the last three steps: something that shone against the dull carpet like a miniature sun. She bent down and picked it up.

It was a gold watch. Clara had never seen a watch quite like it. The dial was no larger than her thumbnail; it seemed to represent the full moon. Around it was a night sky made of black enamel, with two figures set against it: a golden wolf and a silver swan. The swan was suspended in midair, its wings outstretched. The wolf's jaws gaped, its teeth as thin as needles.

*'Madamina!'*

Clara's head jerked up. The puppet master Grisini stood in the doorway of the drawing room. She had seen him leave a quarter of an hour ago.

'You come *apropos.*' He swept off his hat and bowed. 'I want your eyes, Miss Wintermute – your keen, bright eyes. Come and help me!'

Clara hung back. She wasn't sure whether it was proper to speak to him. They had not been introduced, and she didn't know what *apropos* meant. She had a vague idea that *madama* was the proper title for an Italian lady; *madamina* might mean a little lady. She wasn't sure whether Grisini was mocking her or being very polite.

The puppet master stretched out his hands. 'I have lost my automaton watch. Your so-kind butler, Bartletti, told me I might come up the back stairs and search for it – but the light is dim, and my eyes are no longer young. Will you come into the drawing room and help me, little *madama*? It is very rare – *preziosissimo!* – my automaton watch.'

Clara hesitated. She had no wish to follow Grisini into a dim and empty room, but she could think of no polite way to refuse. Close at hand, she could see how disreputable he looked. His tattered frock coat glistened with fog, and there was a patch of sticking plaster under his chin. His words seemed to hang in the air: *madamina, apropos, preziosissimo, automaton watch* . . . ! But *automaton watch* was English and must refer to the object in her hands. Clara smiled with relief. 'I've just found it,' she said, and held out the timepiece.

In a flash he was at her side. He nipped the watch out of her fingers so swiftly that she never saw his hands move. 'Ah! There it is! *Attenti* – I will show you; six o'clock is about to strike. It is time for the wolf to frighten the swan – *guardate!*'

As if in response to his words, the figures on the watch began to move. The wolf's golden jaws gaped and snapped. The swan's wings flapped, allowing the bird to jerk upwards a quarter of an inch. There was a faint sound from inside the watch: a minute hammer striking a tiny gong.

'*Bau! Bau!*' Grisini mimicked it. 'That is how dogs bark in Venice, Miss Wintermute. Do you like it – my automaton watch?'

Clara wavered. She liked the colours of the watch, the richness of the gold and silver against the black enamel, but she pitied the poor swan, who could not fly away. Soberly she said, 'It's beautiful.'

Grisini nodded. '*Sì, molto bello.*' He cocked his head to one side, his eyes alight. 'Would you like it as a birthday present? Shall I give it to you, Miss Wintermute?'

Clara cried, 'Oh, no!' and clasped her hands behind her back. 'I mean, no, thank you. It's very kind of you – but I couldn't take it.'

'*Perchè no?*' Grisini shut his fingers over the watch and opened them again. His palm was empty. He laughed at her surprise, stepped forward, and flicked one of Clara's ringlets. The watch reappeared between his fingers. 'If I choose to give it to you, why not?'

'I don't –' Clara began, but the watch had vanished again. He snapped his empty fingers, and it gleamed in the palm of his other hand. He lost the watch a third time and discovered it behind Clara's sash; he produced it from under her chin; he bent almost double and brought it out from the hem of her skirt. He circled her, his hands fluttering, the watch winking in and out of thin air. Clara felt as if she was being tickled. She wanted to laugh. She wanted to scream.

'Perhaps you are afraid your mother will find out,' Grisini said softly. 'How shocked she was, a little while ago! Oh, yes, I saw! The boy works the skeleton puppet – so I watch – and I hear you laugh!' His grin widened. His teeth were black and yellow, like the keys of an old piano. 'But of course, she is shocked because you are laughing at death. Is that not so? *È vero!* But I say, Miss Wintermute, it is good to laugh at death –'

'I – I wasn't,' Clara stammered, 'I didn't –'

'You did,' he contradicted her. He set his forefinger in the narrow groove above her lips, commanding her silence. 'You have a brave heart, *madamina*.' His finger descended, grazing the lace on the bodice of her dress. Clara thought he was about to lay his hand against her heart, but instead he scooped up her gold locket and held it in the hollow of his hand.

'*Cosa c'è?* It is new, yes? A birthday present? Only I think you do not like it.' His mouth twisted in an upside-down smile, as if he was talking baby talk.

'I do like it,' Clara said desperately.

Grisini smiled at her dishonesty, clicking his tongue against his teeth. 'A very good sapphire,' he said in a pleased tone of voice. 'Siamese?'

'I don't know,' Clara answered. Her mouth was dry.

'The filigree work is well done,' Grisini observed. 'Not quite so well as a Venetian jeweller might do it but very fine.' He turned the locket to catch the light. 'It's the inside you don't like, yes?' He leaned closer. 'Open it up and let me see. I have shown you my treasure; now you must show me yours.'

Clara felt sick. Grisini, the puppet master; Grisini, the foreigner, had touched the lace on her dress and was asking to see inside her locket. Such things did not happen. She gazed at his wriggling, agile fingers and felt a throb of terror lest he touch her again. She yanked the gold chain over her head and held it out to him.

He accepted it gracefully and opened it to see the picture within. Against an ivory background was a weeping willow tree, less than an inch high. Each branch and frond was fashioned from snippets of human hair. 'Ah, so this is for mourning! The hair is from your dead brothers and sisters, I suppose.'

'How did you —?'

'Servants talk, I am afraid, and such a sad story begs to be told. *Povera* Clara!' He held out the locket so that she could take it back. 'But you were not made for weeping, little *madama*. You should laugh – as you did today – and you should dance. You *shall* dance.' He smiled. 'Shall I tell you how?'

His voice was gentle, encouraging. Against her will, Clara's eyes met his. It seemed to her that they were terrible eyes: the whites slightly reddened, the irises as opaque as granite. She could not look away.

'You are weary of mourning, are you not? You want to laugh and to dance . . . and there is something else, yes? No, do not deny it; I can see into your deepest heart. You carry a secret, don't you, *mia piccina*? Something that haunts you and makes you feel you are a very wicked girl . . . ?'

Clara stared at him dumbly. After a moment, she moistened her lips and whispered, 'Yes.'

'I thought so.' He nodded. 'Now, listen to me,' he said, and he lowered his voice still further. His whisper was so muffled that Clara could scarcely hear him. She understood nothing that he said and she did not try. The bit of sticking plaster under his chin moved as he spoke, and she wondered if it might fall off. She could smell the gin on his breath and the Macassar oil that stained his collar, but she did not step away. She stood as if she had taken root, trembling at first, and then still. By and by she was as calm as she had ever been in her life.

*Bau! Bau!* The gold watch was striking. Clara looked down and saw that it was back in her hand. All at once she realised that it was safe to come to her senses. Grisini had gone. The hands on the watch stood at half past six.

# Chapter Six

# Dr Wintermute

Dr Wintermute, I would be grateful if you would look in on Miss Clara.'

Dr Wintermute closed his book, marking his place with one finger. It was eight thirty at night and his first break in what had been a long day. He had been called out before dawn to deliver a baby and returned home just in time to see the performance of the *fantoccini*. At the end of the show, he had seen his daughter disgrace herself, casting his wife into something close to hysterics; before he could calm his wife, he had been summoned to treat an ill-tempered duchess with a stone in her kidney. When he arrived home, his wife was still distraught and his solitary dinner was overcooked. As he sat with his book before the fire, the last thing Dr Wintermute wanted was to be assigned a new duty by his daughter's governess.

None of this showed on his face. Like Clara, Thomas Wintermute could make his countenance a mask. He regarded

Miss Cameron with a look of courteous interest. 'What is the matter, Miss Cameron?'

'She won't stop crying,' answered the governess.

Dr Wintermute kept his finger inside his book. 'I should have thought that today's incident might teach Clara the value of repressing her feelings.' He frowned at Miss Cameron. He had hired her because he thought her stern common sense might balance his wife's excitable nature. 'Let her cry herself to sleep. I don't suppose it will hurt her.'

Miss Cameron did not seem satisfied. After a moment, she said bluntly, 'I don't like the look of her.'

Dr Wintermute set down the book. The simple statement, *I don't like the look of her*, was enough to set his heart hammering. Dear God, if the child was ill . . . He told himself there could be nothing wrong. If Clara had been anyone else's daughter, he would have said she was as strong as a little pony. But the nightmare of the past would be with him till the day he died. When the cholera struck, the children had been taken ill very suddenly. He remembered his wife's face as she wept over the bodies of the children he had been unable to save. As he followed the governess upstairs, he was praying silently, though he wore the same look of calm interest on his face.

Clara was in bed. She lay very still, with her clenched hands on top of the blankets. Dr Wintermute turned up the gaslight so that he could examine her. She looked more like a child who had suffered a shock than one who had misbehaved at a birthday party. Her pupils were dilated. Though her cheeks were wet, she held her facial muscles rigid, as if trying to demonstrate as little grief as possible. At the sight of her father, her chest heaved, but she did not speak.

'Now, then,' Dr Wintermute said soothingly, 'what's all this about, Clara?'

Clara gulped. 'Mamma said –' She could not finish the sentence but gazed at him with tears streaming down her cheeks. She tried again. 'Mamma –'

'Your mamma is in bed,' said Dr Wintermute, 'and you must be like her and go to sleep. Miss Cameron.' He raised his head to look across the room, where the governess stood. 'I think Clara should have a cup of hot milk with plenty of sugar and a teaspoon of brandy. Will you see to it, please?'

Miss Cameron answered, 'Yes, sir,' and left the room.

Dr Wintermute drew a chair beside the bed. He felt his daughter's forehead. Her skin was clammy, and her pulse was a little too rapid. She curled her fingers around his hand. 'Sit up and let me examine you.'

Clara sat up obediently. Her face twisted as she tried to cry without uttering a sound. Dr Wintermute bent over so that he could listen to her chest. 'Have you any pain?'

'No, Papa.'

'Are you dizzy? Thirsty?'

'No, Papa.'

'Have you a headache?'

'No, Papa.'

Dr Wintermute reached in his pocket for a handkerchief, only to recall that he had given his handkerchief to his wife. It occurred to him that he had spent the day ministering to female creatures, and all of them had cried. Clara, reading his gesture, dug under her pillow and drew out a handkerchief of her own.

'My dear, you must stop crying. You behaved badly today, but your mother will forgive you.'

'She won't,' said Clara. 'She told me so. I went to see her after the party – I wanted to say I was sorry – and she said that – that I insulted their memories and that God was punishing her – and the only child He spared her had a – a h-heart of stone.' A huge sob rose in her throat, making her shoulders jerk. 'She said she didn't think she could ever forgive me. She *said* that.'

Dr Wintermute winced. He did not doubt Clara's word. He knew the kind of thing his wife could say when she was beside herself. He often marvelled that Ada, who wept at the sight of a whipped horse or a malnourished child, could be so merciless with her tongue.

'She only loves the Others,' Clara sobbed. 'They c-can't do anything bad because they're dead.'

'Listen to me, Clara.' Dr Wintermute took his daughter's hands and squeezed them tightly. 'Stop crying and listen. Your mother loves you dearly. She should not have said those things to you.'

Clara gazed at him with startled eyes. Dr Wintermute felt a surge of guilt. He had betrayed his wife.

'But you must remember,' he went on quickly, 'we must all remember, how much your mamma has suffered.' He cleared his throat. 'Today wasn't your birthday alone, you know. Your brother Charles Augustus –'

'I know,' Clara interrupted him. 'He would have been twelve years old today. We went to Kensal Green, the way we always do, because it was his birthday, and we went in the mausoleum and cried.' She spoke the last word flatly; crying was an essential part of the outing. 'I hate the mausoleum. I hate seeing the caskets and the space on the shelf next to Charles Augustus – I hate looking at it and thinking that I shall have to lie there one day, all dark and dead and cold. And' – her face twisted, making her ugly in her father's eyes – 'my casket will be bigger than his, because I'm older, which isn't fair, because we're twins –'

'Clara,' Dr Wintermute said, 'please.'

Clara twisted her handkerchief. 'I'm sorry,' she said levelly, 'but it's every birthday and every Christmas and every Easter. And Sundays. And after we cry at Kensal Green, we come home and look at their pictures in the photograph album and pray and cry some more. And every birthday Mamma gives me presents from the Others.' She pointed to the table across the room. 'The lace collar and cuffs are from Selina and Adelaide. And Quentin always gives me chocolates. The toy theatre is from Charles Augustus.' She drew in a ragged breath. 'That was clever, the toy theatre – I *like* it. I miss him. He ought to have been the one who lived –'

Dr Wintermute stiffened. Clara had touched a nerve. He was ashamed of it, but he often found himself wishing that Charles Augustus had been the twin to survive the cholera. It was his most terrible secret. He loved Clara. He was quite sure he loved her, though he sometimes felt he didn't know her very well. But a man needed a son. Dr Wintermute had placed his dearest hopes in his firstborn son. Charles Augustus had been a promising boy, bright and strong and handsome. The deaths of baby Quentin and his other two daughters were deep wounds, but nothing was worse than the loss of Charles Augustus.

Clara's breath was coming in gasps and spasms. Dr Wintermute forced his attention back to his daughter. 'Clara,' he said, 'please stop crying.'

Clara averted her face.

'Your mother will forgive you in time,' Dr Wintermute assured her. 'You must remember' – with a twisted smile – 'you're the only little girl we have. Your mother loves you. As do

44

I.' He forced himself to lean over the bed and kiss his daughter's wet cheek.

Clara clung to him, pressing her face against his sleeve. He could feel her shaking. 'I ought to have eaten the watercress,' she said. 'If I'd eaten the watercress, I'd have –'

Dr Wintermute could bear no more. 'For God's sake, Clara!' he said. 'You must not say these things. You are making yourself ill.' He heard footsteps on the stairs: Miss Cameron was returning with the glass of hot milk. His heart lifted. All at once he could not wait to return to his quiet study, with its glowing fire and decanter of port.

He pried Clara's arms loose and stood up, smoothing his wrinkled coat. Clara looked straight into his face. Her eyelids were red, but her gaze was like a lance. Dr Wintermute had a sudden, uncomfortable conviction that she had seen into his soul. It was a look he was to remember often in the weeks to come.

# Chapter Seven

# The Women in the Mirror

November the sixth was also the witch's birthday. There were no parcels, no letters and no cake; Cassandra did not expect anyone to wish her many happy returns, and she would have been rude if anyone had. She saw no visitors but the doctor, who examined her mutilated hand and tried, once again, to explain that the safest course would be to amputate. Cassandra made use of her good hand to seize the tray of medicine bottles by her bed and hurl it at him. The doctor backed up, stammering apologies, and the servants hastened to show him out.

Exhausted by her tantrum, Cassandra fell asleep and did not awaken until after dark. The pain in her hand was sharper. It throbbed like a drumbeat, making her head reel. She felt like a wolf with its paw in a trap. She wished she had a wolf's courage and could bite off her hand at the wrist, separating herself from the pain.

She sat up and drew the bed curtains, craving cold air. Her thumbnail scratched at the filigree locket, feeling for the spring that would release the fire opal. At last she found it, and the phoenix-stone fell on to the counterpane. Cassandra rubbed it against her swollen hand, rolling it like a child playing with a marble.

The pain changed. It did not leave her but became a fierce and gnawing pleasure. Tears of relief filled the witch's eyes. Cassandra knew that the phoenix-stone would heal her. Underneath the swollen flesh, the bones were knitting. She fixed her eyes on the jewel as it tumbled and twirled.

The colours held her spellbound. For seventy-one years, she had gazed into the stone and never grown weary of it. Sometimes the coloured flames inside it were sharp edged, like sparks or crystals; at other times they were long and sinuous, like eels in a scarlet sea. No pleasure in her life could rival this: the glamour of the shifting colours and the dulling of her pain.

How could she have dreamed of crushing the stone? She had come close to losing it; she had wielded the silver mirror with force enough to shatter the metacarpal bones in her hand. If her arm had not changed direction, she would have lost everything: colour and power and healing. Cassandra shut her eyes at the thought. Then she cried out. Like a seam drawn tight, the skin on the back of her hand was puckering. The opal had raised a blister.

Cassandra shuddered. Then she steadied herself. She worked the fire opal into its filigree cage and shut the clasp. A wave of fever washed over her. She thrust aside the tangled bedclothes and hauled herself out of the bed, seeking the draught from the ill-glazed windows. She drew the curtains and gazed into the darkness.

Outside, the night was icy and serene. A gibbous moon hung above Lake Windermere. She saw its light shimmer on the surface of the water, and thought of how cold the water must be. She wished she were strong enough to leave the house and go down to the lake. The glacial waters would be chill and clean, and she had heard that drowning was painless. Whereas fire –

She shook her head. She was not the sort of weakling who killed herself. While she lived, she would fight. There must be some way to tame the fire opal before the fever consumed her. Even Grisini had said *unless*. There must be a solution, and he had nearly told her what it was. Once again she vowed to herself that she would not send for him; she would never humble herself to ask him for help. Nevertheless –

She turned from the window, catching sight of the mirror over the mantelpiece, and gasped aloud. The reflection in the glass was not her own. A young woman stood lashed to a wooden stake. A crowd of people surrounded her, faceless in the smoke. The woman was burning, and her mouth opened in a soundless scream.

Cassandra wondered if she was dreaming. She looked from side to side, seeking comfort in the presence of familiar things. Carved wood and red damask, gilded chair and dressing table, candlestick and washstand, and the lake outside the window . . . She was awake. She was not dreaming.

Her eyes went back to the looking glass. Another woman had appeared: an older woman this time, with wild hair and a haggard countenance. She, too, was burning – until the smoke blotted her out and the witch beheld a third woman: one whose face reminded Cassandra of her only childhood friend. The third victim of the flames was not Marguerite, but she resembled her: her long curls caught the blaze and soared upwards.

Cassandra raised her hands to block out the sight. Peering through her fingers, she stumbled towards the bed. She drew the bed curtains and dragged the blankets over her head. She squeezed her eyes shut, but the flames still danced, scarlet against the black of her eyelids.

# Chapter Eight

# At the Home of
# Mrs Pinchbeck

Grisini's landlady, Mrs Pinchbeck, was fond of pets. In her narrow house, comprised of three floors, she maintained five dogs, two cats, a parrot and a canary. Lizzie Rose loved dogs, but life at Mrs Pinchbeck's had taught her the melancholy truth that there could be too many. Since coming to live with Grisini, Lizzie Rose had taken it upon herself to see that the dogs were walked twice a day, but the results were not satisfactory. At least one of the dogs – Lizzie Rose suspected Pomeroy, the bulldog – was not housebroken, and the house was pungent indeed. It was also noisy: the lodger on the top floor played the trumpet, the cats waged war in the back alley, the canary was shrill, the parrot strident and the dogs yapped frantically whenever they heard anything, saw anything or smelled anything. The morning after Clara's birthday party Lizzie Rose slept through someone banging on the front door and the eruption of barking that followed. It was only when Ruby, the little spaniel that shared her bed, leaped to her feet and yapped, that Lizzie Rose opened her eyes.

'Shhh, Roo,' she said sleepily. 'Lie down, there's a dear.'

She patted the dog, feeling the tensed muscles under the silky fur. Ruby had begun life as one of Mrs Pinchbeck's dogs but had deserted her mistress when Lizzie Rose came to live with Grisini. Ruby was a morbidly sensitive dog, drawn to anyone in distress; Lizzie Rose, grieving for her parents, found comfort in the spaniel's love. In no time at all, the two were inseparable.

'Broken!' shrieked the parrot from downstairs. 'No good! No more! It's broken!'

Ruby continued to bark. There were strange men in the house. It was not to be borne.

'Lizzie Rose,' whispered Parsefall from outside Lizzie Rose's bedroom, 'it's coppers.'

'Coppers?' echoed Lizzie Rose.

'I seen 'em out the winder. I seen their big 'elmets.'

Lizzie Rose climbed out of bed and scooped up the spaniel. 'Hush, Ruby.' She stepped from her bedroom into the parlour.

What Lizzie Rose called her bedroom was in fact nothing of the kind. Grisini's lodgings consisted of two rooms: his private bedroom and a large parlour. Parsefall slept in a nest of blankets before the parlour fire. When Lizzie Rose joined the household, Grisini – with the air of one offering the jewels of the Orient – purchased a straw mattress and invited her to share the hearth with Parsefall. Lizzie Rose declined the honour. Since Grisini's parlour was cluttered from floor to ceiling, she built herself a little room out of rubbish. It occupied one corner of the parlour: seven feet square, with walls five feet high. The walls were made from old bits of puppet scenery, Grisini's former caravan, fragments of ancient furniture, a shattered bookcase, empty cartons and yellowed newspapers tied together with string. A broomstick draped with a sequined curtain functioned as a door.

Lizzie Rose kept the interior as tidy as she could. She swept out the dog hair and made her bed every day, smoothing the dingy quilt over the lumpy mattress. Though her room was far from elegant, she valued its privacy. She had twice caught Parsefall trying to watch her undress. Though she slapped his face for it, she didn't trust him not to do it again.

Parsefall was fully awake. He slept in his clothes, and they were grimy and creased. 'Grisini's down there too,' he said in a half whisper. 'He must've gone down to cadge breakfast from Mrs Pinchbeck. Then the coppers banged on the door, and she 'ad to let 'em in, didn't she? Grisini won't like it – 'avin' coppers in the 'ouse – and she won't, neither.'

'Policemen in the *house*,' Lizzie Rose corrected him, aspirating the *h*. She glanced out the window. The street was only partly visible. Patches of yellow-grey fog drifted and settled, blocking her view.

'Cut off your nose to spite your face!' screamed the parrot. 'It's broken!'

A shriek from Mrs Pinchbeck came from below.

'*Now* they've done it,' Parsefall observed, not without satisfaction. 'She's 'avin' one of her Spasms.'

Lizzie Rose sighed. Both she and Parsefall were familiar with Mrs Pinchbeck's main complaints: Palpitations and Spasms. Palpitations were eased by hot water, sugar and rum, but Spasms required gin. 'I'd better go to her,' she said reluctantly. 'I hid the gin bottle.'

Parsefall detained her, snatching at her wrist. 'What if they come up 'ere?'

'Don't worry,' Lizzie Rose said gently. 'They won't hurt us –' But Parsefall was not listening. He dashed to his bedding before the fire and attacked the bedclothes with frantic haste.

52

'Parse, they're not going to arrest you for not making your bed –'

Parsefall flung her a look of pure contempt.

'Come along, come along!' Grisini's voice was expansive. 'Watch the stairs, *signori* – they are treacherous! One false step and you'll break your necks!'

Lizzie Rose put Ruby down and withdrew to change out of her nightdress. She pulled a dress over her head and tugged on her flannel petticoat – there wasn't time for outer petticoats, but hers were too limp to make much difference.

'Parsefall!' shouted Grisini. 'Lizzie Rose, my jewel! Come and meet the gentlemen of the police!'

He sounded delighted. Ruby yapped lustily. Lizzie Rose buttoned her dress, shoved her feet into her boots and smoothed her plaited hair. She looked frowsy and it grieved her, but it was the best she could do.

Parsefall stood just outside the sequined curtain. With unwonted tidiness, he had rolled up his bedding and stashed it in the corner. Lizzie Rose fished for his hand and was surprised when Parsefall let her take it. His fingers were ice-cold.

The two policemen appeared fascinated by Grisini's parlour. The room was crammed floor to ceiling with trunks, casks and baskets, which were in turn choked with rags, crockery, rusted ironmongery, empty bottles, tools, brushes, papers and books. Disused string puppets hung from the ceiling: some naked, some bald, others missing an arm or a leg.

'Children, this is Sergeant Croft and Constable Hawkins of Sir Robert Peel's Metropolitan Police Force,' said Grisini. '*Signori*, these are my wards – Miss Elizabeth Rose Fawr and Master Parsefall Hooke.'

Lizzie Rose dropped a curtsy. Her father had told her

how to deal with policemen. 'Meek as a housemaid,' he had impressed upon her, 'and polite as a princess.' She raised her eyes and smiled as if the policemen were her friends. 'How do you do, sir?'

'The children will tell you all that you wish to know.' Grisini raised both hands and flicked his fingers open. 'My dear children, tell them the truth! Tell it all!'

Lizzie Rose and Parsefall looked at each other, puzzled. The constable spoke. He was a swarthy, muscular-looking man, but he struck Lizzie Rose as being friendlier than the sergeant. 'If you don't mind, sir, I'd like to talk to them alone for a bit.'

'Would you, by God?' Grisini sounded impressed. 'Magnificent! I shall await you downstairs!' He bowed to both men and sauntered to the door of the lodgings, swinging it open and shut with a flourish that would have won him an exit applause in any theatre.

Lizzie Rose sniffed. Parsefall was frightened, she could tell. She could also smell the constable, who had had sausages for breakfast, and who, if she wasn't mistaken, had a baby at home. Lizzie Rose smiled at him trustingly. Surely a man with a baby would not be unkind.

'All right, now.' Constable Hawkins countered her smile with a stern look. 'How old are you, girl?'

'I'll be fourteen in February,' Lizzie Rose answered promptly. 'And Parsefall's eleven,' she added, so that Parsefall would not have to speak. Parsefall's age was in fact open to question. No one in his past life had kept track of his birthdays, and Parsefall changed his age whenever it suited him.

'And what relation are you to Mr Grisini?'

'None, sir,' said Lizzie Rose. 'My father was David Fawr, the actor. He died of diphtheria two years ago – my mother too, and our troupe disbanded. Some of my father's friends wanted to take me, but they couldn't afford to keep me. Then one of the actors knew Mr Grisini –'

The constable had stopped listening. 'David Fawr?' he said eagerly. 'Why, I saw David Fawr as William in *Black-Eyed Susan*! I've never forgot him. The way he spoke that speech about the old apple tree –'

'Aspen tree,' Lizzie Rose corrected him. 'Yes, sir, my father was famous for that speech. People used to cry –'

Sergeant Croft interrupted them by clearing his throat. The constable looked as if he couldn't remember what to ask next. The sergeant prodded him. 'Start with yesterday afternoon.'

Constable Hawkins spoke purposefully. 'Miss Fawr, you spent yesterday afternoon in Chester Square, at the home of the Wintermute family.'

'Yes, sir,' agreed Lizzie Rose. 'We had a performance.'

The sergeant took a step closer to the children. 'One of the servants said you had tea with Miss Clara Wintermute,' he said. 'Is that true?'

Lizzie Rose met his eyes fearlessly. 'Yes, sir, it is. It was very kind of her, wasn't it, Parsefall?'

Parsefall raised his eyes and said curtly, 'Yes.'

'Didn't it strike you as uncommon, that a young lady like that should take the trouble to arrange a treat for you?'

'Oh, yes, sir, it was uncommon,' Lizzie Rose said warmly. 'There's not many a young lady as would be so kind. We had strawberry jam,' she added, and smiled at the constable, who smiled back.

'What did Miss Wintermute say to you?'

Lizzie Rose paused, remembering. 'She told us her name. And she said she'd seen one of our shows in the park, only we didn't remember her. We meet so many children when we do the shows. But Miss Wintermute remembered us and asked us to take tea with her. I think she was lonely.'

'Lonely.' The constable exchanged glances with the sergeant. 'Lonely enough to run away from home?'

Lizzie Rose looked startled. 'Run away from home? Oh, no, sir!'

'Did either of you invite her to come here?'

Lizzie Rose shook her head. 'No, sir.' She raised one hand, indicating the room around her. 'She was a young lady, sir. It wouldn't have done; it wouldn't, indeed.'

'Did she say anything – *anything* – about coming here to visit you?'

'No, sir.'

The constable sighed and tried again. 'Did she mention any friends – any plans she had – any places she liked to go?' Lizzie Rose went on shaking her head.

'Did she say or do anything out of the common?'

Lizzie Rose thought. 'She gave us presents,' she said. She appealed to the policemen. 'Let me show you.'

She let go of Parsefall's fingers and went back into her bedroom. A moment later she emerged with a handful of tissue paper.

'She gave us each a little packet to take home,' she explained. 'We each had an orange, a whole one, and a paper cone full of sweets. And she gave me ribbons.' She lifted a coil of ribbon and let the mingled colours fall in spirals. 'Green and blue and white – all the best colours for my hair. She'd only seen me once, but she remembered. She gave Parsefall presents too, didn't she, Parse?'

Parsefall assented glumly. 'Wooden animals,' he said resentfully. ''S'if I woz a baby.'

Lizzie Rose frowned at him. 'Hush. Her brothers are dead. She can't know what boys like.'

For the first time, Parsefall spoke to the constable. 'Did she run away?'

'May have done.' The constable said shortly. 'Housemaid went into her room early this morning to tend the fires. The young lady was gone. We've checked the houses around the square. No one's seen her. We wondered if she might have come here.' He looked around the room as if he expected to find Clara crouching behind an armchair. 'The servant girl said she was very interested in the puppets. Stagestruck, she said.'

Parsefall lifted his chin. 'She liked my skeleton act.' His voice was shaky, but his lips curled in a smirk. 'Laughed herself into fits she did. She wasn't much like a young lady then.'

Lizzie Rose shook her head so hard that her plaits swung back and forth. 'All the same, she wouldn't have run off without telling anyone,' she said firmly. 'It would be a cruel thing to do, after her poor mother lost the others. Miss Wintermute would understand that. She wasn't silly, and she wasn't a baby. She was twelve.'

'Her mother's distraught, that's for certain,' the sergeant observed, 'and her father's no better.' He turned from the constable back to Lizzie Rose. 'Are you sure she said nothing that might provide a clue?'

'No, sir. Could she – could she have been kidnapped?'

The two men exchanged glances again. It seemed to Lizzie Rose that they must have asked each other the same question. But the constable answered, 'It don't seem likely. No one broke into the house. The front door was unbolted from the inside. Windows were all secure – and nothing's missing, though there's plenty of value in the house.'

Parsefall raised his head. 'If you ask me,' he said, 'she didn't like livin' with deaders.'

'Debtors?' repeated the constable.

*'Deaders,'* Parsefall said staunchly. 'All them dead people. She was tired of 'em.'

Lizzie Rose squeezed his hand warningly. 'He means her brothers and sisters,' she explained.

'They was all over the 'ouse.' Parsefall dug his thumbnail into Lizzie Rose's palm. 'Dead pictures and dead-masks. They smear plaster on the deader's face to make the masks – did you know that? 'Orrible, I call it.'

'Parsefall –' began Lizzie Rose.

'All I'm sayin' is, I wouldn't want to be wiv 'em all the time,' Parsefall persisted. 'I don't blame 'er for runnin' away.'

'She didn't run away,' Lizzie Rose snapped.

Constable Hawkins turned to his superior. 'All the same, I'd like to take a look through the rooms.'

'She isn't here,' Lizzie Rose said. 'She wouldn't have run away, but if she'd come here, we'd know it.'

'There was fog this morning,' the sergeant said in a low voice. 'She might've started out somewhere and lost herself in the fog.'

'Very likely,' agreed the constable. 'Still –' He turned from the chaos of the room to Lizzie Rose. 'If you'll let me look behind that curtain, miss –'

'I sleep in there,' Lizzie Rose said, flushing. 'I'm afraid it's untidy.' She wished she had made her bed.

The constable waved her apology aside and ducked under the sequined curtain. Sergeant Croft scrutinised the room, gazing from one corner to the next. He opened a large trunk that contained puppets in their calico bags, and took apart a stack of wicker baskets to make sure there was no child hiding in the largest one. The constable came out of Lizzie Rose's little room and headed for Grisini's bedroom.

'It's *broken*!' screamed the parrot from downstairs.

The sergeant turned back to the children. 'Listen to me, both of you.' He sounded stern. 'You're to keep an eye out for that young lady. If she comes here – or you think of anywhere she might be – you run straight down the King's Road to the police station, you hear me? There might be a reward for you.'

''Ow much?' demanded Parsefall coolly.

'Half a crown,' answered the sergeant.

Parsefall, to whom half a crown was riches, shrugged. His fingers were still clammy. Lizzie Rose marvelled that he could be so frightened and yet so disagreeable. She rubbed her fingers against the back of his hand, trying to tell him that everything was all right.

The constable came out from Grisini's bedroom. 'There's no place anyone can hide in there,' he told the sergeant. 'I've looked in the wardrobe and under the bed. We can search the rest of the house, but my guess is we won't find her. She's out in the streets, lost in the fog.'

Lizzie Rose turned her eye towards the window. The fog was congealing; the buildings on the other side of the street had vanished into thick air.

# Chapter Nine

# The Other Time

After the policemen left Grisini's lodgings, they separated. Constable Hawkins set off to search the attics and question Mr Vogelsang, the trumpeter on the top floor. Sergeant Croft went downstairs to continue his interview with Grisini and Mrs Pinchbeck. From time to time, Lizzie Rose heard a stifled shriek. Evidently Mrs Pinchbeck had resumed her Spasm.

The children waited, straining to hear what was happening below. Parsefall built up the fire and crouched down beside it. Lizzie Rose replaited her hair and made a half-hearted attempt to subdue the clutter in the parlour. When the front door banged shut, they flew to the window.

The two policemen emerged from the house, followed by Grisini. He bowed to them, turned on his heel and headed down the street. The policemen set off in the opposite direction, their heads close together.

'They don't like Grisini,' Parsefall concluded. 'They think he's flimflammin''em.'

Lizzie Rose's thoughts were elsewhere. 'I hope they find Clara,' she said. 'It seems heartless to just go on with the day.'

'It don't seem 'eartless to me,' answered Parsefall. 'I'm 'ungry.'

Lizzie Rose wrinkled her nose at him, but she was hungry too. She reached into her pocket. 'Here's thruppence,' she said. 'You could get us each a penny loaf and some milk. And take the dogs.'

'Why do I 'ave to take 'em?' protested Parsefall, as he did every morning.

'Because if they don't go out and they make a mess, you'll have to clean it up. I cleaned up yesterday,' Lizzie Rose pointed out. 'And I'm the one Mrs Pinchbeck will want to talk to after her Spasm.'

Parsefall was out-argued, and he knew it. He was not skilful with Mrs Pinchbeck's complaints and Lizzie Rose was. He went to get his jacket. Ruby began to frisk around his feet.

'And carry Ruby on the stairs,' Lizzie Rose commanded. 'Her toenails slip out from under her and it frightens her, poor darling.'

Parsefall made a wordless grumbling noise but scooped up the dog. Lizzie Rose returned to her makeshift bedroom. She made her bed and put on the rest of her petticoats. Then she went downstairs to tend to Mrs Pinchbeck.

The staircase of the lodging house was dark and steep. The late Mr Pinchbeck had provided a handrail in the form of a rope screwed into the wall. Since Mr Pinchbeck had been dead nine years and the plaster was crumbling, Lizzie Rose had little faith in this contrivance. She descended cautiously, bringing her feet together on every tread. At last she knocked on the door of Mrs Pinchbeck's parlour.

'Come in, dearie!'

Mrs Pinchbeck lay on the sofa, scanning a newspaper. She wore a poppy-coloured robe and a soiled cap adorned with green ribbons. She had evidently found the gin bottle and was looking more cheerful than Lizzie Rose had expected. Lizzie Rose eyed her warily. Mrs Pinchbeck with a little gin inside her was rakish and lively, but Mrs Pinchbeck with too much gin was inclined to dwell on the day when Titus Pinchbeck, the only man she had truly loved, had been struck down by an omnibus.

Mrs Pinchbeck tossed aside the newspaper and clutched her heart. 'Oh, child!'

That was all Mrs Pinchbeck said, but it was enough for Lizzie Rose, who had spent her life in the theatre. From the deep, foghorn-y sound of Mrs Pinchbeck's voice, it was clear that a play was under way, a play in which Mrs Pinchbeck was the heroine. With light, dainty steps, Lizzie Rose crossed the threadbare carpet and flung herself on to her knees beside the sofa.

Mrs Pinchbeck stretched out her hand to Lizzie Rose. Lizzie Rose caught it and held it against her cheek. Both females turned their bodies away from the back of the sofa, offering three-quarter profiles to the far end of the room.

'Dear Mrs Pinchbeck,' Lizzie Rose said breathlessly, 'are you quite well?'

'Alas, poor child,' Mrs Pinchbeck replied, 'I wonder if I shall e'er be well again. Coppers – first thing in the morning!' She dropped her voice half an octave. 'And oh, child, the way they spoke to me!'

Lizzie Rose clasped her hands. 'How dare they, ma'am?' she cried, her voice throbbing with indignation.

'I don't know how they dared,' Mrs Pinchbeck said darkly, 'but it was something 'orrible – as if I was *common*.' She collapsed back on the sofa. Then a thought struck her, and she raised herself on one elbow. 'Dearest child! Did those fiends lay their wicked hands on you?'

'No, not at all,' Lizzie Rose answered. She almost said that the policemen had been very kind to her but remembered just in time that this was not that sort of play.

'All over the 'ouse, they went,' Mrs Pinchbeck said. 'I couldn't stop 'em. That sergeant wanted to see everything – kitchen and larder and coal cellar and all!' She lowered her voice. 'By the by, dearie, something's gone bad in the larder. I don't know what it is, but the smell is very high.' She waved her handkerchief under her nose. 'P'raps you could help Luce sort it out.'

Lizzie Rose's heart sank. Mrs Pinchbeck's larder was a torture chamber for anyone with a sensitive nose, and her maid-of-all-work, Luce, was the most dismal woman in London. Lizzie Rose made up her mind that cleaning the larder would be Parsefall's job.

Mrs Pinchbeck returned to the drama she was enacting. 'I couldn't bear those strange men lookin' at my boudoir,' she said with a shudder of feminine disgust. 'I've always been very delicate and modest in my ways. "You keep out of there!" I said, and I stood in the doorway. "Move aside!" the copper says to me! And I said to him, "You may cast me aside, you may dash me to the ground as a frail, weak woman, but never"' – Mrs Pinchbeck's voice sank impressively – '"*never* shall you cause me to tremble before you!"'

It was a superb moment. Mrs Pinchbeck thrust out her bosom and flung back her head. Lizzie Rose knelt upright.

Together they struck attitudes to create what was called (in the theatre) a Picture.

They held the Picture for a few seconds, so that the imaginary audience at the far end of the room could applaud.

'Dear Mrs Pinchbeck,' breathed Lizzie Rose, 'how brave you were! How pure!'

'He felt it,' Mrs Pinchbeck said with simple pride. 'I could tell 'e felt it. But that didn't stop 'im.' Her face darkened. ''E was too set on ransacking the house.'

Lizzie Rose's brow puckered. She forgot the scene they were enacting. 'It doesn't make sense,' she said. 'If Miss Wintermute ran away from home, she'd come to see Parsefall and me. She wouldn't hide in your boudoir or creep down to the larder.'

'They think she was kidnapped,' Mrs Pinchbeck said sagely. 'They think Grisini kidnapped her and 'id her in the 'ouse.' She took the gin bottle from under the sofa and poured a tablespoon into her glass. 'It don't matter,' she concluded, and drank. 'They won't find anything, any more than they did the last time.'

'The last time?' Lizzie Rose echoed.

Mrs Pinchbeck eyed the level of gin in the bottle, sighed, and pushed it under the sofa again. 'Must have been eleven, twelve years ago. It was just before I met Mr Pinchbeck and settled down. I was in Brighton, at the Theatre Royal – I was Angela in *The Castle Spectre* – and Grisini was playing at the Dome. We was staying in the same boarding'ouse. And this little boy went missing. He'd come to the Dome to see the *fantoccini*, and afterwards his nurse brought 'im backstage, because he wanted to see up close. And then – the next day it was – he went missing. Everyone thought Grisini 'ad something to do with it, because 'e was a foreigner. So the coppers come to the boarding'ouse. They was all over, poking and prying and asking their questions. But they couldn't prove anything, because Grisini never done it.'

The front door slammed shut. Lizzie Rose heard the sound of barking. Parsefall had returned with breakfast. The parrot, excited by the cries of the dogs, shouted, 'Ruination!' The canary burst into song, beginning with a series of earsplitting chirps and ending with a trill.

Lizzie Rose leaned towards Mrs Pinchbeck, not wanting to lose the thread of the story. 'But did they ever find him?' she said imploringly. 'Did they ever find the little boy?'

'He came back 'ome,' Mrs Pinchbeck said, 'but 'e was never the same after that. Next to an idiot, 'e was. That's what I 'eard. But it had nothing to do with Grisini, and soon afterwards, I met Mr Pinchbeck.' Her voice warmed as she began the familiar story. 'I 'ad on a white muslin gown with pink flowers and a parasol to match, and my 'air was in natural ringlets, as took two hours to put up in papers –'

The door opened. Parsefall came in, oppressed by dogs. Pomeroy, the bulldog, had attached himself to the boy's trousers and hung there, drooling. Punch, the rat terrier, leaped up and down like a hammer on a nail. Puck, the beagle, snarled at Parson, the pug dog, and Ruby was at the rear. The spaniel had caught the leash between her hind legs and was circling with one paw lifted, hopelessly tangled.

'Oh, poor Ruby!' cried Lizzie Rose, and went to rescue her favourite.

'I've got breakfast,' Parsefall said joyfully. 'I asked for stale bread, but the old lady at the bakery said there was only fresh. She said she'd give it to me 'ot an' cheap, if I'd just get the bloody dogs out of the shop.'

'How clever of you, Parsefall,' cried Lizzie Rose, 'and shame on you, using such horrid language in front of a refined lady like Mrs Pinchbeck!'

Parsefall blinked at her. Mrs Pinchbeck was charmed, as Lizzie Rose had intended, and assumed an air of mincing gentility. 'There's fresh dripping in the larder,' the landlady hinted, and Lizzie Rose clapped her hands. She had an unappeasable craving for meat in any disguise.

'Bread and dripping for breakfast!' announced Lizzie Rose. 'I'll run downstairs and put the kettle on, and we'll have a feast.' She reached under the sofa, nabbed the gin bottle, hauled the bulldog off Parsefall's leg and went bravely downstairs to face Mrs Pinchbeck's larder.

Clara slept. Never in her life had she known so dense a sleep: a sleep without dreaming, without the slightest twitch of finger or eyelid. She was as lifeless as a pressed flower. If she had been awake, she could not have said whether her eyes were open or shut. Her mind was empty, freed from guilt and terror and grief. Only the night before, she had spoken of her fear of cold and darkness; now darkness and cold claimed her, and she was not afraid.

# Chapter Ten

# The Photograph

That night Parsefall had a nightmare. It was Ruby who sounded the alarm, sniffing at her mistress's face and whining softly. Lizzie Rose heard Parsefall's laboured breathing and climbed out of bed. She drew a blanket around her shoulders, tiptoed out of her room and knelt down beside the sleeping boy. She wanted to rouse him before he screamed; Grisini did not like being awakened.

'Parse,' she whispered urgently. She took his hand and squeezed it. 'Parse!'

His eyelids lifted, fluttering. He flailed his arms and sat up, straining to see through the darkness. Ruby whimpered and tried to lick his face.

'It's just me,' Lizzie Rose whispered. She put her arms around him and drew him close. He was trembling so hard that her own heart beat faster. She steadied herself, taking deep breaths. If feelings could cross from one body to another, he must catch hers, not the other way around. 'I'm right beside you, Parse.'

Parsefall burrowed into her. She felt the heat of his breath against her shoulder and a few damp spots, tears he would never admit to shedding. Once, after one of his nightmares, he had bitten a hole in her nightdress. Lizzie Rose rocked him back and forth, stroking his hair. It felt greasy and smelled horrid. She tried not to inhale. 'You had a bad dream,' she murmured, 'but the bad isn't real. I'm here, and you're safe.'

For perhaps a minute and a half, they clung to each other. Then he pushed her away. 'Get off me,' he growled.

It occurred to Lizzie Rose that it would be easy to hit him. It would serve him right, and he was certainly within range. She pushed the tempting idea aside and reached for the poker. 'I'm going to stir up the fire,' she whispered. 'You're cold as ice.'

Parsefall wrapped his arms around his knees. He was still quivering, but he didn't argue. He watched as Lizzie Rose put coal on the fire and stirred the embers. As the firelight grew stronger, his narrow little face took on a different cast. By full light, he was a weedy, homely little boy, but now he was weirdly pretty. His hollow cheeks held the shadows, and his pale eyes gleamed silver.

'Now,' Lizzie Rose said briskly, 'what was your dream?'

She knew he wouldn't tell her. He never did. She wondered if he even remembered.

'Nuffink,' said Parsefall tonelessly.

'Do you want to go back to sleep? I'll sit by you.'

Parsefall didn't answer.

'Do you want me to tell you a story?'

She had him there. Caresses he spurned and sympathy he

could resist, but Parsefall loved stories. No one had told him stories in the workhouse. As a figure worker, he had learned the plots of Grisini's puppet plays, but he knew no others. He could not read and he resisted all Lizzie Rose's attempts to teach him his letters. But stories he loved. He said hungrily, 'Cinderella?'

Lizzie Rose smiled to herself. It was his favourite and her masterpiece. She had told it many times over and perfected each detail; if she was in the mood to describe every gemstone on the enchanted coach, or every ribbon on Cinderella's gown, she didn't spare him. 'Wrap yourself up,' she whispered, 'and I'll tell.' She reached for his quilt so that she could wind a cocoon around him.

Something fell from the folds of the cloth, striking the floor with a sharp *plonk*. 'What's that?' hissed Lizzie Rose.

Parsefall's hand moved rapidly, but for once Lizzie Rose was quicker. She snatched the object from him and held it close to the firelight. It was a photograph in a silver frame. 'Parse, where did you –?' Then she knew. 'You stole this!'

'Did not,' Parsefall said automatically.

'You did. You stole it from the Wintermute house. Oh!' Lizzie Rose recalled the frantic haste with which Parsefall had tidied away the blankets that morning. 'That's why you were so afraid of the coppers!'

Parsefall said, 'Woz not,' but without much force.

'You're a thief!' Lizzie Rose cuffed him. 'Oh, Parsefall, for shame!'

Parsefall switched tactics. 'They're rich enough,' he said defensively.

'Rich enough!' Lizzie Rose hissed scornfully. 'All their children dead, and you say they're rich enough! Have you no pity?'

'One of 'em's living',' Parsefall said weakly.

Lizzie Rose cuffed him again. 'Yes – poor Clara!' she said again. 'If she isn't kidnapped and she comes back home. Oh, Parsefall, how could you? Don't you know right from wrong?'

Parsefall opened his mouth and shut it again, as if realising that this was a dangerous question.

'What are we to do?' Lizzie Rose turned the photograph in her hands, reading the writing on the back. '*Charles Augustus Wintermute* – he was Clara's twin.' She brought the photograph closer to her eyes. 'Oh, Parsefall!' she wailed. 'He's in his coffin!'

'No, is 'e?' Parsefall took the photograph and peered at it narrowly. 'I didn't look that close. I thought 'e was sleepin'. He's a real little swell, ain't he?'

Lizzie Rose frowned at him. 'You shouldn't call him a swell now he's dead.'

'It ain't my fault 'e's dead,' Parsefall said, stung. 'They're all dead in that family.'

Lizzie Rose cuffed him a third time. Parsefall slapped back. He did not hit hard, but the blow served to discourage Lizzie Rose. She hugged her knees to her chest and let her head fall forward. 'Oh, Parse! What are we going to do?'

Parsefall shrugged. Then a look of naked fear crossed his face. 'Are you going to tell the coppers?'

Lizzie Rose shook her head. 'No. I don't know if they'd hang you, but they might. Or they'd put you in prison; I don't know which. I suppose' – she considered – 'we *might* send the photograph through the post. That way poor Mrs Wintermute –' She stopped. 'Oh, no, how horrid!'

'What's 'orrid?'

'Don't you see? If you were Mrs Wintermute – and Clara's still missing! – imagine how dreadful to open a parcel and find a picture of your son in his coffin!'

Parsefall said tentatively, 'There's the pawnshop.'

'There isn't,' Lizzie Rose snapped back. 'If you think I'm letting you get a single farthing from this photograph, you're mistaken. You've been wicked – not just naughty but wicked – and you ought to be punished. You ought to be whipped.'

'You can't whip me,' Parsefall said coolly. It was true. Lizzie Rose was taller than he was, but she wasn't strong enough to immobilise him and strike him at the same time.

'No, I can't,' Lizzie Rose admitted mournfully. 'Oh, Parsefall! What's to become of you? You can't read and you don't go to church, and you steal things, and you smell so bad. How are you to grow up to be respectable?'

'You ain't going to tell Grisini, are you?'

Lizzie Rose looked at him as if he had lost his mind. 'Of course I won't. I'm not a telltale. Anyway, Grisini would whip you too hard.' Her eyes flashed; for a brief moment she envisioned herself defending him from a furious Grisini. On the heels of that thought came another. 'Parse –'

'Wot?'

'Today – I was talking to Mrs Pinchbeck and she said there was a child that was kidnapped years ago. It was in Brighton. She said the coppers came after Grisini then too.'

Parsefall put one finger over her lips. He shook his head emphatically and pointed in the direction of Grisini's bedroom.

Both children listened. Grisini's snores were regular and even. 'He's asleep,' whispered Lizzie Rose.

Parsefall's answer was almost inaudible. 'What if he ain't?'

'Parsefall, do you know —?'

'Shhh.' Parsefall was gathering up the blankets. He layered one over the other, making a tent over their heads. Ruby, who was not the sort of dog who tolerated being shut out, clawed at the tent and made piteous noises. Parsefall muttered, 'Bloody 'orrible dog,' raised one corner of the blanket and let her in.

'Grisini don't like it talked about. It wozn't Brighton; it woz Leeds.' He counted on his fingers. 'Four years ago.'

Lizzie Rose protested, 'Mrs Pinchbeck said it was eleven years —'

'No. I remember it. It was winter and there was snow. We woz in Leeds, but we couldn't do the shows 'cos it woz too cold and we woz 'ard up. Then that girl went missin'. She was a rich man's daughter. The coppers came and questioned Grisini. There was talk of locking 'im up. But then the little girl come 'ome safe and sound. After that, Grisini 'ad money again, so we come to London and lived with Mrs Pinchbeck.'

'But that's *two* children,' Lizzie Rose whispered. 'A boy in Brighton, eleven or twelve years ago, and the little girl in Leeds. Parsefall, what does it mean?'

His breath was hot and sour inside the tent. 'Dunno. Only Grisini don't like it talked about.'

Lizzie Rose leaned closer to whisper directly into his ear. 'We ought to tell the coppers.'

Parsefall grabbed her wrist and squeezed it warningly. 'We can't tell the coppers,' he hissed. 'There ain't nuffink to tell. We don't know nuffink.'

'We know that Grisini knew two other children who disappeared. It must mean *something*,' hissed Lizzie Rose. 'Perhaps the coppers could find out what it is. It might help them find Clara!'

'Grisini would kill us,' Parsefall said desperately. He dug his

72

fingernails into her hand. 'If we peached on him, he'd kill us. You don't know 'im the way I do.' He heard his voice rise and lowered it again. 'Promise me you won't go to the coppers.'

Lizzie Rose gave a little shiver. She wasn't promising anything.

# Chapter Eleven

# Constable Hawkins

Five nights after Clara's disappearance, Constable Hawkins left the police station and headed home.

He walked rapidly but remained alert. The night was misty, and he knew how many people lost their way in the city's fogs; he had seen the bodies of men struck down by carriages and trampled by horses; he had examined the corpses of drowned Londoners who had fallen into the Thames. He made his way from street lamp to street lamp, keeping count of the cross streets as carefully as if he was blind.

The fog curdled and thinned. A nearby church tolled quarter past ten. A dog barked shrilly. All the sounds of the night – the clop of hooves, the grinding of iron-shod wheels on stone – were distorted by the moisture in the air. For a moment he thought he heard someone call his name.

A hand reached through the fog. 'Sir –'

The constable halted, pressing his arms to his sides to protect himself from pickpockets. He felt a surge of impatience. His wife was keeping supper for him, and he was hungry. He said gruffly, 'What is it?'

The fog receded, and he caught sight of the person who had touched his sleeve. A tall child with red hair, surrounded by innumerable dogs.

'Please, sir – it's Constable Hawkins, isn't it?'

The child spoke prettily, with just a trace of Welsh accent. All at once the constable knew who she was. 'Why, it's David Fawr's little girl!' he exclaimed. His face softened. 'What are you doing out so late, miss?'

Lizzie Rose dodged the question. 'It's good of you to re- member me, sir. I was wondering' – she stuck her foot in front of Punch, who was trying to mount Ruby – 'if you'd heard any news of Miss Wintermute. The young lady who was lost. I wondered if she'd come home.'

The constable's smile faded. The last week had not been an easy one. Dr Wintermute was a wealthy and important man. He had contacted the Home Secretary, who had made it clear to the police force that Clara Wintermute must be found soon and found alive.

'She has not,' he said shortly.

Lizzie Rose's face fell. She looked down at the leashes in her hand. She hesitated, and the constable took a step closer. 'Here, now, Miss Fawr! Is there something you want to tell me?'

Lizzie Rose met his eyes for a moment and then looked away. He took her arm and half led, half pulled her to the nearest street light. He stooped a little to peer into her face.

She looked tidier than she had the last time they met, though her efforts at sprucing herself up were rather sad. Her bonnet strings were new, and she wore a matching ribbon around her collar. The feathers on her bonnet were waterlogged, and her coat was threadbare.

'You followed me from the police station, didn't you?'

'No, sir,' said Lizzie Rose. 'That is to say – not exactly. I had to walk the dogs, you see, sir.' She averted her eyes, looking to the dogs for distraction. Pomeroy squatted and relieved himself heartily. Lizzie Rose, wincing a little, retreated to the utmost length of the leash. The constable kept pace with her. He spoke almost coaxingly.

'Now, listen to me, Miss Fawr! If you've something to tell me, I want to hear it. It don't matter what it is – I won't be cross. Just you open your mouth and let it out.'

Lizzie Rose raised imploring eyes to his face. '"If it were done,"' she quoted, '"then 'twere well it were done quickly." That's from one of Father's plays, and it's true. If there's something I don't want to do – cleaning up after the dogs or clearing out the larder – it's better to do it as fast as ever I can. So I thought I'd tell you that Professor Grisini – oh, it sounds like nonsense! – but there were other times when children disappeared, and he was there.' She took a quick breath. 'Mrs Pinchbeck told me Grisini was in Brighton eleven or twelve years ago, when a little boy ran away from home. And then Parsefall said there was a little girl who vanished – only that happened four years ago, in Leeds. And both times, the coppers – I mean, the policemen – questioned Grisini. They must have thought he had something to do with it. But in the end, the children came home again, so perhaps it doesn't mean anything, and I shouldn't trouble you. But I thought it was queer, sir.' She gulped. 'And I thought perhaps I should tell you.'

Constable Hawkins said slowly, 'And you thought right, Miss

Fawr.' He fell silent, digesting what she had told him. Grisini, with his foreignness and flamboyance, had made a bad impression from the first. During the last few days, Constable Hawkins had questioned the inhabitants of Chester Square and had found them above suspicion. The Wintermute servants appeared blameless. His thoughts had come to rest on Grisini more and more, if only because he had no one else to suspect. 'Perhaps we ought to search the house again.'

The girl took in her breath. 'Oh, but she isn't in the house! We'd know – Parsefall and I. And the dogs would know. If she was kidnapped, she'd have to be somewhere else. So I thought I ought to tell you that after the puppet show on Clara's birthday, Grisini didn't walk all the way home with us. We – Parsefall and Grisini and me – dragged the caravan as far as Wellington Square, and then Grisini gave us sixpence and told us to go the rest of the way by ourselves. That wasn't like him. The caravan's too heavy for just Parsefall and me – and Grisini doesn't hand over sixpence for nothing.'

'Did he say where he was going?'

'No, sir, but then, he wouldn't.' Lizzie Rose wrapped the dog leashes around her hand. 'Mr Grisini doesn't explain himself, not to us. He tells us what to do, and we do it. But I can't help wondering if he was looking for a place to hide someone. If he were a kidnapper, I mean. He'd need someplace to keep Clara hidden – a stable or an empty house, perhaps.'

The constable considered this. The girl's theory was far-fetched, but it was not incredible. There were plenty of half-wrecked houses in Chelsea where Clara Wintermute might be hidden. It might make sense to search them – and to have Professor Grisini watched and followed.

He dug in his coat pocket. 'I said I'd give you half a crown –'

It was a mistake. Lizzie Rose raised her chin and reproached him with her eyes. 'No, thank you, sir. That isn't what I came for.' She gave the leashes a jerk, gathering the dogs into a pack. 'Good evening, sir.' And by the time the constable had found the appropriate coin, she had gone, her dignity hampered but not overcome by her retinue of unmanageable dogs.

# Chapter Twelve

# November the Fourteenth
# at Kensal Green

Eight nights after his daughter's kidnapping, Dr Wintermute sat inside the family mausoleum, waiting to pay Clara's ransom.

From the outside, the mausoleum looked like a small Gothic church. Inside, it was cramped, dark and bitterly cold. Narrow shelves for coffins lined three of the four walls. Dr Wintermute sat on the centre platform, which had been erected for himself and his wife. One day, they would lie together in peace, surrounded by the children they had lost. Four of his children were already entombed here; whenever he turned his head, he saw the caskets that held their mortal remains. Dr Wintermute thought of how Clara had dreaded visiting this place, and he set his jaw. If Clara came back to him alive, he would see to it that she was never forced to come here again.

He had received an anonymous letter three days ago. The writer had instructed him to go to Kensal Green Cemetery on the fourteenth of November. Dr Wintermute was to hide himself in the family vault until dark, when the cemetery gates were locked. At midnight, he was to go to the road overlooking the Grand Junction Canal and listen for the sound of someone striking the brick wall with a stone. That sound would lead him to the proper place to cast the ransom money over the twelve-foot wall.

For the hundredth time, the doctor raised his hand to his breast pocket, checking to make sure that the packet of money was still there. Ten thousand pounds. It had not been easy to raise so large a sum without attracting the notice of the police. Dr Wintermute could only pray that he had been successful and that no police officer had followed him to Kensal Green. The kidnapper had warned him that any attempt to consult the police would be punished by Clara's death.

Clara's father was no fool. He understood that the arrangements gave every advantage to the kidnapper. Until the next morning, Dr Wintermute could not leave the cemetery. He would not catch so much of a glimpse of his daughter's captor; he had only the kidnapper's word that Clara would be released after the ransom was paid. Nevertheless, he had determined to follow the instructions in the letter. It had come with a spiral of glossy hair: one of Clara's ringlets. The sight of that curl had robbed Dr Wintermute of his last shred of common sense. He could think of one thing only: if there was any chance that Clara could be set free, the ransom must be paid.

A light glanced off the stained-glass window. One of the night watchmen was passing. Dr Wintermute's lips moved. Silently he counted to five hundred, allowing the man time to go away. Then he struck a match and glanced at his watch. Six forty-nine. He blew out the flame.

The time passed with infinite slowness. Thirty-four minutes

past seven. Seven minutes past eight. He would leave the vault at quarter to twelve. It was a five-minute walk, no more, but he must not be late.

He thought of his wife back in Chester Square. Ada shared his vigil. He could almost see her: silent, prayerful, with every muscle rigid and her eyes fixed on the clock. Her anguish over Clara's disappearance had been so great that he had feared for her reason. Then the letter arrived. The dazzling, improbable hope that Clara might be ransomed had changed Ada into a woman he had never seen. Her eyes were tearless; she was charged with energy and decision. There was only one thing to do, she stated: get the money and pay the ransom.

Dr Wintermute agreed. He had assured the inspector that if he received a ransom letter, he would contact the police. Now he broke his word, sacrificing his honour. He believed the kidnapper's threat. He dared not risk Clara's life.

His mouth twisted. Only a week ago, he had thought how little he knew his daughter. Now he seemed to know her through and through. Trifles came back to haunt him. He remembered the slippers Clara embroidered for him, and her frown of concentration on those rare occasions when he found time to play chess with her. He remembered the way she crept through the house on tiptoe when Ada had one of her headaches.

He searched for a happier memory. As a tiny child, he recalled, she was boisterous and robust, a juggernaut of a little girl. Agnes, the nursery maid, had complained of her naughtiness. 'Miss Clara's as noisy and bold as her brother, Dr Wintermute, sir. It's a fine thing for a boy to have spirit, but a little girl ought to be more quiet-like.' It was not long after that Clara became quiet. The deaths of her brothers and sisters had silenced her.

He thought of her face on the night she disappeared: her

swollen eyelids and the eyes that pierced him like a lance. He had feared then that she guessed his terrible secret, and the thought returned now to torment him. Had she known that in his heart, she must always be second to Charles Augustus? It had been true, but it was true no longer. If she came back to him, he would find a way to tell her so; he would clasp her tightly and tell her over and over how much he loved her.

He reached to make sure that the ten thousand pounds was still in his pocket. Clutching the money through his coat, he longed for his daughter and tried not to weep.

# Chapter Thirteen

# November the Fourteenth
at Strachan's Ghyll

The witch dreamed that she was lying on her funeral pyre. Veils of white-hot fire surrounded her, and the brass monkey capered in the smoke. He gibbered and bared his teeth at her. Cassandra moaned. The fire opal on her breast was so heavy that she couldn't draw breath.

She opened her eyes. The flames around her bed trembled, changing from fire to brocade. The curtains of the bed were drawn aside. Grisini stood before her.

He was young again, and somehow she was young too. He wore an embroidered doublet, like a prince in a fairy tale, and his eyes were tender, his smile dazzling. He stooped as if to kiss her mouth, but what he did was sweeter still. With infinite care he slid his fingers under the phoenix-stone, lifting the burden from her heart.

Cassandra cried out. Tears of relief spilled down her cheeks.

Grisini removed the stone from its cage of golden wires. He turned and passed it to the children who had gathered around her bedside. Cassandra croaked his name: 'Gaspare.'

The mantel clock chimed half past eight. Cassandra's eyelids opened. This time she was fully awake: alone, decrepit and in pain. The fire opal weighed upon her heart. Grisini was no fairy-tale prince but the man she hated above all others.

She sat up wearily. Why must she dream of Grisini? And if she must dream of him, why did she dream of him as her rescuer instead of her mortal enemy? She stared into space, pondering the question. Then she flung back the bedclothes and slid out of bed. She hobbled to her dressing table, opened the drawer and took out an iron key.

It had been days since she left her bedchamber, and months since she entered the Tower Room, which was her stronghold. Cassandra had built Strachan's Ghyll around the ancient tower, discarding the architect's warning that the structure was on the verge of collapse. She had cast her most elaborate spells from the Tower Room. It was her fortress and her laboratory.

She unlocked the tower door and bolted it behind her. Fumbling a little, she struck a match and circled the room, lighting the candles in the wall sconces. Panels of black lacquer and mirror glass hung from the walls, multiplying the light from every flame. Cassandra set the last taper in the wall bracket and crossed to the cabinet opposite the door. From it she took a crystal globe as large as a child's head. She set the crystal on the table and dropped into a chair, peering into the depths of the globe.

At first there was nothing to see, only a splotch of dim white – the reflection of her nightdress – and a constellation of tiny flames. Cassandra yawned. She had never been gifted at crystal gazing, and before five minutes had passed, she had given up the struggle to concentrate. Her eyelids drooped. Then her head jerked upwards and her eyes grew wide. A mist was rising inside the glass globe.

Inside the mist was a city – not Venice, with its soft colours and shimmering water, but London, with its lead-grey fogs; and in London, Grisini – not the enchanted prince of her dreams but Grisini as he might be now: cadaverous, seedy and no longer young. Beside him were three small and shadowy figures. Cassandra clicked her tongue in frustration. She could not understand what the children were doing there. But the crystal, unlike her sleeping mind, did not lie. If the crystal foretold the future, the mysterious children had some role to play in her life – and so did Grisini. Always she came back to Grisini, with his claim to secret knowledge, his damnable *unless*.

Cassandra shoved her chair back. She was too weary to think any more. She heaved herself on to her feet – and stepped back.

The mirrors around her were alive. Each mirror held a wraith of a woman, burning. The sheets of glass reflected the image over and over again, like coloured beads in a kaleidoscope. Cassandra lifted her hands to cover her eyes. The women lifted their arms with her. Each pair of blazing hands moved in rhythm with her hands. Each tortured face was her own – and as she recoiled from them, she smelled smoke.

Cassandra gave a great wild cry. Her hand flew to the locket at her breast. She shut her eyes and willed the vision – if vision it was – to *stop*. She told herself that it could not be happening – it must not happen, not ever; she must not burn.

She felt a breath of cooler air and opened her eyes. The figures in the mirror were no longer clear; as she watched them, they became translucent and drifted away like smoke. Cassandra let out her breath. It had been a waking nightmare, no more. There was still time to save herself from a fiery death.

She tightened her grip on the fire opal. It tingled as if it was alive and eager to serve her.

She opened her lips and spoke Grisini's name.

## Chapter Fourteen

# November the Fourteenth at the Juniper Bough

In the gin palace of the Juniper Bough, Grisini swayed and set down his glass. A red mist glowed around him; his skin prickled and felt hot, as if he stood before the mouth of a great furnace. Then the sensation passed.

He reached for his glass of gin. He had drunk scarcely a tablespoon, knowing that he must keep his wits about him. Now he took a large swallow, fixing his eyes on the clock across the room. It had stopped an hour and a half ago, as he had reason to know: he had tampered with the pendulum. If policemen came tomorrow and asked the landlady of the Juniper Bough what time he came or left, she would be unable to answer them.

He reached in his pocket and took out the automaton watch. It was almost nine o'clock, and he wanted to see the hour strike. He cherished a childish fancy that one day the machinery might jam so that the wolf could capture its prey. He imagined the tiny jaws tearing at the swan's feathers; he pictured drops of ruby-bright blood, smaller than grains of sand. He even wondered if such a drama could be engineered, if in all of London there was a clock maker who could alter the works so that the wolf might bite the swan.

He returned the watch to his pocket, reviewing his plans. In another quarter of an hour, he would head back to his lodgings at Mrs Pinchbeck's. There he would assume the disguise he had contrived and take a hackney coach westward, towards the cemetery at Kensal Green.

He congratulated himself on the excellence of his plan. He had chosen his victim well. Dr Wintermute could be relied upon to pay Clara's ransom; a man who had lost four children would stop at nothing to rescue the fifth. Not until the following morning would the doctor understand that his daughter was never coming home. It tickled Grisini to think that he had forced Dr Wintermute to spend the night in the cemetery where his children had been buried. It was a masterstroke, the kind of inspired touch that made Grisini an artist in crime.

He thought hungrily of the ransom money. Ten thousand pounds. Enough money to leave London and live abroad in luxury. Grisini tilted the glass so that the last drop of gin fell on his tongue. He missed Venice but dared not return there. The Venetian police bore him a grudge; so did the authorities of Austria and Spain. He had no wish to return to France, where he had been imprisoned for fourteen years. After weighing the remaining choices, he had booked passage on a ship to Madeira. He wanted the sun. He hated the northern winters, and he was sick to death of fog.

A wave of intense heat broke over him. He swayed, clinging to the counter for balance. One hand came up to his face, tracing a pattern of old scars: furrows where a woman had raked him with her claws. It had happened thirty-eight years ago, in Venice. He had nearly lost an eye.

The scar tissue tingled, but his cheeks were dry. The old wounds had not reopened. He blinked, and the red fog around him cleared.

He raised the empty glass to his lips. His hand was shaking. Why should Cassandra Sagredo summon him after so many years? The thing was unlikely, impossible. Why now, when he was happy in his thoughts, envisioning Madeira and ten thousand pounds?

He set down the empty glass and left the Juniper Bough. After the frowst of the gin palace, the cold of the streets was piercing. It seemed to Grisini that the fog had crept into his bones. He was not well. In the past months, he had been troubled by a hoarse cough and restless nights. He was afraid his lungs were not strong.

He was also deeply bored. Even the puppet theatre failed to amuse him. He was willing to abandon it and eager to be rid of the two children who worked for him. He knew he would never find a boy who suited him better than Parsefall did – the boy's hands were wonderfully deft – but he found he didn't care. He looked forward to a life of idleness, with servants to attend him instead of children.

'Gaspare! Gaspare Grisini!'

He stopped in the middle of the street. It was as if Cassandra had thrown a noose around his neck and yanked it tight. He felt her presence. He even smelled the scent she used to wear: a nauseous blend of myrrh and musk roses.

'Gaspare! I want you!'

He spun like the needle of a compass. If he did not obey her, she could make him bleed. He recalled the night they had parted, when she clawed his face and laid her curse on him. The blood had streamed from him, ounce after precious ounce, pint after pint, not clotting but flowing in eight crimson streams.

'You come, Gaspare! I summon you!'

He lurched forward as if she had released the halter around his throat. As he stumbled through the streets, pictures swam into his mind. He must go north. He would have to go to a railway station, and he knew which one; in his mind's eye, he saw the great arches and tunnels of King's Cross. He glimpsed his destination: a landscape of dark fells and silver lakes. A castle of red sandstone rose before him.

He heard footsteps. He imagined Cassandra tracking him, like Hecate with her pack of hounds, and he panicked. He spied a narrow alley to the left of him and ducked into it, wrapping his arms around his chest as if he could squeeze himself into invisibility. He realised that he was panting and shut his mouth to muffle the sound.

The footsteps passed.

Grisini stifled a gasp of relief. Once again, he touched his cheeks, making sure that the wounds had not opened. All at once he recalled his appointment with Dr Wintermute, and the ten thousand pounds he was about to lose. Ten thousand pounds! He could have screamed with frustration. Why must Cassandra summon him now? Another night – just one – and he would have ten thousand pounds –

His fingers curled into fists. If he could disobey her – for three hours, three little hours, just long enough to collect Clara's ransom . . . In the old days, it would not have been possible. But the witch had grown older; the power of her summons was not as strong as it had once been. Perhaps he could manage it.

He felt his pulse quicken. He had always been a gambler, and though his heart raced with fear, the situation was not without its savour. He turned his footsteps homewards and doubled his pace. He was so intent on his purpose that he was nearly home before he saw the man who followed him through the streets.

# Chapter Fifteen

# The Staircase

Parsefall was rehearsing. He was trying to learn the dance of the ballerina puppet, which Grisini had refused to teach him. Grisini was fond of taunting his apprentice; he was willing to admit that Parsefall had mastered the skeleton dance, but the ballet was more difficult, requiring the finesse of a true artist. The insult ate deep into Parsefall's soul. Whenever Grisini set off for the Juniper Bough, Parsefall took the dancer from her muslin bag and practised. He was determined to prove Grisini wrong.

He propped a mirror against the side of Lizzie Rose's bedroom, positioning it so that he could watch the puppet's movements. He would have liked to practise close to the fire, but Lizzie Rose had laid claim to that territory. She had hauled a basin of water upstairs and was heating a kettle on the hob. Parsefall rolled his eyes at her. Lizzie Rose's propensity for washing things struck him as insane. He was glad he knew better than to waste time like that.

He stood on a chair – he was shorter than Grisini, and the puppet's strings were too long for him. He lifted the perch of the little dancer, and she swung like a child on a swing. He waited patiently until she was still. Then he pulled the hand string. The ballerina raised her arms.

Parsefall began to hum the music of the dance, keeping his eyes on the mirror. He was dissatisfied: the puppet jerked with every move. Though she was beautifully balanced, she was rather light; if she was his, he would experiment with adding weight to her hips. He steadied her and relaxed his hands. The slow, supple movements, each melting into the next, required an almost superhuman delicacy and control. He swore under his breath.

'Don't swear,' said Lizzie Rose automatically. 'It's vulgar.'

'Vulgar be blowed,' countered Parsefall. He knew that Lizzie Rose was only pretending to be shocked. She didn't think swearing was as sinful as stealing or thumbing through Grisini's pictures of naked ladies. 'Listen, Foxy-Loxy, would you get the fiddle and play for me?'

'I'm not Foxy-Loxy,' Lizzie Rose said between her teeth. 'And I'm busy. I'm going to wash Ruby.'

Parsefall wrinkled his nose at her. The day before, Ruby had discovered the source of the foul smell in Mrs Pinchbeck's kitchen. The little spaniel had found a dead rat behind the stove and dragged it forth in triumph. Before eating it – and being extremely sick – Ruby had celebrated by rolling over and over on her prey. The smell was so vile that the dog had been shut in the cellar ever since.

'She'll 'ate it,' Parsefall predicted.

'She hates being alone in the cellar,' Lizzie Rose countered. 'She's been crying all day, poor thing.'

'I'm tryin' to *rehearse*,' Parsefall said in an aggrieved tone of voice. 'That's more important than washin' a dirty dog.'

Lizzie Rose rolled up her sleeves. 'You wouldn't think so if she slept in your bed.'

Parsefall shrugged, giving up. He tugged the string for the dancer's leg, easing her into an arabesque. The standing leg left the floor. He sighed and started over, humming creakily. By the time Lizzie Rose had the dog in the bath, he was beginning to make progress.

A door slammed downstairs. Parsefall dropped the puppet. The dogs in Mrs Pinchbeck's lodgings emitted an earsplitting series of barks and yaps. Ruby leaped out of the basin and raced around the room, spraying the carpet with water.

Parsefall yelped. The dog was headed for his puppet. He snatched up the dancer by one leg, forgetting what he had known since the age of six: a string puppet should always be picked up by its control. The strings tangled. Parsefall shoved the ballerina under a chair so that Grisini would not see.

The door burst open, and Grisini came in.

Parsefall saw at once that something was wrong. There was a sense of heightened alertness about the man, as if he was a predator about to spring. Parsefall kept very still. He fixed his eyes on the carpet so as not to draw attention to himself. He was poised to duck, dodge or flee.

But there was no need. Grisini passed between the children as if they were invisible. He strode into the bedchamber and slammed shut the door.

Parsefall let out his breath. He set his finger to his lips, cautioning Lizzie Rose to silence. He listened to the sounds in the next room. He heard rustles and thumps, the rasp of wood scraping wood, the tinny rattle of drawer pulls. He wondered what Grisini was searching for.

Lizzie Rose wiped her wet hands on her skirt and went after Ruby. She knelt down and forced the shivering dog back into the washbasin. Parsefall cocked his head, still listening. Impelled by some instinct, he went to the window and peered between the soot-stained curtains. When he saw the policeman across the street, he nodded. He spoke in a low voice. 'Lizzie Rose, there's a copper out there. 'E's watchin' the 'ouse.'

Lizzie Rose lifted her head. He saw the fear come into her eyes – fear and comprehension and a look of guilt. She whispered, 'Don't tell Grisini.'

Parsefall shook his head impatiently. ''E knows,' he hissed back. 'Don't you see? That's why –' He broke off, staring at her incredulously. 'God strike me dead, Lizzie Rose, you never went to 'em! You never told 'em wot Mrs Pinchbeck said!'

Lizzie Rose pointed to the door of Grisini's bedchamber. The doorknob was turning. The door opened, and a stranger came out.

Lizzie Rose uttered a faint cry. Parsefall stared. It took him several seconds to realise that the stranger was Grisini.

He had changed his clothes. Grisini's regular clothes were grimy and torn, but they had once been elegant; his tattered frock coat had been cut by a master tailor, and his hat was genuine beaver. The clothes he wore now made him look like a pauper. An overcoat woven of some heavy wool covered him from throat to knee. His boots were clumsy, and his trousers were frayed. The torn brim of a slouch hat cast his face into shadow.

And his posture had changed. He moved heavily, his shoulders bowed. His hands – Grisini's long-fingered, theatrical, gesticulating hands – hung from his wrists like a pair of empty gloves. Here was a beggar like ten thousand others: a man so cheerless and commonplace that no one would give him a second glance. Only the eyes were Grisini's: they were hawk bright and angry.

Grisini took Lizzie Rose's jacket from the back of a chair. He flung it down beside her. 'Go outside,' he said curtly. 'Go and walk the dog. There's a policeman on the other side of the street. You must distract him – speak to him – *fai la civetta*; play the coquette. Make him turn his back on the house.'

Lizzie Rose quailed. The colour drained from her face. 'I can't,' she faltered. 'Ruby's wet. She can't –'

'*Ubbidisci!*' Grisini's voice was a whiplash. '*Subito!* I need to leave the house – quickly and unseen. Obey me, or you will be the worse for it!'

'I can't,' Lizzie Rose said desperately. 'He won't believe me –'

Grisini's hand lashed out. His fingers curled like a hook, snagging one of Lizzie Rose's plaits. He yanked her to her feet so violently that she lost her hold on the dog in her arms. Ruby fell to the floor, squealing with pain.

'How do you know what he will believe?' demanded Grisini. 'What do you know of him?' He twisted both plaits around his hand and dragged her closer, peering into her face. There was a moment of utter silence as he glared into her eyes. Then: 'Have there been words between you?' he inquired, sotto voce. 'Have you betrayed me – *perfida, ingrata*!'

'No,' gasped Lizzie Rose. 'No!' Her voice rose to a shriek. Grisini forced her head down and slapped her viciously, striking at the back of her neck.

Lizzie Rose's knees buckled. Her hands went out to break

her fall, but Grisini jerked her to her feet. Ruby circled them, barking wildly. There was the sharp crack of a second slap. On the third slap, the ring on Grisini's finger cut into Lizzie Rose's neck. A long scratch appeared, beaded with drops of blood.

There was a queer, high noise, as piercing as a pennywhistle. Parsefall had no idea that it came from his own throat. He knew only that his whole body had been set in motion. He leaped like a cat on to Grisini's back, seizing him by the collar. Grisini shook him, but Parsefall tightened his grip, keeping the stranglehold. He swung forward, chest to chest with Grisini. One knee shot out and kicked hard, landing squarely between Grisini's legs.

Grisini swore. Parsefall tightened his grip and kicked again, aiming for the same place. He had learned to fight in the workhouse, and his methods were simple and vicious. He went on kicking until the puppet master doubled over. Then, like Ruby, Parsefall tumbled to the floor.

He was back on his feet in an instant. Lizzie Rose was at his side.

'Quick.' Parsefall seized her hand. 'Out.'

They swooped for the door with Ruby at their heels, and flung themselves headlong down the passage to the stairs. There was no time to strike a light or hold on to the guard rope, but it scarcely mattered. Neither Parsefall nor Lizzie Rose had ever been more sure-footed. They reached the ground-floor landing and hammered at Mrs Pinchbeck's door.

'Old Pinchbeck!' bellowed Parsefall. 'Mrs Pinchbeck, let us in!'

The door was bolted shut. Behind it, the dogs were enjoying a frenzy of barking.

'She's drunk,' Parsefall said bitterly. 'Damn her eyes, she's drunk. I should've known –'

'Parse –' gasped Lizzie Rose, and she pulled him around to face upstairs.

There was a shadow at the top of the staircase. Grisini stood there, swearing softly in Italian. At any moment, he would fly down the stairs and strike them dead. Parsefall flattened himself against the door.

What happened next seemed to happen very slowly. The children heard footsteps, followed by the sound of wood splintering: a crack like a pistol shot, knocks and thuds and a scream like a woman's. The stairwell reverberated like a drum. Then the sounds were muffled, duller: the thud of a man's body as it tumbled and slithered down the steps.

The door behind the children opened. Mrs Pinchbeck stood white-faced, with a candle in her hand. 'What 'appened?'

Parsefall answered at once. 'Grisini.'

'He fell. Down the stairs. We've killed him,' said Lizzie Rose, and burst into fresh tears.

'We might 'ave,' Parsefall said hopefully. 'He was after Lizzie Rose and she runned away. An' then he came after us and the stairs fell apart.' He strained to see up the dark staircase.

Mrs Pinchbeck put her hand over her mouth. The words came out between her fingers. 'He's fallen?'

'Down the stairs,' repeated Lizzie Rose.

Mrs Pinchbeck took a deep breath. The children watched her, prepared for an outburst. But when she spoke, her voice was surprisingly calm. 'I suppose we'd better 'ave a look at him.' She paused, gathering her thoughts. 'There's a looking glass on the chest of drawers in my boudoir. Go and fetch it. Don't let the dogs out.'

Parsefall obeyed. In a moment he was back in the hall with the mirror in his hand.

'That's good,' Mrs Pinchbeck said levelly. 'Now, if you'll hold the candle, we'll see whether 'e's still breathing.'

She pinched the skirt of her dressing gown and started up the steps, clinging to the rope with her other hand. Parsefall followed with the candle and the mirror. Mrs Pinchbeck stepped over Grisini's legs, squatted down and fumbled for his wrist, seeking a pulse. 'Now, give me the glass.'

Parsefall surrendered the hand mirror.

'His 'eart's beating,' said Mrs Pinchbeck. 'A little more light on the face.'

Parsefall raised the candle. The shivering light passed over Grisini's features. His face glistened with blood. There were a few curly hairs growing out of his nostrils.

Parsefall shuddered.

Mrs Pinchbeck adjusted the mirror so that the glass was beneath Grisini's nose. She stared down at the clouded surface. 'He's breathin',' she said in a bemused tone of voice, 'but he's bleedin' like a stuck pig. Which of you clawed 'is face?'

Parsefall curled his fingers into fists. He wasn't sure what he'd done during those frantic moments of attack. ''E's a bleeder,' he said evasively. ''E bleeds more'n other men.'

Mrs Pinchbeck wedged her hand underneath Grisini's skull. When she pulled her hand free, it was coated and dripping with blood. 'Ooof,' she said, wiping her hand on Grisini's coat. 'I suppose we ought to send for a surgeon.' She looked from Parsefall to Lizzie Rose. 'I don't suppose one of you children'd go? Seein' as 'ow I'm in me nightdress?'

Lizzie Rose gave a great sob and sat down as if her legs would hold her no longer. Ruby leaped into her lap and tried to lick her face.

'*I* ain't going,' Parsefall said defiantly.

Lizzie Rose buried her face in Ruby's coat and went on crying.

'Well, then,' Mrs Pinchbeck said, 'I suppose it'll 'ave to be me. It's a pity it's so late, because they always charge more if they come after dark.' She eyed the body dubiously. 'I suppose we could take 'im straight to 'orspital.'

'How'd we get 'im there?' demanded Parsefall.

Mrs Pinchbeck considered. 'We'd 'ave to get an 'ackney coach. An omnibus would be cheaper, but he'd bleed, and we'd 'ave to prop 'im up.'

Lizzie Rose gave a little gurgle of hysterical laughter. Mrs Pinchbeck eyed her narrowly. Then she hauled herself to her feet and descended the staircase. She went to Lizzie Rose and settled back down on the floor, pulling the crying child into her arms. 'There, now, you mustn't take on so. The surgeon may be able to put 'im right.' Then, ''Ere, now!' she said in quite a different tone of voice. 'You've a nasty scratch on your neck! Where'd you get that?'

Parsefall spoke up. 'Grisini slapped her. He was bashin' 'er about.'

Lizzie Rose pulled away from Mrs Pinchbeck's embrace. 'Parsefall defended me.' She smiled through her tears. 'He was as brave as a lion, Mrs Pinchbeck.'

Parsefall felt his lips draw back in a smirk of pride. He couldn't help it.

'That's a very good thing,' Mrs Pinchbeck said approvingly. 'Shame on 'im, striking an 'elpless female!' Her face hardened. 'Serve 'im right if he falls down the stairs. He ought,' she added incoherently, 'to 'ave 'eld on to the rope.'

'He was chasing us,' Parsefall explained. He squatted on his haunches and peered at Lizzie Rose. 'I nobbled 'im good, didn't I, Lizzie Rose?'

Lizzie Rose nodded vigorously. Then a cloud passed over her face. 'Where will we go?'

Mrs Pinchbeck looked blank.

'We can't go upstairs,' Parsefall explained. 'The staircase broke.'

'You can stay in my rooms for the night,' Mrs Pinchbeck said after a moment's thought. 'Lizzie Rose can share my bed, and you can sleep on the sofa.'

'Will you lock the door after you leave?' entreated Lizzie Rose. 'In case he wakes up – and is angry –?'

'I'll lock you in,' promised Mrs Pinchbeck. 'No matter what 'appens, you'll be safe from him tonight.'

# Chapter Sixteen

# The Morning After

Lizzie Rose was awakened by Mrs Pinchbeck's snores. She smelled the yeasty odour of spirits and saw a large blanket-covered mound beside her. At some point during the night, Mrs Pinchbeck had crept under the covers and oozed into the centre of the bed. Ruby, who had fallen asleep on the pillow, had moved to the floor.

Lizzie Rose squeezed her eyes shut and tried to go back to sleep. Her stomach felt queasy. As the events of the night came back to her, the queasiness increased. Grisini had found her out and struck her. Parsefall had rushed to her defence. The staircase had broken, and Grisini had tumbled down and hurt his head. At the thought of Grisini bleeding on the stair treads, Lizzie Rose began to tremble. She wondered why none of them had tried to staunch the bleeding. If they had, would it have helped him? And if they hadn't and he died, were they to blame?

She couldn't lie still any longer. The snores of the landlady struck her as jarring and even disgusting. Lizzie Rose eased herself out of the bed and tiptoed over to the washstand. She would have liked to wash, but there was no water in the pitcher.

She saw Mrs Pinchbeck's looking glass lying on the chest of drawers and picked it up. She twisted, trying to get the glass to reflect the mark on her neck. There was a long scratch that ended in a scab. She thought that her neck looked bruised, but in the dim room it was hard to tell. If she combed out her plaits, no one would be able to see the mark. Lizzie Rose wasn't sure whether to hide it or not.

She was ashamed that Grisini had beaten her, but she wanted someone to see what he had done and be angry on her behalf. She thought of what her father would have said, and her eyes filled with tears. Never in her life had she been treated so roughly. She had seen Grisini cuff Parsefall, but she had been spared such punishment. Lizzie Rose had never liked Grisini but neither had she feared him. Now she grew cold as she thought of what he might do to her once he recovered consciousness.

Ruby whimpered, pawing her knee. Lizzie Rose bent down and fondled the dog's ears, letting a few tears fall on the silky head. Then Lizzie Rose picked up her boots and tiptoed out of the room.

Her nostrils were greeted by an unwelcome smell. One of the dogs had misbehaved in Mrs Pinchbeck's parlour. The room was cluttered with newspapers and empty glasses and bits of clothing. The sofa looked like a rumpled sea of unmatched shawls, with three tousled spheres afloat in the chaos. One of the spheres was Parsefall's head. The other furry-looking circles turned out to be cats.

Punch leaped to his feet and began to bark. Pomeroy, Pug

and Parson swarmed forward. The parrot woke up and shouted, 'It's broken!' Parsefall stirred and began to damn somebody's eyes.

Lizzie Rose squatted, shushing the dogs. Then she sat down and put on her boots. After she had tied the laces, she opened the door leading into the hall and looked up the stairs for Grisini.

There was no body. Shadowy though the passage was, there was no doubt about that. There was only a great dark stain on the stairs and an array of lurid blotches and smears. Lizzie Rose felt her skin crawl as she stared at them.

A small hot hand gripped hers. Parsefall stood at her side.

''E's gone,' Parsefall whispered. His face broke into a bemused smile.

'Do you suppose he's in hospital?'

Parsefall shook his head, confirming Lizzie Rose's thoughts. Now that it was broad daylight, neither of them could imagine Mrs Pinchbeck doing anything as efficient as taking Grisini to the hospital.

'If he died, she might've called in the beadle,' Parsefall suggested. 'When somebody's dead, you call in the beadle.'

'Does the beadle take the body away?'

Parsefall shrugged. He didn't know.

'We ought to have done something to help him,' Lizzie Rose said in a hushed voice. 'We ought to have bandaged his head or –' She hesitated. 'Or poured some gin down his throat.'

Parsefall contradicted her. 'We couldn't.'

'Why couldn't we? Why didn't we think of it?'

'Because we couldn't bear to touch 'im,' Parsefall said reasonably.

Lizzie Rose remembered Grisini lying unconscious on the stairs. Her shoulders twitched in an involuntary shudder.

'You see?' Parsefall pointed out.

There didn't seem to be much point in arguing with him, so Lizzie Rose said, 'We ought to put a lamp on the stairs for Mr Vogelsang-on-the-top-floor.'

Parsefall shrugged again, as if to say she could bother with that if she wanted to. Lizzie Rose went back to Mrs Pinchbeck's lodgings, found a lamp, kindled it and positioned it close to the broken step. The bloodstains looked even more ominous in the lamplight.

'What'll we do now?' Parsefall asked her.

Lizzie Rose considered. The gnawing in her stomach was worse than ever. She wondered if something to eat would help. 'Why don't you take the dogs out and buy some breakfast? I'll tidy the parlour and see to the fire.'

'Ain't got no money.'

Lizzie Rose hesitated. She hadn't either, but she had seen sixpence on Mrs Pinchbeck's chest of drawers. She supposed they could pay it back once the stairs were safe to climb.

'We'll borrow from Mrs Pinchbeck,' she said. 'She'll be hungry too, when she wakes up.' She thought for a moment. There was nothing cheaper than bread and milk, but as always she longed for meat. 'You might buy a mutton pie.'

Parsefall, who had been about to argue about having to take the dogs out, shut his mouth at the mention of the mutton pie. In less than a minute he had pocketed the sixpence and collected the dogs.

Left alone, Lizzie Rose turned her attention to the dog's mess in the corner. She got rid of it, cleaned the canary cage and built up the fire. Once that was done, she circled the room, folding shawls and newspapers and retrieving a tray of sticky glasses and empty plates. She had a vague hope that tidying the room might make the world seem less chaotic. By the time Parsefall was back with the mutton pie, the parlour was transformed. The fire was bright, the worst of the clutter had been sorted through, and the table was set for three.

An hour later, when Mrs Pinchbeck emerged from the bedroom, the children had finished eating and begun a game of cards before the fire. They looked up from their game and asked, almost in unison, 'What happened to Grisini?'

Mrs Pinchbeck caught hold of the nearest armchair and staggered theatrically. Lizzie Rose leaped to her feet. 'Oh, Mrs Pinchbeck, I'm sorry! It's just that Parsefall and I have been so anxious – do sit down, and let me give you a slice of mutton pie!'

Mrs Pinchbeck sat down heavily. Lizzie Rose poured her a cup of milk and brought the last slice of pie. It was not a very large slice, but it had taken all Lizzie Rose's self-control not to eat it. Mrs Pinchbeck, who didn't seem to be feeling well, regarded it without enthusiasm. She glanced over at the table where the gin bottle had last sat. The bottle had been replaced by a china Cupid on a piece of paper lace.

'Please, Mrs Pinchbeck,' Lizzie Rose said, 'can't you tell us about Grisini? Is he in hospital? What did the surgeon say?'

Mrs Pinchbeck sighed. 'I don't know,' she said blankly.

'Don't know?' echoed Lizzie Rose.

'I knew it,' Parsefall said triumphantly. ''E's dead, ain't he?'

'He ain't in 'orspital,' Mrs Pinchbeck said, 'and I don't suppose 'e could be dead, because he walked out of 'ere last night on 'is own two feet.'

It was the children's turn to look blank. Mrs Pinchbeck took a forkful of pie and swallowed carefully. 'It was like this.

Last night, after I locked you in, I headed off for Church Street. There's an apothecary lives over there, name of Mr Whitby, and I thought he might be cheaper than a surgeon. Only on the way, I 'ad to pass the Cock and Bottle' – referring to a nearby public house – 'and it struck me as 'ow I'd seen Mr Whitby in there once or twice. So I went in and the barmaid said to me, "Why, Bella Pinchbeck, you're as white as a sheet!" And "Bella Pinchbeck, you're all a-tremble!" And I was,' she added stoutly. 'I always *was* delicate. Of course, I'd made meself strong for your sakes. But after a bit, the strain was too much for a poor frail woman, and I turned faint and fluttery and was all in a swoon. The shock took 'old of me.'

'Did you see the apothecary?' Lizzie Rose asked tactlessly.

'I did not,' answered Mrs Pinchbeck with asperity. 'And if I had, 'e'd 'ave been worried about me. I 'ad Spasms an' dizzy spells an' I don't know what all. All my friends at the Cock and Bottle said they'd never seen anyone so pale and trembly, and they made me sit before the fire and drink a glass of spirits. It was to bring me back to meself, as it were.'

Lizzie Rose looked at Parsefall, and Parsefall looked at Lizzie Rose. They knew the rest of the story without being told.

'So I drank it,' Mrs Pinchbeck said unnecessarily, 'and it was a good thing I did, because I was in ever such a state. The spirits did me good, but I still wasn't meself, so they gave me a bit more and bade me stay by the fire. So I did, and by the time they closed, I was well enough to get back on my feet. But by then the fog was bad, very bad indeed, and I daren't go wandering off looking for Church Street, because what if I was to fall into the river? So I come back 'ome. But when I opens the door, Grisini was gone. He weren't there.'

The children were silent. They were recalling the bloodstains on the staircase. How had a man who had lost so much blood managed to get to his feet and leave the house?

'Do you think 'e'll come back?' asked Parsefall.

'I don't see why he wouldn't,' Mrs Pinchbeck answered. 'All 'is things are here, and it's not every landlady that would give 'im such fine rooms for five shillings a week. And keeping the caravan chained in the area too, which is inconvenient, but I don't complain of it.'

Five shillings a week. Lizzie Rose felt her stomach tighten as she realised that if Grisini were gone, she and Parsefall would have to come up with five shillings a week. She laid her hand on Mrs Pinchbeck's arm. 'Has – has Grisini paid the rent this week?'

'He 'asn't,' Mrs Pinchbeck said, 'because 'e said the takings was bad. He were a shilling short last week, and he promised me 'e'd pay this week, with an extra sixpence for my trouble.' She took a last gulp of milk and set her cup down. All at once, the trouble in Lizzie Rose's face seemed to strike her. ''Ere, now! You ain't worried about that, are you?'

Lizzie Rose opened her mouth to speak but found her voice was only a faint croak. 'Just now I don't – of course we'll pay – only –'

'I ain't turning orphelings into the street,' Mrs Pinchbeck said grandly. 'I 'aven't the 'eart. It's one thing if you 'ad the money, but if you 'aven't, you can' – she thought for a moment – 'you can 'elp Luce around the 'ouse. Tidy up.' She raised her hand in a graceful flourish, drawing attention to the improved state of the room. 'Or 'elp in the kitchen. Or with the dogs.'

Lizzie Rose's eyes filled with tears of relief. 'Oh, Mrs Pinchbeck!'

Mrs Pinchbeck nodded majestically. All at once the dramatic

108

possibilities of the situation struck her full force. She rose from the chair, flung out her arms and gathered both children to her bosom. Parsefall didn't want to be held, but she caught him off balance and lugged him against her. Lizzie Rose, understanding what was required for the scene, clasped her arms around Mrs Pinchbeck's neck. The landlady smelled of sweat and bacon grease and dogs.

'Poor little lambs,' crooned Mrs Pinchbeck, 'poor little orphelings! You've 'ad a dreadful shock! But don't you be afraid!' Her voice deepened and grew strong, as if there was an audience beyond the front window. 'You shan't be 'omeless as long as Arabella Pinchbeck's in the world! As long as Arabella Pinchbeck's alive,' she vowed, 'there'll be a roof over your 'eads! And Arabella Pinchbeck 'erself will comfort and protect you in your distress!'

Parsefall pulled himself free. 'Wot distress?'

'Any distress,' Mrs Pinchbeck retorted testily. 'Losing your guardian.'

'That ain't distress,' said Parsefall.

# Chapter Seventeen

# An Unexpected Discovery

Grisini did not come back. Each morning when Parsefall awakened, he listened for the sound of his old master's footsteps. When he heard only Lizzie Rose and Ruby, he smiled to himself and went back to sleep. He had no more nightmares. By the time ten days had passed, he was happily convinced that Grisini had bled to death in the London streets.

Mrs Pinchbeck and Lizzie Rose were not so sure. They reasoned that if Grisini had been strong enough to leave the house, he might have been strong enough to survive his injuries. The police returned to the house, first asking to see Grisini and then demanding to know his whereabouts. Mrs Pinchbeck treated them to a dramatic account of Grisini's injury, ending with a Spasm so harrowing that the constable sent Parsefall to the nearest public house for a pennyworth of gin. The policemen left the house deeply shaken; Mrs Pinchbeck dried her tears and set about finding a workman to fix the broken staircase. She toyed with the idea of renting out Grisini's bedroom but could not quite make up her mind to do so.

Parsefall was tempted to occupy the empty room himself. Never in his life had he slept in a comfortable bed. All the same, he felt it might be dangerous to sleep in Grisini's. He told himself he would wait until Grisini's body was found. He looked forward to this macabre discovery, even going so far as to envision a pauper's funeral for his dead master. He had seen many a penniless corpse dragged through London as the street urchins sang:

> 'Rattle 'is bones
> Over the stones.
> 'E's only a pauper
> Who nobody owns.'

The idea of serenading Grisini with this chorus was delicious, but days went by and the body was not found. Parsefall had little time to wonder over its whereabouts. He had work to do. However delightful it might be to imagine Grisini's corpse on a handcart, the death of the showman was a loss to the puppet theatre. The scarlet caravan was too cumbersome for two children to manage alone, and the acts had to be shortened and simplified.

Parsefall flung himself into the task of working out the alterations. For the first time in his life, he regretted that he could not write. It would have been easier if he had been able to keep a record of the changes he envisioned. As it was, he had to practise the altered shows again and again, until he knew them by heart.

He was displeased to find that Lizzie Rose showed little

interest in learning her new roles. She spent long hours in service to Luce, Mrs Pinchbeck's maid-of-all-work. For years the slatternly Luce had toiled for Mrs Pinchbeck, ill paid and dog tired, never doing more than half the work assigned to her. When Mrs Pinchbeck explained that Lizzie Rose was to help with the housework, Luce's dull eyes glistened.

Lizzie Rose had always tended the dogs because she liked dogs; she had always straightened and tidied because she craved order. Now she carried coal and hot water up and down the stairs, scrubbed out the chamber pots, blackleaded the stove and riddled the ashes. Within two weeks, her clothes acquired a patina of oily filth, and she was prone to tears and temper. She snapped at Parsefall every time he spoke to her.

Parsefall was too busy to take much notice. He hammered together one of Grisini's old wagons and contrived a new stage for the theatre, one that was small and light enough to be hauled by a single person. He spent long hours practising with the *fantoccini*, perfecting his work with the acrobats and the magnetic skeleton. He fancied he was as good as Grisini with the variety acts, except for the ballerina. He had not practised the ballet dance since the night of Grisini's accident. The ballerina had disappeared.

He found it one afternoon when he was searching Lizzie Rose's bedroom for a spare penny. He espied a small pointed foot, sticking out from under a chair. Parsefall scooped up the puppet, only to see that its face and bosom bore the imprint of teeth marks. One arm was missing, and the tulle skirt hung like an unwrapped bandage.

Parsefall gave a howl of fury. He had no doubt which of the dogs had mauled the puppet. He tucked the dancer under his arm and stamped downstairs to Mrs Pinchbeck's chambers. The door was ajar. Parsefall smacked it open and strode inside.

Mrs Pinchbeck had gone out. Lizzie Rose was in the back room, changing the sheets. Ruby was making a nuisance of herself, following her mistress from one side of the bed to the other.

Parsefall held up the puppet. 'Your bloody 'orrible dog –' he began.

'Don't you use that language to me!' snapped Lizzie Rose.

'Look what she done!' Parsefall shook the puppet in Lizzie Rose's face. 'She near chewed off the 'ead. I could tack on another arm,' he said plaintively, 'but the face is spoiled for good. And the boozum's ruined – just look at the boozum!'

'It wasn't Ruby,' Lizzie Rose said indignantly.

'Must've been,' argued Parsefall. 'She's the only one that comes upstairs.'

Lizzie Rose could not deny it. She turned her back, heaved up the mattress and slapped it down on the bed ropes. A cloud of dust flew up, accompanied by a sour smell. Both children sneezed.

'I been a-workin' and workin',' Parsefall complained bitterly, 'trying to get that bally dance in me 'ands, and then your bloody 'orrible dog steals the puppet and chews 'er up. Now I'll 'ave to change puppets, and the weight'll be different –'

Lizzie Rose gazed at him stonily. 'Hand me that sheet.'

Parsefall glared at her and did not help.

Lizzie Rose's eyes flashed. With dangerous briskness, she reached past Parsefall, snatched the sheet, snapped it into the air and brought it down on the mattress. She bent over and began to tuck in the edges, pounding the mattress in a way that would have been a warning to anyone but Parsefall.

'*I* can't sew,' Parsefall said pointedly. 'I can get one of the lady puppets out of the wicker chest, but you'll 'ave to make her a skirt that sticks out.' He waited for a response and added, 'I can't do everyfink. Besides, it ain't fair – it woz your dog and I'll have all the trouble of restringing her –'

Lizzie Rose uttered something between a growl and a scream and threw the counterpane at him. Then she sat down on the bed and burst into tears.

Parsefall disengaged himself, blinking – the corner of the quilt had caught him in the eye. He gazed warily at Lizzie Rose. He hated it when she cried. He liked a good fight, but Lizzie Rose's tears took all the joy out of battle. When she cried, his stomach knotted up. And she always cried. Lizzie Rose couldn't seem to lose her temper without shedding tears.

'*Your* trouble?' echoed Lizzie Rose. Her face was crimson. 'It seems to me that I'm the one as has the trouble. It's me who has to sweep out the ashes and empty the slops –'

'Yes, but you don't 'ave to,' Parsefall pointed out. 'The Louse is supposed to do all that. Besides, I've took the bloody dogs out – and last night I went to the chop'ouse for supper –'

'Yes, because you were hungry. You don't do a single thing to help me,' declared Lizzie Rose. 'You're a lazy, thoughtless, selfish boy!'

'I ain't,' Parsefall defended himself. 'I bin workin' on the show –'

'The show!' Lizzie Rose cried scornfully. 'Playing with puppets when I –'

'I ain't playin'!' Parsefall flung back at her. 'I bin changin' the show so it'll work wiv two people. I've thought the whole thing through – every scene. We'll 'ave to bring back the Babes in the Wood –'

'We can't do the shows without Grisini,' said Lizzie Rose.

'We'll 'ave to,' Parsefall shot back. He was so astonished that he forgot to be angry. ''Ow else are we to live?'

Lizzie Rose, astonished in turn, stared at him.

'It'll be Christmas soon,' Parsefall said. 'Last year at Christmas, Grisini and me made five quid a week. Only we 'ave to rehearse – *you* 'ave to rehearse, because you ain't good with the puppets; you float 'em, and you jerk the strings –'

'Parsefall,' Lizzie Rose spoke with maddening patience, 'things are different now. Grisini's gone.'

'I know 'e's gone!' shouted back Parsefall. 'I woz there when he bashed in 'is skull! Now that he's gone, it's up to me to plan the shows. I've done the 'ard part,' he said soothingly, 'the proper work. All you 'ave to do is rehearse and do as you're told.'

Lizzie Rose got to her feet, leaving the bed half made. She marched out of the room with her head up and her chest heaving. She slammed the door of Mrs Pinchbeck's lodging so hard that the dogs began to bark and the parrot screamed, 'No good! No more! It's ruined!'

Parsefall opened the door and followed her up the stairs, accompanied by Ruby. 'If Grisini's dead, the business's ours,' he called after her. 'The puppets and all. We can make our fortunes.'

Lizzie Rose put her hands over her ears. She stalked into Grisini's chambers and flounced into her bedroom, dashing aside the sequined curtain as if it was a door she wanted to slam. Ruby darted under the curtain. Parsefall halted outside.

'Only we 'ave to *rehearse*!' he shouted.

There was no answer. Parsefall waited on the other side of the curtain. He heard Lizzie Rose whimper, 'Oh, Ruby!' followed by a series of sobs and sniffs.

After a stretch of silence, he inquired, ''Ave you stopped cryin'?'

'Yes,' answered Lizzie Rose. 'Come into my room. I want to talk to you.'

Parsefall drew aside the curtain and went into the dim little room. Lizzie Rose sat with Ruby in her lap. Her face was still red, but she seemed to have regained her composure. Her tear-streaked face looked both older and younger than usual.

'Parse,' she said, 'you're younger than I am, and –'

'No, I ain't,' Parsefall said glibly. 'I'm thirteen, same age as you.'

Lizzie Rose glared at him. 'You're younger,' she contradicted him, 'and even if you weren't, you're a baby and a fool, so it comes to the same thing. You don't seem to understand that things are different now. When Grisini was our master, the shows were our living, but he's left us. If Mrs Pinchbeck were to throw us out, you'd have to go back to the workhouse and I'd have to live on the street. There's girls younger than me on the street and it's a bad, bad life. So you see' – her voice shook – 'we must be grateful to Mrs Pinchbeck and do everything we can to help with the housework – and the dogs – and everything.'

'But there's no end to that,' Parsefall said, baffled that she should not see what was so clear to him. 'There won't be no end to the 'ousework, 'cos the Louse is lazy, and Mrs Pinchbeck won't do anyfink but lie on the sofa and say how good she is to us.'

'She *is* good,' Lizzie Rose said despairingly. 'Our lodgings are five shillings a week. That's thirteen pounds a year, Parse – and poor Luce gets only six; she told me so. And we don't just need rent; there's food as well.' Her eyes filled with tears. 'We eat so much.'

Parsefall sat down on the bed, one leg under him. He leaned

towards her. 'But don't you see? All this 'ousework – there ain't any money in it. You'll be cleanin' the slops and haulin' coal the rest of your life if that's all you do. You've got to find time to rehearse –'

'I can't.' Lizzie Rose scooped Ruby from her lap and set her on the floor. 'I'm run off my feet as it is, can't you see? Parse,' she said earnestly, 'if you could only help a bit, it would make things so much easier. I don't mind the hard work so much as the smells – the chamber pots and the things in the larder that've gone bad – and the dogs, you don't take them out near often enough –'

'I can't do all that,' Parsefall objected. 'I 'aven't got time. Besides, all that 'ousework would make me 'ands too stiff to work the *fantoccini.*'

Lizzie Rose lunged at him. She grabbed his jacket and shook him. Then she seized a handful of hair and yanked. Parsefall pulled away, crying out as if she had stabbed him with a red-hot poker. Lizzie Rose, guilt stricken, stepped back. 'I really don't see,' she said with a despair that was worthy of Mrs Pinchbeck herself, 'what I'm to do. I do nothing but work from dawn till dusk, and you won't help me' – she relapsed into tears – 'because you're a horrid, wicked, selfish boy.'

Parsefall felt the familiar knot beginning to form in his stomach. Ruby pawed at Lizzie Rose's skirt, whimpering mournfully.

'I only said we ought to rehearse,' muttered Parsefall.

'Rehearse, then,' Lizzie Rose said stonily. Her head came up, and tears glittered on her cheeks. 'Go ahead and rehearse, while I work myself to death –'

'I can't,' Parsefall said, returning to his original point. 'Your bloody 'orrible dog ruined my puppet. *Our* puppet,' he corrected himself, 'wot's part of the show.'

Lizzie Rose flung the curtain to one side and flounced over

to the wicker trunk where the old puppets were kept. She threw open the lid. 'There are puppets in here,' she said frostily. 'Do you want me to choose one for you, or is that something you're willing to do for yourself?'

'I can't sew,' Parsefall began, but Lizzie Rose was rummaging through the puppet bags.

'Here's one with a stick-out skirt,' she said, feeling through the muslin bag. 'Take this one, and leave me alone – I've too much to do –'

Her voice broke off as she drew the puppet out of the muslin bag. She took in her breath sharply. 'Parse –'

The puppet in her hand was beautifully made and entirely suitable for a dancer. She had black ringlets and a snow-white frock. Her complexion was delicately pink and white; her Cupid's-bow mouth wore an enigmatic simper. Around her neck was a locket smaller than a pea. The jewel in the centre flashed blue fire.

'Parsefall,' whispered Lizzie Rose. 'It's Clara.'

# Chapter Eighteen

# Awakening

'I'm going to be sick,' announced Parsefall.

The words startled Clara. The sound of her name had roused her from a long and dreamless sleep. Two enormous children were staring down at her. Beyond them was a vast and dingy room, larger than a cathedral. Swaying just above Clara's face was an inverted flame, red-gold in colour: it was the tassel end of Lizzie Rose's plait. The tassel moved higher, and Clara's position shifted. Lizzie Rose leaped to her feet. Clara fell, and her head struck the floor.

Clara felt the impact but no pain. Her eyes were fixed; she had no choice but to watch the scene before her. Lizzie Rose rushed to fetch a chamber pot. Quickly she collared Parsefall and set the pot before him. She wrapped one arm around his forehead as he vomited.

Clara tried to turn away and found she could not. The spectacle of Parsefall was enough to make her own gorge rise, but she could neither close nor avert her eyes. She lay stock-still, baffled by the immensity of the room and the presence of the children. She had no idea how she came to be there. She strained to think back, but memory eluded her. A single image passed before her mind's eye: the streets at night, and a tall shadow detaching itself from the fog.

Parsefall wiped his mouth on his sleeve. 'Tastes 'orrible.'

'I know.' Lizzie Rose released him. 'Do you think it's over?'

'Dunno' was Parsefall's discouraging reply.

The children sat in silence for a moment. It struck Clara that she had been spared the sickly odour of the chamber pot. She stared past the children, taking stock of the cavernous room. The snuff-coloured paint was peeling, and there were string puppets hanging from the ceiling. *This must be where the children live,* thought Clara, *where they keep their puppets. This must be Grisini's house . . .* The name *Grisini* rang a bell. Grisini was the man she had met in the streets.

Lizzie Rose released Parsefall and twisted sideways so that she was facing him. 'Parse,' she said tentatively, 'I'm sorry I frightened you. I didn't mean the puppet was really Clara –'

*But I am Clara,* Clara wanted to protest, and then the word *puppet* struck home. All at once she understood. Her skin prickled, as if someone was walking on her grave; she felt as if she was trembling, but she never stirred. No puppet could stir, unless the worker touched its strings – and Clara had no strings. Her limbs were lax, disjointed. Nevertheless, she tried to speak: *I am Clara!* A wave of grief washed over her as she failed to make a sound.

'Because it can't be,' went on Lizzie Rose. 'Things like that can't happen. It was just such a shock to see her – it, I mean

120

– because of the ringlets and her birthday frock. She looks so real.' Her hands closed around Clara's waist, lifting her from the floor. Clara's head flopped back.

'She *is* real,' Parsefall said in a thread of a voice. 'Grisini must've –'

Lizzie Rose's fingers tightened. 'He couldn't have, Parse. People can't do things like that. Magic spells – and evil magicians –' There was a brief, pregnant pause. 'They're only in plays.'

Parsefall leaned in closer; Clara was forehead-to-chest with his grimy shirtfront. His fingernail scraped the side of her neck. 'Look at the gewgaw she's wearin'. It's the same one she 'ad on that day.'

'Her birthday locket,' gasped Lizzie Rose. 'She showed it to me.' She bent down to examine it. 'Oh, Parse, look! It opens – just the way hers did! And inside there's a tiny, tiny picture – made of little weenie bits of hair –'

'It's *'er*,' insisted Parsefall. 'Grisini did her.'

*Yes*, thought Clara. *It was Grisini*. She concentrated on each syllable, willing the words to reach him.

'People can't change into puppets,' argued Lizzie Rose.

'Grisini could change 'em,' Parsefall said staunchly. 'You don't know 'im. Not the way I do.' He lowered Clara to his lap. 'I'll warrant that's 'ow he did the other ones. He kidnapped 'em and changed 'em, and the coppers wouldn't find 'em, even if they woz in the same room –'

'They opened the trunk,' Lizzie Rose interrupted. 'The police did, remember? When they were looking for Clara, they opened that very trunk!'

Parsefall nodded, evidently following her thoughts. 'If

they'd opened the bag, they might a-seen 'er – but they wouldn't 'ave believed their eyes. Not once she woz changed. He changed 'er.'

'But how?' Lizzie Rose sounded as if she might cry. 'Oh, Parsefall, I can't believe it! How could he – and why –?'

'For the money,' Parsefall answered promptly. 'Clara was rich, weren't she? And 'er brothers and sisters woz all deaders. He must've known 'er father would pay to get 'er back again. He must've done the same thing to that girl wot went missin' in Leeds.'

'Parsefall, he couldn't –'

'Why couldn't 'e?' persisted Parsefall. 'It were safe enough, if the children was changed. Nobody'd find 'em. Then after he got the money, he could change 'em back an' send 'em 'ome.'

*Change me back,* thought Clara. *Please.*

'How can you know that?' demanded Lizzie Rose. 'How can you be so sure?'

Parsefall didn't answer. Lizzie Rose leaned forward and seized his arm, giving him a little shake. The movement made Clara tumble from Parsefall's lap to the floor. She found herself staring at the side of the chamber pot. The handle was sage green and shaped like an ear.

'Leggo-a-me!' Parsefall said shrilly. 'I don't know wot I know. I don't look back – not when it's about Grisini. There's a black place in my mind wot 'e made, and if I think about 'im too much, I fall into the black place. So I don't do it. See?'

Lizzie Rose struck her hands together. 'I can't believe it. That puppet can't be Clara Wintermute – and Grisini can't – couldn't – work a spell like that! He might have been wicked, but he wasn't clever enough to turn flesh and blood into –' She stopped.

'Into wot?' jeered Parsefall. 'Wot's she made of, then?'

Once again, Clara was taken up by Lizzie Rose. One work-roughened thumb rubbed Clara's cheek.

'She ain't wood,' Parsefall pointed out, keeping tally on his fingers. 'She ain't chiny. She ain't cloth, and she ain't papery-mash. Wot is she, then?'

'I don't know,' Lizzie Rose said faintly. 'She feels like wax – or soft leather – and oh, Parsefall, I think she's *warm* –'

*I'm not wax,* Clara thought. *I'm myself. Only I can't move.*

'Look.' Parsefall pinched Clara's wrist between his thumb and forefinger. 'She's got ten fingers. Puppets only 'ave eight.' Clara felt a draught on her lower limbs. 'And look under 'er frock. She's got things on underneaf. Real puppets never 'ave nuffink underneaf.'

'Don't look under there, Parsefall.'

'Why not?' demanded Parsefall. 'You're lookin'.'

'That's different,' Lizzie Rose said firmly. 'It's very naughty for little boys to want to know about ladies' things. And besides, she'd hate it if she were alive –'

'She's alive,' Parsefall said. He corrected himself. ''T'any rate, she ain't dead. Not all the way. Look at 'er.'

*I am alive,* Clara agreed silently. *Listen to him. I can see you; I can hear you; I have feelings. Grisini changed me – I don't know how he did it, but he changed me –*

She tried to retrace the steps that had brought her to Grisini. On the night of her birthday, she had cried herself to sleep. She had awakened a little before midnight, possessed of the idea that there was something of the utmost importance that she had to do. Without knowing what it was, she dressed herself in the clothes she had worn earlier that day. She crept back to her bed and reached inside the pillowcase, where she had hidden Grisini's watch. Once the automaton watch was in her hand, she understood. She must find Grisini before the watch struck twelve, and give it back to him. Quickly, on tiptoe, she descended the stairs and unbolted the front door.

She knew that the streets were dangerous at night; she had never walked through them alone. But she did not hesitate. Swiftly she made her way to the King's Road and down to Sloane Square. There she waited, hugging herself against the cold. When Grisini appeared, he bowed and held out his hands. Then she was afraid. Every cell in her body shrank from him; she felt as if he was some great carrion bird, whose touch was contamination. She dropped the automaton watch into his cupped hands. After that, she remembered nothing.

A large black knob appeared before Clara's eyes. It had a bristly reddish halo around it. A curl of pink cartilage flicked out of the halo. Something wet and warm slicked across Clara's face.

Lizzie Rose shrieked, 'Ruby!' She stood up, clutching Clara to her breast like a favourite doll.

Clara heard Parsefall mutter, ''Orrible little dog.'

'Parse, what are we to do? If it's Clara – only it can't be – how are we to keep her safe from Ruby? We'd better put her back in the trunk.' Lizzie Rose snatched up the puppet bag. 'If we put something heavy on top –'

*No!* thought Clara. Her mind flashed to her brother, locked up in his casket in the mausoleum. She thought of herself, motionless in the trunk, with the lid pressing down upon her. *No! Don't bury me alive!*

'She won't like it inside the trunk,' Parsefall said, as if he had heard.

'How do you know?' demanded Lizzie Rose.

'Well, you wouldn't like it, would you?' retorted Parsefall.

'Stuck in a box like a deader! She'll like it better out 'ere.' He reached for Clara. 'I could string her,' he said tentatively.

*Yes,* thought Clara at once. *Please.*

'String her? Like one of the other puppets?'

'We need a dancer,' Parsefall said defensively. 'She's dressed like a bally dancer, and she's about the right weight. She won't 'ave nuffink else to do, will she?'

Clara waited, her face hidden against the bodice of Lizzie Rose's dress.

'Parse,' Lizzie Rose said slowly, 'if it is true – I can't believe it, but I do – if it's really Clara, and Grisini changed her – how on earth are we to change her back?'

# Chapter Nineteen

# Another Awakening:
# Strachan's Ghyll

The bedchamber was unfamiliar. The man with the bandaged head raked it with his eyes, searching for clues as to where he was. No gas lamps shone outside the pointed windows, and he heard none of the London street noises. It was night, and he was in the country.

He lifted himself on one elbow. At the far end of the room was a chair like a throne, and in that chair sat a woman. Her back was turned to him, but he could see the lustrous fabric of her dressing gown.

He heard the woman muttering. 'The Tower. That's danger or a fall. Nine of Swords and the Wheel of Fortune. Then there's the Magician – a man of genius – and the woman subduing the lion – Strength. The Two of Cups – but that doesn't belong; that's love.'

The woman's voice was familiar. It was shaky with age and deeper in pitch than he remembered it. It was Cassandra's voice and she was reading the *tarocchi*. The Tower, the Wheel of Fortune, the Nine of Swords. They were all Tarot Cards.

'The Hanged Man, reversed. That's someone trapped between life and death. Perhaps I am the Hanged Man. And Death – perhaps that's mine. And the Devil – that's a liar; that's Grisini.'

The man with the bandaged head recognised his name. He was Grisini, and this must be Cassandra's house. He raised one hand to his face. The furrows she had carved into his skin thirty-eight years ago were ragged with fresh scabs. He remembered the staircase breaking beneath him and the blinding pain when he cracked open his skull. Later he had come to himself and crawled out of the house: dizzy, feeble, bleeding but with just enough strength to obey Cassandra's summons. Weak though he was, he had remembered the policeman stationed across the street. He had stumbled down the cellar steps and crept out the back door through the lavatory. Either the simple ruse or his disguise protected him, for he was not followed. He had a dim recollection of a railway station and an endless journey by train.

Cassandra rose from her throne. Grisini watched her warily. She was no longer as tall as she had been. Age had gnawed her bones and bowed her broad shoulders. She had grown coarser and heavier, but she was magnificently dressed. Her dressing gown was woven from some changeable fabric, saffron yellow where the light struck it, blood red in the folds. Around her neck was a filigree locket containing the gem he had tried to steal. At the thought of the fire opal, he experienced a mixture of terror and desire: terror lest the stone be used against him, desire that he might wrest it from Cassandra and make it his own.

Cassandra spoke, using the Venetian dialect they had once

shared. Enemy though she was, he welcomed the caressing tones of his mother tongue. 'So, Gaspare. You are awake.'

He licked his dry lips. 'How long have I been here?'

'Nine days. I summoned you, but you didn't come.'

'I suffered an accident.'

'Yes, and lost your way. In the end, you came to the railway station in Windermere. You were out of your wits, railing in Italian, unable to walk or tend to yourself. I had you brought here.' Her lip curled. 'My housekeeper would not wash you, you were so foul. I had to ask the groom.' She added deliberately, 'You've grown old. I shouldn't have known you.'

He smiled at the crude attempt to wound him. They had both changed since last they met, but she was twenty-three years older than he was, and she had aged badly. She looked ill; her eyes were feverish, and her colour was unnaturally high. He selected his words carefully. 'To me, you are as beautiful as you ever were.'

It was a double insult. She bared her teeth at him, the unhealthy colour in her cheeks deepening. 'How dare you, Gaspare! I could have let you die –'

'And would have, no doubt, unless you wanted something.' He took a shallow breath. 'What do you want, Cassandra? You summoned me here; you bandaged my head; you put me to bed in a very luxurious room . . . This house must have cost a fortune. You've done well for yourself.'

'If I have, you haven't,' she said spitefully. 'I thought it was your destiny to be a great man. What became of you?'

Grisini's smile faded. 'I've never sought the things you care about. You've always had a swinish love for comforts and luxuries, have you not? Trinkets and feather beds and sweets to suck upon. Whereas I –'

'Yes, you.' The pronoun was an insult. 'What have you sought?'

'Knowledge. Secrets. I studied magic in Budapest, Paris, Prague. My misfortune was that my experiments were too daring, and I was found out. I was imprisoned for fourteen years.'

He tried to speak as if there was something heroic about a long term in prison. In fact, those fourteen years had almost broken him. His arrest had been violent and unexpected: he had been beaten unconscious and stripped of the tools he used to work his enchantments. Those years in prison haunted him still: the hunger, the hard labour, the monotony. By the time he was set free again, his powers had all but left him.

'Why were you imprisoned?'

He made a small, impatient gesture. 'I told you: I was experimenting. There was an accident. A child died.' He saw her features contort in a grimace of disgust. 'What, are you shocked? Have you grown sentimental? Magic power cannot be had for nothing. There must always be some sacrifice. You of all people ought to know that.' He changed the subject. 'And you? What use have you made of your time?'

A hunted look came over her face. 'I've doubled the Sagredo fortune,' she shot back. 'I've travelled; I've gambled; I've entertained. Men have courted me and I've collected them like butterflies. I've gathered marvels and curiosities; I built this house.' She flung open one hand, indicating the high ceilings, the Venetian windows, the carved and gilded furniture. 'There is not a single caprice – not one – that I have not indulged.'

'How happy you must have been.'

She looked daggers at him. He laughed under his breath, because he could see that her life had been a burden and a misery. Her hands came together as if she wanted to wring his neck. For the first time he noticed that her left hand was bandaged. He forbore mentioning it but repeated his former question. 'What do you want, Cassandra?'

He spoke her name as he once had, lingering over each syllable. He remembered how her eyes used to kindle when he spoke like that. She had fought against her love for him like a fish on the hook, but he had once had the power to soften her.

Her colour darkened. 'That night in Venice – the night we parted – you spoke of the stone I wear around my neck. You said you knew its history. I didn't care to listen to you then, but I will listen now. Tell me what you know.'

He wondered if he could disobey her. Weak though he was, he craved the game of thwarting her. But as he hesitated, she cupped her right hand around the filigree locket. He felt a wave of feverish heat. 'Speak.'

He sighed. 'Among jewellers, it was called the phoenix-stone –'

'I remember that. What else did you learn?'

'Less than you think, perhaps. I had to piece together the story, and it is far from complete. The stone had a bad reputation among jewellers; it was considered unlucky. I consulted my fellow magicians. After that, I had the good fortune to discover a parchment in the Libreria Sansoviniana –'

'Never mind your good fortune. Tell me what you found out.'

Her impatience intrigued him; he wished he had time to think through what it might mean. 'The story began more than three hundred years ago, with the burning of a witch.' He heard her intake of breath. 'According to the legend, she was possessed of great wealth. The fire opal was a treasure from the New World. How she came by it, no one knows. But someone feared her, or envied her good fortune, and she was accused of practising witchcraft. In one telling of the tale, the accuser was her brother; in another, it was her lover. Who can say? What does it matter? What matters is that she was found guilty, and her property was forfeit. Her lands were seized, and so was the fire opal. She was burned at the stake. With her dying breath, she cursed those who had stolen from her.' His eyes shifted to Cassandra's face. 'You've gone pale. What is it?'

He did not expect her to answer, but she did, driven, perhaps, by the same motive that had led her to consult him. 'I've seen her. The witch, burning at the stake. In my dreams, and – when I look in the glass.'

'Ah!' He raised himself to a sitting position. 'Have you seen the other ones?'

Cassandra turned away from him and began to pace, the hem of her dressing gown rasping against the carpet. 'What do you mean, the other ones?'

'The other women who burned. The opal is known as the phoenix-stone because the fires recur. Almost everyone who possessed it died by fire. One woman was struck by lightning. Another perished in a house fire; that was said to be an accident. But there were other women who set themselves ablaze. Madwomen, suicides. One woman left a letter behind. She said that the women she saw in her looking glass had driven her insane.'

Cassandra halted in midstep. Then she reversed and resumed pacing, the train of her gown uncoiling like a scorpion's tail.

'Here's the curious thing: the stone itself always escapes the blaze. Always. That's part of the pattern. A woman inherits the stone or steals it. She may not fall under its power right away. But the more the stone is worn, the more it is handled, above all, the more it is used to make magic, the stronger its power grows.

In time, it maddens and consumes its owner.' He shot a malicious glance in her direction. 'I warned you years ago, didn't I? Your hand is bandaged: have you been setting fires? You burned yourself, perhaps?'

'No.'

'But you see the other women in the looking glass.'

She inclined her head.

'You must wish I had stolen it, all those years ago.'

'I wonder,' she said very slowly, 'if you could steal it now.'

It was an invitation. She crossed the carpet haltingly, as if every step hurt her. He was seized by a frenzy of rash desire, and he raised himself on one elbow. In spite of his knowledge of the stone, in spite of the curse she had placed on him, his hand shot forward, fingers trembling. The witch leaned over him so that he might seize it. His fingers fastened themselves around the gold chain.

Then she recoiled, wrenching the chain away from him so that his fingertips smarted. She seemed to shimmer and swell before his eyes. She was a giantess wreathed in flame. He fancied that he could see inside the filigree locket, where the red stone pulsed like a racing heart. The air around him darkened, and he swooned.

When he opened his eyes, he saw that the witch had retreated. The scars on his cheeks oozed blood, and the back of his head felt tender. Grisini said bitterly, 'Your curse holds,' and Cassandra heaved a sigh of mingled frustration and relief.

'That night in Venice,' she said, 'you said *unless*. You told me that the stone would consume me *unless*. What did that mean?'

He felt too ill to speak. He knew that blood was soaking through the bandages on his head.

'Answer me! The fire will consume me *unless*. Unless what?'

'Unless the fire opal is stolen.'

Hope dawned in her face. It was swiftly replaced by mistrust. 'You tried to steal it, but you couldn't.'

'I was not a child.'

His vision was beginning to blur, but he saw the look that came over her face, the sudden alertness. It was as if she understood something she had failed to grasp before. He hazarded a guess. 'You stole it, didn't you? Weren't you a child at the time?'

'I was thirteen.'

An idea flashed through his mind like a comet. He wanted to clap his hands and crow with laughter and drum his heels with joy. In one flash of inspiration, he saw how he might gain the power of the fire opal – the power, not the doom of it. He thought of the children he had planned to discard as useless. They would not be useless now. He lowered his eyelids, scarcely daring to breathe. Cassandra must not see the triumph in his eyes.

He searched for words to distract her. 'Thirteen,' he repeated, 'exactly! You were a child on the threshold of womanhood. A remarkable time in life. For the child believes – everything! And feels – everything! So much life, instinct, vital force – and then the first stirrings of adult desire. Everything is potent, volatile . . . ! Why do people sacrifice infants in the Black Mass? It makes them feel wicked; that is something, of course, but what strength is there in a suckling babe? If one wants power, there is far more power in *children* –! The women who did not burn survived because the phoenix-stone was stolen from them. And the thieves were always *children*!' He was out of breath. 'When I tried to steal from you – I failed – I was twenty-three – I was *too old* –' The room went dim. He panted open mouthed, like a dog.

Cassandra hastened to his bedside. She kept one hand

133

around the filigree locket but pressed the other against his cheek. He knew that she was only healing him so that she could go on questioning him, but the sensation of warmth was exquisite. He wanted to give himself up to it but instead forced himself to think. How might the children be summoned to Cassandra's house? He could write to them from his sickbed, but they would be loath to come. At their last meeting, Parsefall had kicked him, and he had beaten Lizzie Rose.

It was several minutes before Cassandra spoke to him again. 'Do you truly believe a child could steal the phoenix-stone?'

He was ready for her. 'Why not put it to the test? By a stroke of good fortune, I can provide you with two children: my apprentices in London. They're the right age, more or less, and the little boy is a trained pickpocket. Show him your jewels, and give him the run of the house. He won't disappoint you.'

Cassandra looked dubious. 'A little boy?'

'Not so very little. He's quite old enough to be dishonest. I took Parsefall from the workhouse five years ago. A clever boy. A good thief, an even better figure worker.'

Her eyebrows rose and she gave a *tchha* of laughter. 'Lud, Gaspare! You still play with your string puppets?'

'Why not?' Her amusement nettled him. 'My father was in the profession; so was my grandfather. The puppets are in my blood.' He changed the subject. 'If you think a girl is more likely to serve you, I have one of those too. Her name is Lizzie Rose Fawr, and her parents were theatrical people. They died, and I took her in out of charity.'

Cassandra uttered a snort of disbelief. 'Is she a pickpocket too?'

'Not a pickpocket, no. When you first meet her, you will

be struck by her air of innocence. It is misleading. She's a deceitful little puss, in spite of her pious airs. You must not let her deceive you.'

'I am not easily deceived.'

Grisini was greatly tempted to laugh. He closed his eyes as if the conversation wearied him. 'Write to them. Invite them here. Tempt them. One or the other will steal the phoenix-stone from you.'

*And whichever it is,* he thought, *will be my puppet and my slave. If Parsefall steals it, he will use it according to my commands. And if it is Lizzie Rose . . . She has not yet learned fear, not as the boy has, but I shall enjoy teaching her.*

'Very well, then. Write to the children and invite them here.'

'It will be better if you write to them. They're ungrateful little beggars and dislike my society. You may have to lure them here – and you'll have to address your letter to the girl. The boy can't read.'

'You have taught him nothing?'

'On the contrary, I have taught him everything. How to animate the puppets, how to ease a purse out of a waistcoat pocket . . . But reading, no. That is not one of his accomplishments. The girl can read. Invite them both.'

'Or perhaps all three,' Cassandra said shrewdly. 'Remember, Gaspare, I have sat by your bedside. You have dreamed and raved in your sleep. Tell me, if you please: who is Clara Wintermute, and what is all this about a ransom of ten thousand pounds?'

# Chapter Twenty

# Of Purse Strings
# and Puppet Strings

Parsefall was washing his hands. Lizzie Rose, who knew how seldom he washed, would have rejoiced over this, but Lizzie Rose was out, and the only witness to this unusual event was Clara. Clara lay on the mantelpiece, facing a streaked and spotty mirror. From this vantage point, she could see most of the room, a thing for which she was grateful.

Clara had spent the last week on the mantelpiece. It was one place, Lizzie Rose reasoned, where Ruby could not reach her. Lizzie Rose might have doubts as to whether it was possible that anyone could be changed into a puppet, but she took care to keep Clara out of harm's way. Clara was not sorry to be safe from the dog, but she was weary of lying in the same place for days on end. She felt stranded. She found herself listening for noises in the street below: the sounds of hoofbeats and carriage wheels, the tolling of the bells and the battle cries of the cats. She looked forward to the hours when the children were at home and she could hear their conversations.

The mantelshelf was cluttered. In the past few days, Lizzie Rose had taken to cleaning the lodgings. Whenever she found something of value, she placed it next to Clara. Gazing into the glass, Clara could see three snuffboxes, a pair of opera glasses and a photograph in a silver frame. The frame looked oddly familiar, but it faced outward: Clara could see only the back of it.

Parsefall's splashings ceased. He wiped his palms against his filthy trousers, walked directly to the mantel and picked up Clara. He carried her to the puppet gallows and laid her on the floor. Then he hunkered down next to her. From his jacket pocket, he took a reel of black thread, a lump of beeswax and a needle.

*He's going to string me,* thought Clara. She wanted to stretch her painted lips and shout for joy.

Parsefall bit off a piece of thread, sucked one end and inserted it into his needle. He knotted a string close to her left temple – Clara realised that there must be a screw there – and pulled the string through the perch that hung from the gallows. Clara rose in the air, neck bent, body dangling. Parsefall lowered her until her left foot was flat against the floor. He knelt back down and threaded the string through the screw on the other side of her head. *It's not right,* Clara wanted to tell him, *my right knee is sagging.* As if he heard her, he reached up to adjust the string.

Clara thrilled to his touch. As the strings passed through her limbs, she felt as if her bones were full of air. She longed for Parsefall to lift the crutch off the gallows. She imagined herself dancing on the tips of her toes, light and supple and free. She wondered if Parsefall were thinking the same thing. She seemed to hear the sound of coins dropping into a tin box and the patter of applause.

A door slammed downstairs. 'It's broken!' the parrot cried triumphantly. There was a fanfare of barking. Clara heard Lizzie Rose's footsteps on the staircase and the skittering sound of Ruby's toenails. The door opened, and the dog rushed in, circling the room at top speed.

Parsefall yelped and yanked Clara into his arms. For a moment, Clara's head rested against his chest, and she could hear his heartbeat. It was fast and strong. She felt him lift her; the spaniel was jumping at his knees. Lizzie Rose said, 'Ruby! Come here!' as she set off in pursuit. Ruby eluded her, making a wide circle around the carpet. After another lap of the room, she settled down by the hearth, her black lips open in laughter and her pink tongue showing.

'Bloody 'orrible dog,' said Parsefall.

'She isn't,' said Lizzie Rose indignantly. Her eyes fell on Clara. 'Oh, Parsefall! What are you doing with Clara?'

'I 'aven't 'urt her,' Parsefall said defensively. 'All I done was string 'er a little. She likes it.'

'She can't like it. She isn't –' Lizzie Rose began. She shook her head, dismissing the subject. 'Never mind that now. I have to talk to you.'

Parsefall turned his back on her. He replaced Clara's perch on the gallows and said automatically, 'I ain't done nuffink.'

'"I *haven't* done *anything*,"' Lizzie Rose corrected him. She unbuttoned her coat and threw it over the arm of a chair. Then she reached into her muff and brought out a lady's purse made of grey silk. 'I found this today. Have you ever seen it before?'

'No. Where woz it?'

'In Grisini's room, stuffed inside the mattress.' Lizzie Rose wedged her fingers into the mouth of the purse. She brought out a handful of glittering objects. 'Look, Parsefall! There was a man's gold watch – not Grisini's, with the wolf and the swan, but a different one, very large and heavy – and these two bracelets, one set with sparkling stones and the other one with pearls. I think they're real pearls, not fish scales and glass. I took the gold watch to the pawnbroker, and oh, Parse! Mr Grimes gave me ten quid for it!'

'Ten quid?' echoed Parsefall disbelievingly.

'Ten quid,' Lizzie Rose repeated. 'It was real gold – a gold repeater, Mr Grimes said. Perhaps I shouldn't have parted with it – it must be worth a fortune if he gave me that – but I was so flustered, I couldn't think. I took the ten quid, but all the way home I kept thinking how strange it is that Grisini should have had such things! He always said we were so poor. But he must have known what was in the mattress – it was horribly lumpy; I don't know how he slept on it – and then I looked at the purse, and –' She held it out to him. 'Parse, see how the purse strings are cut? They aren't worn or frayed; they're sharp at the ends. I think a lady must have been wearing this purse and someone cut the strings with a pair of scissors – and I think the someone was Grisini. I think he was a cutpurse – and a pickpocket – and I think he *stole* these things, all these things!'

She paused, allowing Parsefall time to respond.

'A gold watch worth ten quid,' Lizzie Rose repeated. 'And bracelets set with jewels.' Her voice grew hard. 'There were nights when we went to bed hungry because he said there was no money. Parse, you must tell me. Did you know Grisini was a thief?'

Parsefall hesitated. Clara wished she could see his face. 'What're you doin', pryin' through Grisini's things?'

'I have to,' Lizzie Rose said flatly. 'Mrs Pinchbeck told me to clear out Grisini's bedchamber. She's invited young Mr

Pinchbeck to stay with us at Christmastime, and she wants him to have Grisini's bed.'

'Old Fitzmorris?' Parsefall repeated incredulously. 'What's she want wiv 'im?'

'He's her stepson,' Lizzie Rose said, so bleakly that Clara understood that Lizzie Rose disliked Fitzmorris Pinchbeck even more than Parsefall did.

''E almost twisted my ear off last year,' Parsefall complained, 'just for 'aving a pick at the pudding.'

'It was worse for me,' Lizzie Rose flared. 'He kissed me under the mistletoe. Twice. And he has a horrid wet mouth.'

There was a brief silence. It seemed to Clara that Lizzie Rose had the better claim to be pitied. But Parsefall's mind had left Fitzmorris Pinchbeck. 'What're you going to do wiv the ten quid?'

Lizzie Rose sighed. She sank down beside the fire, wrapping her skirt around her hands to warm them. Ruby trotted over and flopped down next to her. 'You haven't answered my question,' pointed out Lizzie Rose. 'Did you know Grisini was a thief? And if you did' – her voice grew stern – 'why didn't you tell me?'

'Because he'd a killed me!' Parsefall shot back, exasperated. 'You saw wot 'e did when you peached on him! He'd a killed me if I told you!'

Lizzie Rose bent her head over Ruby. She fondled the spaniel's ears and dropped a kiss on her head. Then: 'Parse –?'

'Wot?' demanded Parsefall.

'Did you steal any of the things I found?' Lizzie Rose asked. 'I know you stole the photograph from the Wintermute house –'

*What photograph?* wondered Clara.

Parsefall said unwillingly, 'I mighta stole one of the bracelets.'

'Oh, Parsefall!'

'I 'ad to,' Parsefall said irritably. 'You don't know how it was. Grisini told me to steal things. I 'ad to do what he told me, didn't I?'

'Tell me.' After a moment: 'Tell me. I'm not going to scold you, but you must tell me the truth.'

Parsefall turned away from Lizzie Rose. He picked up his needle, knelt down before Clara and passed the thread through her left shoulder. He said slowly, 'When I was at the work'ouse –'

As his fingers closed around the puppet's torso, a picture came into Clara's head: the interior of a grim brick building and two rows of trough-like beds. It was like no place that she had ever seen, and yet she had no doubt that it was a real place: the workhouse where Parsefall had lived when he was very small. For a moment it was as if she was there herself. She was shivering with cold, and one of the bigger boys had taken her blanket. The man in the bed next to hers was sick, coughing up gobbets of blood-streaked phlegm . . . Clara wished she could shake her head from side to side. She wanted to dislodge the memories that entered into her mind as the strings passed through her limbs.

'I think I woz five or six. An' Grisini came and said he wanted a boy for 'is apprentice. So Grisini, he took three of us outside and we 'ad to play a game wiv 'im. He had a 'andful of little thin sticks, all alike, and he dropped 'em and we had to pick 'em up one at a time, wivout moving any of the other ones.'

'Spillikins,' interrupted Lizzie Rose, voicing Clara's thoughts. 'What?'

'It's a game. It's called spillikins. Go on.'

'We played that game – spillikins – and I woz the best. 'E said I woz clever with me 'ands. So he took me away wiv 'im. And I was willin', 'cos by that time, me muvver and all was dead, and I didn't want to stay in the work'ouse no more.'

'"*Any* more,"' Lizzie Rose corrected him. 'Go on.'

'So I went wiv 'im. And he showed me the puppets. He did the show by 'imself those days, and people would watch, an' my job was to pick their pockets. It weren't 'ard, because they woz watchin' the show –'

More pictures swam into Clara's mind: a gold bracelet, studded with blue-green stones, and a stout lady in a large bonnet, who watched the puppet show as happily as a child of six. It was an easy matter to sidle up close to the woman, unclasp her bracelet and catch it when it slipped off. Clara could almost feel the bracelet in her hands. The metal was still warm from the woman's wrist.

'An' I wozn't never caught. An' if the takings woz good, then Grisini'd take me to the cookshop and give me wotever I wanted for supper.' Parsefall's voice was husky with gratitude. 'I thought I was in 'eaven. I watched the shows, and he'd let me play wiv the puppets, and I learned how to work 'em. We went to fairs, an' I saw the horse races and the jugglers and the swells. And then, after a while, Grisini started teaching me to work the puppets, and he could see I woz going to be good. So he 'ad me with him in the booth, an' I didn't steal so much. He liked the puppet theatre. He liked it as much as I do. The devil couldn't hold a candle to Grisini in wickedness, but he woz good with the *fantoccini*. He liked 'em.'

'Yes,' agreed Lizzie Rose, 'he was good with the *fantoccini*. He might have made an honest living for himself. But he was a bad, disgraceful man, Parsefall, and it was very wrong of him to teach you to steal. You mustn't do it any more. Not ever.'

'I won't,' Parsefall said with a prompt willingness that Clara, at least, found unconvincing. 'Only now that we've got ten quid, what'll we do with it?'

'I suppose,' Lizzie Rose said reluctantly, 'we ought to pay rent to Mrs Pinchbeck.'

'That's a waste,' Parsefall declared. 'You've been working your fingers to the bone to pay Mrs Pinchbeck. It ain't right for 'er to have the money too.'

Lizzie Rose did not argue. Perhaps she agreed with Parsefall. She spoke in a low voice, as if confiding a secret to Ruby. 'I wish I could have a new dress. This one is so tight and greasy – and it *smells*.' She lifted her head. 'Only we ought to save, Parsefall – that is, if we don't pay the rent to Mrs Pinchbeck. And I suppose' – still more reluctantly – 'we ought to take Grisini's things to the police station because they're stolen goods. Only that might get us into trouble, and I don't see –'

Parsefall interrupted her. 'I'm 'ungry,' he said piteously. He sounded weak and almost babyish. 'I'm *ever* so 'ungry,' he repeated, in case she had missed the point.

'So'm I,' admitted Lizzie Rose. 'It'd be lovely to go to the cookshop and order a proper feast, wouldn't it? I suppose we could spend just a little. I could get a new dress for sixpence. Do you think it would be wrong to spend a whole sixpence on myself?'

Parsefall was already on his feet. His pinched little face was bright with excitement. 'We could go to the Egyptian 'All,' he said.

'The Egyptian Hall?' echoed Lizzie Rose.

'It costs a – a shillin',' Parsefall said. He hesitated before

143

the last word, and Clara understood why: for him and Lizzie Rose, the spending of a shilling was an enormity. 'The Royal Marionettes – that's what they call *fantoccini* – are playing there; they're doing *The Bottle Imp*, same as we do. Only wiv pyrotechnics,' he added, 'which is fireworks, and they 'ave over two 'undred puppets. I've 'eard about 'em. They say the puppets is life-size, and they're all string, no wires to 'em, and they've got mouths that open and shut. We could go to a cookshop,' he suggested, warming to his theme, 'and 'ave an 'ot dinner. And then we could go see the Royal Marionettes. They're the best,' he added, and then added a word Clara had never heard him use. '*Please.*'

There was a brief silence. 'Is that what you want?' Lizzie Rose said in a bemused tone of voice. 'If – if you had a shilling of your own, that's how you'd spend it?'

Parsefall jerked his head in an unqualified yes. 'You could 'ave a shillin' for your dress,' he said recklessly. 'For a shilling, you ought to be able to get something bang-up to the mark. We could 'ave supper,' he added, and Clara caught his sense of exhilaration; he saw a radiant evening before him: a full belly first, and the splendours of the Royal Marionettes to follow. 'We could 'ave supper and see the show. And we could do it tonight – if you put your togs on right away.' He swung Clara off the gallows, set her back on the mantel and picked up Lizzie Rose's muff. He shied it at her, and she caught it. 'Come on, Foxy-Loxy. It starts at eight.'

Lizzie Rose burst out laughing. She scooped Ruby off her lap and stood up. 'Very well, then,' she said, and her cheeks were pink with excitement. 'Why shouldn't we? We'll go. We'll go tonight.'

144

# Chapter Twenty-one

# The Egyptian Hall

The evening began well.

They did not take the dogs. As they strolled side by side, it dawned on Lizzie Rose that her hands were empty; there was no caravan to push and no dogs straining at the leash. She said in wonder, 'I haven't even a market basket,' and Parsefall, following her thoughts, favoured her with one of his lopsided smiles.

The traffic was heavy, making progress slow. Mingled with the stink of the river and the reek of horse manure were fainter, more appetising smells: crumpets, fried fish, saveloys and mutton pies. The children sniffed appreciatively but passed their favourite baked potato stall without a second glance. Tonight they would dine like lords and ladies, with meat and gravy, bread and butter, oysters, pudding and table beer. Parsefall, whose flat little stomach was already growling, would have chosen a tavern at random, but Lizzie Rose had other plans. She announced that she would go nowhere where the table linen was unclean. 'We don't eat the cloth,' Parsefall protested, but Lizzie Rose paid no heed. The sovereign inside her muff was no ordinary coin; it was a magic amulet that was to provide them with an evening of splendour and enchantment. To Lizzie Rose, cleanliness was enchanting, and she meant to have it. Parsefall was mystified but fell in with her desires.

After almost an hour of wandering, they entered the Royal Saxon, where the cloths were white, starched and recently laundered. A waiter appeared, a swarthy giant with the battered nose of a prizefighter; when Lizzie Rose smiled at him, he bowed and led the children to their table. They ordered extravagantly, and he filled their plates with a benign dignity that seemed to applaud their appetites. For once, Lizzie Rose had all the roast beef she wanted and enough milk to turn her tea white; to her delight, her teacup had rosebuds on it. Parsefall devoured most of an eel pie, slurped innumerable oysters and amused Lizzie Rose by making castanets of the shells. By the time the children left the Royal Saxon, their bellies were stuffed to the point of discomfort, but they did not complain.

Outside, the darkness had thickened, and a mizzling rain was falling. The church bells tolled seven o'clock. 'It starts at eight,' Parsefall said urgently, and hurried Lizzie Rose through the Haymarket towards Piccadilly. The streets were jammed with carriages full of elegantly dressed people bound for the theatre. Men in sandwich boards sauntered back and forth, advertising the shows; a fire-eater plied his trade on one corner, a Bible seller on another. There were a great many idlers: men in top hats and girls with painted faces. To Lizzie Rose's distress, one young man exclaimed over the colour of her hair, wished her a drunken good evening and dogged her footsteps.

'Wot's 'e want?' demanded Parsefall. 'Where d'you know 'im from?'

'I don't know him,' Lizzie Rose said shortly. She dodged between two carriages, jerking Parsefall along with her. 'Men come here to stare at women. He thinks I'm pretty.'

'Blinkin' fool,' Parsefall said, not entirely to Lizzie Rose's satisfaction. 'Come on, Foxy-Loxy. He can't 'urt you just by lookin'.'

Lizzie Rose was not so sure. She was relieved when they reached the Egyptian Hall. It was a queer-looking building, she thought, with two nearly naked statues above the central door. She supposed they were heathen gods, though they wore wigs. It seemed odd that supernatural beings should be unable to provide themselves with adequate hair.

'Come on,' urged Parsefall. 'Let's go in.'

They passed through the papyrus columns and went inside. The interior of the Hall was colourful and outlandish, adorned with a riot of hieroglyphics and statues: crocodiles and sphinxes and hawks in wigs. Lizzie Rose had little time to admire them, for Parsefall was in a hurry to secure their seats. They paid their shillings, plunged through the crowd with more force than good manners and planted themselves in the third row.

Parsefall craned his neck, looking upwards. Lizzie Rose's eyes followed his. Far above their heads was an immense chandelier, glittering like a tree encased in ice; before them was the stage, curtained in olive green. Nestled in the folds of the stage curtains was a smaller theatre, a pavilion in gold-and-silver brocade. 'For the *fantoccini*,' whispered Parsefall; the new term *marionette* was still strange to him. There was an orchestra. 'Nine players,' said Parsefall, counting on his nine fingers. When the musicians began to tune their instruments, he whirled around and shushed the people in the fourth row with such passion that they stopped talking for nearly a minute.

The show started. To begin with, there was a conjurer and a man with trained dogs. The conjurer had brown curls and a teasing smile; Lizzie Rose fell in love with him at once but forgot him when the dogs came in. There were two of them, dressed in pink and blue satin, and they danced a minuet on their hind legs. Parsefall was restless; he wanted the Royal Marionettes. When at last the curtains of the small stage parted, he leaned forward like a thirsty man about to take a drink.

For the next two hours, he never took his eyes off the stage. Beside him, Lizzie Rose watched the show, but from time to time her eyes came back to rest on Parsefall's face. He was spellbound, and no wonder; the world before him was sharp edged, exquisite and eerily alive. There were knights and fairies, demons and clowns, sword fighting, slapstick and the ballet; there were fireworks and water cascades. The showmen had used every material to its best advantage: looking glass, pasteboard, paint and wax; wood, cloth and papier-mâché. The figure workers might not be as deft as Grisini, but their show was far more spectacular; Grisini's equipment was tatty by comparison.

'They 'ave a *giuoco di luce* – that's a stage machine Grisini told me about' were Parsefall's first words after the curtain fell. 'That's 'ow they did the fireworks and waterfalls an' all. But their puppets ain't life-size – that's a take-in. The Mother Shipton was the biggest; she mighta been three foot tall, but she was closer to two.' He reached up, feeling his bony chin. 'The mouths move wiv a wire from the chin to the top of the 'ead; they must be weighted so they stay shut unless you pull the string. That scene when the man in *The Bottle Imp* woz dying an' the medicine bottles danced with demons in 'em – wiv all the demons mouthin' and mockin'– that was the best thing I've ever seen.'

'Oh, yes! Wasn't it horrid?' exclaimed Lizzie Rose. 'It made my flesh creep. And wasn't the transformation scene lovely, with the fairy grotto –?'

'That was lit gauzes.' Parsefall snapped his fingers. 'It were quick, though, weren't it? They must 'ave people just to change the scenery. The figure working weren't too bad. The same worker did the lead females – the fairy queen and Lucretia – did you notice? It were the same style –'

'Parse,' Lizzie Rose interrupted gently, 'I think they want to close the theatre now. We're the only people left –'

'I know that,' Parsefall said, to her surprise. 'I'm waiting to talk to 'em.' He jerked his head towards the stage, and his eyes narrowed. 'I mean to work for 'em,' he said. 'I 'eard they woz good, but I didn't know –'

'But, Parsefall,' protested Lizzie Rose, 'we have to stay together. And besides, they wouldn't let you in. You know how it is with puppet workers. It's almost always a family company, and they pass down their skills from father to son. They wouldn't want you.'

'Why wouldn't they?' demanded Parsefall. 'Even the best of 'em ain't better than Grisini, and Grisini taught me. They wouldn't 'ave to pay me at first – I could be an apprentice –'

'Parsefall,' Lizzie Rose said thoughtlessly, 'you're a *little boy.*'

The minute the words left her lips, she regretted them. Parsefall did not think of himself as a little boy. His face reddened. In another instant, he was out of his chair. He dodged around the two front rows of seats and leaped on to the stage, narrowly missing the footlights. Then he lifted the edge of the curtain and ducked underneath.

'Parsefall!' Lizzie Rose called, but it was too late. She heard voices backstage, a man shouting and another swearing, and then Parsefall's voice, speaking rapidly and pleadingly. He was answered by a low growl. A moment later, the curtain bulged outward, as if someone had stumbled against it. Lizzie Rose left her seat. She reached the edge of the stage as Parsefall came out through the slit between the curtains. For one dreadful moment, she was afraid he was crying, but though his face was working, his eyes were hard and dry.

'They don't want me. Let's get out' was all he said, and he jumped down from the stage. He darted forward so that she had to run to keep up with him, and when she tried to put an arm around him, he struck at her, knocking her muff to the floor.

# Chapter Twenty-two

# The Rocking Chair

Parsefall couldn't sleep. He was plagued by two powerful enemies of slumber: hurt pride and an upset stomach. His stomach muscles jerked and strained, trying to subdue the half-digested mess inside: oysters, mashed turnips, eel pie, sausages and a pudding compounded from treacle and suet. A wave of nausea passed over him, and he wondered if he was going to be sick.

He shifted, sat up in bed and swallowed hard. Parsefall detested being sick. It wasn't the sour taste he loathed or the mess; he hated being forced to part with anything that was rightfully his. He opened his mouth, hoping to belch. A faint hiccup rewarded him.

He wondered if Lizzie Rose was awake. He knew that she was cross with him, and he didn't altogether blame her. She had tried to console him after his rejection, but her pity was salt in the wound; he'd been nasty to her all the way home. Once they were back in their lodgings, Ruby – bloody 'orrible Ruby – had started in where Lizzie Rose left off, trailing after him with sad eyes and pawing at his trouser legs. He had sworn at the dog and aimed a kick in her direction. That was when Lizzie Rose lost her temper. She'd called him a horrid cruel beast, and he'd answered back in kind, greatly relieved that she had stopped pitying him. They ended the evening by shouting insults at each other and retiring to bed in icy silence.

Parsefall sighed, wishing he trusted his stomach enough to lie back down. The room was cold, and he was sleepy. He wrapped the thickest blanket around him like a cocoon. Outside, a cat yowled. Parsefall shivered a little. He wondered what time it was. The fire on the hearth had burned low, but a street lamp shone through the grime of the window. It made Grisini's old coat rack look like a humpbacked crone. Parsefall glanced from corner to corner, making sure nothing stirred in the shadows.

Clara was staring at him.

Parsefall felt the hair on his arms rise. She lay on the mantel with her head twisted outward, and her glass eyes caught the glow from the street lamp. It was a trick of the light, no more. But looking back at the mantel, he could not rid himself of the idea that she was awake. 'Lemme alone,' he whispered, but her gaze was unblinking.

'Damn yer eyes,' Parsefall said. 'I don't 'ave to look at you.' He turned his back to the mantel. He folded his lumpy mattress so that it supported his shoulders, easing himself into a half-reclining position. He swallowed, shut his eyes and drifted into sleep.

In his dream, he heard a rhythmic sound, repetitive as the

song of a cricket. It was the creak of a rocking chair, and in the rocking chair sat Grisini. The puppet master lurched back and forth, smiling a little. Parsefall yelped, twitched and woke himself up.

He sat up in bed. Grisini wasn't there. He listened, wondering if Lizzie Rose had heard his cry, but there was no sound from her bedroom. He thought of calling her, remembered the quarrel and clenched his teeth to keep from whimpering.

Grisini was dead. That was the thing he was counting on, the thing he had to remember. Grisini was dead, and there was no rocking chair in the room. Parsefall remembered Grisini's rocking chair. It had broken one day, and Grisini had cracked the frame apart and thrown the fragments on the fire. Parsefall twisted about, gazing at the dying coals, half expecting to see the shards of burning wood.

He raised his eyes to the mantelshelf. Clara was still staring. Her glassy eyes were piercing, as if she saw through his skin to the nightmares he carried inside. He felt a surge of rage that overcame his fear, and he squirmed out of his cocoon. He wasn't going to put up with her one minute longer. He would take her into Grisini's room and hang her from the bed frame. Or perhaps he'd shut her up in the wicker trunk; he was almost sure she hated that. Even better, he would throw her on the fire; burn her, like a witch . . .

He reached up and caught hold of the wooden perch, but his hands were shaking and he dropped her. Clara fell face up on to the carpet. Parsefall squatted down and picked her up.

She felt different from the other puppets. They were sticky with shellac, and their clothes were limp and greasy. Clara's frock was crisp and clean, and her skin was soft. Her body emitted a faint heat. Parsefall's anger melted away. He lay back down, clasping the puppet against his unquiet stomach.

Almost at once, he felt better. As he lay there with one hand draped over her, he fancied that she sympathised with him, that she understood his terror. The idea was comforting. He pulled her closer. She was warm and strong and solid. As if he was stretching out a hand, he tried to think himself inside her, to imagine the thoughts that passed through her mind.

The answer came at once. She felt trapped. She *was* trapped, locked in her puppet body, unable to speak or move. She wanted him to finish stringing her: to give her life. And he could do it. He might not be welcome at the company of Royal Marionettes, but he could liven up Clara. Tomorrow he'd start working with her, rehearsing the ballet dance he'd copied from Grisini. Lizzie Rose wouldn't like it – she didn't think Clara ought to be treated like an ordinary puppet – but it wasn't any of Lizzie Rose's business. She'd abandoned the theatre; she'd rather do housework. Very well, then; he'd put together a show without her. He'd start his own company.

He began to review the possibilities, subtracting the acts that called for two figure workers. He might start with the sailor's hornpipe – he'd have to get the audience clapping to provide a beat for the dance – and then the circus acts, followed by the ballet. He could take Grisini's old music box and wind it up, so that Clara would have music for the dance. That would work. Then he would end with the skeleton puppet. It wouldn't be as good without music, but it was his best act; it had to go last.

'I'll finish stringing you tomorrow,' he whispered to Clara. 'It won't take long. We'll practise the bally dance – and soon we'll do the shows. Lizzie Rose won't come with us, but we'll get along by ourselves, won't we?'

He did not bother to imagine the response from the puppet in his arms. He was drowsy now, and his nausea had almost passed. He dragged the coverlet up to his shoulders and fell asleep. Even as he slept, his fingers twitched, rehearsing the movement of the puppets.

# Chapter Twenty-three

# The Streets

Four days later, Clara was packed inside the new wagon and hauled off to perform her first show.

She was swathed in a muslin bag, so she couldn't see. As the wagon rattled through the streets, she hung from the puppet gallows, swaying back and forth with every bump and jerk. She heard the din of the crowded city: the scraping of wheels against cobblestones, the clip-clop of hooves, the shouts of coachmen and costermongers. The wagon's progress was fitful: Parsefall was too small to make anyone give way to him, and he was forced to travel in zigzags, dodging foot traffic and coaches alike. Once or twice, Clara heard someone swear at him. A woman shouted, "Ere, now!' and a man bellowed, 'D'you *want* to end up under the 'ooves?' Undaunted, Parsefall answered with oaths of his own.

The wagon swerved and jolted for more than an hour. The streets grew quieter; they were entering a less crowded part of the city. Clara felt the wagon back up and strike something hard. A moment later, the gallows rose into the air; Parsefall was lifting it. His hands fumbled for Clara's bag, loosening the drawstring. He drew her out, and at last she could see.

They had come to a square in Pimlico. There was a large rectangle of garden surrounded by iron palings, and the houses around the square were white columned and prosperous looking. It was very like Chester Square, and Clara felt a wave of homesickness.

Parsefall set to work at once. He pushed the wagon close to the iron palings, so that the fence would be at his back. Clara understood why. Performing alone, he had no one to guard his puppets. He reached into the wagon and unpacked the drum, the music box and a toy horn. He shoved the horn into his mouth. As he prepared the theatre for the show, he blew a series of ear-splitting blasts. Between the blasts, Clara heard childish voices from the other side of the fence. There were children playing in the garden. Parsefall was hoping to attract them.

He set the gallows at right angles to the stage, pinned back the curtains and unrolled the backdrop. He arranged a black cloth over his head and mounted the wagon. Picking up the drum, he began to play.

Clara listened with misgivings. Who would come? The day was raw; the sounds of the horn and drum were faint; the wagon was gimcrack and rickety and small. But luck was with Parsefall. The children's voices grew louder. They had heard the horn and followed the sound. The gallows vibrated as Parsefall reached for one of the *fantoccini*.

The show began. Clara could not see the audience, but she heard ripples of laughter and gasps of delight. After a quarter of an hour, she heard the staccato whirr of machinery: the winding up of the music box. It was her cue. She felt herself being lifted off the gallows and flown through the air. She ended up centre stage, in front of the painted backdrop.

She was surprised by the size of the audience. A governess with three children, a nursemaid carrying a baby, a red-faced clergyman, an errand boy with his hands full of envelopes ... So far, so good – but beyond this crowd of respectable-looking people was a sprinkling of paupers. She saw a chimney sweep and two ragged girls, evidently sisters. There was an ancient man with black teeth and an idiot grin, and a drunkard in a red kerchief.

It was the drunkard who stood closest to the stage, close enough to touch her if he chose. Clara quailed at the sight of him. He was thickset and unshaven. He seemed fascinated by the puppet show. He stood head cocked, hands dangling, rocking back and forth in time to the music.

Clara was afraid of him. She wished she could close her eyes and shut out the faces of the crowd. But her eyes were wide open and the music box was tinkling. Parsefall was tugging at her strings.

She rose on the tips of her toes, her arms coming together, her wrists crossing. One of the ragged girls gave a coo of admiration. Clara stretched out her left foot, toe pointed, and lifted her arms to pose. The perch raised her, and she floated into a leap. She obeyed every motion of the strings; her limbs were as light as flower stems and as smooth as water. The crowd was silent, held in thrall by the silvery music and the little dancer in the white frock.

A thrill of joy ran through Clara. She was moving with such lightness and sureness that she almost fancied that she moved by herself. The drunken man jerked his thumb at her and said, 'Look at that!' and she wanted to smile at him. Why, he was – she searched for the right word and found it – *innocent*. He might be coarse and dirty and drunk, but he was as hungry for enchantment as she had been at her birthday party.

The music was slowing down. Clara kept time. She gave one final cat leap, lowered her arms and sank into a curtsy. The old man with the black teeth clapped like a child, elbows out. The others joined in, and there was a round of excited applause. Clara wanted to laugh with happiness. She felt Parsefall's triumph ripple through his hands and down her strings. She wanted to dance again. But the perch was yanking her away, swinging her past the curtain; she felt the hook at the top clamp over the gallows rack. It was time for the skeleton to dance. Clara swayed back and forth, her strings still quivering. Little by little, the swaying stopped, and her body hung slack and still.

# Chapter Twenty-four

# The Legacy

Lizzie Rose sat by the fire, mending a torn shirt for Fitzmorris Pinchbeck. She sewed with her nostrils quivering and her mouth screwed up, pulling the thread so taut that the cloth nearly gave way. The shirt reeked of hair oil, and the seams under the arms were yellow with perspiration. Lizzie Rose almost shuddered as she stitched, and Ruby, who lay close beside her, had a worried look on her furry face.

The detested Mr Pinchbeck had come two weeks early to celebrate Christmas, and there was no prospect of him leaving anytime soon. His trade was selling artificial teeth, but he had recently lost his place, and he found Grisini's old bedroom very comfortable. He would have liked the entire floor for his use, but when he said so, Mrs Pinchbeck brandished a lace-edged handkerchief and swore that she could never, never be so cruel as to turn helpless little orphelings into the street. Mr Pinchbeck responded by saying that he hoped the little orphelings were grateful for his stepmother's charity. Every day, he thought of new ways for them to show their gratitude. Parsefall was to bring his shaving water, polish his boots and run his errands; Lizzie Rose was to make his bed, tend his fires and mend his clothes.

This was bad enough, but it was not all. To Lizzie Rose's great disgust, she found favour in Mr Pinchbeck's eyes. He patted the sash of her pinafore, chucked her under the chin and teased her with sucking noises that sounded like kisses. Lizzie Rose did everything she could to escape his attentions. She dressed herself in her shabbiest clothes and spoke to him as rudely as she dared. It was a wet December, but she spent much of her time out of doors, walking the dogs. During the worst downpours, she took shelter in the secondhand shops and hunted for winter clothing. She told herself she must spend as little as possible, but the money from Grisini's pawned watch seemed to burn a hole in her pocket. She bought herself a servant's dress, a red flannel petticoat and a warm nightgown. For Parsefall, she bought two pairs of thick stockings, galoshes and a heavy wool coat. The coat was a little too large for him, but that was an asset; he could wear his old jacket underneath.

She clipped the last thread on Mr Pinchbeck's shirt, set it aside and wiped her hands on her apron. The mending basket was still full: Mr Pinchbeck had given her five pairs of his horrid stockings to darn. Lizzie Rose reached instead for Parsefall's old jacket. He'd complained that there were holes in his pockets, and she'd promised to patch them.

The right-hand pocket bulged. Lizzie Rose smiled a little. Parsefall was always picking up odds and ends and storing them in his coat. She fished inside and found a cache of rubbish caught between the jacket and the lining: two bills addressed to Mrs

Pinchbeck, an advertisement for Cooke's travelling circus, an oyster shell, several hairpins, a large piece of coal and a letter.

It was the letter that caught her attention. It was sealed with red wax and a single letter: *S*. Though the envelope was soiled and creased, the spiky writing was still readable. The letter was addressed to Gaspare Grisini at Danvers Street. Someone had written *Urgent* beneath Grisini's name and underscored it in black ink.

Lizzie Rose drew her bottom lip between her teeth. No lady ever read a letter unless it was addressed to her. All the same, the letter was marked *Urgent*, and the date on the postmark was more than two weeks past. After a moment's thought, she broke the seal and unfolded the letter, slipping the envelope into her apron pocket.

*My dear Gaspare,*

*It has been many weeks since I heard from you. If you were a different man, I should be anxious; as it is, I am impatient. Why have you not answered my letter? I have very little time left. The doctor tells me that I shall not live to see another spring.*

*I do not expect you to pity me. Nor do I pity myself. I have lived a long life and enjoyed more than my share of the world's goods. Now I can hold on to nothing – not my fortune nor my jewels nor Strachan's Ghyll. That is why I am asking you to come to me and to bring your apprentices with you. You will think me an old woman in my dotage, but I tell you, my mind is fixed on those children.*

*You wrote to me that they are orphans, without a penny in the world. I think of them, left to your tender mercies, and a strange fancy comes into my mind: why should they not inherit my wealth? I have no one of my blood to succeed me, and the prospect of playing fairy godmother amuses me. I think I should like to enrich your two hardworking orphans. But of course, before I arrange their legacies, I must first meet the children face-to-face and make sure that I like them.*

*Now for the journey. You must come north to West-morland. Leave London from King's Cross Station and take the train to Lancaster, from thence to Kendal and then Windermere. I believe first-class tickets are something like fifteen shillings, so I enclose five pounds for the journey. The sum should prove ample. At Windermere, the proprietor of the Black Bear will allow you the hire of a coach. You may come to Strachan's Ghyll at any hour, day or night. I have told my housekeeper to prepare rooms for you and the children.*

*I pray you, come soon. I have no time to waste.*

> *Yours most truly,*
> *Cassandra Strachan Sagredo*

Lizzie Rose reread the letter, first with astonishment, then with wonder. She could not doubt that she and Parsefall were the children referred to in the letter. It sounded as though the unknown woman was very rich; she had referred to jewels, and Strachan's Ghyll must be the queer name of her house. *I think I should like to enrich your two hardworking orphans.* Lizzie Rose clasped the letter to her breast. She felt as if she was living in a play. In the theatre, legacies arrived during the fifth act, when everything was at its worst. Some offstage person would die, clearing the pathway for a happy ending. A legacy meant rescue, luxury and the promise of happiness.

Lizzie Rose unfolded the five-pound note that had fallen into her lap. Lancaster, Windermere, Westmorland . . . She wished her father's atlas had not been sold. She wasn't quite sure where Westmorland was, but she thought it was almost as far north as Scotland. What if she and Parsefall made the long journey only to be turned away? Cassandra Sagredo was evidently a friend of Grisini's, but Grisini had vanished without a trace. Would Grisini's children be welcome without him? Perhaps Lizzie Rose should write to Mrs Sagredo and ask if it might be so.

It would be an awkward letter to write. Lizzie Rose could think of no delicate way to phrase it. She would have to begin by explaining why she had opened a letter that wasn't addressed to her. Then she would have to find some way to hint that though Grisini had disappeared, she and Parsefall were still available to be enriched. She must sound grateful but not greedy – and then, if Mrs Sagredo persisted in inviting them, Parsefall would have to be induced to make the journey. It was unlikely that he would want to abandon the puppet theatre during the holiday season. Only yesterday he had come home with two shillings ninepence halfpenny and the joyful conviction that business was picking up.

The front door slammed. The parrot shouted, 'Ruination! Wipe your boots!' and was told by a nasal voice to 'Stow it!' There was the sound of Mr Pinchbeck's heavy tread on the stairs. Lizzie Rose's smile faded. She reached down, picked up Ruby and tiptoed into her makeshift bedchamber, drawing the spangled curtain across the doorway. If she kept still and made no sound, Mr Pinchbeck might pass into the next room without suspecting she was at home. She cupped her fingers around Ruby's muzzle and waited, scarcely daring to breathe.

# Chapter Twenty-five

# A Member of the Audience

Clara hung from the gallows in Parsefall's wagon. It had been a wet week, and the clatter of the wheels was muffled by the sound of splashing. Parsefall slogged through an icy stew of mud and straw, horse manure and urine. Inside the wagon, Clara was spared the worst of the mire, but she could not help remembering the days when she rode through London in her mother's carriage. If she walked, it was in the park with her governess; if they had to cross a street, Miss Cameron paid to have a path swept clear. No crossing sweeper ever lifted a broom to sweep a path for Parsefall. It was only too clear that he had no halfpennies to waste on cleanliness. Parsefall cursed the sloppy streets, but only because they slowed him down. He had a show to give, and his mind was on his work.

In the past weeks, Clara had come to look forward to the puppet shows even more than Parsefall did. When he lifted the perch and pulled her strings, her bloodless body seemed to tingle, and she felt as if something quickened inside her. She could almost imagine that her limbs stretched and swayed by their own free will. It was not true, of course. But she wondered if one day it might be true – if somehow Parsefall might help her to cross the border between paralysis and life. With every touch, the bond between them grew stronger. When he played upon her strings, Clara glimpsed the splendours and glooms that haunted his mind. She shared his appetite for prodigies and wonders, for a world where spangles were stars and skeletons frolicked until their bones fell apart.

She knew his fears and his weaknesses. The spectre of Grisini lurked in the darkest corners of Parsefall's mind. Parsefall hated foggy days, not just because they were bad for business but because he was afraid that Grisini might be following him, masked by the fog. Hunger was another, lesser spectre, and with hunger came guilt. Parsefall was shocked by how much money he spent on sausage rolls and penny buns. He lied to Lizzie Rose about his daily earnings and concealed from her the shameful fact that he'd bought something to eat. Now and again he bought two buns and put one in his pocket, but if it was his ambition to take the second bun home to Lizzie Rose, he never achieved it. Almost before he knew it, the treat was out of his pocket and between his teeth. He gobbled every crumb, sucked the sugar from his fingers and despised himself for his greed. Lizzie Rose would scarcely have believed that her adopted brother possessed so tender a conscience: Clara knew better. She recognised guilt, even when it was only a shadow in someone else's mind.

On that raw day in December, Clara was holding an arabesque, her profile to the audience, when a man strode towards the stage. Clara saw him only from the corner of her eye, but she knew him: a man with hair as dark as hers, broad shouldered and prosperous. She wanted to gasp, to cry out to him. Parsefall spun the perch, making Clara pivot *en pointe*. When she stopped spinning, she was facing her father.

He was as pale as death. She saw him elbow his way forward, close to the front of the stage. Her father, who never shoved, her father, who never shouted, was shouting: 'Where did you get that puppet?'

Parsefall's hand jerked, making Clara jump straight-legged into the air. He swung her offstage, around and behind the backdrop.

'*Where did you get* –?' Dr Wintermute's voice was thunderous. His hand reached under the backdrop and seized Clara's legs.

Parsefall did not let go. Clara's head strings went taut; she felt the screws grind against her temples. Her father gripped her so tightly that his arm shook. A thrill ran through her like an electric shock. *Why, he loves me,* she thought in amazement. The idea was new to her. If anyone had asked her, she would have said that of course her father loved her; good fathers must always love their children. But she had always known how deeply he mourned Charles Augustus. She was the twin who should have died. Now, feeling the tremor in her father's hand, she understood that she was precious to him, and she wanted to weep for joy.

One of her head strings snapped. Parsefall shouted, 'Leggo!' The audience was murmuring, upset that the show had been interrupted. Parsefall shrilled, 'Gimme back my puppet!' and the bystanders backed him up: 'That's right!' 'Give 'im 'is puppet and get out of the way!'

'Come on, guv'nor!' shouted a boy from the back of the crowd. 'Give it up and let the show go on!'

'It isn't right to steal a poor boy's puppet,' said an elderly woman. 'That's his living.'

Dr Wintermute didn't seem to have heard. 'I know you!' he cried out. 'You're Grisini's boy! I saw you the day my daughter was kidnapped. Grisini made that puppet, didn't he? He kidnapped her. He took my Clara.' His voice broke. 'Tell me what he did with her.'

'Grisini's gone,' Parsefall shot back. He corrected himself. ''E's dead. Bashed 'is brains in. Leggo-a-me!' His voice rose, enlisting the help of the audience. 'Leggo-a-me puppet, sir! Don' 'urt me! I ain't done nuffink!'

His ploy was effective. Clara heard a rustle from the other side of the curtain. A man said, 'Bloomin' shame.'

The elderly woman quavered, 'Stop, sir! If you hurt that boy, I shall call a constable!'

Parsefall squealed like a pig. Dr Wintermute released Clara and came around the side of the wagon. He seized Parsefall's collar, holding him prisoner. 'What do you mean, he's dead? He can't be dead. How can he be dead?'

Parsefall shook himself like a wet cat. He twisted and squirmed. In the scuffle, Clara fell from his hand, landing face up on the cobblestones.

Two hands reached for her. One hand was large, clean and strong, a hand that she had loved all her life. The other hand was small and filthy, with one finger missing. In an instant, Clara knew which hand she wanted to capture her. *Please!* she begged. As if he heard her thoughts, Parsefall snatched her up and crammed her inside his jacket.

*Run!* thought Clara. She wanted beyond everything to get away. If her father, who loved her, wrested her from Parsefall, he would take her back home again. Her mother would weep over the puppet that resembled her lost daughter. Clara would hang on the wall, next to the death masks of the Others. She would never dance again; she would lose all hope of coming back to life.

She felt Parsefall leap sideways. There was a scuffle. She heard the rattle of the coins in the money box and a series of thumping sounds. Parsefall was packing up the wagon.

'Stop! Thief!' Dr Wintermute was shouting, but Parsefall leaped forward. The wagon wheels swashed over the cobbles. *He can't get away*, Clara thought despairingly. *He can't go fast enough if he has the wagon, and he'll never abandon the wagon —*

A horse whinnied. A man shouted, 'Bloody 'ell!' Parsefall fell headlong, sprawling. Men were shouting, and a woman was screaming.

A gruff voice spoke. 'Whoa, now! Steady, now!'

Her father was entreating everyone to remain calm. He said, 'Let me help; I'm a doctor —' In an instant, Parsefall was back on his feet and running full speed, one arm around Clara and the other towing the wagon.

He veered to the right. There was a scraping noise: the wagon catching on the corner of a brick building. Parsefall dragged it free. He was panting now, and Clara could hear his heart beat double time. The music box was still tinkling.

Little by little, his pace slowed. His gasps turned to wheezing sounds. When at last he came to a stop, he opened his jacket. Clara's head fell back. She found herself staring at a single pair of wet trousers, pegged to a clothesline. A cat mewed nearby. Parsefall had brought her to an empty courtyard.

Parsefall took Clara from his jacket and examined her with narrowed eyes. Her head flopped so that her ear touched her shoulder, and her right elbow faced forward. Her left knee bent the wrong way. Parsefall frowned and wiped her sodden skirt against his coat sleeve, an act that did no favours either to Clara or the coat. Then he set her back on the gallows, knelt down on the pavement and began to unravel her strings.

# Chapter Twenty-six

# In Which Dr Wintermute Recovers a Lost Object

Grisini's boy had provoked an accident. His flight through the streets had caused a collision between a closed carriage and a hansom cab. The cabbie had been thrown from his seat, and the woman inside the carriage was sobbing hysterically. The accident gave the boy an advantage; he found a gap in the snarled traffic, forced the wagon through it and disappeared like an eel into its burrow. Dr Wintermute saw that further pursuit was futile. He was bound both by conscience and by training to tend to anyone who was hurt. Nevertheless, it cost him dearly to abandon the chase.

He helped the cabbie to his feet, made sure that there was no head injury and turned his attention to the woman. She was heavily pregnant and panic-stricken. Dr Wintermute examined her and assured her that all was well. He advised her to return home, loosen her corsets and spend the rest of the day in bed. Once she had promised to follow his orders, he returned to the cabbie, who was nursing his arm to his chest. Dr Wintermute diagnosed a sprained wrist. He wrapped it tightly, using his own muffler as a bandage.

After the cabbie drove off, Dr Wintermute made his way to the kerb. He felt shaken. The puppet's face swam before his mind's eye: heart shaped, pink cheeked, with Clara's smile frozen on its lips. Why had Grisini created a puppet in the image of his daughter? How – and when – and what hideous thing did it mean? Dr Wintermute's first impulse – to go to the police station – seemed futile. The existence of the puppet proved nothing. He could not tell a police constable how the sight of it had pierced his heart.

He began to walk, not knowing where he was going. He realised after a time that he had missed the cross street that would have taken him home. In the weeks since Clara's disappearance, Dr Wintermute had come to dread the house in Chester Square. The atmosphere of grief was stifling, as if the walls had thickened, blocking every breath of air and ray of light. He knew it was his duty to be strong for his wife, but he could not help Ada. In his worst moments he shrank from her. Her anguish increased his own.

He had resumed work in early December. It comforted him to be of use again. When he was with patients, he was himself once more: calm, skilled, compassionate. When he returned home, he changed back into a man he could not respect: a husband too heartsick to ease his wife's pain, a father who had failed to save even one of his five children.

He became aware that he had wandered into Chelsea. It was a poor section of town, and the narrow houses looked bleak and cheerless. Rubbish lay thick underfoot, and the stink of the polluted river made him wish that he could pull his muffler over his nose. Then it struck him: Professor Grisini lived in Chelsea. He recalled the letter he had written, arranging for the showman to perform at Clara's party. He remembered the address, even the house number.

His step quickened as he made his way to Danvers Street. The police had assured him that they shared his suspicions of Grisini; they had promised to keep a close watch on him, even stationing a constable to watch Mrs Pinchbeck's lodgings at night. Yet they had failed. The officer detective had been forced to admit that Grisini had eluded them. The puppet master had left London, and his unreliable landlady could provide no clue as to where he might be. Now Grisini's boy had blurted out that his master was not missing but dead. Dr Wintermute told himself that it could not be true. He scanned the housefronts for numbers. A servant girl walking her mistress's dogs skimmed past him. To his surprise, she went straight to the house he was seeking.

She went up the front steps and went in without knocking. After a split second, the door swung back open. There was a cry of distress. Dr Wintermute rushed forward.

He stopped on the threshold, confused. A young man in a plaid overcoat and chimney-pot hat held the maidservant prisoner; he had both arms around her waist and was planting a series of smacking kisses on her lips. The girl squirmed and struggled, her face screwed up with distaste. The room was alive with barking dogs. Their leashes were twisted together and caught inside in a moth-eaten muff, which bounced over the carpet like a sixth dog.

The servant girl entreated, 'Oh, stop, *please*!' and Dr Wintermute did stop, startled by her voice. The girl was slatternly; her skirts were too short and her apron was soiled, but she spoke in the accents of a young lady. His sense of chivalry awakened, Dr Wintermute seized the man and swung him around with such force that the chimney-pot hat flew off. 'Release her, sir!'

The young man looked blank. He had a fleshy face with a mouth like a baby's. It was the sort of face that Dr Wintermute instinctively disliked. Moreover, the man smelled of gin. The girl, seeing her escape, ducked away from the two men and went after the dogs. Dr Wintermute had thought she was a young woman; she was almost as tall as the man who had tried to kiss her. Now that she knelt on the floor, he saw that her figure was childishly slight and that she wore her hair in plaits. She was only a year or two older than his Clara. A thrill of rage passed through him, and he turned back to the young man with murder in his eyes. 'How dare you molest this young person?'

The young man attempted a conciliatory grin. He jerked his thumb towards the ceiling, pointing to a bunch of mistletoe tied with red ribbon. 'Good Lord, sir! It was only a kiss! Christmastime, you know!'

'It is not Christmas yet,' Dr Wintermute said coldly, 'nor does Our Lord's birthday grant you the liberty to force yourself on a defenceless child.'

The young man reddened. 'There warn't any 'arm in it.' He turned to the girl as if he expected her to defend him. '*She* don't mind, do you, Lizzie Rose?'

The servant girl scrambled to her feet. 'I do mind,' she said indignantly. 'I do, indeed! I hate it when you kiss me!'

'You see, sir.' Dr Wintermute's voice was steely. 'Your conduct is offensive.' He picked up the man's hat and held it out. 'I believe you were on the point of leaving. Pray do not allow me to detain you.'

The young man looked baffled. 'I don't know what right you 'ave to tell me to leave the 'ouse,' he said. 'Not your 'ouse, is it? It's my stepmother's 'ouse, and I'm passin' Christmas wiv 'er. No 'arm in that, is there?'

'That remains to be seen,' Dr Wintermute said coldly. He strode to the door and held it open. 'Sir.'

The man stared at him stupidly. Then he gave up. With tipsy dignity, he edged past Dr Wintermute. He misjudged the height of one of the steps, stumbled without falling and descended to the street. Dr Wintermute shut the door sharply and turned back to the girl.

'Thank you, sir.' The girl placed one broken boot behind the other and sank into a curtsy. It was not, Dr Wintermute observed, the usual servant's bob but a graceful and elaborate gesture, such as a dancer might make on the stage. All at once he knew who she was. She was one of the puppet master's assistants, and he had seen her on the day of Clara's birthday party. His heart beat faster. Perhaps she might know something of Grisini.

'Are you here to see Mrs Pinchbeck, sir?'

She had pronounced her *h*'s. Dr Wintermute examined her curiously. She reminded him of someone, though he could not think whom. 'I think I would rather speak to you. My name is Dr Wintermute. You may remember me from the day of my daughter's birthday party.'

'Oh!' The girl brought her hands to her lips. 'You're Clara's father!'

Dr Wintermute winced. 'Yes. I'm Clara's father.' He took a deep breath, composing himself. 'You worked with Professor Grisini, did you not?'

'Yes, sir. I'm so sorry – about Clara.'

'Would you be so good as to grant me a little of your time? I should like to ask you some questions.'

'Of course, sir. Come upstairs, sir. Just let me – the dogs –' As she spoke, the girl took a key from her pocket and unlocked the door to the left of the staircase. Hastily she dragged the bulldog, the pug, the beagle and the rat terrier towards the door, untied their leashes and pushed them through the opening. Then she relocked the door and picked up the red spaniel. 'Thank you. If you'll follow me, sir –' She stopped, her eyes raised to the bunch of mistletoe. Dr Wintermute divined what she was thinking.

'Would you like me to take that down?'

'Oh, yes, please!'

The ceiling was low; it was no trouble for Dr Wintermute to catch hold of the red ribbon and un-tack the mistletoe. The girl nodded her thanks and headed up the stairs. The staircase was steep, dark and narrow. Dr Wintermute noted that some of the steps had been patched with wood from a packing crate. He glanced at the hand rope that served as a banister, noted the crumbling plaster around it and grimaced.

At the top of the stairs, the girl set down the dog. She led him down a narrow passage and unlocked the door. 'Come in, sir.'

Dr Wintermute went inside. He was well aware that there was poverty in the world, but he had never seen anything like the gaudy squalor of Grisini's chambers. In one corner there was a sort of playhouse built out of rubbish, with a spangled curtain for a door. Clotheslines had been strung from one wall to the next, bearing an assortment of string puppets: some missing arms and legs, some naked, all with oversize heads and staring eyes.

'This way, sir.' The girl edged her way through the clutter to the fire. She drew a stained armchair close to the hearth. She knelt before the fire, added a few lumps of coal and held out her hand for the mistletoe, which she placed in the midst of the flames. 'Pray sit down, sir.'

'You have no chair,' Dr Wintermute pointed out.

'I like to sit by the fire.' The girl patted her lap, and the red spaniel leaped into it. All at once Dr Wintermute caught hold of the idea that had eluded him. Why, this girl was Cinderella, with her sooty dress and wistful eyes. He half smiled at the fancy.

'I'm afraid I don't know your name.'

'I'm Lizzie Rose – that is, Elizabeth Rose Fawr, sir.'

'Professor Grisini is not your father?'

'No, sir. My father was David Fawr.' She spoke with pride; evidently David Fawr had been someone of importance in her world. 'Grisini took me in a year and a half ago.'

'Do you know where he is?'

The girl shook her head. 'He's gone, sir. I think – I believe he's dead.'

'Is he?' He spoke with such intensity that she drew back, gathering the spaniel closer to her breast. 'I need to know. I was told he was not in London. The police want to speak with Mr Grisini. Have you any clue as to where he might be?'

He watched the girl's face, alert for any signs of fear, of cunning, of knowledge withheld. But she met his eyes candidly. 'He fell down the stairs,' she said, 'and then he went away. That's all we know, sir.'

'The stairs of this house?'

'Yes, sir. He was in a temper, and the stairs gave way and he struck his head.' She bit her lip. 'He – there was a lot of blood – and Mrs Pinchbeck – she's our landlady – went to fetch the surgeon, but Grisini must have come awake after she left. He wandered off by himself. He never came back.'

'But he was alive. He must have been alive when he left.'

'Yes,' the girl said unwillingly, 'but he never came back. Everything he owns is here – his clothes and the theatre and the puppets –'

At the word *puppets,* Dr Wintermute leaned forward. 'The puppets. He makes them, doesn't he?'

For the first time, the girl looked wary. 'Some of them, yes, sir.'

'Did he make the one that looks like my daughter?'

She gave a little gasp. 'Oh, sir! You saw that puppet?'

'Today. In Ebury Square.'

'Oh!' the girl said again. 'Oh, no, how cruel!' She pushed the spaniel off her lap and stood up. 'Might I fetch you a glass of spirits, sir? I believe Mrs Pinchbeck –'

Dr Wintermute caught hold of her hand, detaining her. 'What do you know about that puppet? When did he make it? And why? He scarcely knew my daughter. Why did he make a puppet in her image?'

The girl withdrew her hand. 'I don't know,' she said unhappily. 'He didn't tell us about things like that.' She added unconvincingly, 'The puppet isn't so *very* like Clara –'

'It is exactly like her,' Dr Wintermute contradicted her. 'For God's sake, if you know anything, you must tell me! When did Professor Grisini leave here? What was the date?'

The girl hesitated. Her hands twitched; she was counting on her fingers. 'It was eight days after the birthday party. The fourteenth.'

Dr Wintermute closed his eyes. His heart seemed to stand still. At the same time, he was quite composed; the worst had happened and nothing could ever hurt him again. He heard himself speak quite calmly. 'I was at Kensal Green that night.'

'I don't understand.'

'Kensal Green is the cemetery where my children are buried,' Dr Wintermute said. He was astonished to hear himself confide in her; he had told no one but Ada what had happened that night. 'I had a letter from a stranger – I thought it was Professor Grisini – telling me to go to Kensal Green cemetery with ten thousand pounds. That was the price of my daughter's ransom.'

The girl nodded. He saw horror dawn in her eyes.

'At midnight, I was to go to the wall overlooking the Grand Junction Canal and listen for the sound of someone striking the bricks from the opposite side. I was supposed to throw the ransom money over the wall. I waited all night, straining my ears for the slightest sound. But I heard nothing. No one came. I wondered if the kidnapper had been followed, if he'd lost his nerve. But I told myself, *He must want the ransom money.*' He clenched his hands as he spoke the words. He had repeated them to himself a thousand times. 'He *must* want the money. Why else would he kidnap my daughter? He kidnapped her for the ransom money, and once the money was paid, he must release her. Afterwards, I dared not tell the police. The kidnapper still had Clara. He might write again. I prayed that he would, but no letter came. After a week, I went to the police detective and asked what progress had been made with my daughter's case. He said there had been no progress. I asked him about Professor Grisini. He told me that Grisini had left London and that they were trying to trace his whereabouts. Now you tell me' – he needed to inhale but was afraid that if he took a deep breath, he would burst into tears – 'that he was injured, perhaps mortally, and that it happened on the night of the fourteenth. He may have bled to death. If he did, then Clara – my Clara – may still be a prisoner.' Once again, he shut his eyes. Behind his eyelids were a dozen Claras, all in pain and deadly peril: Clara in a shadowy cellar, dying of thirst; Clara shivering with cold and fear;

Clara lying stock-still, her skin waxen and faintly blue. His throat closed and his face twisted.

'Oh!' said the girl. He heard the rustle of skirts as she crept closer. 'Oh, please, Dr Wintermute, don't – don't give way! I believe – I truly believe – that Clara is alive! Somehow, someone will find her, and she'll come home again!'

'How can you believe that? What do you know?'

'I don't know anything. But I'm sure it must be so –' She was crying too; the tears slid down her freckled cheeks. 'If Grisini – if he was hiding her – it would have been somewhere safe, and –' Her words made no sense, and perhaps she knew it, because she gave up on them. Instead, she reached over the arm of the chair and stroked his coat sleeve. The gesture went to his heart. He sobbed aloud, and she murmured wordlessly, as if she was his mother and he was her child.

He had no idea how long he wept or how long the girl knelt patiently at his side, patting his coat sleeve and making soft sounds. But at last he became aware that something was scratching his knee. The spaniel was trying to climb into his lap. The dog's face, with its wide eyes and slender nose, was so like the girl's that Dr Wintermute gave a brief, hysterical laugh. He realised that he felt a tiny bit better. Crying had eased him. How strange that he should have found comfort in this filthy kennel of a room, in the company of a stranger. He felt a sudden irrational desire to lean back in his chair and fall asleep. He knew that if he did so, his Cinderella would not shame him for it. She would stay beside him, stroking his coat sleeve.

He cleared his throat. 'I must go home. My wife worries when I am late. Forgive me for –'

'Oh, sir, please! There is no need.'

He bowed, accepting her kindness. She got to her feet to see him out, and he waited until she turned her back before reaching into his pocket. He knew better than to offer her money. Incredible though it might be, she seemed to consider herself a young lady; he must not insult her by treating her as a beggar. Stealthily he drew out three sovereigns. He would leave them on the mantelpiece to be found later. His eyes passed over the objects on the mantel. There was a grey silk purse, two snuff-boxes and a pair of glittering bracelets. And –

'Where did you get this photograph?'

The girl spun around to face him. 'Oh!'

'Where did you get it?' Dr Wintermute scarcely recognised his own voice; it was so low and threatening. 'This is my son – my dead son!'

The girl raised her hands in mute appeal. The spaniel, sensing a threat, barked twice. Dr Wintermute took a step forward and stopped. He was a gentleman, and a gentleman must not strike a female under any circumstances. But the sound of his voice was as savage as a blow. 'You're a thief.'

'I'm not. I didn't take it –'

'You robbed my house.' Dr Wintermute was breathing hard. 'I see I was mistaken in you. I thought you were honest. Perhaps a police constable will be able to force the truth out of you –'

'No!' The girl caught his sleeve, gazing imploringly into his face. 'Please don't tell the constable!' She seemed to sense that her plea could not move him and changed tactics. 'It was Grisini who stole that photograph! It was *Grisini*!'

'If it was Grisini, why are you so afraid?' demanded Dr Wintermute.

Her tears began to fall again. 'I'm not afraid. Only, *please*, sir, don't tell the constable. You don't know how it is with us – how hard –'

He would not hear her. He shook off her arm, clasping the photograph to his chest as if it was a thing that could wrest itself free. He rattled down the dark staircase with the girl at his heels, pleading with him to listen, begging him not to go to the police. But he was deaf to her entreaties; he shook her off when she sought to detain him and slammed the door when he went out.

# Chapter Twenty-seven

# Flight

Parse!'

Parsefall halted in the middle of the street. Lizzie Rose spoke to him from a narrow space between two shops. Parsefall glowered at her. He was tired, cold and footsore; he wanted to go home, not stand in the streets talking to Lizzie Rose. 'Wot is it?'

Lizzie Rose caught hold of his sleeve. 'I have something to tell you.'

She reached for the wagon handle and dragged the wagon into the alley where she had been hiding. Parsefall followed. He saw that she was looking purposeful and unusually tidy; she wore her new black dress and had pinned up her hair, so that she looked older than she was. Parsefall eyed her with distrust. It wasn't like her to come to meet him, unless she was walking the dogs, and for once there were no dogs. 'Wot is it? Wot're you doin' here?'

'I've been waiting to warn you. You mustn't come home.'

Parsefall's face fell. He'd been afraid to return to his usual haunts after Dr Wintermute accosted him and had hauled the wagon clear over to Brompton Road. It was unfamiliar territory, and he had only earned sixpence. He was looking forward to the dubious comforts of Mrs Pinchbeck's house: to taking off his boots and making a nest of blankets before the fire. 'Why not?'

'Because we're in trouble. Dr Wintermute – you remember, he's Clara's father –'

Parsefall made a face. 'Ol' Wintermute,' he said bitterly. 'I seen 'im. Strike me dead if 'e didn't try to yank Clara off the stage! I 'ad to make a run for it – he'd a prigged her if –'

'That's not the worst of it,' Lizzie Rose interrupted. 'Listen to me, Parse! After Dr Wintermute saw you, he came to Mrs Pinchbeck's to question me –'

'Damn 'is eyes,' interjected Parsefall.

Lizzie Rose frowned. 'Don't use such vulgar language! It isn't his fault, poor man! It was a dreadful shock for him, seeing Clara like that – and oh, Parsefall, when he was about to leave, he saw the photograph on the mantel –'

'Wot photograph?' demanded Parsefall. He had honestly forgotten that he had taken anything from the Wintermute house.

'The photograph of his dead son. The photograph you *stole*,' snapped Lizzie Rose. 'It would have been all right if he hadn't seen that. He's a kind man, really – he caught that horrid Fitzmorris trying to kiss me and pitched into him – but when he saw that photograph, he spoke as if he hated me. He thought I robbed him. I said I didn't –'

'You peached on me,' Parsefall accused her. He didn't quite believe it, but he watched her narrowly. She drew herself up, eyes flashing.

'I never! I told him Grisini stole it. Only he didn't believe me, and oh, Parse –'

'Oh, never mind,' Parsefall said irritably. He was vastly relieved; she hadn't betrayed him. 'You didn't peach on me, but you botched the lie. I mighta known. You're no good at lyin'. You're never goin' to make your way in the world if –'

'Be quiet!' hissed Lizzie Rose. 'Don't you hear what I'm trying to tell you? Dr Wintermute saw that photograph, and he thinks one of us stole it. He's going to the coppers to tell them. They'll come to the house and question us again. That's why I came to warn you.'

The knot in Parsefall's stomach tightened. If the coppers were looking for him, he dared not go home. He tried to imagine where else he could go. It was too cold to spend the night in the streets, and he'd rather freeze to death than go to the workhouse. 'Where'm I to go?'

'That's what I'm trying to tell you.' Lizzie Rose took a deep breath. 'You must give me the wagon, so I can take it back to Mrs Pinchbeck's. Then you must go to the coach stand on the King's Road and wait for me. I'll bring our things – I can haul the wicker trunk by myself if I put it on the wagon – and we'll take a hackney coach to King's Cross Station.'

Parsefall gaped. 'King's Cross? That's 'alfway across the bloomin' city!'

Lizzie Rose hissed at his language. 'That's why we're taking a hackney coach. Only we must be quick – to catch the train.' She reached into her muff and pressed a coin into his hand. 'You try to get us a coach. I shan't be long – I've packed the trunk, so I need only go home and take the puppet stage off the wagon and strap on the trunk –'

'The *train*?' Parsefall echoed. He had never been on a train.

'We're going to Westmorland. To Windermere,' Lizzie Rose corrected herself, but the correction was wasted: Parsefall had never heard of either place. 'It'll be all right, Parse. I haven't told you, but there's a kind lady there that wants to take care of us –'

Parsefall's hackles rose. 'Wot kind lady? Wot's she want wiv us?'

'She's dying,' Lizzie Rose answered, sidestepping his question. 'I don't have time to tell you just now. I'll explain it in the coach.' She tugged at the wagon, which stuck in the mud. Parsefall dodged around her, planting himself in her path.

'Who is she? I ain't goin' unless you tell me.'

'Her name is Cassandra Sagredo. She's someone who knows Grisini –'

'Grisini!' Parsefall caught hold of the wagon handle and jerked it away from her. 'If that ain't just like you! Thinkin' some old woman's goin' to *take care* of us!' He spoke the words with savage mimicry. 'Wot's she want wiv us?'

'She wants to give us a legacy. She wrote and invited us to come. I started to write back, but I couldn't think of the right words – but it's all right: she said we could come anytime. A legacy's *money*, Parsefall. She's dying and she's rich and she wants to give away her money –'

'People don't give away money,' Parsefall pointed out.

'They do when they're dying and don't need it any more.'

'They don't give it to us,' Parsefall countered. He clenched his fists and shoved them into his pockets. 'Sounds to me like a take-in. I'm not goin' 'alfway round the world to be taken in by a friend of Grisini's –'

'Yes, you are,' Lizzie Rose contradicted him. 'The coppers are going to come after us – don't you understand? If they find out you took that photograph, they'll send you to prison – or

Australia. I don't know which. Only I won't let them.' She looked suddenly fierce. 'I won't lose you. So we must go away, and we must go tonight, before the coppers come.'

Parsefall hunched his shoulders. Everything was happening too fast. He did not want to leave London, and the prospect of taking a train was daunting. The chance of inheriting money was too slight to outweigh his fear. Parsefall knew about money. It could be found in the streets, if one were very lucky; it could be stolen; or it could be earned. No one gave it away. 'I ain't goin',' he said, but there was a note of uncertainty in his voice.

'Yes, you are,' Lizzie Rose said grimly. 'I'm not letting the coppers take you. I've planned everything – I pawned the bracelets and the snuffboxes – and I packed, and I found out about the trains. This may be our chance, Parsefall.' Her voice was shaky but resolute. 'I want that money. I'm tired of working like a slave, and I want to get away from that horrid Fitzmorris. So we're going, and you needn't say one more word, because if you argue with me, I'll *drag* you.' She bared her teeth at him; for a split second she looked like a mad dog. He was so taken aback that he forgot to hold on to the wagon, and she yanked the handle away from him. She was six paces away before he came to his senses.

He ran to catch up with her. 'What about the puppets?'

'What about them?'

'I need 'em,' Parsefall said. 'You'll pack 'em, won't you?'

'Parse, there isn't room –'

'You 'ave to,' Parsefall insisted. 'If this old lady cheats us, 'ow are we to earn our living? Besides, there's Clara.'

Lizzie Rose winced at the sound of Clara's name. 'I'll pack Clara,' she conceded. 'But there isn't much room in the trunk, Parse. I couldn't tell Mrs Pinchbeck that we're leaving, but I shouldn't think she'd throw away the puppets; heavens, she never throws anything away! After a little time, we'll come back to London and sort things out –'

'I need 'em.' Parsefall heard the panic in his own voice and amplified it, knowing that Lizzie Rose was always tender towards him when he acted like a little boy. 'I don't want no clothes – I can wear what I 'ave on – but I must 'ave the puppets. I *need* 'em.'

Lizzie Rose sighed. 'Very well. I'll pack as many as I can wedge in.'

'And the backdrops,' persisted Parsefall. 'You can roll 'em up – they won't take much room. I can't paint like Grisini – we got to 'ave the backdrops.'

Lizzie Rose looked a little desperate, but she nodded. 'Very well! I'll pack the backdrops – only you must go *now*, Parsefall – to the cabstand in the King's Road. I'll come as soon as I can – it'll be safest if we catch the night train.'

Parsefall jerked his head in acknowledgement. He shoved his hands in his pockets and watched until she disappeared into the dusk.

# Chapter Twenty-eight

# The Journey

It was fully dark by the time the children met at the coach stand in the King's Road. The cabbie unstrapped the wicker trunk from the wagon and loaded it into his coach. To Parsefall's anguish, the wagon was left behind; there was no time to return it to Mrs Pinchbeck's if they were to catch the night train.

The journey began easily enough. The driver of the hackney coach navigated the London traffic with surprising ease. It was only when he brought them to King's Cross Station that he named his fee, a price so high that even Lizzie Rose, who wished to think well of him, knew they were being cheated. She could think of no other way to punish the cabbie than to refuse his help with the luggage. She raised her chin haughtily and nodded to Parsefall to take one handle of the wicker trunk. She gripped the other handle, shifted the burlap sack in her arms and descended the steps of the coach. Together they hauled the luggage into the railway station.

Inside the station, all was confusion: crowds of hurrying people, pyramids of luggage and great clouds of smoke. Parsefall inhaled the sulphurous air in short puffs, like a nervous horse. Lizzie Rose steered him towards the booking clerk. Bravely she took out her purse and requested two first-class tickets.

The booking clerk looked startled. He knew his passengers at a glance, and it was clear to him that Lizzie Rose and Parsefall belonged in a third-class carriage. But he sold them the tickets and summoned a guard to take charge of their luggage. The guard led the children down a long platform, opened the coach doors and hoisted the trunk into the luggage rack. He reached for the burlap sack, but Lizzie Rose told him that she preferred to hold it in her lap.

Parsefall whispered, 'Is that Ru –?' but Lizzie Rose shushed him. She waited until the guard had gone before admitting that Ruby was inside the sack. No, she hadn't told Mrs Pinchbeck, but that didn't mean she was stealing. No, she didn't know if animals were allowed inside the coaches. She had drugged the dog with a large saucer of rum and milk and hoped that Ruby would sleep through the journey.

Parsefall was impressed. According to his lights, Lizzie Rose had stolen a dog and was defrauding the railway, two things of which he approved. He lolled back against the leather upholstery, admiring the first-class coach.

The coach door opened. A cross-looking man in a clerical collar sat down on the far end of Parsefall's seat. When the door opened a second time, it admitted a stout man, his peevish wife and a nursemaid with a crying baby. The man frowned at the children and stepped back outside the coach, where he held a low-voiced argument with the guard. Lizzie Rose caught the words *paupers*, *dirty* and *most improper*. The nursemaid with the baby settled down between Parsefall and the clergyman, to the disgust of both. When the stout man returned and took his seat, the carriage was full.

The baby's sobs rose to a scream. The nursemaid bounced and patted it, but the baby refused all comfort and shrieked as if it was being disembowelled. Parsefall rolled his eyes. The coach began to vibrate. There was a blast from a trumpet – a series of rumbles – and the train surged into the darkness of the December night.

Parsefall peered out the window. They were travelling in a cloud of coal smoke and red cinders. The baby's screams sank to an incessant wail, less piercing than its screams but no less irritating. Parsefall's eyes met Lizzie Rose's. He placed his fists together and gave a vicious little twist of one hand. Lizzie Rose nodded, her eyes thoughtful.

Several hours passed. Then a whistle blew, and lights appeared in the darkness. Doors opened and slammed. Lizzie Rose heard a man bellow, 'Soup!' and saw passengers hurry out of the train, intent on purchasing supper. In less than a quarter of an hour, the trumpet blew and the train started up again. Lizzie Rose closed her eyes, wondering if she might sleep through the remaining hours. Before she had time to grow drowsy, the stout man drew a hamper out from under his seat. Lizzie Rose's nostrils twitched. She smelled chicken-and-leek pie, ripe cheese and oranges. Parsefall leaned forward, eyes glistening, hoping to partake of the feast. But the husband, the wife and the nursemaid behaved as if there were no other people in the coach. When they finished eating, they wrapped the leftovers in napkins and returned them to the hamper.

The train rattled onward. The night was frosty, and the padded seats felt as hard as iron. Parsefall squirmed and shivered.

Lizzie Rose's toes ached with cold, and she tensed her jaw to keep her teeth from chattering. She was grateful for the warmth of the dog in her lap.

The whistle shrilled. The train slowed. They had come to another station. This time the clergyman left the train. Parsefall, who had taken a strong dislike to him, hoped he would not return. But before a quarter of an hour had passed, the man reappeared with two dry jam puffs, which he thrust into the hands of the children. '"Whosoever shall give to drink unto one of these little ones a cup of cold water shall in no wise lose his reward,"' he thundered.

Lizzie Rose, who recognised the Bible verse, said, 'Thank you, sir.' Tears of gratitude and humiliation filled her eyes. She accepted the jam puff and tried to nibble it daintily, as if she wasn't hungry. Parsefall wolfed his down and looked around for the cold water. He might have demanded it if he hadn't been distracted: the burlap sack in Lizzie Rose's arms was moving, and a faint whine issued from it.

The spaniel's head emerged from the sack. The nursemaid gave a little shriek. The stout man muttered an oath and shouted for the guard, but the trumpet blared, signalling that the train was about to move again.

They reached Lancaster at three in the morning. Lizzie Rose and Parsefall wrestled the trunk from the luggage rack and dragged it to a corner of the railway station. Parsefall went exploring and found the lavatories. When he returned, Lizzie Rose took Ruby for a walk. She bought two cups of tea and a sandwich, which the children shared: five knobs of gristle swaddled in stale bread.

They waited for three more hours. When at last the next train arrived, the guard showed the children to a second-class carriage. Parsefall glanced at Lizzie Rose to see if she would object, but she took her place on the hard wooden seat without a murmur. Parsefall yawned as the train shot out of the station. He was sick of watching the red sparks, and it was too dark to see anything else. He turned to ask Lizzie Rose how much longer they had to travel, but saw that she had fallen asleep. Her face was very pale. Parsefall studied her narrowly and held his tongue.

While Lizzie Rose slumbered, Dr Wintermute lay awake. For once, he was not thinking of Clara. He was thinking of Lizzie Rose. He recalled her stricken eyes when they parted. 'You don't know how it is with us – how hard –' He hadn't let her finish the sentence. Now, in the dark, he finished it for her: *You don't know how hard our life is.*

It was true. He didn't know, but he could imagine. He had seen her shabby lodgings and sat by her meagre fire. He remembered the darns and patches on her frock, and the way the sole of her boot parted from the upper. How could he, who had lived in comfort all his life, condemn her for stealing? The girl had no one to provide for her, no one to protect her. He remembered the beefy young fellow who had kissed her and regretted that he hadn't punished the man with his fists.

He thanked God he had not gone to the police station, as he had threatened to do. The girl might be telling the truth, after all; the photograph of Charles Augustus might have been stolen by Grisini or even by the boy in Ebury Square. Perhaps if he questioned her a second time – kindly and patiently – she might tell him the truth about the matter. At the very least, he could apologise for his rash behaviour, provide money for her immediate wants and make sure that the beefy fellow left her alone.

He turned the thought over in his mind, and found, to his surprise, that it eased him a little. He closed his eyes and promised himself that he would return to Danvers Street that very day.

'Oh,' breathed Lizzie Rose. Her breath came out in a white mist. She stood with Ruby on the platform at Windermere, gazing over the wide space around her.

The children had slept through the last stage of their journey. The guard had shaken them awake. Now groggy, thirsty and stiff with cold, they stood on the platform with the wicker trunk between them.

They had come to a new world, a world of immense space and ample light. Everything was foreign, majestic and sublimely clean. Three inches of pristine snow lay on the grass. The sky was coldly blue. White clouds soared like galleons overhead, shadowing the snowy fells. The train station stood in the midst of steep hills: great, curving humps, one beyond the other, like a pod of whales breaching and diving.

Parsefall whistled. He had expected Windermere to be like London or Leeds: another city, with rows of begrimed houses pressed tightly together. He shook his head in amazement. 'It's like scenery,' he said at last. 'Like a painted backdrop.' He could give no higher praise.

'I never thought it would be like this,' Lizzie Rose said. Her voice caught, and her eyes brimmed over.

'It ain't nuffink to cry about,' Parsefall said disapprovingly.

'No,' agreed Lizzie Rose. She brushed her cheeks with the tips of her fingers. 'We'll have to hire a gig,' she said, and turned to face the station.

A man in a rough jacket came towards them. He spoke to

them in a voice that was gruff but not unkind. Lizzie Rose did not catch his words, but they ended with something that sounded like *strawns-gill*.

It took Lizzie Rose a moment to decipher this. She had thought of Strachan's Ghyll as *stratch-hans-guy-el*, not *strawns-gill*. The man jerked his thumb over his shoulder, indicating a carriage drawn by two chestnut horses. He repeated, 'Are you bound for Strachan's Ghyll?'

'Yes, please,' said Lizzie Rose. 'That is, if that's where Mrs Sagredo lives. She invited us to stay. I have her letter with me –'

'Madama,' the man corrected her, taking off his cap. 'We call her Madama; it's what she prefers. She had one of her fancies today and thought you'd come.' He replaced his cap and picked up the trunk, heaving it on to his shoulder as if it was weightless.

Parsefall emitted a squeak of protest. The man grinned at him. 'Don't you mind, now! I'm supposed to carry your things, and I'm not likely to drop 'em. I'm Mr Fettle, coachman. Footman too, when Madama needs one. My mother's the housekeeper at Strachan's Ghyll.'

Parsefall darted a nervous look towards Lizzie Rose. He didn't like the idea of Madama's fancies – how had the woman known they would come? But Lizzie Rose only tugged Ruby's leash and answered, 'Come, Parsefall,' as if he was as bound to obey her as the spaniel was.

# PART TWO

# ICE

STRACHAN'S GHYLL
Winter 1860-1861

# Chapter Twenty-nine

# Strachan's Ghyll

Parsefall had never ridden in a private coach. The inside was leather and tufted velvet, and there were two travelling rugs on the seat: glossy pelts from some immense black animal. 'Look, Parsefall,' exclaimed Lizzie Rose. 'Fur rugs! Isn't that kind?' She wrapped one end of the rug around Ruby, who was once again swaddled in the burlap sack. 'Poor Roo,' she crooned. 'She's cold.' Ruby shivered theatrically. Lizzie Rose kissed her and made loving little noises that set Parsefall's teeth on edge.

He hauled the travelling rug around his shoulders and tried to anchor it in place by leaning back against the seat. The fur smelled queer, and he sneezed. He could have cried. He was half frozen, and everything familiar was hundreds of miles away. For the first time since the journey began, he thought of Clara, crammed into the wicker trunk. She had no choice as to where she was going; neither did he. His stomach growled, and he wished they'd bought two sandwiches at Lancaster. There weren't any coffee stalls or baked potato stands in this clean, cold country, and they couldn't eat the snow off the trees.

He shut his eyes and tried once more to sleep. Time passed, then: 'Parsefall, look!'

Lizzie Rose sounded so excited that he left his seat and joined her at the coach window. They were approaching a red stone building, half castle, half cottage. It was attached to a high wall with an open archway. The house had a small turret, deliciously capped with snow. It looked like a piece of scenery for the puppet stage. 'Is that it?' asked Parsefall.

'I hope it is,' Lizzie Rose answered. 'It's like something from a fairy book, isn't it?'

Parsefall shrugged; he had never seen a fairy book. The horses drew the coach through the archway, but they did not stop, and Lizzie Rose looked crestfallen. 'I suppose that was the gatehouse.'

Parsefall wondered what a gatehouse was. He said, 'Huh,' in a skeptical tone of voice.

'Very rich people have gatehouses,' explained Lizzie Rose, 'at the entrance to their estates. I suppose Mrs Sagredo is very rich.'

Parsefall repeated, 'Huh,' and clenched his teeth to keep them from chattering.

'She must have been expecting us.' Lizzie Rose sounded as if she was reassuring herself. 'She sent the carriage. That was good of her. I hope she won't be very distressed that we've come without Grisini.'

Parsefall stuck out his tongue to show what he thought of Grisini, but Lizzie Rose was too lost in thought to rebuke him. The horses drew them into an avenue of trees. The branches had not been trimmed and pressed close, tapping the sides of the coach and sending down miniature snowfalls. Parsefall tensed. He could navigate the thickest traffic and the narrowest alley, but he didn't like being surrounded by trees. They seemed alive to him: they had too many fingers.

When at last the trees parted, the children saw the house: a castle of red sandstone. The gatehouse had mimicked the larger building; this was the real Strachan's Ghyll, and it was forbidding, not picturesque. It stood in a circle of hollies, and the verdant green of the leaves made the stones look blood red. A round tower leaned over them at a menacing angle, as if daring them to take shelter. Even to Parsefall's ignorant eyes, it looked unstable. Lizzie Rose said faintly, 'It's very grand, isn't it?' and the carriage came to an abrupt stop.

The carriage doors opened. Mr Fettle let down the steps so that the children could climb out. Parsefall wondered why the coachman hadn't driven them all the way up to the house. He looked to Lizzie Rose for enlightenment, but she was busy with Ruby, who was whimpering, *I-want-to-go-out.* Lizzie Rose extracted the dog from the burlap sack and set her down. Ruby squatted in the snow.

Parsefall gave a snort of disgust. He started up the brick walkway to the great house. He had a queer instinct that someone was watching from within, and he eyed the windows nervously. They were pointed, with stained glass at the tops and small square panes, like scales. Three broad steps led to the entrance. The doors were arched and carved like church doors, and the hinges were black iron, cast in the shape of butterflies.

He raised one hand to the knocker, and the door opened from within.

\* \* \*

201

From her tower, the witch surveyed the children. She had sat by the window all morning with a spyglass in her lap; it was by her order that the carriage stopped a little distance from the house. She wanted to see the children before they saw her.

Why hadn't they come sooner? It had been weeks since she'd written; what had taken them so long? She had banished Grisini from the house, lest his presence frighten them; she had told the servants to expect two children who must be treated as honoured guests. Cassandra had unearthed treasures from her collections and strewn them about the rooms, hoping to stimulate the children's appetite for plunder. Each day, she had hoped for their arrival, only to be disappointed. Then that morning, she had awakened knowing that the children were on their way. They would come – at last, at last! – and one of them would deliver her from the phoenix-stone.

But they were not as she had pictured them. Her wistful fancy had conjured up a brute of a boy, a painted minx of a girl: two ripe young criminals who would have no scruples about stealing from her. The children who crept out of the coach were younger than she had thought they would be. They looked malnourished, especially the boy; probably the girl, being older, took the lion's share of the food. What had Gaspare said about the girl? *She's a deceitful little puss, in spite of her pious airs.* But it didn't seem to Cassandra that either of the children looked particularly deceitful; they looked exhausted and defenceless. She lowered her spyglass. She had seen neglected children before. The streets of London were full of them. But one did not look at them there. One averted one's eyes.

The girl stooped in the snow, opening the sack she had been clasping to her breast. A small red dog emerged.

It was a spaniel. Cassandra's lips parted in surprise. Marguerite had kept a spaniel as a pet, a red-and-white spaniel named . . . Fanchon? Ninon? Cassandra couldn't remember. She must not fret over useless memories. She must think only of her current plight and of the children who might rescue her. One of them must steal the fire opal. Their poverty, deplorable as it was, would serve her well.

Only which of the two would deliver her? Which was the more promising, the greedier, the more vulnerable? Cassandra heard the rattle of the front doors opening. She had no doubt that her housekeeper would welcome the children properly. Mrs Fettle was a stiff, tiresome old thing, but she knew her duty.

Cassandra shifted in her chair. It was time to return to her bedchamber. The thought of the walk down the passage wearied her. She wished she could ring for one of the servants to help her, but they had no idea that she still frequented the Tower Room. Even if she shouted for them, they would not be able to enter. She had bolted the door from inside.

She raised her hand to the gold locket. The filigree that encased the phoenix-stone was lukewarm. Her lips shaped a single word: *Which?* She shut her eyes, trying to concentrate on the question, wishing she could force a prophecy from the stone.

Her head flopped to one side, and she gave herself up to sleep.

At first there was no coherent dream, no story: just slumber and nonsense. She was unwinding a tangle of embroidery silks, sorting through the different colours: scarlet and sea green and peacock blue and white . . . They were snarled and knotted, and she couldn't draw the threads free. Then, with a suddenness that made her twitch, she was in Venice. She was standing at the threshold of an open door, blinking at the sunlight. She was twelve years old again, at school in the convent of Santa Maria dei Servi.

There was a draught of chilly air and a whisper of laughter. Marguerite stood behind her, so close that Cassandra felt the younger girl's head against her shoulder. It was Carnival time in Venice, and one of the convent doors had been left unlocked. The two girls exchanged glances. With one accord they stepped out and shut the door behind them. Quivering with suppressed laughter, they ran down the street.

Only the wind pursued them. It was a boisterous wind that drove the clouds across the blue sky and scattered confetti on the cobblestones. Sunlight flashed and skipped over the waters of the canal. It had rained the night before, and the cobbles were still damp; the girls' shoes slid on the rain-washed stone.

They ran hand in hand, steadying each other in the slippery places. Up one street and over a bridge; through a courtyard and under a dim *sottoportego;* back out in the sunlight and over the hump of another bridge, stone bridges and wooden bridges, over a dozen of them, until they found themselves in the great piazza. The balconies were hung with flags and waving banners, and there was a puppet booth set up beside the bell tower.

The two girls raced up to it. In the centre of the miniature stage was a string puppet, a girlish figure in a white frock. No, not a puppet but a child, a living child only thirteen inches high. She smiled and raised one hand. Her fingers opened, small as the spines of a sea urchin. In the centre of the tiny palm was a pulsing heart: scarlet and sea green and white and peacock blue . . . Cassandra knew it for what it was: the fire opal.

She cried out harshly and awoke. She blinked, trying to make sense of her dream. Some of it was not a dream but a memory;

she recalled that long-ago day when she and Marguerite escaped into the streets. Only the part about the puppet stage was a dream or perhaps a vision: the part with the child who was a puppet, or the puppet who was a child . . . Cassandra's mouth dropped open. How could she have forgotten the child Gaspare had kidnapped? In her mind's eye, she saw him again, with the bloodstained bandages around his head; he had been weak and dizzy, and she had forced him to confess every detail. He had imprisoned Clara Wintermute in the body of a puppet. Was it possible that the other children had brought Clara with them to Strachan's Ghyll?

Cassandra's mind raced. That captive child would be easy prey. Above all things, Clara Wintermute would desire the magic power that would break Grisini's spell. Nothing would be simpler than to tempt her with the fire opal. It only remained for Cassandra to devise some way of speaking to Clara in her paralysed state. It could be done; with the power of the cursed stone, it could be managed. Cassandra thought of the intricate, draining spell she would have to cast and wanted to groan with weariness.

How sick, how sick she was of magic! With her one good hand, she pushed herself to her feet, forcing herself to a standing position. The spyglass clattered to the floor and rolled under her chair. Under her weight, the floorboards creaked, emitting a sound like the squeal of an animal in pain.

# Chapter Thirty

# Servants' Talk

Ruby was whining, asking to be taken out. Lizzie opened her eyes and sat up in bed. Above her head was a canopy of creamy linen, embroidered with fantastical birds. She was in the White Room at Strachan's Ghyll.

She threw off the bedclothes and slid out of bed. She spied her boots beside the washstand and shoved her bare feet into them. Ruby leaped off the bed and trotted to the door, making it clear that she wanted to go out *now*. The spaniel was keenly aware of how disgraceful it would be to make a puddle in the house. She whimpered imploringly.

Lizzie Rose scanned the White Room, searching for her clothes. The light was dim, and she wondered how long she'd slept. She hobbled to the window, found the curtain cord and drew the curtains.

Outside, the sun had almost set. The White Room over-looked the slope of lawn that led to Lake Windermere, and the frozen lake reflected the colours in the sky: grey and lilac, pale rose and flaxen yellow. The trees on the shore cast deep shadows on to the ice, rimming the lake in black. Even as Lizzie Rose took in the beauty of the view, her mind was at work, unravelling the events of the day.

She had come to Strachan's Ghyll only that morning. The housekeeper, Mrs Fettle, had greeted the children with three statements that brooked no argument: One: they would see Mrs Sagredo when, and only when, Mrs Sagredo asked to see them; Two: they would have an early dinner at noon; and Three: after dinner they would want baths. At this last assertion, Parsefall rebelled; he had never in his life wanted a bath, and he wasn't ashamed to say so. Mrs Fettle turned a deaf ear to his protests. It was perhaps fortunate that the dinner, when it arrived, was sumptuous: roasted chicken with bread sauce, apple fritters and marmalade pudding.

The children ate ravenously and drank a large pot of tea, loading their cups with lashings of cream and emptying the sugar bowl. Afterwards, they were sent upstairs to bathe. Lizzie Rose suggested timidly that if it would save trouble, she could bathe first, and Parsefall could use her bathwater; they might even share a room, as they were brother and sister. Parsefall growled, 'You ain't my real sister'; Mrs Fettle snapped out, 'Most improper!' and the children were assigned bedrooms at the opposite ends of the corridor.

Replete with roasted chicken, exhausted and rather cowed, Lizzie Rose watched as two sullen housemaids prepared her bath. Screens were set before the bedroom fire, and cans of steaming water were brought up in relays, along with Turkish towels, a sponge and an unused cake of Pears' soap. Once the servants were gone, Lizzie Rose shed her clothes and climbed into the bath. She was luxuriating in hot water and sweet-smelling lather when one of the housemaids returned. To Lizzie Rose's embarrassment, the woman invaded the shelter of screens and gathered up Lizzie Rose's dirty clothes. Without uttering a word, she carried them off, leaving a lace-trimmed nightdress in their place.

Now Ruby yipped, her cries mounting to a crescendo. Lizzie Rose looked desperately around the room. She couldn't go outdoors in her nightgown. Her eyes went to the wardrobe. Inside, there might be a dressing gown or even a cloak. The key was in the lock . . . Feeling like a thief, she crossed the room and turned the key.

A whiff of strong perfume rose to her nostrils: sweet musk roses and another, more metallic smell, reminiscent of something or someone she disliked. Nevertheless, she stood transfixed, for inside the wardrobe were gowns such as she had scarcely imagined: iridescent taffetas and silk brocades, India muslins, cashmeres and velvets. A flash of black-and-white caught her eye. It was the trim on a jade-green coat, and it was ermine. Lizzie Rose had seen ermine on theatrical costumes, but that had been rabbit fur daubed with blacking. This was the real thing: tiny pelts as soft as gossamer and whiter than pearls. The precious fur edged the coat sleeves and the yoke around the shoulders.

Ruby shifted her weight from paw to paw, moaning with impatience.

With fingers that trembled, Lizzie Rose lifted the garment from its hook and slid her arms into the sleeves. The coat was loose and warm and deliciously heavy; it hid her nightdress, reaching to the tops of her boots. Lizzie Rose cast a glance over her shoulder. Across the room, the looking glass reflected a stranger: a princess with loose red hair and startled eyes.

The transformation was so arresting that Lizzie Rose would have liked to look at herself a little longer, but she dared not. She picked up Ruby's leash, fastened it to the dog's collar and opened the door.

The frantic dog lunged into the passage. She headed for a narrow staircase at one end of the passage: Lizzie Rose hoped it was the servants' staircase; with luck, it would lead to the servants' hall and the back door. She followed the dog down two long flights, ending up in a vaulted cellar. She smelled kitchen smells: coal smoke, onions, vinegar and cloves. Her hand was on the knob of the kitchen door when she heard a woman's voice. Lizzie Rose stopped. She didn't want the servants to see her in the coat she had borrowed from the White Room.

'After we've served her all these years, you'd think she might do something for us. But no, not she! She'd rather take in a pair of dirty little beggar children and leave her money to them.'

Lizzie Rose's heart gave a leap. So Cassandra Sagredo did mean to leave them her estate! She wound Ruby's leash around her hand, caught between warring emotions: relief that the legacy was forthcoming; anger at hearing herself called a dirty little beggar; shame that in wanting Mrs Sagredo's money, she was coveting what might be left to someone else. She understood now why the housemaids had been so cross when they prepared her bath.

'And now we've got to wait on them,' continued the sharp voice, 'which'll mean carrying trays upstairs four times a day, not to mention the coal scuttle. Why, Essie and me are worn to a thread – hauling all that bathwater up the stairs! I've half a mind to leave here and seek another place.'

'You'll do nothing of the kind,' Mrs Fettle contradicted her.

'Which of us has ever managed to leave here? If Madama wants you to go, she'll dismiss you. Otherwise, you'll stay and do as you're told.'

A third voice spoke up plaintively. 'All the same, Mrs Fettle, it is hard – respectable people having to wait on children like *them*. It isn't as if they were any kin to her. What do you think she wants them for?'

'It's not for me to say why she does what she does,' answered Mrs Fettle, 'and it's not for you to ask.'

A fourth voice spoke up. 'At any rate, they won't be hard to cook for. They won't want no *polenta* or foreign messes. They ate every scrap from them trays! Picked the carcass clean and licked out the inside of the sugar bowl. I 'ad to laugh – there wasn't a lump left. I feel sorry for 'em – poor little toads!'

'Aye.' It was a man's voice: Mark Fettle's. 'They'll be glad of a few good meals. The girl has a sweet face, I thought.'

'All the same, she's nothing but riff-raff, and I'll warrant she's no better than she should be,' argued the first voice. 'First foreigners and now riff-raff! I shouldn't wonder if they're crawling with lice, the pair of them –'

Lizzie Rose lifted her chin. She no longer cared that she was wearing a coat that did not belong to her. As she swept into the kitchen, her posture was queenly and her cheeks were scarlet.

'Forgive me for disturbing you.' She was not sorry to see the consternation caused by her entrance. 'I must take the dog out. If you will be so good as to return my clothes as soon as possible, I should be grateful.'

She espied the door at the other end of the room and made her way to it, stepping out into the winter landscape. The cold was piercing, and the light had faded. The shadows on the snow were faintly blue. Lizzie Rose took a shaky breath. 'Come, Ruby,' she said and led the dog down the path to the lake.

The golden wolf barked four times. Grisini watched the tiny jaws close and returned the watch to the pocket of his dressing gown. He had walked for only eight minutes; he had meant to walk for ten. Breathing heavily, he lowered himself into the armchair before the fire.

He glanced around the room, checking to make sure that it was tidy. In a little while, one of Cassandra's servants would come with food and tend the fires. He made sure that the servants always found him in bed. The witch must think he was still bed-ridden. She must never suspect that each day he dragged himself around and around the small room, resurrecting his strength.

He leaned back, watching the fire through half-closed eyes. He wondered, as Cassandra had wondered, why the children had not come. He thought of them with longing: Parsefall, who already feared him, who would obey him absolutely; Lizzie Rose, who had yet to discover what terror and obedience were. Which would be his own particular Bottle Imp, his personal genie? Who would assume the curse of the fire opal, while allowing Gaspare Grisini to taste its power?

His lips opened in a yawn. He was still weak from loss of blood, and the exertion of walking had tired him. He had better return to bed before he fell asleep in the chair. He stood up and started to leave the room. As he did so, a noise reached his ear – a high-pitched and much-detested noise: the barking of a dog.

The barking was familiar. It was Ruby's bark, which he had cursed a score of times. Grisini went to the window and peered out, screening the dusk for a moving figure. His eyes found them quickly: a girl in pale green and a small patch of dark red, connected by the straight line of the leash.

They had come. The children had reached Strachan's Ghyll. Grisini smiled to himself and made his way back to bed.

# Chapter Thirty-one

# The Witch's Stronghold

Clara. Clara Wintermute.'

Clara opened her eyes. Then she recalled that this was impossible. Her eyes were fixed and could not open or shut. But her eyelids twitched and she felt her upper and lower lashes meet; she even fancied she could hear them. She blinked a third time and was flooded with joy. She was *moving*.

She screwed her head sideways. Her cheek rasped against cloth – Parsefall had freed her from the wicker trunk and placed her on a chair. He slept by the hearth on a bearskin rug and looked oddly small. With a jolt, Clara realised that she was as big as he was. She filled the chair like a person, not a puppet: her skirt fell over the edge of the seat and one foot dangled. Her other foot was tucked in the crook of her knee. She felt pins and needles in it.

She sat up, easing the foot out from under her. The blood rushed back, hurting her so that she caught her breath. She could feel pain; it was a miracle. She was alive.

'Clara Wintermute. Come to me now.'

Clara stood up. Never before had she heard that voice, but she knew she was bound to obey it. She wanted to rouse Parsefall, to show him she wasn't a puppet any more, but instead she headed for the door. Favouring the ache and prickle in her foot, she limped out into the hall.

The corridor was darker than Parsefall's room, because there was no fire. Why, then, were the shadows tinged with red? Clara felt the first stirrings of fear. She recalled the night after her birthday party, when she wandered the murky streets in search of Grisini. Her footsteps slowed. She stopped before a heavy door in a curved wall.

'Clara. Come into my tower.'

Clara opened the door. The Tower Room was hung with mirrors: silver mirrors with gilt frames and sheets of dark lacquer that glistened like water. Candles had been placed so that the quivering flames gleamed against the icy glass and plumbed the depths of the lacquer. Reflections darted from wall to wall, light to dark, dark to light, until the eye was baffled by innumerable flames. Lines of red paint hooked and spiralled across the bare floorboards, tracing the pattern of a labyrinth. At the heart of the labyrinth was a chair like a throne and a massive, ancient woman.

Clara felt a surge of panic. Quickly it subsided, leaving behind a weird sense of amusement.

*What a pretty little puppet! No wonder Gaspare was tempted to meddle with her!*

Clara didn't understand the joke. Nevertheless she put up her hands to cover her mouth and giggled in sympathy.

'Shut the door and bolt it. That's good. Now, come back and stand still. I want to look at you.'

Clara obeyed. On her way back, she tripped over the uneven floorboards and caught herself just before she fell.

*She's clumsy. As I was.*

'Please, ma'am, who are you?'

'I am Cassandra Strachan Sagredo. You may call me *Madama*, as Grisini does.'

Clara twisted her hands together. She wished she could find the words to ask how she had been set free from Grisini's spell. But her thoughts shuttled back and forth like the flickering lights; she could not fasten upon them. After a long pause, she moistened her lips. 'Is Grisini here?'

'Gaspare? No. He wouldn't dare set foot in this place. This is my tower, my stronghold.' The old woman's voice softened. 'You are quite safe here. My powers are greater than Grisini's are. So long as you are with me, there is nothing to fear.'

Clara didn't believe it. She squeezed her fingers together and lowered her eyes to the floor. Against her will, she found herself thinking of Grisini, of his mocking *Bau-bau!* and the gold watch with the silver swan on it.

'Ah, the automaton watch!' Cassandra lifted her hands; one was bandaged like a mummy's paw. 'So that's how he cast his spell on you! Years ago, I gave him that watch. He was my pupil in sorcery, Gaspare was; he pretended to love me, and I –' She shrugged. 'You know how it is. Someone pretends to love you, and you give too much away.'

Clara thought confusedly, *Her pupil. In sorcery. She's a witch.*

In the same breath: *I mustn't frighten her. I must go slowly.*

'Come closer.' The witch's voice was low and kind. 'You've never been inside a magic tower, have you? You may be quite at home here; indeed, you belong here. Look around and see what you can see.'

*How can I belong here?* But Clara didn't speak the words aloud. She revolved slowly, her hands behind her back. A tall cabinet inlaid with mother-of-pearl caught her eyes. It was fitted with rows of little drawers, perhaps three dozen of them.

'You may open the drawers.'

Clara opened one at random and found it full of pearls. Another held crystals, glinting green and yellow; she scooped them up and let them trickle through her fingers. The third drawer rattled when she opened it, revealing a collection of chalky white sticks. With a shudder, Clara realised that they were the bones of some hapless animal. She shut the drawer quickly. *I ought to have locked that one. It shocked the poor little doll!*

Clara giggled again. She wiped her contaminated hand on her skirt and turned her attention to a bookcase with glass doors. On top of it was a great crystal ball; the shelves below were crammed with books so huge and black that they could only be Bibles.

'Not Bibles. Grimoires. Books of spells,' explained Cassandra. 'You may open them if you like, but most of the spells don't work. What makes a spell work is passion – fear or desire or rage –'

Clara nodded. That made sense to her.

'Witchcraft begins with passion. You've a world of strong feeling locked up inside, haven't you, Clara Wintermute? You think it makes you weak, but it doesn't. It might make you strong, if you knew how to use it.'

Clara cast down her eyes. Frightened and dubious she might be: she was also fascinated. What if the witch were telling the truth? What if passion could somehow be converted into power – even into magic? If Clara were a witch, she wouldn't have to be good; she wouldn't have to be sad. She might free herself from

Grisini's spell and be happy for the first time since the Others died.

'Step into my labyrinth and follow the painted lines. I want to know you better.'

Mutely Clara stepped into the maze. The arches of her feet tingled, and she felt curiously giddy, as if she had been twirling round and round on a swing. Gingerly she traced the convoluted path, her footfalls as regular as the tick of a metronome. At each narrow turn, she spun counterclockwise. Fragments of memory played before her mind's eye, each one awakening a different response: pity, surprise, amusement. Clara saw herself at the Others' funeral, dressed in mourning. Then the funeral was over, and she was shrieking with laughter at her birthday party. Another twist of the path and Clara was small again. She knelt in the mausoleum beside her Mamma; she was cold and bored and she wanted to go home, but she knew better than to say so. The walls of the mausoleum turned to vapour, and Clara heard the tinkle of a music box. She was a puppet, dancing in the chill November air. The red lines jackknifed, and Clara was alone in the nursery, balancing before the looking glass. More than anything in the world, she longed for proper ballet shoes, so that she could stand on her toes. Three steps forward, and it was teatime, a rare sunny day, and she was sulking because she didn't want to eat her watercress –

Clara stiffened. No one must know about the watercress. She was suddenly and acutely aware that the witch had been following her thoughts as she wound her way through the maze. *Stop it, stop it!* she thought frantically. *Get out!* She opened her mouth to shriek the words, but no sound came. Deliberately she brought her foot down on one of the painted lines, breaking the rules of the labyrinth. She stumbled sideways, staggering until she touched the rough stones of the tower wall. She leaned against it, feeling sick.

'You've done well.'

Clara lifted her head to stare.

'When I sought to invade your thoughts, you resisted me. I thought you were strong, and I was right. Now, go to the table across the room and choose one of the *tarocchi*. I want to see which one you choose.'

Clara paused, not recognising the word. But after a moment – *Tarocchi are Tarot Cards, stupid child!* – her legs dragged her to the great carved table and she stood looking down at the cards. They were larger than ordinary playing cards, and the images on them were haunting: a woman holding a silver crescent, a skeleton with a scythe, a tower struck by lightning.

'Choose one.'

Clara had already chosen. Her card showed a dancing man in a white smock and green leggings. He stood on one pointed toe with his hands behind his back. Silently she crossed the floor and offered the card to the witch.

'Ah, the Hanged Man!' The old woman's face lit up. 'But you're holding him the wrong way.' She turned the card, and Clara saw it properly; it was not a dancer, but a man hanging upside down with a noose around his foot. 'See how he's a prisoner, with his hands tied behind his back? That's your card. I thought I was the one who was trapped –'

'Trapped?' echoed Clara.

'You're trapped, aren't you? You're caught in Gaspare's spell. You're a puppet.'

'I'm not,' Clara said. She lifted her palms to show there were no strings.

The old woman's smile broadened, baring her ugly teeth. 'Look in the glass.'

Clara wheeled around. There were the flames, floating in the mirrors like drowned suns; there was the tall cabinet and the woman in her throne-like chair. But she, Clara, had no reflection. She opened her mouth to ask, *Where am I? Why can't I see myself in the glass?*

'You're inside the stone.'

Clara could have wept. She asked, 'What stone?' and clenched her teeth. She must not cry before this horrid old woman.

*Horrid, am I?* But Cassandra's cruel grin was gone and she spoke gently. 'Come here. I'll show you.'

Clara had no wish to draw near. But her feet towed her forward, and she knelt before the old woman as if they were granddaughter and grandmother. Cassandra bent towards her, her age-spotted hands fumbling for the chain around her neck. At the end of the chain hung a cage made of golden wires. The cage broke open, releasing a red jewel as large as an eye. It fell on the old woman's scarred palm.

Clara had never seen anything like it. Gazing at it, she had no difficulty believing that she was inside it. It was a whole world, a red sea, a bloody womb, a beating heart . . . She wanted to close her eyes against it. She wanted to go on looking at it for the rest of her life.

'You see how beautiful it is? And beauty is only the beginning. There's power in it – power to gain, power to heal, power to break down the barriers between minds. That's how I can speak to you. I brought you inside it, so that I could see into your heart.'

Clara stretched out her hand. She did not dare to touch the

gem but rested the tips of her fingers against Cassandra's wrist. The contact seemed to intensify the bond between them.

'Would you like it, Clara? It could be yours to keep. Only, I cannot give it to you. You will have to steal it from me. Have you the courage to steal from me, Clara?'

Clara stared into the depths of the stone. She felt the witch's mind holding her, lulling her.

'Listen, and don't be frightened,' murmured Cassandra. 'Let me tell you who you are.'

Clara did not stir. She wanted to hear what the old woman thought.

'I see you, Clara Wintermute,' murmured the witch. 'I see you at home, where you are unhappy, as I was, when I was a child. My mother deserted me and my father neglected me, even as yours does. You seek to please your parents, to comfort them, but they don't love you; you know they will never love you, don't you?' She caressed Clara's hand. 'And so your heart breaks, and your home is a prison. I know all about it. That's why I want you to have the stone. With the magic of the fire opal, you will win your mother's heart; you will fill your father's house with joy. Think of it, Clara! If you want to dance, you may. Whatever you want will be yours for the taking. Only first you must dare – dare to steal from me –'

'How?' interrupted Clara. She needed no further persuasion. She envisioned herself dancing in a rain of rose petals. The applause broke against her ears like thunder; her parents were clapping in the front row.

'I have cast a spell, Clara: a spell that will bring you back to life. Your desire is the key; you need only wish for the stone, and you will be yourself again. Wish with all your heart! If your wish is strong enough, your strings will snap and Grisini's spell

220

will be broken. Then you must come to my room – and steal! You will have to pry open the locket and remove the stone, and' – the old woman's voice grew rough and deep; something feral gleamed in her eyes – 'I will fight you for it. No, don't shrink away from me! If you use all your strength – all! – you may defeat me. Think of what you might gain! It's your last hope, you know – your only hope of being human and happy once more.'

*But you're not human,* Clara thought rebelliously. *And I don't believe you're happy.* She raised her eyes to the witch's face. Deliberately, with terrifying ease, Clara crossed the boundary between them, and all at once, she *was* Cassandra. She was old and ill, thirsty and feverish; pain gnawed at her joints and bit deep into her left hand. She was haunted by nightmares; she wanted to die; she was terrified of dying; she was surrounded by flames –

Clara snatched her hand free. She scrambled to her feet. 'You're not happy!' she cried accusingly. 'You're in pain – dreadful pain! I can feel it – I can see into your thoughts, just as you saw mine. The spell works both ways, doesn't it?'

'Yes,' conceded Cassandra. She was breathing heavily, and her face was ashen.

'You're miserable!' said Clara. 'And you're frightened to death, because of that *thing*! Now you want me to take it – but I won't! It's a trap!'

'Someone must take it,' the old woman said desperately. 'Someone. If it isn't you, it will have to be one of the others.'

*The Others.* Clara clutched the locket at her breast. She thought of the snippets of hair inside it: all that was left of her brothers and sisters. 'You can't hurt them! They're dead!'

'They're not. They're here,' snapped Cassandra.

Clara gazed at her, aghast. She realised she had misunderstood. The witch was talking about Parsefall and Lizzie Rose. She stammered, 'I – I won't let you. I'll warn them.'

'How? You're a puppet. You can't speak; you can't move –'

Clara shook herself like a wet dog. She turned to flee, as if she could escape the witch's power by physical force. She reached for the door handle, only to find it wasn't there. She stopped, bewildered. She could not find the way out. She could not sort out where the walls were and what was mirror glass: what was reflected and what was real. She whirled clockwise, and the uneven floorboards tripped her. In a heartbeat, she was on her feet again, only to see that the silver mirrors were darkening. All around her were women with haggard and desperate faces, women wrapped in tendrils of coiling smoke.

Clara shrieked, 'Help me!' She clenched her fist around the sapphire locket, as if the Others were good angels who could rescue her. Her frantic mind dredged up a single hope: earlier that night, when she'd entered the room, Cassandra had been facing her: Cassandra's chair must be opposite the door. Clara turned her back on the witch. She leaped for the door.

She never touched it. The red light dimmed. When Clara's vision cleared, she was staring down at Parsefall, who lay like a sleeping giant before the fire. She – small and inert, a puppet once more – was back in the armchair, with one foot clamped in the crook of her knee.

# Chapter Thirty-two

# A Meeting with Madama

Madama was not well. When Lizzie Rose asked Mrs Fettle when she might meet the mistress of Strachan's Ghyll, the housekeeper said that Madama had passed a bad night and would see no one but the doctor. The children were not to leave – Madama had been very insistent on this point – but they must be very quiet, and the dog must be quiet as well. If the dog misbehaved, it would be shut up in the stables.

Lizzie Rose assured Mrs Fettle that Ruby would be the best of good dogs and scuttled back to her bedroom. It worried her that Mrs Sagredo was so ill. Lizzie Rose had been hoping that the old lady would welcome them and make them feel at home. She began a prayer for Mrs Sagredo's recovery: 'Please, God, don't let her die until –' She stopped in mid-sentence. Until what? It horrified Lizzie Rose to realise that what she feared most was not that Cassandra Sagredo might die, but that she might die before she decided to leave her money to the children. Hastily Lizzie Rose amended her prayer: 'Dear God, please make Mrs Sagredo get better and live a long time,' but her feelings of guilt were not easily banished. Neither was her desire for the legacy. At Strachan's Ghyll, she and Parsefall were sheltered and fed and safe. There were no policemen, no Luce and no horrid Fitzmorris. To wake every morning in a clean bed, with a fire in the grate and breakfast on a tray, was an extraordinary privilege; to know that someone else had to carry the coals and empty the slops was a blessed relief.

In spite of these luxuries, the days that followed were anxious ones for Lizzie Rose. Her conscience was fretful, and it worried her that she could not make friends with the servants. She spent most of her time in Parsefall's bedchamber, rehearsing with the puppets.

The Green Room, which Mrs Fettle had allotted to Parsefall, was a stately chamber, richly decorated with tapestries, Gothic fretwork and serpentine marble. It took Parsefall less than twenty-four hours to despoil it. The four-poster, with its curtains of bottle-green velvet, struck him as the perfect place to erect his theatre, so he stripped the bed and piled the blankets on top of the bearskin by the fire. He unpacked the wicker trunk and strewed the carpet with puppets and backdrops, scraps and tools. Lizzie Rose worried that the mess made work for the servants, but Parsefall didn't care. If he had been a duke, he could not have cared less what the servants thought.

On their fourth evening at Strachan's Ghyll, the children were busy with the puppets when the door of the Green Room opened and Mrs Fettle addressed them. 'Madama wishes to see you. You're to come at once.'

Lizzie Rose felt her stomach tense. Here was the interview

for which she had waited. She scrambled to her feet, wishing she was wearing her own clothes. Parsefall's clothes had been returned to him two days ago, cleaned, mended and pressed; Lizzie Rose's frocks hadn't. She had been forced to adopt the ermine-trimmed coat as a sort of day dress.

Mrs Fettle turned her back, assuming that the children would follow her. Lizzie Rose caught Parsefall's sleeve. 'Let me do the talking,' she whispered. He jerked his head in agreement, and they pursued Mrs Fettle down the passage. The housekeeper opened a pair of double doors and stood aside to let them pass.

Lizzie Rose halted in the doorway. The room was radiant with candlelight and lined with crimson damask; the bed hangings were sulphur yellow and blood red. Beneath the smell of coal smoke and wax candles, Lizzie Rose detected another scent, a weird, inhuman odour, like hot metal.

'The children from London, ma'am. Miss Fawr and Master Hooke.'

'Close the doors behind you,' commanded a voice from the bed.

Lizzie Rose obeyed but not quickly enough. A small red figure darted between the doors and frisked over the carpet. Ruby halted before the high bed, barked impetuously and launched herself upwards.

Lizzie Rose cried, 'Oh, ma'am! I beg your pardon!' and hastened to the bedside.

She was startled to hear Mrs Sagredo laugh. It was a jarring sound: creaky and rasping and too low for a woman's voice. As Lizzie Rose bent under the canopy to retrieve the dog, something caught on her sleeve. She started and looked up. The thing that had touched her was a silken cord, and shinnying up the cord was a brass monkey with a dreadful grin. Lizzie Rose thought she had never seen an uglier ornament, and she gazed warily at the woman who had chosen it.

She was a thickset woman, with a large head and a wide square brow. Lizzie Rose had expected Cassandra Sagredo to be frail and aristocratic. Instead, she was ruddy and full bosomed, with a nose like the snout of a sow. A close look revealed that her brilliant complexion was unnatural: she was powdered white and painted red. Her eyes were bloodshot, and she breathed unevenly.

Lizzie Rose reached for Ruby. To her surprise, the dog eluded her, scampering over the invalid's lap. The spaniel turned in a circle and sat down, wedging her rump against the old woman's side. Cassandra Sagredo ran her hand down the dog's spine. 'Ah,' she said, and the monosyllable spoke of pure pleasure.

'I thought you didn't like dogs,' said Lizzie Rose.

'Who told you that?' demanded Cassandra Sagredo. 'Fettle? Fettle doesn't know what I like. Perhaps I'll confound Fettle.' She grinned, looking uncannily like the monkey on the bed cord. 'So! You are Elizabeth Rose Fawr, and you are Parsefall Hooke. What have you done with my old friend Grisini?'

It was the question Lizzie Rose had been dreading, but she was ready for it. 'I'm very sorry, ma'am, but I have bad news. Back in November, Professor Grisini fell down the steps of our boardinghouse. He hit his head, and I'm afraid he wasn't quite in his right mind, because he wandered off into the streets and didn't come back.' She paused for Mrs Sagredo's exclamation of dismay, but the old woman scarcely batted an eye. 'We couldn't find out what became of him. And Parsefall and I hadn't anyone to look after us, and we were in such straits! So when I saw your letter –'

'You read it,' interrupted Mrs Sagredo.

Lizzie Rose flushed. 'I did, ma'am.' Unconsciously she

assumed the pose of a suppliant, clasping her hands. 'I do beg your pardon, ma'am! I know how wrong it is to read other people's letters –'

Cassandra interrupted her again. 'Oh, fie! Don't be such a little prig! I always read other people's letters. The world would be a very dull place if one had nothing to read but one's own letters. What I want to know is what took you so long. I wrote to you weeks ago.'

'Parsefall takes in the post,' explained Lizzie Rose. 'He left the letter in his pocket and I didn't find it right away. When I did find it, I hoped it might be from someone who could offer us comfort and advice. Your letter sounded so very kind.' She faltered on the last word, aware that it didn't ring true. 'I'm afraid you must think us very bold to have come –'

Cassandra cut her off with a flick of the hand. '"Be bold, be bold but not too bold!" Do you know that old rhyme? I've always liked it. But now you must tell me: Did you really come all this way for comfort and advice? Or were you hoping to inherit my fortune?'

Lizzie Rose gave a little gasp. She felt the blood rush to her cheeks and knew she was red to the roots of her hair.

'Tell the truth and shame the devil!' mocked Cassandra. 'It was the money you came for, wasn't it? Why not say so? You're like the cat that wants to catch fish but won't get its feet wet! Well, come on, girl! Answer my question!'

Lizzie Rose did not trust herself to speak. To her astonishment, Parsefall came to her rescue. 'We got our feet wet.' He stepped forward, jamming his hands in his pockets. 'Didn't we take the night train from London? We woz on that train for hours, and there woz a baby in the carriage wiv'us, screaming its bloody 'ead off. Lizzie Rose an' me wanted to wring its neck,

227

didn't we, Lizzie Rose? Then after we come, Old Fettle made us bathe in 'ot water, whether we wanted to or not. I call that gettin' our feet wet.' Scornfully he turned to Lizzie Rose. 'I told you it woz all flimflam. We come all this way, and she ain't going to fork over the stumpy.'

Lizzie Rose shut her eyes. When she dared to open them, she saw that Mrs Sagredo was gazing at Parsefall as if he was some exotic animal at the zoo. 'What's that you say, boy? I didn't catch half of that. Tell me: what's *stumpy*?'

Parsefall did not deign to speak. He removed one hand from his pocket and rubbed his thumb against his forefingers.

'I see. So *stumpy*'s money. And I'm to fork it over, am I? Well, my little man, you shan't be disappointed; I mean to fork over my stumpy, and you shall have your share. Come here and let me look at you! You're missing a finger. What became of it?'

'Dunno.'

The old woman caught hold of his wrist, unfolding his fingers so that she could trace the lines on his palm. 'Why, you're a thief!'

'He isn't,' Lizzie Rose said hotly.

'He is. I can see it in his hands. Quite a nimble one, aren't you, boy? A pickpocket – and clever with the puppets, just like Gaspare.' Mrs Sagredo narrowed her eyes at Lizzie Rose 'What about you? Are you a thief too?'

'No, ma'am, I'm not.'

'Where d'you get the coat you're wearing?'

Lizzie Rose lifted her chin, determined to defend herself. 'From the wardrobe in the White Room. I borrowed it because I had nothing to wear. Your servants took my frocks away.'

'Those were my orders,' Mrs Sagredo said indifferently. 'Fettle said your things weren't worth mending. I told her you could have my cast-offs. Didn't you see the other gowns in the wardrobe?'

'I saw them,' Lizzie Rose said, tight-lipped, 'but I didn't think it proper –'

'Take any gowns you want and have the servants make them fit you. The house is full of fripperies – gowns, stockings, petti-coats. I don't want them; I'm too ill. Well? Aren't you going to thank me?'

Lizzie Rose gritted her teeth. 'You're very kind, ma'am.'

'I'm all kindness,' the old woman said with a savage grin. 'Kindness and stumpy! Do you know what day it is?'

The sudden change of subject took Lizzie Rose aback. She raised her eyes to the ceiling, mentally counting on her fingers. 'Why, it must be nearly Christmas!'

'Just so. Tomorrow will be Christmas Eve. And because I am all kindness, I have thought much about your Christmas presents. You must have gifts from me; I insist upon it. You may choose what you like from the things in this house.'

Parsefall looked blankly at Lizzie Rose. She shook her head.

'You may begin now.' Cassandra spread her hands. 'Here and now – in this very room. Go to the table before the fire, and take anything you like! Think of it as treasure trove! Go and choose! Be bold!'

Unwillingly Lizzie Rose turned to face the hearth. There was a table spread with a white cloth and a tempting array of objects: small animals carved from amber and jade; fragments of lace; leather masks and ivory fans; enamelled watches; silver penknives; and a wicked-looking pistol with gilded steel mounts. An open jewel box held bracelets and necklaces, all coiled and entwined like serpents in a snake pit.

'You are suspicious.' Cassandra lingered over the last word, as if it was *luscious* or *delicious*. 'I don't blame you. But I assure you: you may explore the entire house and take anything you like. The rooms are all unlocked – except the Tower – the Tower isn't safe. But except for that one room – and except for one thing – you may go wherever you will and take whatever pleases you. And tomorrow evening, Christmas Eve, you must show me what you've chosen. That will help me decide what to leave you in my will. Why aren't you taking anything?' She spoke pettishly: a child on the verge of a tantrum. 'Fettle brought those things up just for you. Look – and desire – and *take*.'

Lizzie Rose hung back. She was determined not to show any interest in the objects on the table. But Parsefall went forward and dipped his fingers into the jewel box. There was a flash of green and gold. 'Catch!'

Lizzie Rose's hands opened instinctively. Something hard and metallic stung them, and when she looked down, she was staring at a necklace of heavy gold, set with square green stones.

'Go ahead. Keep it.' Cassandra Sagredo leaned sideways to watch her. 'What use will it be to me in my coffin?' Her voice grew sharp. 'What's the matter? Aren't my emeralds good enough for you?'

'It isn't that, ma'am –'

'Try them on. And call me *Madama*, not *ma'am*. Put on the necklace and look in the glass. There!'

Lizzie Rose turned to face the tarnished mirror. One of her plaits hung in front of her shoulder. She could not help appreciating the contrast between the glinting green stones and her red hair. Tentatively she touched the gold links.

'You like that, don't you, little Vanity?'

Lizzie Rose made up her mind. She reached behind her neck

and undid the clasp. She crossed to the table and returned the necklace to the jewel box. 'It's very kind of you, ma'am, but I think I would rather not.'

Cassandra mimicked: '"I think I would rather not." Lud, but you *are* a precious one, aren't you? Such blushes, such a virtuous air! If Gaspare hadn't warned me –' Her words caught on a laugh. She choked so violently that Lizzie Rose hastened to the washstand to pour her a glass of water.

Cassandra took the glass with a shaking hand. She gulped the water and cleared her throat. Under the powder, her skin was a curious shade of grey. The red paint on her cheeks looked pathetic and grotesque.

'Help me sit up. There is something else I must tell you. I must warn you against the one thing you may not take.' She dropped the empty glass on to the counterpane. 'Lift me up.'

Lizzie Rose slid one arm under the old woman's shoulders. The hot-metal smell was very strong.

'Give me another pillow. And take that pitying look off your face – it's mawkish. Now – I'll show you.' She raised her voice. 'Come here, boy! You must see this too.'

From around her neck, she held out a gold chain with a round locket. One yellowed fingernail found the catch, breaking the sphere in two, and releasing a red gemstone. Lizzie Rose was reminded of the cracking of an egg.

Cassandra scooped up the jewel, holding it in the hollow of her hand. It didn't glitter but glowed like a red-hot coal. Against the carmine red of the stone, other colours curled and dissolved: peacock shades of blue and green, dim white and pale yellow.

'Look, but don't touch. It's a fire opal. Have you ever seen anything like it?'

Lizzie Rose shook her head.

'Look at it – its size and depth and sheen! Few fire opals have such play of colour. It is extraordinarily rare. The stone is worth more than the whole house and everything in it. But that is only the beginning. There's magic in it. In your wildest flights of fancy, you could scarcely imagine what it might do for you – but here's the cruel thing: I will not part with it. Lay even a finger on it, and you will be a thief. And what thief would be bold enough to steal my fire opal?'

'But we're *not* thieves,' protested Lizzie Rose. 'We wouldn't dream of taking it, would we, Parsefall?'

Cassandra bared her teeth in a crooked smile. 'I wouldn't speak for him, if I were you. He's a bold one, ain't you, boy? I wouldn't put it past him to creep in here while I was asleep. It could be done, you know; I sleep very soundly, and the clasp on the locket is loose.' She lowered her voice to a whisper and spoke directly to Parsefall:

*Be bold, be bold but not too bold,*
*Lest that your heart's blood should run cold!*

'Your blood wouldn't run cold, would it, boy? I like that about you. I like you altogether.' She sounded surprised. 'It's been years since I liked anyone. I wonder what it means.'

Parsefall said, 'Huh,' and scratched his ear.

Lizzie Rose gazed from one perplexed face to another and felt an unaccustomed pang of jealousy. Unlikely as it might seem, the old woman had taken a fancy to Parsefall. Lizzie Rose told herself that she ought to be glad of it. She was aware that most people preferred her to Parsefall, and it wasn't fair. Nevertheless,

232

she felt shaken, as if Madama's partiality had wounded her in some way. She looked down at Ruby, who seemed to be enjoying the comforts of Madama's bed, and a new lump rose in her throat.

'I will see you both tomorrow,' said Cassandra. She ran her hand over the spaniel's back. 'You will come in the evening and show me what you chose for Christmas. Now, go.' She closed her eyes. 'Take your pretty little dog and go.'

# Chapter Thirty-three

# The Wolf and the Swan

Clara hung from the gallows, close to Parsefall's sleeping place. It was eleven o'clock at night, and she was wide awake. Though she could not stir, she was hard at work, straining to cast a spell that would allow her to communicate with Parsefall and Lizzie Rose.

She was no witch, and she had no idea how to work her spell. But she had devised a ritual, and over and over she practised it.

She began by recalling the night Cassandra's magic had brought her to life. She pictured herself swelling until she was full-size; she envisioned herself crossing the carpet and going out into the passage. She went first to the White Room, where Lizzie Rose slept. Her spell – if spell it was – was hampered by the fact that she had never seen the White Room; Parsefall hadn't taken her there. Even so, she strove to imagine it, and the name was some help to her.

She found her way down the dark corridor and stopped before the door. Calling on all her powers of memory, she thought of what it was like to operate a doorknob. If she could imagine the doorknob, she told herself, she could open the door.

She worked hard, framing every detail of her vision. She saw her hand go out and her fingers curl around the knob. She twisted her hand clockwise, so that the knuckle of her thumb stood at twelve o'clock; she called to mind the click and creak of the latch. She conjured up the sensations that followed: the swing of the door as she opened it and the carpet brushing the soles of her shoes.

She imagined the White Room. It was lit by moonlight, as clean and pure as a lily. Lizzie Rose lay sleeping with her red hair loose on the pillow. Clara stood at the end of the bed, grasping the footboard. She tried to remember how it felt to speak: the sensation of air filling her lungs, the play of muscles in her throat. With all the strength she could muster, she thought the words she wanted to say:

*Lizzie Rose! Listen to me! There's danger! Madama's a witch, and the fire opal's evil! Don't let her trick you into taking it! Whatever you do, don't take it!*

The figure in the bed never stirred. Clara imagined herself raising her voice: *Lizzie Rose, there's danger here! Take Parsefall and leave Strachan's Ghyll!*

There was no response. Clara remembered what Cassandra had said: *What makes a spell work is passion – fear or desire or rage* – Clara prayed that her passion might be strong enough. She thought the words a third time, intensely, trying to convey the urgency of the danger. She turned from Lizzie Rose and retraced her steps.

Once again, she opened and shut the door. She could almost hear it: the click of the latch and the thud of the door against the wooden frame. *I have warned Lizzie Rose,* Clara thought, desperately hoping that this was true. *Now I must warn Parsefall.*

She imagined herself flitting down the hall. She opened the door of the Green Room – *click-thud* – and went to the hearth where Parsefall slept. *Parsefall! Listen to me! It's Clara! I've come to warn you. Madama's a witch, and the fire opal is evil!*

She saw him twitch in his sleep, and her heart leaped. Had he heard her? Perhaps in his sleep, in his dreams . . . His face was pale. Clara imagined herself hunkering down beside him, touching his hand to wake him. She felt a surge of protective love.

Suddenly her vision changed. She slipped into Parsefall's mind smoothly and completely; it was as easy as sliding her hands into her fur muff. The Green Room vanished, and she was within his dream, seeing the shadows that haunted his sleep.

His dream was not a pleasant one. Clara stood beside him in the dormitory of a dim brick building. The room was desolate and prison-like, and she understood that once again they were in the workhouse. Parsefall was small in his dream, no more than five years old. His head was shaved, and he clutched a bundle of rags to his chest. It was human shaped: a doll.

She laid her hand on his shoulder. 'Parsefall!'

He squinted as if he didn't know who she was. 'Eppie?'

'No,' Clara said. 'I'm Clara. Listen to me, Parsefall –'

His features blurred. It was as if she saw him through a wall of moving water. Then the water stilled and she saw that he had aged. He was taller now and gazed straight into her eyes. Clara spoke in a rush.

'Parsefall, listen to me. The red stone that Madama wears

round her neck – the fire opal. You mustn't take it. No matter what happens, you mustn't. It's dangerous.'

'Why?'

'Madama wants you to take it. It's hurting her. It'll hurt you.' Clara seized upon a new way to explain. 'Remember that play you did, with the Bottle Imp? The stone is like that – there's power in it, but the power's bad. So you must keep away from it, and you must warn Lizzie Rose –' She stopped, for again he was changing. His body dwindled and he was a small boy once more.

'Who're you?' Parsefall asked. His voice was higher, his pronunciation less distinct. 'Where's Eppie?'

'Who's Eppie?' asked Clara, but before he could answer her, she knew.

'Eppie's me sister,' Parsefall said. His face twisted and he began to cry. 'She gi'me her rag doll. She's dead,' he said, and his cry rose to a howl of raw misery.

In an instant, Clara's arms were around him. She pressed his head against her front, trying to hold him as softly and strongly as she could. It was like clasping a bird that had no feathers; he was nothing but breath and bone. 'Don't cry, oh, don't,' she said with stupid tenderness, but his body melted away. She was back on the gallows, in the Green Room. The connection between them had been lost.

Clara fought to regain it. She repeated her warning, hoping to hammer it into his mind. *Parsefall, listen! You're in danger here! Don't take the fire opal! It's like the Bottle Imp!* But he had gone deeper into sleep, and she could not reach him.

The door of the Green Room opened.

*Who's there?* wondered Clara, but she could not turn her head to see. She heard soft footsteps. They hesitated beside the empty bed. Then a shadowy figure came into view: a tall, thin man in a ragged frock coat. *Grisini!* thought Clara, and she went cold all over. She wanted to shriek at the top of her voice: *Look out, Parsefall – wake up!*

But her panic was voiceless. Grisini lowered himself to his hands and knees, crouching over the sleeping boy like a werewolf. The firelight threw his shadow on the ceiling. Then, with a brutal lurching movement, he clamped one hand over Parsefall's mouth and pinned him down by kneeling on his thighs.

Parsefall's eyes flew open; the whites gleamed. His arms thrashed, but the blows he struck were feeble. His resistance was frantic but short-lived. After a few seconds he stopped struggling.

'*Stai zitto!*' hissed Grisini. 'Not a word, or I will tear out your throat! You are surprised, *si*? You thought – no, you hoped – that I was dead.' He shifted his weight, twisting so that he sat on the boy's legs. 'I assure you, I am very much alive. And I have forgotten nothing.'

Parsefall's face was unreadable, but Clara seemed to feel his thoughts. They were like splinters of glass when a mirror breaks: jagged, brittle, darting in all directions. He knew he was going to be hurt, but he didn't know how or how much. He fastened his eyes on Grisini's face, desperate to anticipate what might happen next.

'I remember how you kicked me – *disgraziato, ingrato*! But if you will obey me, we will be friends once more. *Senti.*'

Grisini lifted his hand from Parsefall's mouth. *Scream!* thought Clara, but Parsefall was too wise to scream. The hour was late and the servants were abed. Lizzie Rose was at the far end of the corridor.

'You have met Madama, yes?'

Parsefall drew his chin close to his chest, nodding. Grisini picked up the poker. There was a hideous moment when Clara thought he was going to use it to hurt Parsefall, but he only leaned forward to stir the fire. The room grew brighter, and Clara saw her kidnapper more clearly. He was unshaven, and his face was seamed with fresh scars. Grains of snow clung to his boots. *He came from outside the house,* thought Clara, and she wondered whether Cassandra knew he was there.

'When you met her, did you notice the locket around her neck?'

Parsefall jerked his chin towards his chest.

'Did she show you the stone inside?' Another jerk. 'What colour is it?'

'Red.'

'And how big?'

Parsefall lifted his hands, crooking his fingers to approximate the size of the fire opal.

'*Va bene.* We are speaking of the same stone. Now, listen to me. I want that stone for myself. Do you understand me?'

'Yes.'

'You must steal it.'

*No!* thought Clara. She saw Parsefall swallow and grimace, but he did not speak. The boy's silence seemed to exasperate Grisini. He caught hold of Parsefall's ear, digging his fingernails into the tender lobe, drawing blood. Parsefall inhaled sharply.

'Listen to me! I was your master once! *Non ti scordar* – I will be your master still! What I tell you to do, you do. Do you understand that, my little pickpocket? Or must I remind you –?'

'No,' shot back Parsefall. 'I'll steal wot you want – only' – he shut his eyes for a fraction of a second before he went on – 'if I give you the stone – will you go away and leave me and Lizzie Rose alone?'

There was a moment of utter silence. Grisini shifted his position. Parsefall winced.

'You wish me to leave you? I, who took you from the workhouse, who have been more than a father to you? I taught you my trade: how to bring the *piccoli* to life, how to pick a pocket, how to pick a lock . . . *Ingrato!*' He flung up his hands to express disbelief. The thumb and finger of his right hand glistened with Parsefall's blood. 'Still, if that is what you wish, we will part. Bring me the fire opal and I will trouble you no more.'

Parsefall did not relax a muscle. 'Do I go and get it now?'

*No!* Clara shrieked silently.

Grisini spoke at the same instant. 'No. *Piu tardi.* Day will be better than night – I have questioned the servants, and they tell me that Madama sleeps during the day. It will be best if you enter her room when she lies sleeping. Your nimble fingers will do the rest. And not a word of this to Lizzie Rose – not one word! Or it will be the worse for her. For her as well as for you, *capisci?*'

'Yes.'

'If you fail me, I will be obliged to hurt you. You know I should like nothing better.'

Parsefall didn't speak. A tremor ran through his body.

Grisini nodded his satisfaction. '*Va bene.* As soon as you have the stone, you must bring it to me. You will find me in the gatehouse – do you know where that is? Go out the front door and follow the path away from the house. Bring me the stone, and from that day on, you will see no more of me. But until then, I will haunt you, lest you neglect your duty. Otherwise, you might say, *Ah, my old master! He has forgotten me!* But even as you speak the words, I will be at your elbow!' He opened his eyes wide, mimicking Parsefall's astonishment. 'I can enter the house whenever I like; I can come into your room at any hour –'

240

He was interrupted by a shrill, sweet chiming. Grisini slipped his hand into his pocket and brought out the automaton watch. His fingers, still wet with Parsefall's blood, caressed the edge of the dial. He listened until the twelfth chime rang out. '*Mezzanotte*. It is apropos, *sì*? The wolf snaps its jaws at the swan, but the bird cannot fly away. They are always together. If you want to escape from me, *figliolo*, you will have to bring me that stone.'

'I will.'

Grisini shifted his weight until he was on all fours. Gingerly he found his balance and raised himself to a standing position. Moving stiffly, he crossed the room and went out into the corridor.

Parsefall got up. He could not stop shaking. After Grisini left, he stood facing the door, terrified lest it open again. He scarcely breathed. He wished he could hear Grisini's footsteps descending the great staircase, but the walls were too thick or the carpet too soft – *or Grisini was outside the door, waiting to come back in*! Parsefall shivered. He touched his torn earlobe. It was still dripping, and he put his fingers in his mouth to lick them clean. Warm tears stole down his cheeks, gathering inside the collar of his nightshirt.

He kept still for some time. Then he crept to the door, rocking from toe to heel with each step, making no sound. He thought longingly of Mrs Pinchbeck's cramped house, where only a spangled curtain separated him from Lizzie Rose. Lizzie Rose had always tried to comfort him when he was afraid. He thought of how indignant she would be if she could see the blood on his ear. All at once, he wanted her desperately, all the more because he could not go to her. Even if he was brave enough to venture into the corridor, he dared not confide in her. Only by saying nothing could he protect her from Grisini.

He ran his fingers over the doorplate. There was a keyhole but no key; he could not lock Grisini out. Even if there had been a lock, it would have been no good; Grisini was a skilled picklock. What Parsefall needed was a secure hiding place, a room with a bolt on the inside of the door –

*I know a room with a bolt on the door!*

The words rang inside his head, as sharp and clear as the chime from Grisini's watch. Parsefall shook his head as if there was a bee in his ear. He raked the room with his eyes, selected a chair and carried it on tiptoe to the door. He wedged it underneath the doorknob. The chair was heavy, but the back of it was full of pointy little holes, crosses and teardrops. He didn't know if it was strong enough to withstand an attack from Grisini.

He went back to the hearth. As he neared the mantel, his glance fell upon the puppet gallows. Clara's glassy eyes shone like water in the dark, and he had a weird fancy that she had been crying too. He lifted her perch. His hands were shaking so hard that she quivered like a twanged string.

He scooped her up and held her in his arms. He settled down cross-legged with Clara in his lap, mounting guard with his face to the door. Little by little, he shifted to a reclining position. Then he fell asleep.

When he opened his eyes, he stood before the door to the Tower Room. It was still night, but there was a lamp at his feet: a lamp and Clara, who lolled untidily against the wall. He was gripping something thin and sharp: two of Mrs Pinchbeck's wire hairpins. They had been twisted together to serve as a picklock.

It took Parsefall a few minutes to understand that he was awake. He realised that he had been sleepwalking – and in his sleep, he had determined to pick the lock of the Tower Room. Why? He stared at the tool in his hand. The tower was dangerous. Mrs Fettle had warned the children not to go there, and so had Madama. Why, then, was he wanting to go inside? There was no point in it – but after a moment, he dropped to his knees and inserted the pick in the lock.

It was a simple lock, the kind Grisini had taught him to pick when he was seven years old. In less than a minute, Parsefall had the door open. On the inner side was a heavy bolt: solid iron, three-quarters of an inch thick. Somehow he had known it would be there.

He picked up the lamp and started into the room. He halted and yelped in terror. Phantoms surrounded him: ghosts of children clad in white. Parsefall spun around. They moved with him.

They were his reflections. He halted in mid-flight, his hand vibrating so that the mirrored lamps quaked. Once he was sure that none of the children were ghosts, he took a deep breath and examined the room around him.

It was peculiarly warm. He could feel dust and grit under his bare feet. The tower was unsafe and therefore uninhabited. He tested the floorboards with his weight. They wiggled a little, but they didn't feel as fragile as Mrs Pinchbeck's staircase. He was light, not like Grisini; Grisini might fall through the floor, but he wouldn't.

And Grisini would not be able to come here. He might pick the lock, but he wouldn't be able to get in. The iron bolt would keep him out, the bolt that could be worked only from the inside of the room. Parsefall cast his eyes over the gloomy tower and nodded his satisfaction. Here he would be able to sleep, safe from whatever ghastly surprise Grisini might choose to inflict on him.

He eyed the mirrors, appraising them. They would be

excellent for rehearsing with the puppets. If he stood on the table, he would be able to see his work from every angle. He let out his breath. For the moment, at least, he had found a sort of sanctuary. He would bring the bearskin rug into the room, and Clara – he would certainly bring Clara. He set the lamp on the floor and went out into the passage to fetch her.

# Chapter Thirty-four

# The Treasure Hunt

Lizzie Rose paused under the stone arches of the Great Hall, preparing to explore the house.

She was in no mood to do so. She had awakened with a headache that the acrid smell of Strachan's Ghyll did nothing to appease. The memory of last night's meeting with Madama was still fresh in her mind: the hideous old woman, the brass monkey, the troubling beauty of the red stone. She recalled Madama's instructions for the day: the children were to explore the house and choose their Christmas presents. Lizzie Rose was quite certain that the invitation to take what she liked was a test, a trap. She knew she needed her wits about her and wished that her head would stop pounding.

She had hoped to warn Parsefall against taking too many Christmas presents, but he was unaccountably absent, and this too, was a source of worry. Thus far, every morning at Strachan's Ghyll had begun the same way: Lizzie Rose wrapped the velvet coat around her nightdress and went outdoors to walk the dog. On her way out, she passed through the kitchen and asked the servants to send two breakfast trays up to the Green Room. That morning she'd found the Green Room deserted. It was clear that Parsefall had been there – he had seized upon his full share of porridge and hot rolls, bacon, jam and tea. But he himself had disappeared, and Lizzie Rose hadn't seen him all morning.

She stood at the window with Ruby at her side. The long windows were made of small panes of cloudy glass; they diluted the colour of the sky and gave a greenish cast to the snow. Lizzie Rose scanned the landscape, searching for a thin boy in a grey jacket. She gave herself a little shake. Parsefall hated the cold; he had to be somewhere in the house. Perhaps she would find him as she hunted for her Christmas present.

She began her task in the Great Hall. With its black-and-white floors and heavy oak furniture, it seemed centuries old. The swords and shields on the walls held no charms for Lizzie Rose. She wondered what the point was of such a huge and dismal room. The fireplace was so large that no amount of coal could heat it, and the wind swept down the chimney and rattled the windowpanes. Shivering, Lizzie Rose snapped her fingers at Ruby, and they passed into the music room.

It was smaller than the Great Hall and more feminine, with a suite of gilded furniture that looked too frail to sit on. The harp's strings were broken and the piano was out of tune. Ruby yipped happily, trotted to the hearth and sniffed, searching for mice. Lizzie Rose went on to the next room.

If the music room had been almost empty, this room was overstocked. It was a cabinet of curiosities, crammed with antlers, stuffed birds and animal bones. There was a spiral horn that could only have come from a unicorn and a tiger skin on the wall behind it. The pelt was the first thing Lizzie Rose had seen that could serve as a cloak or a shawl. She unpinned it from the wall and draped it around her shoulders, grateful for the extra warmth. She swept her eyes over the cases on the opposite wall.

There were a great many of them. It seemed to Lizzie Rose that there was nothing that Madama did not desire, did not collect. She gazed on seashells and fish skeletons and corals that looked like tree branches. There were glass trays full of butterflies and a magnifying glass; Lizzie Rose took up the glass and examined the designs on the dead wings. They were as intricately lovely as bits of stained glass but sad: how could anyone be so cruel as to kill a butterfly? Lizzie Rose set down the magnifying glass and picked up a conch shell to listen for the roar of the sea.

The last cabinet in the room was filled with miniature portraits, painted on ivory and framed in gold. The colours were so fresh and delicate that it was some time before Lizzie Rose noticed that all of the subjects were gentlemen. Below each frame was a lock of hair tied with a narrow ribbon. Every shade of hair was represented: browns ranging from wheat to stained walnut, auburn and black and blond and grey.

Lizzie Rose's mouth opened in a silent O. A lock of hair was a keepsake, a token of true love ... Why, this was a catalogue of Madama's admirers! Lizzie Rose looked over her shoulder to make sure she was alone. Then she counted, smudging the glass with her fingertip. Forty-eight miniatures; forty-eight locks of hair. She murmured, 'It isn't even respectable,' and caught herself on the brink of a laugh. It seemed incredible that somewhere in this world there were, or had been, forty-eight men who had fallen in love with the vulgar, unbeautiful and odious Mrs Sagredo.

Her smiled faded as she turned away. She was a little ashamed

247

that she had laughed. It struck her that for Cassandra Sagredo, the men in the miniatures were no different from the butterflies in the glass trays. They were specimens, not people. The old woman couldn't have loved any of them, or she wouldn't have lumped them together in a single display. What she had cared for was the number, the variety – and the fact that all forty-eight men had surrendered a lock of hair. Grimacing, Lizzie Rose left the room, heading into the library.

She found more collections there: old cameos, antique coins and a case full of daggers with sharp blades and jade handles. There were two wooden globes, one of the heavens and one of the earth, each so large that Parsefall could have sat cross-legged inside of them. The bookcases were crammed with leather-bound volumes. One of the spines caught Lizzie Rose's eye. Her face lit up. Within five minutes, she had chosen two books. As she started to leave the library, her eyes fell on a small portrait in an ivory frame.

It did not seem to belong with the other pictures in the room. They were handsome but grim: dark seascapes and sombre still-lifes of silver goblets and half-peeled lemons. This picture was not only frivolous but friendly. A young girl leaned towards the viewer with a puppy in her arms. Her hair fell in loose curls to her shoulders, and her lips, childishly red, were parted in a smile.

Lizzie Rose found herself smiling back. She stood on tip-toe and lifted the frame off the wall. She dusted it with her sleeve and read the inscription on the back: *From Marguerite. In remembrance.*

Parsefall eased shut the doors of Madama's room. He knew that Lizzie Rose was occupied downstairs, and the servants were having their midday meal. He had spent the morning collecting valuables from Madama's house and stuffing them in a pillowcase. Now he stood just inside the closed doors, with his pillowcase in one hand and a lump of red wax in the other.

He had discovered a supply of red candles in the Tower Room. He had lit one and moulded the melted wax, shaping it into a ball while it was still warm. His plan was to open Madama's locket, remove the jewel and replace it with the wax. Seen through the wires of the gold filigree, the wax might resemble the red stone. He didn't think the old woman would be fooled for very long, but the sham stone might buy him time enough to get away from Strachan's Ghyll. He cast a speculative eye over his victim. The old lady lay fast asleep, with her mouth ajar and spittle leaking on to the pillow. Her sleeping body appeared huge and sow-like. He told himself he wasn't afraid, but it wasn't true. He had a queer feeling about stealing the fire opal. The act seemed both perilous and strangely familiar, as if he had dreamed about it.

He lowered his pillowcase to the floor, taking care so that the objects inside wouldn't clink and wake the sleeping woman. He crept close to her bed. Opening his mouth, he stowed the ball of wax between his lips. He would need both hands to open the locket.

A rush of adrenaline swept over him. He welcomed it, knowing that it would steady his hands and quicken his wits. He shook his hands to loosen his fingers and reviewed his plan for the last time. Open the locket; take out the fire opal. Replace it with the wax. Shut the locket; tiptoe out of the room; pelt down the road to Grisini. Seeing Grisini again would be the worst part, but after that, things got easier. He'd have to tell Lizzie Rose that he'd stolen again. She wouldn't like it, but she'd know what to do next. She'd work out the trains, and they'd light out from Strachan's Ghyll as quick as ever they could.

He squatted down, eye level with the top of the mattress. The gold locket rested on the coverlet, close to the old woman's armpit. He could see the gemstone through the gold filigree. It was as red as strawberry juice. The colours in it frothed like beads of boiling syrup. His fingers twitched. He wanted to touch it, even if it burned him. He wanted to roll it between his fingers and watch the colours flash and spark –

> *Be bold, be bold but not too bold,*
> *Lest that your heart's blood should run cold!*

The old rhyme sang in his head. He braced his fingers against the gold filigree. His thumbnail found the tiny clasp. It slid to one side as if it had been oiled –

Cassandra Sagredo awoke. She thrashed, and he leaped back, dodging her flailing hands. He coughed out the ball of wax and saw it roll under the bed. The old woman hissed at him, not like a serpent but like some enormous cat. Her mouth was red and dark, and the breath that issued from her stank as though she was already dead. She screamed at him: 'What do you want? Why are you here? Get away! Get out!'

# Chapter Thirty-five

# The Bottle Imp

Cassandra couldn't see straight. Someone was shouting and it was several seconds before she recognised that it was she. Her throat felt raw from screaming. The room tilted, and she thought she might faint. She curled both hands around the fire opal, ready to defend it with her life.

There was a boy in the room. He was the one she'd been screaming at. Small and ashen faced, with faded clothes and un-combed hair, he could not have looked more harmless. His eyes darted towards the double doors, and she saw him brace himself to make a run for them. She skewered him with a glance. 'Why are you in my room? What do you want?'

He said, 'Nuffink.'

Her jaw dropped. All at once, she grasped what he was doing in her room and why she'd been screaming. He had come to steal the fire opal.

And she had stopped him.

She could have thrown back her head and howled with frustration. She wanted to spew curses, to claw the air and pound the bedclothes with her fists. She choked back her rage, desperate to believe that the opportunity had not been lost. The boy had been prepared to steal from her. Perhaps he would try again.

'I've frightened you.' She tried to soften her harsh voice, to impersonate a frail old lady. 'I was having a nightmare. I'm so sorry.'

The boy didn't believe a word of it. She opened her mouth to call him by name but couldn't remember what it was. That sort of thing happened to her more and more often, and it drove her mad. She fancied that his name began with a *P*. An unusual name, too grand for this rat of a boy. Peverel? Phineas? She gave it up. 'What's your name? I've forgotten it.'

'Parsefall.'

'I'm sorry I frightened you, Parsefall. I was startled.' She tried to gather her wits. She wondered if she could convince him that she was unaware that he'd been on the verge of robbing her. It would be best if he thought of her as a pathetic old lady, too simple to suspect him and too weak to defend herself. She quavered, 'Did you come to my room to find a Christmas present?'

His eyes narrowed. She had provided him with an explanation for his presence in her room. He was willing to adopt her lie, but it was clear that he didn't trust her. 'You said we could take things from anywhere in the 'ouse.'

'Indeed I did,' Cassandra said warmly, 'and I laid out a number of things in this room. Did you come for one of them?'

The boy screwed up his mouth, refusing to commit himself. Cassandra lost her temper. She was frustrated and ill, and she was already weary of pretending to be a kindly old lady. 'I'm cold,' she snapped, 'and the blankets are on the floor, where I can't reach them. Get me a glass of wine. There's a bottle and glass by the washstand. Fetch it!'

The sharpness in her voice spurred him to action. He fished up the fallen bedclothes and lobbed them at her. She watched impatiently as he found the wine and poured her a glass. She drank it all in one draught and held out the glass to him. To her surprise, he took it. She saw that roughness suited him better than her simulated kindness. She supposed he was used to being scolded and ordered about.

'I want another glass. You have one too.' She indicated a silver goblet on the table. 'Take that one. We'll drink together.'

He looked surprised but went back to the decanter of wine and poured two glasses. He took a gulp and licked his lips. It was evident that he'd never tasted port before.

'So. You came here for a Christmas gift.'

The boy dropped his head and slurped the wine as if it was soup. The action hid his face.

'I told you: you may take what you like. I only want to know what it is. It was something on the table, wasn't it? Something you saw last night?'

Parsefall glanced over his shoulder. 'The pistol.'

Cassandra smiled. 'I thought that might appeal to you. If you want it, it's yours. Go and get it.'

He looked a little taken aback, but he crossed the room to claim the prize. 'Is it loaded?'

'I don't know,' Cassandra answered truthfully. 'Pull the trigger and see.'

He gaped at her, turned the pistol towards the window and fingered the trigger. Cassandra shook her head. 'Not like that.

You have to cock it. Here, bring it to me.' She held out her hand, and he approached, carrying the pistol muzzle down. 'Stand back.' She cocked the pistol, aimed it at one of the mirrors and pulled the trigger.

Nothing happened.

'No gunpowder,' Cassandra said morosely. She dropped the weapon on the counterpane. 'I'm not sure if we have any gunpowder in the house. Perhaps we could order some from the village.'

Parsefall's face was a study. All at once, it broke out in an incredulous grin. It had been a long time since anyone smiled at Cassandra like that, and she was absurdly pleased. Her cheeks felt warm, and she wondered if she'd drunk too much. Then her smile faded. She could not afford to be sentimental about the boy. Whether she liked him or not, she meant to use him. If she succeeded, she would be his doom.

Her eyes lit on the pillowcase halfway across the room. 'What's that?'

Parsefall tensed. 'It's me Christmas presents. You said I could 'ave wot I like.'

'I said it and I meant it. Bring it here and show me. What did you take?'

The boy heaved the pillowcase on to the bed and opened it. 'Candlesticks, mostly,' he said. 'There woz a lot of 'em. I took the silver ones. I left you the chiny ones, because they ain't worf much.' He peered into the bag, unaware of Cassandra's amusement. 'There woz a clock wiv a metal lion on it. I took that. And an inkwell – it's tarnished, but I fink it's silver. And a fan.' He spread the fan open. 'Them sticks is muvver-of-pearl an' gold leaf. Then I opened the drawers in all the bedrooms an' found wipes.' He brought up a fistful of handkerchiefs. 'They're silk, an' some of 'em 'ave lace at the edge. I can sell 'em down the pawnshop when I gets back t'London.' He looped a rosary over his fingers, eyeing it appraisingly. 'An' Jesus. I took 'im too.'

Cassandra was impressed. The boy had a good instinct for what was valuable. He had done a creditable job of plundering the house.

'Ma'am?' Parsefall was watching her warily. 'Did yer mean it – what you said before? Will I keep 'em? You ain't going to call the coppers?'

Cassandra saw her opportunity. 'When you say *coppers*, do you mean policemen?'

He nodded.

'I hate coppers,' Cassandra said promptly. 'They're vulgar and tedious, and I won't have them in the house.' She saw his brow clear, and she decided to elaborate on the lie. 'Last year, when a thief broke in and stole the silver, Mrs Fettle wanted to call in the coppers, but I forbade it.'

He looked dubious. Cassandra changed her tack. 'Besides, why would I call in the police when you haven't stolen anything? I said you might take anything in the house – except one thing, of course. You haven't done anything wrong. Have you shown me everything you took?'

Parsefall shifted his weight, lifting one leg to scratch the back of the other. His eyes widened in a look of specious innocence.

Cassandra sighed. Wearily, she lifted her hand, cupping it around the gold locket. The effort it took to see into his mind made her feel faint. 'Less than five minutes ago, when you went to the table for the pistol, you palmed my emerald necklace, the one your sister didn't want. It's in your trouser pocket,' she said flatly. 'And earlier this morning, you took two rings from the Florentine chest in the Blue Room. One's set with a ruby and the other with a yellow diamond. The diamond's good, by the way – don't let the man in the pawnshop tell you it's a topaz and cheat you. You wrapped the rings in a handkerchief and hid them in the lining of your jacket.'

Parsefall looked dumbfounded. He ducked his head and rubbed the back of his neck.

'You may keep the rings. You may keep everything.'

'Why don't you want 'em?'

Cassandra said irritably, 'I told you. I'm dying. I shan't need them. Aren't you curious about how I knew where you hid my jewels?'

'Woz the servants spyin' on me?'

'No. I found you out because of my stone. I told you it was magic,' retorted Cassandra. 'Would you like to see it again? I'll let you look at it.'

'Wot for?' demanded Parsefall. 'If I can't 'ave it, why do you want to show it to me?'

It was an intelligent question, one Cassandra was not prepared to answer. She paused to think. 'I want to show you a trick.' She nodded at a glass globe on the mantelpiece. 'Fetch me that case.'

The boy brought the case and laid it in her lap. Inside, perched on a branch of coral, were two stuffed hummingbirds. Their bodies were scarcely larger than a bumblebee's. Cassandra hugged the fire opal with her fingers. 'Watch.'

The heat of the phoenix-stone came slowly and with it a wave of nausea. Seconds passed, and nothing happened. Cassandra squeezed the stone tightly. One of the dead birds began to move. It cocked its tiny head, and the wings began to pump up and down. The iridescent colours of the feathers appeared: lime green and ultramarine, glittering gold and violet. Now the second bird was fanning its wings and jerking its head, and the ghost of a twitter came from inside the glass globe: a thin, eldritch sound.

The boy said, 'Is it clockwork?'

Cassandra's concentration wavered. One of the birds stopped moving, its beak ajar. The other dropped its wings.

'No, it's not clockwork. It's the stone.' She forced a smile. 'What do you think of that, Master Parsefall?'

Parsefall hunched one shoulder. 'It ain't bad,' he said, 'but I know an old Chinaman who does birds better. He uses shade puppets.'

'That's puppetry,' Cassandra said scornfully. 'This is magic.'

He bristled. He came closer to examine the case, running his hands over it to feel for hidden wires or strings. Cassandra saw the stump where his fourth finger ought to be, and a new idea came to her. 'Don't you ever wonder what happened to you?' she asked softly. 'Wouldn't you like to find out how you lost your little finger?'

The boy's pupils dilated. He put the maimed hand behind his back.

Cassandra opened the locket to release the stone. She rocked it back and forth between her thumb and forefinger. 'Would you like to touch it? You can't take it, because that would be stealing, but you may touch it, if you like.'

He drew closer still. Cautiously, as if he was afraid of being burned, he laid one finger against the crimson gem. Cassandra had invited the touch, but she found it disturbing. It was as if he had kissed her mouth. She breathed shallowly, forcing herself to remain motionless.

Suddenly he recoiled. It was as if he'd received an electric shock: he jerked back his hand, breathing hard. He took two

257

steps backward, his gaze inwards, as if he was trying to remember something.

'Wot if it's like the Bottle Imp?'

Cassandra said, 'What bottle imp? What are you talking about?'

'It was a play we used to do wiv Grisini,' explained Parsefall. 'There was this man, and he had a bottle wiv a n'imp inside it, like a demon. The demon could grant wishes, but the wishes never worked out proper. An' whoever took the bottle, if 'e didn't get rid of it, 'e was going to burn in hell.'

'How did it end? Did the man go to hell?'

'Not the principal puppet,' Parsefall said, as if she'd asked a stupid question. ''E can't go to hell, 'cos he's the hero, innee? He tricked somebody else into taking it – the wicked Spaniard with the moustaches – and then 'e went to hell. The Bottle Imp dragged 'im down, and there woz flames.'

Cassandra's skin crawled. 'But that was only a story.' She spoke lightly, trying to regain the ground she had lost. 'My fire opal is real. Demons and bottle imps – they're things in stories. You wouldn't be frightened by a story, would you?'

Parsefall shouldered his pillowcase and stepped away. 'How do you know we ain't *in* a story?' he demanded, and was out the door before she could think of a response.

# Chapter Thirty-six

# The Miniature

Lizzie Rose stood outside Madama's room, steeling herself to go in. It was past teatime on Christmas Eve, and she had been summoned to show what she had chosen for her Christmas presents. Lizzie Rose had made up her mind to behave like the youngest daughter in the fairy tales she loved. The youngest daughter always preferred the humblest gift: a rose instead of a diamond, a blessing instead of a fortune. Things always seemed to turn out well for her. Even so, Lizzie Rose dreaded the interview to come. 'She can't eat me,' she muttered, but that was sheer bravado. Cassandra Sagredo might not stoop to cannibalism, but she could humiliate Lizzie Rose and make her cry. That was bad enough.

Lizzie Rose shifted her stack of books from one arm to the other and adjusted the tiger skin around her shoulders. In only a few hours, she had grown fond of the tiger skin. It was bracing to look down and see her arms wrapped in yellow fur and black stripes. Tigers were courageous animals, she reminded herself. She opened the double doors and marched into the room.

Her changed costume was not lost on Cassandra Sagredo. The old woman barked with laughter. Ruby, who had followed Lizzie Rose, woofed in response and sprang on to the bed.

'Outlandish,' commented Cassandra. She smacked the bed-clothes, inviting the dog to settle down beside her. Ruby bounded across the blanket hills and licked the old woman's fingers.

Lizzie Rose said pointedly, 'Good evening, ma'am.'

Cassandra fondled the dog's ears. 'I suppose you think "Outlandish" is a poor way to begin a conversation?'

'I didn't say so, ma'am.'

'No, you didn't. Polite child. Polite-child-in-a-tiger-skin. You like furs, do you?'

'No, ma'am. I don't think I do.'

'Why ever not?'

Lizzie Rose thought a little. The old woman sounded almost friendly, and it occurred to her that talking to Cassandra Sagredo was rather like talking to Parsefall: manners were not strictly necessary. 'I think it must be very agreeable to be a tiger. I don't know much about India, but I believe it's warm, and there are jasmine flowers . . . To live in the sun and be fierce, and then to die because someone wants your skin . . . I think that's sad. If I were a gentleman, I wouldn't shoot tigers.'

'Then why did you take the skin? Don't you like it? Didn't you *want* it?'

'I *didn't* take it,' answered Lizzie Rose. 'Not to keep. I only borrowed it, because the house is so cold –' She stopped. Madama's room wasn't cold at all. No matter how draughty the rest of the house might be, the sickroom was stifling and pungent.

'That dress of yours isn't very warm, is it?'

260

'No, ma'am.'

'Or very pretty, for that matter. I thought Fettle burned it.'

Lizzie Rose's chin came up. 'I don't think Mrs Fettle had any right to take my clothes. I paid sixpence halfpenny for this dress.'

'A fortune.'

Lizzie Rose bit her tongue. She was tempted to tell this pampered woman that sixpence halfpenny *was* a fortune. One could buy six penny loaves for sixpence: six frugal suppers for Parsefall and herself. Remembering just how frugal some of those suppers had been, Lizzie Rose was seized with the impulse to tell Mrs Sagredo even more. She wanted to throw her problems in the old woman's face. She wanted to tell someone how frightened she was of hunger and poverty and ending up on the streets.

Instead she defended herself. 'You said I might explore the whole house and have anything I liked. I found my clothes in the ragbag belowstairs. I had nothing to wear, so I took them back.'

'The White Room wardrobe is full of things to wear,' argued Cassandra. 'Beautiful things. Didn't you even look at them? Didn't you *want* them?'

Lizzie Rose blushed. She had, in fact, looked at the gowns. There was one – a gown of creamy silk, embroidered with butterflies and wild pansies – that she had not been able to resist trying on. It was thirty years out of fashion and several sizes too big for her, but she had stood transfixed before the mirror, astonished that anything could make her look so pretty. If she had known how to make it fit her, she wouldn't have been able to resist it. But the silk was so exquisite that she couldn't bear the thought of ruining it – and that meant asking for help from the servants. The thought of Mrs Fettle's disapproval had settled the matter.

'Well? Cat got your tongue?'

'I did look at them,' admitted Lizzie Rose, 'and I like pretty things, but I couldn't – I didn't –' She sighed. 'My own things are best.'

Cassandra snorted disagreement. 'Your things are hideous. It's a shame – you're not a bad-looking girl. Fetch one of the candlesticks from the mantel. I want to look at you properly.'

Lizzie Rose set her books on the dressing table and returned with a three-branched candelabrum. Candlelight flashed across the face of the brass monkey. Like Madama, the monkey seemed to be sneering.

'What a nose you have!' exclaimed Cassandra. 'A nose like a vixen's – but that's what will make you a beauty when you grow up. If it weren't for your red hair and long nose, you'd only be pretty – but with that nose, you'll do better. The great actress Siddons had a nose like that. Men will stare at you and think that your nose is too long, but they'll go on staring. Haven't you started to think about that sort of thing – gentlemen and gowns and admirers?'

The word *admirer* reminded Lizzie Rose of Fitzmorris Pinchbeck. Her lip curled. 'No, ma'am.'

'Just as well. Lud, what a waste of time! When I was young, I was always in love with some man. Not that I was a beauty. "A big girl" – that was what they used to call me. Hateful phrase. I was too big and I could never endure tight lacing, but I knew how to make men look at me. I had many admirers in my heyday. One man put a bullet through his head for love of me – though I admit he was inordinately stupid. You don't believe me, do you?'

Lizzie Rose took a moment to consider. She recalled the glass case with its hairy relics, and it suddenly seemed less macabre than pathetic. She stared at the old woman, trying to catch a glimpse of the coquettish girl who had craved the attentions of men. It was difficult to imagine. No wonder Mrs Sagredo needed her souvenirs. They were proof of an impossible past.

'I do believe you, ma'am. I saw the cabinet downstairs. The one with the little portraits of all your admirers.'

'Oh, that,' Cassandra said fretfully. 'That was . . . Well. It was all so long ago.'

Silence fell between them. Lizzie Rose returned the candlestick to the mantel. Cassandra settled back against the pillows. Ruby sighed deeply and stretched out flat.

Cassandra broke the silence. 'If you don't want dresses and you don't want men, what do you want? Tell me that. Don't stop and think – just tell me, quick as ever you can. I want to know.'

A swarm of images darted through Lizzie Rose's mind. She wondered if she dared broach the subject of the legacy. Even a fraction of Madama's wealth would make such a difference! She envisaged herself and Parsefall living a whole new life, and in less than a second, she had conceived of a home for them: a cottage by the lake, complete with honeysuckle and deep, cosy chairs covered with flowered chintz. She pictured Parsefall sitting at a desk while she helped him with his schoolwork. Because she was in charge of constructing the scene, he didn't pull away when she put her arm around his shoulders; he didn't tell her she wasn't his true sister. She saw herself in the cream silk dress, reading fairy stories before the fire or skating on the frozen lake with her hands kept warm in a dear little muff. She thought of feeding Ruby a mutton chop every evening and there being meat enough for all three of them.

She caught herself up. These were selfish wishes. The youngest daughter in a fairy story should have a mind above mutton chops and silk dresses. The youngest daughter would think only about the people she loved. Dutifully Lizzie Rose thought of her own beloved, and all at once she knew what she longed for more than anything in the world. 'I want the people I love not to have died.'

The old woman uttered an exasperated noise, something between a snort and a growl. 'That's no good; that's impossible. You must want something other than that. Your brother took half the house – what did you take?'

Lizzie Rose set the books on the bed. Cassandra frowned. 'What's this? Shakespeare in three volumes? Faugh!' She flipped the covers open and shut. 'Do you really want Shakespeare? I've always found him dull.'

'My father loved Shakespeare,' Lizzie Rose explained. 'He used to say you could read Shakespeare your whole life long and never grow weary of it.'

'I'd be weary by the end of the first page,' Cassandra said acidly. She shoved the books away. 'What's this? Ah, something livelier!' A look of mischief passed over her face. '*Tom Jones*! Gracious, child, what made you choose that? It's' – her mouth twisted mockingly – 'not suitable for a young lady.'

'It must be suitable,' Lizzie Rose said stoutly. 'It was Father's favourite novel.'

'Have you read it?'

'No, but I shall.'

Cassandra nodded. 'Good. It will open those innocent eyes of yours. What else? Two books, a borrowed tiger skin and –?'

'A seashell,' Lizzie Rose said, reaching into her apron pocket. 'I thought it was the best one in the case. It reminded me of Brighton. Father and Mother took me to Brighton once.'

Cassandra Sagredo took the seashell on her palm. It was a

miracle of loveliness: a milky spiral with a heart of orange pink. 'Is that all? No jewels?'

Lizzie Rose thought wistfully of the emerald necklace she had turned down. 'I don't need jewels.'

'Fiddlesticks! Every woman needs jewels! What else is in your pocket?'

Lizzie Rose set down her final and favourite choice: the portrait in the ivory frame. 'I found this in the library. I think it's ever so pretty –' Her voice faltered.

The witch's hand darted out, fingers curled. 'Give me that.'

Lizzie Rose surrendered it. Cassandra sat stark still, gazing at the portrait in her hand. Her mouth worked. She raised her head and looked straight at Lizzie Rose. 'You little bitch.'

Lizzie Rose's head came up sharply. She had spent most of her life in the theatre, and she was familiar with foul words. But she was not used to being sworn at. David Fawr had shielded his wife and child from such disrespect. Even Grisini, who had beaten her, had not insulted her with such language. Her eyes filled with tears. 'How dare you?' Her voice shook with outrage. 'How dare you speak to me that way? I don't want your books – or your pictures – or your horrid money! I won't be spoken to like that!'

She spun on her heel and started for the door. But to her astonishment, Cassandra cried out to her. 'Come back!' the old woman commanded. 'Come back! If I insulted you, I beg your pardon!'

Lizzie Rose stopped with her hands on the doorknobs. She had never found it easy to hold out against an apology. She felt that this was a dreadful weakness in her nature, but she couldn't help it.

'I beg your pardon,' Cassandra said again. She was panting, as if the apology had taken a physical toll on her. 'You couldn't have known. No one knows.'

Lizzie Rose asked, 'Knows what?'

Cassandra evaded the question. She stared at Lizzie Rose as if she'd never seen her before. Abruptly she said, 'Give me your hand.'

Lizzie Rose said, 'Why?' but Cassandra held out her own hand, palm up. After a moment, Lizzie Rose slipped her work-roughened hand into the old woman's fat claw.

Cassandra bent her head. Her eyebrows drew together, and her eyes narrowed until they were almost shut. She was so still that Lizzie Rose wondered if she was falling asleep. Then the old woman opened her eyes. 'You're good,' she said flatly. It was not a compliment but an accusation. 'Gaspare lied. He said you were deceitful. You're good, God help you, and God help me. Horribly, inconveniently good.'

Lizzie Rose didn't know what to say. She had never been able to make up her mind whether she was a good person or not. From books, she had gathered that if you thought you were good, you probably weren't, because thinking you were good was conceited. On the other hand, she knew how hard she tried to be good, and she couldn't help thinking that Madama's word *inconvenient* was entirely apropos. It had not escaped her notice that being good was often very inconvenient. 'Ma'am –'

'Well? Don't stand there twisting your hands. If you want to ask me something, ask! And call me *Madama*, not *ma'am*.'

'Madama – when did you speak to Mr Grisini about me?'

The old woman's face was suddenly guarded. 'Months ago. I don't remember the exact date.' She dismissed the subject with an imperious wave of her hand. 'I'm sorry I insulted you. If you want the painting, take it. It's an insipid thing, and I have no use for it.'

Lizzie Rose looked from the old woman to the girl in the picture. 'Did you know her, ma'am? Was she your daughter?'

'No. I had no children.'

'She was dear to you?' Lizzie Rose suggested, but Cassandra answered vehemently.

'No. She was a girl I knew at school. When she died, she left me her portrait – I can't think why. It's been seventy years since I saw her.'

Lizzie Rose fetched the cushioned stool by the dressing table. She sat down, folding her hands in her lap. 'Tell me about her,' she coaxed. To her surprise, the old woman gazed off into the distance and began to speak.

# Chapter Thirty-seven

# An Unfinished Confession

Her name was Marguerite Tremblay. I met her in the convent at Venice – but no, I must begin earlier than that.

'When I was eleven years old, my mother ran away from home. She was a great beauty, and she caused a great scandal. For a long time, no one would tell me what had become of her. The servants told me she was dead, but we didn't put on black and there was no funeral. I eavesdropped until I found out the secret. My mother had chosen to abandon my father and me so that she could disgrace herself with a man.

'Her disgrace spread to all of us. We were no longer received in society. No one came to the house. My father – who had once been fond of me, I believe – was afraid I would grow up to be like my mother – foolish and faithless. It was an intolerable time for him, and he decided to leave England. My father was a scholar of the natural sciences, and he had friends in Padua.

'So we set off to Italy. The journey was a long one, and we were both bad travellers. My father scarcely spoke to me. But at last we reached Venice. I'd been sick on the road – foreign food disagreed with me – but I was not seasick in Venice. When we glided down the Grand Canal, I lifted my head to gaze about me.

'You have never seen Venice, I suppose? I tell you that there is nowhere on earth more beautiful. We floated between two rows of palaces: flesh pink or fawn coloured or pale green or tawny . . . and the world was drenched with light. The light of Venice was unlike anything I'd ever seen. So soft, like candle flames shining through a seashell . . . The water was glassy green, and everywhere you looked there were rippling shadows and reflections. Beauty like that can break the heart. I ached with longing – and I began to hope. I had a strange fancy that in Venice, I would find everything I'd lost: even my father's affection.

'Of course I was wrong. My father had brought me there to be rid of me. He enrolled me in a convent school of Santa Maria dei Servi. The Venetians greatly disliked foreigners, and I cannot think how he persuaded the nuns to accept me. But take me they did, and my father moved on to Padua. I begged him to write, and he promised that he would. But he didn't.

'To say that I was unhappy doesn't begin to tell you the state of my feelings. The convent was a prison to me. The other girls despised me. My father had taught me only a little Italian – and it was not Venetian but pure Tuscan. The Venetian girls slurred their words, so I couldn't understand them. They laughed at me. I was a foreigner, a big clumsy girl. My clothes didn't fit – I was growing too fast, and everything was tight. There was not a single soul that I liked or who liked me. I seemed to grind my way through each day, longing for night-time so that I could weep.

'Then Marguerite came to the convent. She came from New

France, in North America. She spoke no Italian, only French and English. Because I spoke English, she attached herself to me. I did not seek her friendship. She sought mine. I thought the other girls would shun her, as they had shunned me. But when they mimicked her bad Venetian, she laughed with them, and in time she became everyone's pet. You must understand that she had many things that I had not. Her papa had a fortune from the fur trade. She was very pretty, and her gowns had been made in Paris. She always had the best of everything, from ribbons to lapdogs.

'You asked if she was dear to me. The shoe was on the other foot: *she* cared for *me*. Her nature was affectionate, and she was as eager to please as her own lapdog. When I had headaches – I had dreadful headaches in those days – she used to sit by me and bathe my forehead with lavender water. She had many friends, but I was her first, and, she used to say, her dearest. She always called me that: her dearest friend.

'I thought she was a fool, to love me so much when I cared so little for her. But there was a reckless streak in her that I admired. We used to slip out of the convent, especially when it was Carnival and the streets were full of people making merry. None of the other girls dared. Those were my happiest times in Venice – those times when we escaped together. It was then, and only then, that Venice kept her promise to me. The city was so gay and so beautiful . . . And we were never caught.

'There was one way in which Marguerite and I were alike. She was motherless too, and there was a shadow over her mother's name. When Marguerite was six years old, the house caught fire, and her mother perished in the flames. Marguerite had been told that it was a tragic accident. But Marguerite believed – and I have no doubt she was right – that Madame Tremblay set the fire herself: *she died by her own hand*. Her father denied it. But though Marguerite was a silly child, she was a child, and a child has a special instinct for what is being hidden. Marguerite remembered her mother's fits of rage and melancholy, and she was quite certain that her mother had been mad. I have told you that Marguerite was not dear to me; I envied her too much to be fond of her. But I pitied her too, because of her mother.

'I remember the day I hated her most. It was her birthday – our birthday – because that was the curious thing: Marguerite was a year younger than I, but we shared the same birthday. The year that I was thirteen and Marguerite was twelve, Monsieur Tremblay asked the nuns for permission to give his daughter a birthday party. The sixth of November fell during Carnival time –'

Lizzie Rose's head jerked up. 'The sixth of November!' she repeated. 'But that's Clara's birthday!'

Cassandra Sagredo flinched as if someone had thrown a glass of water in her face. Lizzie Rose realised that the old woman was in a vulnerable state, stranded somewhere between the present and the past.

'I'm sorry.' Lizzie Rose laid a hand on the coverlet. 'I shouldn't have interrupted. But there's a girl I used to know, and November the sixth was her birthday –'

Cassandra didn't ask who Clara was. 'November the sixth?' she repeated. 'November the sixth? Are you sure?'

Lizzie Rose nodded. 'I'm sorry I interrupted, Madama. I won't do so again.'

Cassandra leaned sideways and jerked the bed cord. 'You won't have the chance. I've spoken too long and told too much.

Run along – that's a good child. Fettle will attend to me. Take your little treasures and let me sleep.'

Reluctantly Lizzie Rose gathered up the books and the seashell. She didn't want to leave. She wanted the rest of the story. But Madama would brook no argument. She held out the portrait to Lizzie Rose. 'Here, take it. You want it – I don't.'

Lizzie Rose snapped her fingers for Ruby. On her way out, she set the little painting on Madama's dressing table.

# Chapter Thirty-eight

# The Bolt on the Door

It was Christmas Eve. Under the table in the Tower Room, Clara lay beside Parsefall and listened to the sound of distant church bells tolling the hour for Midnight Mass. Beside her, Parsefall muttered and twitched in his sleep. Clara wondered if he was dreaming of Grisini. *Grisini's not here*, Clara soothed him. *He can't get in. There's a bolt on the door.*

She didn't think Parsefall heard her. But after a little while, he sighed deeply and his restless movements ceased. Clara relaxed her vigilance. She was drowsy. The church bells had fallen silent, and the sleeping tent Parsefall had made in the Tower Room was dark and close. He had covered Madama's table with a counterpane that fell to the floor on all sides, leaving just a slit for ventilation. Underneath the table were eight wool blankets, innumerable pillows, a satin-covered eiderdown and the bearskin rug.

*Clara! Clara Wintermute!*

Cassandra's voice shattered the stillness. The darkness under the table shifted and billowed. Now it was a cloud streaked with brilliant colours: tantalising scarlet and sullen gold, deep cobalt and acid green –

*Clara Wintermute! I summon you now!*

Clara felt herself grow larger. She rolled over and crept forward, careful not to bang her head on the underside of the table. Outside the sleeping tent it was only a little less dark. The light that stole through the casements was lacklustre; a small moon shone in the sky. Clara scanned the mirrors, hoping to see some gleam of reflected light from her white frock, some sign that she was really there.

She saw nothing. Once again, she wasn't really moving: she wasn't real. The idea that she could crawl out from under the table was sheer fancy, part and parcel of Cassandra's spell.

*Clara! I must speak with you.*

Clara paused with her hand on the doorknob. *Why?*

The witch's response was immediate, furious and oddly jumbled. *It is your fate, Clara . . . I have learned more of you . . .* Clara caught the words *phoenix-stone*, *destiny* and *birthday*. The rest was unintelligible. It was as if the witch were too impatient to put her summons into words.

*She's changed,* mused Clara. The first time Cassandra summoned her, each word had been crisp and strong. *She isn't as powerful as she was before. If she was, I should have obeyed her by now.*

Clara lifted her hand and stared at it through the dimness. *Of course, I'm not really moving,* she reminded herself. *I'm a puppet. That's Grisini's spell. And Madama can reach into my mind and read my thoughts and tell me what to do. That's her spell.*

*But I'm not obeying her. Not yet. That's my spell.*

*Spell* wasn't the right word, not really. But the idea that she had the power to delay her obedience made a thrill run down Clara's spine. She set the flat of her hand against the door, dramatising her resistance. *No. I won't come to you.*

The witch punished her. Clara felt a wave of heat that made her gasp. The reddish cloud surrounded her; sparks of colour pricked and singed her skin. Clara steeled herself. *It's not real,* she told herself. *None of this is real. I'm not really standing before the door; I'm only imagining it. I'm not really being burned. It's a spell.*

The witch responded to her thoughts with a bellow of frustration. *If you won't come to me, Clara Wintermute, I will come to you! And you will be sorry for it!*

*You can't. I'm in the tower. And the door's locked.* Even as she framed the words, Clara quailed. What if the power of the phoenix-stone was strong enough to break down the door? All too soon, she heard footsteps in the corridor. The tread was heavy and uneven – the footsteps of someone who was weak and old and perhaps dizzy. Clara's head swam as she caught the witch's vertigo. She slumped against the door for support. The red fog enveloped her, and her throat felt parched; her eyes ached with the heat.

Something rustled behind her. Startled, Clara whirled and saw Parsefall in the mouth of his tent. He crouched on his hands and knees, low, like a frightened cat. It was too dark to read the expression on his face, but Clara knew what he was feeling. He believed that Grisini had found his hiding place. For Parsefall, it was Grisini on the other side of the door.

The doorknob rattled. Cassandra yanked and pounded, shaking the door in its frame.

Clara turned to face the door. She thought of Parsefall's terror, and fury rose within her. She recalled the tantrums she used to throw when she was young and naughty, before the Others died. She kicked the door savagely. *Go away! You can't come in!* Willfully she reverted to her younger self. She shrieked and stamped her feet; she hammered on the wood until her fists went numb. *Go away! Go away! Leave us alone!*

There was a great thud, the sound of a heavy body striking the floor. Clara froze. The walls seemed to ring with silence. *I've killed her,* Clara thought with horror. But no: a muffled groan came from the other side of the door. Madama was calling for help. A second moan and then silence. Clara felt her muscles go slack. The shadows around her congealed. She could no longer see the faint light from the windows.

She was back under the table, on the bearskin rug.

She listened as Parsefall got to his feet and tiptoed across the room. He went to the door but dared not unbolt it to see who had collapsed in the corridor. After a short time, he crept back to his tent shelter. He lay stiffly, his heart beating double time, and it was almost dawn before he slept.

# Chapter Thirty-nine

# Christmas at Strachan's Ghyll

Lizzie Rose slept late on Christmas morning. Even before she was fully awake, she remembered what day it was. 'Christmas,' she said groggily and wondered whether this would be a good Christmas or a bad one. Last year's Christmas, the first after her parents died, had almost broken her heart, but every other Christmas had been good.

She tossed aside the bedclothes and padded across the carpet to the window. A light snow had fallen during the night, and the sun on the snow was dazzling. Bits of dry grass, tawny as wheat in harvest time, reached up through the snow, and the sky was clear blue, tinged with lavender. 'It's Christmas,' Lizzie Rose told Ruby. 'Let's make it a merry one, shall we, Roo?' Ruby danced in circles, suggesting that it was not only Christmas but walk time and breakfast time: two of her favourite things on earth.

Quickly Lizzie Rose dressed herself and slipped down-stairs to the servants' hall. The servants were seated at the table, consuming bacon and porridge. 'Merry Christmas!' sang out Lizzie Rose.

No one smiled or returned her greeting. Lizzie Rose felt herself flush. She clasped her hands in front of her, put up her chin, and waited.

At long last Mrs Fettle answered her. 'I'm afraid none of us are very merry this morning, Miss Fawr. Madama suffered an attack last night, and we had to send for the doctor.'

'Oh, dear! I'm so sorry!' said Lizzie Rose. 'Is she very ill?'

'She's poorly,' replied Mrs Fettle. 'She's had spells like this before, but each time it's worse. The doctor says it's a wasting fever, and her heart's bad. Still, she's pulled through before, and she'll likely pull through again.' She addressed the other servants. 'The doctor says she's not to be left alone, so you'll sit with her this morning, Esther, and Janet'll stay with her this afternoon.'

Esther and Janet looked glum. Lizzie Rose cleared her throat. 'I could sit by her.'

'That won't be necessary,' said Mrs Fettle, as if the offer had offended her. 'You're a guest, not a servant. That reminds me: Madama bade me tell you that you're not to leave Strachan's Ghyll. Whatever happens, you and your brother are to stay on here, and as soon as Madama's better, she'll have the lawyer in and settle what's to be done about her will.'

Lizzie Rose heard a faint hiss from either Esther or Janet; she wasn't sure which one. She squeezed her hands tighter. 'I'm very willing to help, ma'am, if there's anything I can do.'

'You can take that dog out before she makes a mess on the floor,' Janet retorted, so pertly that Lizzie Rose looked daggers at her and took as long as she dared leaving the house.

\* \* \*

It was still Christmas, and the sun was shining. The air was sweet and bracing, and it seemed that Madama's offer of a legacy was an honest one, after all. Lizzie Rose reminded herself of these good things and plucked a sprig of holly to adorn her coat. It was Christmas, and she would celebrate by letting Ruby off the leash.

The dog sprang forward and raced down the lawn to the lake. In the roseate glow of morning, Lake Windermere appeared enchanted, reminding Lizzie Rose of her father's old tales of underwater fairies and the sword Excalibur. Then another memory assailed her, more personal, more poignant: the Christmas she had spent in Northumberland when she was six years old.

She remembered it with the utmost clarity. The theatre was shut down because there was cholera, but she was too little to understand what that meant, and she was delighted by the holiday. Her parents had taken her to the vicarage where her mother had grown up. There was a pond below the churchyard, and her mother and father taught her to skate. Superimposed against the Cumbrian landscape, Lizzie Rose saw her parents once again: her father's peaked eyebrows as he skated backward, her mother's rosy cheeks and hazel eyes.

How long ago it seemed! Tears gathered in Lizzie Rose's eyes, dulling the clarity of the winter day. She stood and wept until Ruby bounded over and pawed at her skirt.

The dog's intervention did the trick: Lizzie Rose laughed a little and squatted down to caress the squirming, silky body. Her parents were her good angels; she could not remember them without also remembering how truly they had loved her. 'It's Christmas, Roo,' said Lizzie Rose, and because the dog still looked concerned, she took off her mitten and threw it as hard as she could. Ruby charged after it, delighted that her mistress's grief had given way to a game of fetch.

Obligingly Lizzie Rose received the mitten and tossed it again and again. It occurred to her that unless she was mistaken, her mother's ice skates were at the bottom of the trunk the children had brought to Strachan's Ghyll. Lizzie Rose had hoarded – and packed – every remnant of her parents' lives. Now that she was nearly fourteen, she might be able to wear her mother's skates. She clapped her hands to call Ruby, pried her mitten out of the spaniel's jaws and started up the hill to the house.

In the kitchen, she wiped Ruby's paws. Then she went upstairs to have breakfast with Parsefall. For the second morning in a row, she found the Green Room deserted. Parsefall's nightshirt lay on the carpet like a shed snakeskin, and his breakfast tray held nothing but crumbs. Where was he? He had seemed all right last night at dinner – a bit surly, perhaps; he hadn't been in a very talkative mood . . . Lizzie Rose raised her eyes to the tapestry, as if the knights and ladies in the Green Room might offer some clue as to Parsefall's whereabouts. She had a queer sense that something was missing, something that she was used to seeing there.

Her eye fell on the wicker trunk. She flew to it and knelt down, rummaging until one hand closed around a metal blade. Yes: there were her mother's skates. The blades were only slightly rusted; the leather straps were only a little mouldy. She measured one skate against her boot and saw that it would fit very well.

Ruby let out a moan of extreme anguish, publishing the fact that she was about to die of starvation. Lizzie Rose set down the skates and went to her breakfast tray. She tore the crusts off her toast and flung them to the dog, one piece at a time. Then she sat down and ate her breakfast, sharing her bacon and allowing Ruby to lick the porridge plate. After three cups of much-sweetened tea, Lizzie Rose tucked a lump of sugar into her cheek and set off to find Parsefall.

She searched every room but in vain. Upstairs, downstairs, Great Hall, cellars ... If Mrs Sagredo had not been ill, Lizzie Rose would have shouted for him; as it was, she crept through the house on tiptoe, like a thief. She began to feel rather cross. The metallic smell of the house irked her, and her head was starting to ache. Where was Parsefall? He must be avoiding her, hiding from her on purpose. For the second time that day, Lizzie Rose felt her eyes well up with tears. She did not deserve such treatment; she should not have to be all by herself on Christmas Day.

She stalked back to the Green Room, bundled herself up in the jade velvet coat and picked up her mother's ice skates.

Outside, the weather had changed. The fickle sky was overcast, and snow flurries drifted through the damp air. The lake was dull white and the fells looked translucent. It was like standing inside a moonstone, thought Lizzie Rose. Shivering, she went back to the kitchen and fetched a broom to sweep the snow off the ice.

She started down the brick path, sweeping as she went. The rhythmic movement warmed her, and she began to breathe deeply, drawing the pure air into her lungs. 'At any rate, it's a live cold,' she remarked to Ruby, who pricked up her ears. 'In the house, it's a dead cold.'

Ruby had no opinion of this. She didn't know one kind of cold from another, but she knew immediately and without doubt that Lizzie Rose was beginning to feel better. She wiggled her red rump and bounced forward, sending clouds of drifted snow up in the air.

281

Lizzie Rose went on sweeping. Close to the lake's edge was a short flight of steps flanked by stone urns. She brushed the steps free of snow, sat down and buckled the ice skates around her shoes. She drew the straps uncomfortably tight, remembering that her father had insisted upon this. Clinging to an urn for balance, she stood up. Delicately she minced to the edge of the lake.

She slid one foot on to the ice and then hesitated. She had told no one what she was doing, and she might drown, if the ice wasn't thick enough to hold her. Aloud she said, 'But not right next to the shore,' and stepped forward.

The ice held. She didn't slip. She tried to remember what her father had taught her. All at once she seemed to hear his voice: 'One foot behind the other, and the toes turned out, my Rose. Bend the front knee and push off from the back.' Lizzie Rose adjusted her feet and launched herself forward.

She glided. It was an almost-forgotten sensation, joyful and free. Another stroke and she began to pick up speed. 'Keep bending the knees,' shouted her father, and she took his advice, though it made her shins ache. The ice was not even and Ruby was in her way, but Lizzie Rose's face broke into a blissful grin. She spread her arms like wings and took another stroke.

It was even better than she remembered. Up and down the edge of the shore she skated; much hampered by Ruby, who leaped at her skirts, barking shrilly. As Lizzie Rose tried to dodge the dog, her right skate skidded, and she crashed downwards. The slickness of the ice broke her fall. She knelt on one knee and shifted her weight upwards. In an instant she was skating again, stroking with greater force.

Little by little, the old skill came back to her. She tottered back to fetch the broom and swept a small rink for herself, discovering that the ice was smoother away from the shore. If the cold weather held, she would sweep a larger rink every day. She would bring a length of clothesline from the scullery and tether Ruby to one of the stone urns so that the spaniel wouldn't trip her. Perhaps she could learn to skate a figure eight on one foot, as her father had done. Perhaps she might teach Parsefall; perhaps she wouldn't. It was glorious, having the whole lake to herself. Lizzie Rose caught the tip of her skate on a furrow in the ice, tilted wildly and saved herself from falling just in time.

Her headache had vanished. So, too, had her sense of cold; she was sweating inside the green velvet coat. From time to time she glanced up at the sky. The great clouds were parting, showing shreds of watery blue. Shafts of sunlight turned the lake to mother-of-pearl.

'It's Christmas,' Lizzie Rose said, for the third time that day. She leaned against the wind like a sailing ship, and her mind was peaceful and clear.

# Chapter Forty

# The Wintermutes' Christmas

In London, Christmas morning arrived wrapped in fog. Dr Wintermute was awakened by the pealing of the church bells. He did not rise at once but stared up at the ceiling, shrinking from the day before him. He hoped that one of his patients would need him, so that he wouldn't have to spend the whole of Christmas Day at his wife's side. It would be a hideous holiday for both of them. He longed for it to be over.

He waited until the clock struck seven before he rose. He washed and dressed mechanically, then descended the stairs to the breakfast room. Last Christmas, the staircase had been adorned with holly and white ribbons. Clara had pleaded for red ones, but Ada had insisted on white, as being more suitable for a house in mourning. Dr Wintermute wished he had taken Clara's part. He tried to remember Clara's presents from last Christmas. Had there been a doll? Or had the doll been from the year before? He wasn't sure. Ada would remember, but he knew he would not ask her.

He stopped before the door of the breakfast room, wondering if his wife would be at the table. Sometimes she asked for a tray upstairs. Since Clara's disappearance, she had eaten very little. As a medical man, he disapproved; as a parent, he felt that her thinness was seemly, a tribute to Clara. His own appetite shamed him, surfacing with ruthless regularity. He might be heartsick, but he was also an active and hardworking man; his stomach insisted on breakfast, luncheon, tea and dinner. Even now, in his holiday misery, he smelled broiled kidneys and ham, and his nostrils twitched hungrily. He opened the door and went in.

Ada drooped before an empty plate. With some relief, he observed that she was drinking tea; she would take a little nourishment from the milk and sugar she mixed with it. He bent and kissed her, careful not to speak of Christmas.

She turned her head away. Since Clara's disappearance, she seemed to dislike his touch. He told himself that the rebuff was not deliberate; he must not let it rankle. Silently he filled his plate and sat down at right angles to his wife.

As he unfolded his napkin, Ada spoke. Her voice was so low that he missed the beginning of the sentence, but he caught the words 'Kensal Green.'

Dr Wintermute cleared his throat and tried to speak in a neutral tone of voice. 'My dear, I shall not accompany you to Kensal Green this morning.'

Ada put down her teacup with a suddenness that made the china ring. 'But we always go to Kensal Green on Christmas Day.'

'Yes. But not today.' He realised that he sounded brusque. 'I beg your pardon, my dear. You must recall the last time I was at Kensal Green.' He looked away from her and caught sight of his own reflection in the glass over the mantel. For one split second, he failed to recognise himself and regarded the reflected image as a patient. *A man of robust middle age; prosperous, well nourished but suffering from melancholia and nervous strain . . .*

Ada said again, 'We always go to Kensal Green.'

'Yes. Perhaps that was a mistake.' He knew he was on dangerous ground, but he went on. 'I have sometimes thought that it made Clara unhappy to visit Kensal Green every Christmas. I've even wondered if we mourned our dead children at the expense of the one who lived –'

His wife's head came up sharply. The tears in her eyes brimmed over and began to fall. He reached for her hand, but she stood up quickly, eluding him.

'Ada, my dear, forgive me! I didn't mean –'

'You did, you did!' She swayed and caught hold of the back of the chair. 'You meant that *I* made her unhappy – that *I* forced her to mourn. It's true, it's true! I was unkind to her the very day she disappeared. It was her birthday, and that hideous puppet show – I wouldn't let her laugh – I wouldn't forgive her –' She caught her breath on a sob. 'If she ran away, I was to blame –'

'You were not,' he interrupted sharply. He got up and tried to take her in his arms, but she shrank from him. 'Ada, she didn't run away. I am convinced of that. She was kidnapped – and that mountebank Grisini, that monster, had something to do with it.' He pulled up short, wondering if he should tell her of his recent conversation with Lizzie Rose. He decided not to; Grisini's wards had vanished, and the landlady had no idea where they had gone. 'If anyone was to blame, it was I – I allowed that blackguard into this house! But how could I have known? Clara wanted him, and I wanted to see her happy –' He forced himself to lower his voice. 'If we blame ourselves, if we blame one another, we shall both go mad.'

Ada had buried her face in her hands. She was sobbing so hard that he could not distinguish her words. 'Ada, what are you saying?'

She let her hands fall and gazed at him with such bitterness that he took a step back. 'You do blame me,' she contradicted him, 'and it's true. I didn't love her the way I did the others. How could I, when I knew she might be taken away? I bore you five children, Thomas. Five children in eight years – I carried them in sickness and bore them in pain. You don't know what that's like. No man knows. But I loved them, truly I loved them – and then the cholera came, and they were taken from me. All but Clara. I wanted to love her. I tried – I *did* love her, but then she was taken too.' She pressed her knotted hands against her breast. 'I was a bad mother, I know I was, but I swear to you, Thomas, I never wanted them to die; I never wanted any of them to die –'

'Ada, hush.' He opened his arms, but she shook her head, guarding the distance between them. 'I know you loved them. You must not torment yourself like this. Let the dead bury the dead.' It was not what he had intended to say, but the Biblical phrase seemed strangely apt. 'No matter how much we grieve for them, we can't bring back our children. The death masks and the photographs and the portraits ... They're *things;* they're not our children.' He had a sudden vision of himself lifting the death masks off the wall and wrapping them tenderly in cotton wool. He could do it if he chose; he was the master of the house. 'Our

287

children are with God, Ada. They don't need us to visit them on Christmas Day. They are with God, in heaven.'

'And Clara?' He saw her eyes narrow as she drove her point home. 'Where is Clara?'

# Chapter Forty-one

# A Christmas Gift

Darkness fell early on Christmas Day. When Lizzie Rose came in from skating, she settled in the Green Room and lay in wait for Parsefall. She took up her mother's Bible and passed the time reading the Christmassy bits from Matthew and Luke. By the time Parsefall appeared, she felt that she had been refreshed in body and spirit, and she hailed him sweetly: 'Merry Christmas! Where have you been all day?'

Parsefall blinked at her. He fished in his pocket and drew out a glittering object. ''Ere,' he said briefly, and dropped it in her lap. 'Merry Christmas.'

It was the emerald necklace. Lizzie Rose was both touched and slightly appalled. 'Oh, Parsefall, you mustn't! I'm sure Madama wouldn't want – but how dear of you! But, oh, Parsefall, I haven't anything for you! If we'd stayed in London, I'd have bought you a proper jackknife for Christmas – I meant to –'

Parsefall slipped out from under her arm. 'Don't need a jack-knife,' he said magnanimously. 'The old lady gave me a pistol – only it won't shoot. Put yer gewgaws on, and let's 'ave a look.'

Lizzie Rose held the necklace on the tips of her fingers, as if she was about to play cat's cradle. 'I'm sure I mustn't keep it. I told Madama I didn't need jewels, and I don't think she'd approve –'

'Who cares wot she thinks?' demanded Parsefall. 'I knew you wanted 'em. I saw you lookin' at 'em that first night. So on Christmas Eve, I went into Madama's room and took 'em off the table. An' Madama knew I took 'em, and she didn't make me give 'em back. So you can 'ave 'em, and if she don't fork over the stumpy, we can take 'em to the pawnshop an' live like kings and queens.'

Lizzie Rose was about to argue with this plan of action, but at that moment the door opened, and Esther came in with the dinner tray. Madama's illness hadn't deprived the servants of their yearly Christmas dinner. The tray was loaded with roast goose, sausages, mashed potatoes, peas, bread and butter, mince pies and plum pudding. The sight and smell of so much food put an end to all conversation. Lizzie Rose dragged a table before the fire and spread the cloth. Parsefall set the chairs in place. Ruby leaped on to one of them and made off with one of the sausages. A brief scuffle ensued; the spaniel took refuge under the bed, and Parsefall pursued her there, determined to reclaim the sausage. Esther finished setting out the dishes and stalked out, disgusted. In due time, the sausage was relinquished, the dog was pardoned, and the children took their seats at the table.

Lizzie Rose spread her napkin on her lap and unfolded Parsefall's, as a gentle reminder that he might wipe his hands on it, instead of the tablecloth. Parsefall nipped a piece of goose off the serving platter, twirled it in his mashed potatoes and bit off the end, as if it was a carrot.

Lizzie Rose opened her mouth to criticise his table manners but remembered that they had more important matters to discuss. 'Parsefall, where were you today? I looked for you this morning, and I couldn't find you. Then I went skating on the lake – oh, Parsefall, it was so beautiful! I wanted to take you with me, but you weren't anywhere in the house. Were you hiding from me? Parsefall,' she coaxed, 'do tell. Where have you been?'

Parsefall shovelled another chunk of goose in his mouth. His throat bulged; he looked like a snake ingesting an egg. 'Slept all day,' he said curtly. 'Couldn't sleep last night, could I? Bloomin' servants kep' me awake, carrying on about Madama. She was right outside my door last night, did you know that? They had to get Mark to take 'er to 'er room, and she was so 'eavy he 'ad to drag 'er.'

'Out in the hall!' exclaimed Lizzie Rose. 'I didn't know she could walk!'

Parsefall nodded sagely. 'I thought she woz bedrid too, but she ain't. She's a downy one, ain't she?'

Lizzie Rose passed Ruby the gristle from her drumstick. 'If you mean she's dishonest, I suppose she might be. Though,' she added, trying to be fair, 'she never *said* she couldn't walk. We only thought so because we never saw her out of bed. I wonder what she was doing, wandering about the house at night.'

'Up to 'er tricks,' Parsefall said cryptically.

Lizzie Rose wondered what kind of tricks an elderly lady could play, all alone in the middle of the night. 'I don't distrust her as much as I did,' she confessed. 'We talked on Christmas Eve, and she seemed kinder. And she *is* planning to leave us something in her will – Mrs Fettle said so.' She frowned, realising that once again she had become distracted. 'If you were asleep all day, where were you sleeping? You weren't in here – I looked for you. Why did you hide yourself away?'

'I woz in a room with a big bed,' Parsefall said evasively. 'I woz tired of this room.'

'All these rooms have big beds,' countered Lizzie Rose. 'And I looked through every one. Then I came back and looked here –' All at once she knew what she had missed before. 'Parsefall! Where's Clara?'

Parsefall gave a little jump. Then he shrugged. 'Dunno. Must've laid 'er down somewhere.'

'I don't understand you,' said Lizzie Rose. 'You *were* hiding from me – and you're not telling the truth about where or why, and you'd never leave Clara just *somewhere*. I thought you were avoiding me because you were cross – but you wouldn't have given me a Christmas present if you were cross. Parsefall, what *is* the matter? Have the servants been horrid to you? Are you afraid of Madama? If you tell me what's worrying you, I can help – in fact, you must tell me, because I mean to have the truth.'

Parsefall made a face. He snatched a slice of bread from the plate and used his forefinger to butter it, taking great care to ensure that the butter was slathered from crust to crust. He was stalling; Lizzie Rose knew it, and she suspected that he knew she knew it. Finally he muttered, 'I wish we could go back t'London.'

'Back to London?' echoed Lizzie Rose. 'Parse, we can't. The police –'

'Maybe we could go see Old Wintermute,' Parsefall said desperately. 'Maybe we could give him the emeralds and ask 'im to tell the coppers 'e made a mistake –'

'I don't think that would work,' said Lizzie Rose. 'Dr Wintermute isn't the sort of man who tells lies to the police.

Besides, there's the legacy to think of. Madama told Mrs Fettle that she's going to send for a lawyer –' All at once she stopped. 'Parsefall, what happened to your ear?'

Parsefall fingered the torn earlobe. He looked extraordinarily furtive. 'Dunno. I 'ad a scratch on it, and then I picked it.' He fitted the action to the word, plucking at the scab with his fingernail.

Lizzie Rose shuddered. She wasn't squeamish about many things, but she couldn't bear the way Parsefall dug at himself when his skin was broken. He scratched himself ceaselessly, like an animal; she had once seen him eat one of his scabs. She cried, 'Oh, don't! It's too horrid! Do stop, or you'll start bleeding again!'

Somewhat to her surprise, he did as she asked. He reached across the table to take another sausage. 'I don't like it 'ere,' he complained. 'I didn't want to leave London, but Old Wintermute was after us, an' you made me, so 'ere we are. But there's nuffink for me to do 'ere but go round and round the 'ouse and see wot there is to pinch.' He pointed to the Bible on the sofa. 'I can't read, like you can. I can't sit an' sew, like a girl. There ain't no audience – there ain't even any streets – no penny gaffs, no magic lantern, no Egyptian 'All. And it's cold outside and me boots is thin, and I don't see wot the old lady wants wiv all them trees. So I goes round inside the 'ouse, an' then you start a-carryin' on, saying that I'm *worried*. I ain't worried, but strike me dead if I ain't blue-devilled, wot wiv 'aving nuffink to do.'

Lizzie Rose leaned her elbows on the table. She knew this was not good manners, but she didn't care. She stared at him so intently that he wrinkled his nose and stuck out his tongue. There were dark shadows under his eyes she hadn't seen before. He looked pale and even ugly; every muscle in his face was tight.

She had told him that she meant to have the truth. Now she

saw that the truth could not be forced out of him. The more she pressed him, the more he would lie. And he was lying. He was afraid of something; she could smell it. Whatever it was, she couldn't protect him – not if he went on hiding from her.

An idea came into her head. She gave a little sigh and changed the subject. 'The days are so long here. We ought to rehearse the puppets.'

His eyes kindled. Lizzie Rose went on cannily.

'We shall have to be quiet, because of Madama, but we ought to work on the new show, just in case there isn't any legacy. I don't know the new acts, not properly – and you'll have to teach me to be a better figure worker, because I still float the puppets. Will you do that? And perhaps I could teach you skating in return.'

'We could rehearse,' Parsefall said cautiously, but his eyes had brightened. 'I'll teach you.' And as a token of goodwill, he rolled the rest of his bread into a ball and tossed it in the air for Ruby to catch.

# Chapter Forty-two

# The Gatehouse

They rehearsed in the Green Room. Parsefall tried to persuade himself that he was safe as long as it was daylight and Lizzie Rose was with him. He wanted to believe that Grisini would wait until dark before he returned to the house. But the puppet master's words echoed in Parsefall's ears: *I can enter the house whenever I like. If you fail me, I will be obliged to hurt you.*

And Parsefall had failed. He hadn't succeeded in stealing the fire opal, and he dared not make a second attempt on the stone. Clara had warned him against it, and he couldn't get into the old lady's room. Since Madama's collapse, the servants had taken turns watching over the sick woman. Parsefall racked his brain, but he could think of no way out of the dilemma. He had never learned to think ahead more than a day or two, and he was too frantic to weigh his choices.

So he rehearsed. When he was busy with the puppets, he was not afraid. Grisini and Madama were only shadows, compared to the solid little manikins on the stage. Parsefall worked tirelessly, ardently, and he saw to it that Lizzie Rose kept pace with him.

Lizzie Rose divided her time between the puppet theatre and the lake. The weather remained cold, and she went skating every afternoon. 'You should come too,' she said earnestly. 'It's *good* outside – so pure, with the lake and the snow and the fresh air.'

Parsefall did not love fresh air. In his experience, it was apt to be cold. He tried skating once and found it a failure. His ankles were weak, and they buckled. After that, when Lizzie Rose went skating, he retreated to the Tower Room.

There was a spyglass in the room. Using it, Parsefall could see the stone urn where Ruby was tethered. If the dog was tied up, Lizzie Rose was skating; if the long rope hung slack, Lizzie Rose was on her way back to the house. Parsefall listened for her footsteps on the back stairs. When he heard them, he unbolted the tower door and darted across the hall to the Green Room.

He was in the Green Room late one morning when he heard Lizzie Rose shouting for him. There was a note of panic in her voice. 'Parsefall! *Parsefall!*' The door swung open, and she burst in, gasping for breath. 'Parsefall – listen – it's dreadful – but I have to tell you –' She took a great gulp of air. 'Grisini's here.'

Parsefall felt as if the wind had been knocked out of him. ''Ere? In the 'ouse? Now?'

'No. Not now. Not in the house.' Lizzie Rose flung her skates to the floor. 'He's in the gatehouse. He's living there. I saw him –' She broke off. 'Why, you knew, didn't you?'

Parsefall widened his eyes, dramatising his astonishment. It was a weak effort and a belated one.

'You've known ever since we came here, haven't you? That's what's been wrong with you! Oh, Parsefall! Why didn't you tell me?'

'He told me not to. 'E said he'd hurt you.' Parsefall's voice cracked. He was almost afraid to look at Lizzie Rose. He lied to her so often and she always believed him. Now that he was telling her the truth, it stood to reason that she wouldn't. But her face was transparent, revealing a series of emotions: scepticism, shock, pity, indignation.

She commanded, 'Tell me what happened.'

He bent his head. He didn't want to remember Grisini crouched over him. The carpet snagged his attention. Mossy green, with a score of other colours zigzagging through it: sallow gold and rosy brown and blue grey and black . . .

'Parsefall, tell me!'

He parried the question with one of his own. 'What'd 'e say to you?'

'Nothing. He was asleep. He didn't see me.' Lizzie Rose shuddered. 'I was skating, and I was thinking about – oh, everything. I know it's heartless to wonder what will happen after someone dies, but I was wondering what Madama might leave us in her will. I was wishing we could live close to the lake. And then I remembered the first morning we came and how we both liked the little gatehouse with the tower. So I wondered – if I asked Madama – if perhaps she might give us the gatehouse.'

Parsefall began to understand. He went to one of the chairs before the fire and sat down. Lizzie Rose shrugged off her coat and knelt by his feet, with Ruby close at hand. 'I decided to look inside. I didn't think anyone lived there, so there wouldn't be any harm in peeking in the windows. I took off my skates and walked down to the gatehouse. The ivy's all over the windows, but there was one window on the ground floor . . . I looked through, and I saw Grisini! He was asleep in an armchair, as still as wax – oh, Parsefall – I thought he might be dead. I almost hoped it. But he twitched, just a little, and I knew he wasn't.' She hugged Ruby. 'I was dreadfully frightened. I ducked under the window-sill and crept away, and I didn't run until I was past the trees. It was queer, because he was asleep, but I was so afraid!'

'I know.'

'I ran till I had a stitch in my side. I kept thinking he might be behind me. But then it came to me that Madama must have lied to us. Because if he's living in the gatehouse, she must know, mustn't she? And when we first met her, and we told her Grisini was gone, she didn't seem a bit interested. And I remembered something I overheard when we came here. One of the servants said, "First foreigners and then riff-raff." I was so cross that she called us riff-raff, I didn't stop to think who the foreigners might be, but she must have meant Grisini.' She took a deep breath. 'How long have you known he was here?'

Parsefall's mouth was dry. He thought back to the night when Grisini crouched on top of him. He couldn't find the words. Ruby squeezed out from Lizzie Rose's embrace and leaped into his chair. Uninvited and unwelcome, she set about making her-self at home in Parsefall's lap.

Parsefall moistened his lips. 'He come in the middle of the night. The night before Christmas Eve, it were. He 'eld me down – wiv his 'and on me mouf – and told me I 'ad to steal that fire opal from Madama. He wants it. But he daren't steal it for 'imself.'

'Why not?' breathed Lizzie Rose.

''Cos it's dangerous,' Parsefall answered. 'It's magic –

powerful – but it's bad for the one that steals it. Clara told me so. She – she comes to me in my sleep.' He saw the shocked look on her face. 'Almost every night, I dream about Clara. She says Madama's a witch and the stone's cursed, like the Bottle Imp – and summink bad'll 'appen if I take it. But if I don't, Grisini'll come after me. And I don't know 'ow long I can 'old out.' He stopped, clenching his teeth. 'I know you don't believe me.'

Lizzie Rose had gone pale. 'I do believe you,' she said breathlessly. 'I dream about Clara too. She comes and stands at the foot of my bed, and I know she wants to tell me something, but she never speaks.'

'She's tryin' to help,' Parsefall said in a low voice. 'That night, after Grisini came, I wanted to find a place where 'e couldn't get me. I woke up with a picklock in me hand, right outside the Tower Room door. I think Clara tol' me to go in there. After I went in –'

'You went in the Tower Room?'

'I needed a place to 'ide, didn't I? The locks in this 'ouse are no good – a baby could pick 'em. But the Tower Room has a bolt on the inside of the door. Grisini can't get in.' He dumped Ruby off his lap and got up. 'Come on. I'll show you.'

Lizzie Rose followed him to the door, but she looked worried. 'But the tower's unstable,' she protested. 'Mrs Fettle says so. She says –'

Parsefall snorted, dismissing her fears. He led Lizzie Rose down the passage and held open the tower door. Once they were inside, he shot the bolt. 'See?' he whispered. 'It ain't so bad.'

Lizzie Rose did not seem to share his opinion. She gazed around the tower, noting the tent shelter he had built. Then her eyes travelled to the mirrors and the panels of black lacquer on the walls. She circled the room, examining the red lines of the maze, the spell books in the bookcase, the Tarot Cards that Parsefall had swept off the table on to the floor. 'Oh, Parsefall,' she whispered, 'the *smell* . . .'

Parsefall sniffed obligingly. His shoulders lifted in a faint shrug.

'This is . . . a witch's tower,' Lizzie Rose said. 'It's true what Clara says to you. Madama's a witch, and Grisini's a bad magician, and I don't know what they want from us, but it can't be anything good.' She opened one of the drawers in the cabinet, glanced inside and shivered. 'We must go away.'

She turned slightly. Against the dark wood of the cabinet, her red hair seemed to blaze, and her face was very pale. For the first time, Parsefall realised that she was beautiful. He thought of posing a puppet like that, motionless against a dark backdrop. Cinderella, perhaps, when the stepsisters left her alone and desolate on the night of the ball.

Then the meaning of her words sank in. 'Where?' he cried. 'Where'll we go? We can't go to London.'

Lizzie Rose considered. 'We'll go to Carlisle.'

'Wot's Carlisle?'

'It's north,' Lizzie Rose said hesitantly. 'It's on the rail line. When we were in the second-class carriage, I heard one of the gentlemen say he was staying on until Carlisle.'

'Why'll we go there?'

'Because they'll expect us to go south. Madama and Grisini. They don't know that the police in London are looking for you because of the photograph you stole. They'll take it for granted that we'll go back to Mrs Pinchbeck's. So we'll trick them and go north, to Carlisle.'

''Ow?' demanded Parsefall. He remembered their last journey by rail. It had been endless and unnerving, but at least they had known where they were going. He thought of the acres of empty land around them – to Parsefall, it was a wilderness – and wondered if they would even be able to find the train station.

'It won't be easy,' admitted Lizzie Rose, 'but there must be a village nearby. I've heard church bells. So we'll try to find the village, and if we see anyone on the road, we'll ask where the train station is. We'll buy third-class tickets – I have the rest of the ten quid from the pawnbroker.'

Parsefall brightened. 'We 'ave Madama's gewgaws,' he reminded her.

'No. I think we'd better leave Madama's things behind. They're too rich for us. Think, Parsefall! If she decided to send after us, she could say we'd stolen those things. Nobody'd believe she gave them to us.'

'Wot about the puppets?'

'We'll need them,' Lizzie Rose said after a moment's reckoning. 'Once we get to Carlisle, we'll have to find work as soon as we can. You must do your best with the theatre, and I'll help you – or I'll look for a place as a maid-of-all-work.' She bit her lip, and Parsefall realised that she, too, was appalled by the journey ahead. 'Only we mustn't take the wicker trunk, because it takes two of us to carry it. It may be miles to the train station.'

''Ow'll we carry the puppets?'

Lizzie Rose thought. 'I'll sew the muslin bags to our coats,' she said, after a moment. 'We'll look dreadfully queer – though I can put my shawl over the lumps – but we must have our hands free. I'll sew as much as I can today, so we'll be ready to leave tonight –'

301

'Tonight?' repeated Parsefall, and his voice came out in a squeak.

'Tonight,' Lizzie Rose said, so gravely that he understood that she had no intention of losing time. 'We're in danger here, Parsefall. We shan't stay here another night.'

# Chapter Forty-three

# The Maze in the Tower

At eleven o'clock that night, they stole from the house, unlatching the kitchen door and creeping out into the garden. Both children were heavily laden and wore several layers of clothes. It was snowing, which made Parsefall curse under his breath. 'Don't worry,' Lizzie Rose assured him in a whisper. 'It'll stop soon; it's only flurries,' but the flurries were as large as halfpennies, weighing heavy on the children's eyelashes and drenching their cheeks.

They passed through the kitchen garden and started down the hill. Ruby pranced against her leash, overjoyed that they were taking a walk in the middle of the night. Parsefall muttered, 'Bloody 'orrible dog,' but he was uneasy. Why was Lizzie Rose leading them towards the lake? Perhaps she knew of a shortcut that would bypass the gatehouse. It was only when they reached the two stone urns that he confronted her. 'Why'd we come 'ere?'

Lizzie Rose gave a little jump. 'How queer! I don't know why. I suppose I wasn't attending.'

'Well, 'adn't you better *attend*?' said Parsefall. He knew she hated sarcasm, but he was too frightened to be careful of her feelings. She was in charge of getting them away from Strachan's Ghyll. He needed her not to make mistakes.

Lizzie Rose glared at him. Then she spun on her heel and started up the path, taking such long strides that he had to trot to keep up with her. He said, 'We show up too much against all this bloomin' snow.'

Lizzie Rose frowned at his language but pointed to the trees surrounding the house. The trees might serve for cover. She squeezed between two large hollies, and Parsefall followed suit. The holly leaves scratched and plucked at him, catching his cap and the puppet bags on his back. The noise was deafening. He found it hard to believe that no one in the house heard it. Nevertheless, he was grateful for the shelter. The space between the house and the shrubbery was like a tunnel: private, dark and close. Behind him, Lizzie Rose gave a little cry. She had caught one of her plaits on a holly twig. He waited for her to free herself, glad for the moment of rest. He hadn't realised how much the puppets weighed, and walking was arduous.

'Parsefall,' Lizzie Rose said in a low voice, 'we're at the tower.'

Parsefall opened his mouth to jeer at her. Of course they were at the tower; the curved wall to the side of them could be nothing else. Then he understood her meaning. They had lost themselves in the shrubbery, and they'd circled three-quarters of the way around the house, missing the front drive. Once again they were behind the house, looking down the sloping lawn to the lake.

'We'll go back,' Parsefall said resolutely. 'This time, once we get to the lane, we'll make a run for it.'

Lizzie Rose gave his hand a quick squeeze. 'That's right. We'll run when we get to the gatehouse. The snow will muffle our footsteps.'

Parsefall hoped she was right. He tugged his jacket down in front. The weight on his back dragged at his collar, half choking him. He would have liked to unbutton his coat, but Clara was inside, curled up like an embryo against his chest. He could not risk dropping her in the snow.

'This way,' said Lizzie Rose, and they set off at a jogtrot, heading for the lane.

Cassandra stood by her bedroom window, gripping the fire opal in her unbandaged hand. She had awakened quite suddenly, knowing that something was wrong. Something was not only wrong but missing, and she didn't know what it was. The servant who had been assigned to sit by her all night had deserted her, but that was nothing, Cassandra thought; that would not rouse her from a sound sleep. She sensed that she had suffered a distinct and dangerous loss – and all at once she knew what it was. The children were leaving the house. They were her last hope, and they were leaving. 'Don't leave,' she croaked, as if they could hear her. 'Stay. Stay.' She clutched the phoenix-stone until her palm blistered. The pain was so great that she thought she might vomit or faint. She couldn't afford that; she must summon all her strength and cast the spell to bring the children back.

She slid her hand between the buttons of her nightdress, pressing the jewel against her heart like a leech. She cried out, not weakly but in strong outrage. The skin between her breasts puckered and shrivelled. Numbness followed the pain, and then a steady warmth. The sting and throb became almost comforting.

Her mind was clear again. She thrust the stone back into the locket and peered out the window. She saw three small figures, dark against the snow. As her gaze fell upon them, they changed direction, veering back towards the house. Even from a distance, she could sense their bewilderment, and she almost pitied them. But they must not leave her. No one must ever leave her. She turned her back on the window and lurched forward, moving in a drunken zigzag, grabbing the furniture for balance. First the armchair – then the mantel – then the bedpost – the dressing table – the doorknobs. She wrenched open the doors and staggered out into the corridor.

The candles in the hall were lit. Cassandra rested against the door frame, gathering strength. There was a small table halfway down the hall, and she steered for it, tacking back and forth like a ship. When she reached it, she fell against it. The candlestick on the table rocked; the candle tilted in its socket. The tip of the flame caught the sleeve of her nightdress.

She stared at it, watching the flame swell and the white cloth char. So. It was going to happen, then: the doom she had feared so long. She was going to die by fire. First her nightdress would catch and then the outer layer of her skin, and then the burning agony would possess her whole body. Her mind accepted it and went dead.

But her body, after one moment of frozen horror, was determined to fight. It flung itself against the floor, writhing against the carpet like a dog rolling in carrion. Both hands beat at the flames again and again, long after the last spark had been extinguished. The witch smelled smoke and singed cloth.

The fire was out. She had survived it.

She felt a childish urge to thank God for her deliverance – as if God had anything to do with her. The idea made her laugh a little. She set her palms against the floor and scrabbled until she got her knees under her. She stood up and staggered down the passage to the Tower Room.

She found the door unlocked and went inside. The matches were in the top drawer of the tall cabinet. Cassandra's hands shook as she lit the candles in the wall sconces. She hadn't been inside the tower since the day the children came, and with faint surprise she noted the mess that Parsefall had made. The tent shelter was in her way. Cassandra set her whole weight against it and shoved it against the wall, kicking aside Parsefall's pillows. She dragged the blankets and the bearskin to one side, hating them for being so cumbersome.

She returned to the cabinet and withdrew a dagger with an ebony handle. With one practised movement, she sliced the blade across her arm, letting the wound gape. The fat under her skin glistened like silver. After several seconds, the blood began to flow: first sullenly, then rapidly. She let it drip on to the knife blade. Then she took out the phoenix-stone, twirling it between her fingers until it was coated with blood.

She shut the stone back in the locket and bent forward, dragging the blade of the dagger along the lines on the floor. She shuffled backwards and forwards, tracing the pattern, casting the spell. When she finished, she wrapped her fingers around the filigree locket. She shut her eyes. 'Clara Wintermute!'

The girl's face appeared at once. It was as distinct as if it had been painted inside the witch's eyelids. Cassandra snarled aloud. 'Why are they leaving me? How dare they? What made them decide to go? Answer me!'

Clara's expression was mutinous. Her mouth drew back in a

stubborn line. She was fighting, trying to hold back every syllable. But the witch's power was overwhelming, and at last Clara's lips parted. Her voice was scarcely audible. Cassandra caught only a single word: *Grisini*. Then the girl's face faded, as if it had been painted in watercolour and sponged away.

The witch uttered a shriek of rage. Grisini! Fool that she was, she had forgotten him. Why had she allowed him to stay on in the gatehouse? Why hadn't she foreseen that he would meddle with the children? Cassandra shut her hand around the gold locket. She spoke his name with murder in her voice: 'Gaspare Grisini!'

She saw him, and he was asleep. He looked frail and peaceful: an old man taking his ease in a soft bed. 'Gaspare!' she bellowed, and the puppet master opened his eyes.

An idea flashed through Cassandra's head. She would punish him, and she would make use of him. She would – what was his phrase? – catch two pigeons at the same time. At the thought of what she meant to do, her lips drew back in a yellow-toothed smile, for it was her turn to be the master and his to play the puppet.

'Parsefall,' Lizzie Rose said, on the verge of tears, 'there's something wrong.'

Parsefall was too weary to answer. It seemed to him that they had been tracking back and forth across the lawn for hours. His feet were icy and his teeth chattered. The snow had stopped falling. The moon slid out from under a cloud, pouring grey light on to the trampled lawn.

'Those are our footprints,' said Lizzie Rose. 'We've been going in circles.'

Parsefall stared at the pattern in the snow. It was extraordinarily regular, and with a jolt he recognised it. 'It's the maze. On the Tower Room floor – the red lines that woz painted there! We been making the lines wiv our tracks – over and over –'

'It's a spell,' Lizzie Rose said despairingly. 'We can't leave. She cast a spell on us so we can't leave.'

Parsefall did not ask who *she* was. He looked sideways at Lizzie Rose. If Lizzie Rose didn't give up, he wouldn't.

'We'll have to turn back,' Lizzie Rose said wretchedly. 'We can't go on like this. We won't get anywhere – and we'll freeze to death.'

'We 'ave to go back,' agreed Parsefall, and with dull fear in their hearts, they broke the pattern of the maze and started back to the house.

# Chapter Forty-four

# The Puppet Master

Inside Parsefall's jacket, Clara was uncomfortably warm. She was imprisoned in a puppet bag, flattened between two layers of clothing. She listened to Parsefall's heartbeat as he entered the house. It quickened as he mounted the grand staircase. *Turn back,* she wanted to cry, but her jaws were fused together, and if Parsefall sensed her warning, he paid no heed.

Cassandra said, 'Come in.' Her usual waspish tones had softened to a mellow contralto. 'Come to the fire and warm yourselves! You must be dreadfully cold!'

Clara doubted it. Even through the layers of clothing, she felt the hellish heat of the room. She thought that Parsefall must feel it too; he was fumbling with the buttons on his jacket. He stuffed Clara under his arm and let his jacket drop to the floor. She felt his muscles tense: he was nerving himself to accuse the witch. 'You cast a spell on us!'

'I did,' admitted Cassandra. 'I didn't want you to go away.'

Lizzie Rose took up the battle. 'I don't see what right you have to keep us here. Why shouldn't we be allowed to leave if we want to?'

'Because I didn't wish it. And because it's not what's best for you.' Clara heard the rustle of silken skirts: Cassandra was approaching. 'You may dislike me, my child, but you're safer with me than you would be alone, out in the wicked world. Haven't you been comfortable here, safe and warm and well fed? I wish only to look after you, and, in a very short time, you will inherit everything I have.' Another rustle and her voice sharpened. 'That bag you're holding, boy! Is that Clara?'

Parsefall snarled, 'Leave 'er alone!'

Lizzie Rose asked, 'How do you know about Clara?'

Cassandra sighed. 'I've known about Clara ever since she was kidnapped by that human plague, Gaspare Grisini. I know, too, that you were trying to escape from him tonight. What I don't know is why. Tell me why you fear him and I will protect you.'

There was a brief silence. *Don't tell her anything*, thought Clara, but Lizzie Rose answered. 'Grisini wants Parsefall to be a thief. He came into Parsefall's room in the middle of the night and threatened to hurt him if he didn't steal from you.'

'Ah,' said Cassandra. 'Of course. I ought to have known –' She stopped. 'Never mind. Grisini is in my power, and I shall see to it that he never hurts you again. I will punish him before your very eyes, and you will see that I am your friend.'

She sounded close at hand. Parsefall took a sudden step back but not quickly enough: Clara felt the witch seize the puppet bag. Cassandra tore the limp muslin, releasing Clara from her cocoon. The glare stung Clara's eyes: the witch's room was hung with scarlet and gold, ablaze with firelight and candlelight.

'There!' Cassandra said briskly. 'Don't worry – I shan't hurt her. I only want her to be able to see.' She glided to the window and hooked Clara's crutch over the curtain rod.

It was an excellent vantage point; Clara could see the whole room. There was the tumbled bed, with Ruby lying sphinx-like upon it; there were the other two children, with their clothes all lumpy and dishevelled. By contrast, Cassandra was resplendent; she had swept her hair up on top of her head and secured it with a jewelled pin. With her swollen body and billowing yellow gown, she appeared inhuman: a pyramid of fire with the head of an ogress.

The doors swung open, and Grisini came in.

He wore a queer assortment of clothes: his tatty frock coat, a pair of satin knee breeches and his nightshirt, which was tucked into the breeches in front but not in back. At the sight of him, Lizzie Rose stiffened. Parsefall's face went blank, and he jammed his hands in his pockets.

Cassandra stretched out her hand and pointed to the floor. Grisini bowed but not low enough; Cassandra glowered until he went down on one knee. He covered his heart with his hand and spoke deferentially. 'Madama.' His face was ashen, the half-healed scratches on his cheeks emphasising his pallor.

*He's afraid of her,* thought Clara.

Cassandra circled him, her train hissing. 'Don't speak as if you wish to flatter me! I am disgusted with you, Gaspare! These children are under my protection; how dare you seek to frighten them?'

Grisini shifted. The kneeling position was evidently painful. He spread his hands in a dumb show of innocence. *'Madama, lo prometto –'*

'Speak English, if you please. The children are here to witness your humiliation. I would not have them miss a word. And don't waste my time with lies. I caught them trying to escape – not from me but from you. What have you done to them?'

Grisini started to rise, but the witch glared at him, forcing him back to his knees. He flourished one hand in the direction of Lizzie Rose. The gesture was elegant, almost balletic: the palm up, the outer fingers curled, the smallest finger pointing to the ceiling. '*Nulla*. I have not touched her –'

'Is that true?' Cassandra twisted around to face Lizzie Rose. 'If it isn't, tell me. Whatever injury he has done you, I will avenge.'

'It isn't me,' said Lizzie Rose. 'He struck me once, but it isn't me. He's cruel to Parsefall.'

Cassandra pivoted, facing Grisini. Her lip curled. 'So. You ill-use the boy. I'm not surprised. His hand – is that your work?'

There was a sudden appalled silence. Clara felt as if she might cry out. But Parsefall did not make a sound. He didn't seem to be following the conversation.

'That was – discipline,' Grisini answered at last, pronouncing the last word with the utmost delicacy. 'It was necessary that the boy should obey me. Have I not been a second father to him? Did I not feed him and teach him my art? Should he not obey me?'

Lizzie Rose stared at him in horror. Then she began to cry. Ruby emitted a yap of alarm, leaped off the bed and ran to her mistress. Only Parsefall showed no emotion. He fixed his eyes on the carpet. *He's trying not to hear,* thought Clara. *He doesn't want to know.*

'You are a monster, Gaspare.' Cassandra's face was twisted

313

with loathing. 'You are both more wicked and more trivial than I ever dreamed of being.' She stalked to the window, raising one hand to point out Clara. 'The Wintermute child – I suppose she was another of your experiments?'

Stiffly Grisini got to his feet. '*Ah, Madama,* forgive me. I can no longer kneel. I am an old man, a poor man. Let us come to an agreement.' His voice wavered as if he was on the point of tears, but his eyes were dry. 'If you want these' – he flung out one hand, casting an invisible net over Parsefall and Lizzie Rose – 'you must have them, of course. How should I deny you? But the little girl, I beg you, leave her to me. Her father is willing to pay and I give you my word of honour that I will send her home again once the money is mine. Give me the girl, so that I may not starve, and I will trouble you no more.' He reached upwards. The tips of his fingers brushed the hem of Clara's skirt.

*No!* Clara screamed silently, and Parsefall shouted the word at the same time. He darted past Madama. 'You leave 'er alone! Don't touch 'er!'

'Do you hear him, Gaspare?' Madama came forward, spreading her fiery skirts to make a barrier between Parsefall and Grisini. 'I forbid you to touch Clara. As for your enchantments, you shall cast no more of them. Give me the automaton watch.'

Grisini threw out his hands. They were shaking. '*Madama,* I have it not. I have lost it.'

'It's in the right-hand pocket of your frock coat,' Cassandra said sharply. 'Give it to me or I will make you bleed to death here and now. Give it back.'

She held out her hand for the watch. From her high perch, Clara could see the old woman's palm; it was seared and

314

bloodstained. Grisini slapped the watch into it so savagely that Cassandra flinched. Then, as if the glittering timepiece was rubbish, she flung it into the fire. A strangled sound came from Grisini's throat.

'And now,' said Cassandra, 'tell me, Gaspare. Do you bleed?'

Grisini grimaced. He touched the back of his head and looked at his fingers. They shone crimson. He smiled a sickly grin. '*Sì, Madama.*'

'And shall go on bleeding until I choose to stop it.' Cassandra looked from Lizzie Rose to Parsefall. 'You see how I avenge you, my children? You see how great my power is? This man will never harm you again. He is *my* puppet.' She raised her arms, spreading her fingers as if manipulating strings. 'See? I can make him bleed, and I can make him dance.'

Grisini's body twitched. He held up his hands, palms out, as if he was about to play a clapping game. He bent his knees and cocked his foot, tapping the heel against the floor. Then he capered, his head flopping from side to side. Beads of blood sprouted from the scratches on his cheeks; blood darkened his shirt collar and glistened against the dull black of his frock coat. The witch lifted her hands, and he leaped straight up in the air. Cassandra snapped her fingers, and he fell to his knees with a cracking sound. Instantly he was up again, striking his heels against the floor and spinning like a top. He was short of breath, wheezing and whimpering with pain.

'Stop it!' Lizzie Rose seized the witch's arm. 'Stop it! It's horrid!'

'Are you mad?' Cassandra shook off Lizzie Rose. 'Think of what he has done to your brother! Shall I not punish him? Shall I not have my revenge?'

315

'Not like that!' Lizzie Rose averted her eyes from the dancing man. 'Stop it – oh, please, stop him dancing!'

Cassandra shrugged and let her hands drop. Grisini tumbled down on to his hands and knees. He cringed like a whipped dog.

'If I stop punishing him, will you agree to do as I ask?'

Lizzie Rose jerked her head so that her tears caught the light. Clara couldn't tell if she was shaking her head or nodding.

'The thing I will ask is no evil thing, and you will come to no harm. Will you promise? Or shall I go on tormenting Sior Grisini?'

Grisini moaned. Lizzie Rose gulped. 'I promise.'

Cassandra cleared her throat. 'Gaspare. The young lady has seen fit to have mercy on you. Get up and get out of my sight.'

Grisini struggled to his feet. He tottered to the double doors and went out. Clara could hear him on the great staircase, his footsteps growing softer as he descended.

Cassandra held out her hands to Parsefall and Lizzie Rose. 'Come here.' Her voice was weaker than before; the last spell had diluted her strength. She guided them to the sofa and fell on to it with a sigh of relief. 'Now I will tell you what to do.' She turned to Lizzie Rose. 'Marguerite?'

Lizzie Rose stared at her. 'Ma'am?'

Cassandra shook herself. 'Forgive me. I meant Lizzie Rose, of course! Listen, my child, I want to speak to your brother alone. You must take the dog and go to your room and climb into bed. Will you do that?'

Lizzie Rose leaned past the witch, looking into Parsefall's face.

'I shan't keep him long, and I shan't harm him,' Cassandra assured her. 'Five minutes. You promised to obey me.'

'Parsefall ought to be in bed too.'

'He shall be. But first I want a word with him. If you disobey me, I shall have to recall Gaspare and make him dance again. Will you do as I ask?'

'Yes,' Lizzie Rose said reluctantly, 'but you mustn't say anything bad to Parsefall.'

'Run along, now, and take the dog with you. I shall send Parsefall after you in five minutes.'

Lizzie Rose snapped her fingers to Ruby. She stopped by the door to look back, but Parsefall didn't meet her eyes. As the double doors shut, Cassandra bent forward and spoke softly. 'Tell me, Parsefall. Did you like seeing your master dance?'

Parsefall didn't answer. His eyes were bleak. After a moment, he bared his teeth in a joyless smile.

'One can develop an appetite for such things. Would you like to have that power over Grisini?' Cassandra pried open the filigree locket. 'You hate him, don't you? After what he did to you –'

'I don't remember,' Parsefall interrupted loudly. 'I don't remember! It were something bad, but I dunno wot it was.'

'Don't you? Even now? Your sister understood; that's why she was weeping. Do you remember nothing?'

'No. There's a black place – inside my mind.'

'Then I bid you remember.' Cassandra lowered her voice to a whisper. 'That is your task. Change into your nightshirt and climb into bed and dream – at once, at once.' She touched the fire opal to his cheek; it was the most delicate of caresses. 'When you dream, you will remember.'

*He doesn't want to remember,* Clara wanted to scream. *Leave him alone!* She watched as Parsefall walked to the door. He moved like a clockwork figure.

'I had to,' Cassandra said aloud after the boy left the room. She wasn't talking to Clara but to herself. 'I had to.' Wearily she returned the stone to its cage and shut the locket with a small sharp click.

# Chapter Forty-five

# The Black Place

Outside the witch's bedchamber, Parsefall headed for the Tower Room. A figure at the far end of the hall beckoned to him, and for a moment, his heart stood still, because he thought it was Grisini. Then he recognised Lizzie Rose. She beckoned again, holding her finger to her lips.

Parsefall hesitated. His orders from Madama were clear. He was to put on his nightshirt, to dream, to remember – but she had not told him where to sleep. At the back of his mind was a shadowy conviction that he would be better off close to Lizzie Rose. He tiptoed down the hall towards her.

Lizzie Rose led him into her bedroom and shut the door. The White Room, with its pale wool hangings and rose-coloured curtains, looked safe and inviting. The bed had been turned down, and there was a good fire on the hearth. Parsefall began to undress. As if from a great distance, he heard Lizzie Rose questioning him, asking if he was quite well. He answered her curtly, without knowing what he said.

The witch had told him to put on his nightshirt; she hadn't known that he was wearing it next to his skin. He kicked off his boots and removed his outer clothes. When he had finished undressing, he saw that Lizzie Rose had stripped the blankets off her bed, so that he could have his usual nest beside the fire. She was watching him through tears. A wave of fatigue washed over him, and he turned away and crawled between the blankets.

He fell asleep, not by stages but immediately, as if he was falling off a cliff. His body had no time to relax and his muscles knotted and twitched. The dream claimed him at once. The floor beneath him tilted, like the board of a seesaw. Then he heard a creaking sound, the sound of the rocking chair.

'*Parsefall.*' It was a girl's voice, not Grisini's. She stood beside him in the darkness. 'Parsefall, I'm here. I'll stay with you.'

*Who are you?* Before he was able to shape the question, he sank deeper into his dream.

His eyelids fluttered. He was no longer in the White Room but in a third-rate lodging house. A dingy light made its way through streaked windows. He saw the curved arm of a rocking chair, grotesquely enlarged, and the frayed sleeve of Grisini's frock coat. Grisini was sitting in the rocking chair, and he – Parsefall flinched in his sleep – was sprawled across Grisini's lap. He was very small. Too small: Grisini could cup his fingers around Parsefall's skull.

But it was not Parsefall's skull that Grisini was holding; it was Parsefall's right hand. Grisini held it between his thumb and forefinger. As the chair rocked, Parsefall's head lolled back, and his left arm swung like a pendulum.

'You see what happens when you are disobedient,' Grisini murmured. His voice was as soft as the hum of a contented bee. 'You become a puppet – my puppet – but you have too many fingers for a puppet, so' – he picked up a file – 'I shall shave them off.' He began to rub the file against the outside of Parsefall's hand. There was no pain, but Parsefall could see tiny pieces of flesh breaking off. His finger was being filed away.

Parsefall wanted to weep. He wanted to beg Grisini to stop; he wanted to promise never to disobey again; he wanted to howl with outrage. But his face was as stiff as rawhide and he could not draw breath. He lay limp in Grisini's lap, one knee twisted backward and the left arm swinging.

'Nine fingers left,' said Grisini. He sounded pleased. 'Most puppets only have eight. Shall I take off one on the other hand, for the sake of symmetry? Or are you prepared to obey me from now on?'

Parsefall could not answer. He felt Grisini pinch his other hand between two giant fingers, and again he longed to speak so that he might promise perpetual obedience. The chair rocked, and his body tilted dizzily. If only Grisini would drop him; if only he could slide to the floor, away from Grisini; if he could get away from Grisini for even a second –

'*Parsefall!*' It was the girl's voice again; in some unfathomable way, she was following him through the nightmare. 'Parsefall, you're dreaming! Wake up and you'll escape from it – wake *up!*'

The rocking chair slid out from beneath him. Grisini disappeared. Parsefall turned and saw Clara. Her white dress shone in the dimness; her eyes were wide with shock and compassion. '*Wake up!*'

He tried to kick, to open his mouth and scream himself awake. The sound that came from him was hoarse and strained, scarcely a whisper. He made another sound, louder than the first, and at last he drew breath and shrieked as he had never shrieked in his life.

The scream was good. It separated him from the nightmare in which he was mute. In a moment, Lizzie Rose was at his side, holding him tight. 'Parsefall, it was a bad dream, only a bad dream –' Ruby was whining and pawing at him, trying to climb into his lap. 'Shh, Parse. It's all right, you're safe now. I'm here –'

He held up his hand, inches from her eyes. 'It woz Grisini,' he gasped. 'He shaved off me finger. Grisini did. I'm going to kill 'im.'

Lizzie Rose's arms tightened. She rocked him back and forth. 'Shh, now, Parse –'

Parsefall wouldn't let her finish. ''E did it, he did. You know it, Lizzie Rose. He changed me like he did Clara. An' he took off me finger. You know how puppets only 'ave eight of 'em – 'e did it on *purpose* – and I'm going to do the same to 'im – change 'im and file off his little finger, all 'is fingers, one by one, and I'll take a knife an' gouge out his eyes –'

'Shhh,' Lizzie Rose whispered, 'hush, Parse; hush, you *can't* –'

'I can,' Parsefall shot back at her. He pulled himself free. 'Just like Madama did. I can do anyfink I want to, if I get that magic stone. I'm going to steal it.'

# Chapter Forty-six

# Fire and Ice

*I'm going to steal it.* From her high perch in Cassandra's room, Clara heard Parsefall's words and knew that he meant them. Any moment now, he would enter the double doors and steal the fire opal. The stone would be his doom: he would inherit both the witch's power and her despair.

And Clara could do nothing to stop him. She couldn't bar the doors against him; she couldn't even shout out a warning. She was as helpless as she had been when she was little and cholera struck the Wintermute house.

Her mind flashed back to those desolate days. The Others had fallen ill, and she alone had been spared. Her papa had quarantined her in the attic; her mamma had given her a china doll and told her that she must play very quietly, or her brothers and sisters would not get well. Clara remembered crouching in the narrow space between the wall and the bed, hugging her doll, afraid even to whisper. But her silence had not saved the Others. Now she was silent again.

What had the witch said to her, that first night at Strachan's Ghyll? *You need only wish for the stone, and you will be yourself again. If your wish is strong enough, your strings will snap and Grisini's spell will be broken.* If Clara wished, she might save Parsefall; she could save him if she stole the stone herself. The curse would fall upon her. Clara shut her eyes in terror.

The room went dark.

She opened her eyes and the room reappeared. She blinked, unable to believe that she could open and close her eyes. Her chest hurt, as if her heart were struggling to beat in a space too small for it. *I will*, thought Clara. *I will steal the stone. I will wish for it with all my heart.*

An unseen hand plucked her strings. Clara felt them, taut against the holes in her flesh. She swayed and twisted, shifting her weight as if she was on a swing. There was a soft *pfffft* as a head string snapped. Clara's head flopped sideways. Then she raised her chin. She could do that; she could lift her head and clench her fists. She curled her fingers and wrapped her thumbs around them. Fiercely, joyfully, she hammered the air, yanking the threads that ran through her palms. Her left knee stung as a leg string gave way. Another string twanged, then another. There was a rush of air – a sensation of falling – and a hard landing, one that rattled every bone in her body.

Clara stumbled to her feet and ran to the witch's bed. Cassandra was as pale as death, but her eyes glittered. 'I caught you, I trapped you!' she panted. 'I knew I could do it! I saw into your mind, and I knew you loved the boy. Love is always a trap!' She bit off the last word so fiercely that spittle shot from her mouth.

Clara plunged under the bed canopy. The witch hissed and retreated, protecting the filigree locket with both hands. Clara wedged her thumbs into the hollows of the old woman's fists, prying open the gnarled fingers. She snatched the locket with such force that the gold chain gave way. Once the locket was in her hands, Clara leaped back. She cried out in pain. 'It's burn-ing me!'

Cassandra gasped like a fish out of water. 'Yes, it'll burn you,' she panted. 'It's burned me for years. It's more powerful – if you let it hurt you.'

Clara stared at her reddened palm. She had cherished a hope that she might destroy the stone by consigning it to the flames. Now she saw that she could not fight fire with fire. A weird fancy swept into her mind. 'Wait,' she whispered. She flew to the window and opened the casement. The frigid air came in like a blessing.

She gazed out the window. Her eyes took in the fresh-fallen snow, the floating stars, the immense white saucer of the lake. The lake . . . With shaking hands, Clara gathered snow from the window ledge. She found the clasp that opened the locket and released the fire opal.

The gemstone fell on to the mound of snow. Clara caught her breath. She had never seen anything as beautiful as the flam-ing jewel against the white crystals. The play of colour mesmer-ised her: blood red and grass green and peacock blue . . .

The sound of a moan shattered her reverie. 'Please,' sobbed Cassandra. 'I want it back. Give it back.' The witch was crying open mouthed, like a child; her mouth and her chin were slick with mucus. Clara shuddered. She clapped the jewel between two handfuls of snow and clasped it against her breast. She turned her back on the witch, passed through the double doors and started down the grand staircase –

Grisini was watching her.

He stood at the foot of the stairs, clinging to the newel post for support. There was a lamp there, and the dim light made the blood on his cheeks look black instead of red.

'Clara!' he said in a happy whisper. 'Little Clara! You have the phoenix-stone, haven't you, *mia piccina*?' He beckoned, his fingers spinning like the spokes of a wheel. 'From this night on, we will share the stone's magic, you and I! The stone will be yours, and you will be mine! *Vieni qua, madamina!* Come, my little puppet!'

*Puppet.* Clara froze. Then her mind pitched forward, frantically reviewing her choices. The front door was at the foot of the stairs, but Grisini could creep up behind her while she wrestled with the lock. If she fled back upstairs, she ran the risk of leading him to Parsefall. For a fraction of a second, she considered surrendering the fire opal: why shouldn't Grisini suffer the stone's curse? Then she imagined what he might do, given its magical powers, and she steeled herself to outwit him.

She looked down the staircase. The darkest part was halfway down, equidistant from the lamps at the top and the bottom. Clara crept downwards, seeking the privacy of the shadows. With one hand she broke the chain of her birthday locket. Then she shrieked, 'Take it!' and hurled the locket at Grisini.

There was a metallic clang as it struck the tiles. Grisini fell to his hands and knees, searching. Clara darted down the staircase and dodged past him. She sprinted into the Great Hall, passing the high windows that overlooked the lake. *The lake,* thought Clara as she crossed the threshold into the music room. When she reached the library, she heard Grisini utter a bellow of rage: he'd found her birthday locket and discovered that it was a decoy. Clara screamed too. She wanted to rouse the household

– but there was no time to wait for help to come to her. She must get out of the house and on to the lake.

Grisini was closer now. The darkness between them was stifling and rank, polluted by his presence. Clara found the servants' staircase and scuttled down the narrow stairs as fast as she could. The cellars were pitch-dark, and she lost her way. At last she blundered into the kitchen and lifted the latch of the back door.

It was strangely light in the snowy garden. The sky was not dark but a weird pinkish colour, like wine diluted with ashes and water. The trees were sharply black against the sky. Clara bent down and scooped up more snow. The kitchen door slammed. She leaped forward, running downhill. She lost her footing but jumped to her feet and dashed forward on to the lake.

The ice was solid. Clara slipped and slid, venturing further and further from the shore. Her fingers were numb around the dripping snowball. She heard the sound of Grisini's feet scuffling through the snow and turned to see where he was.

He paused at the lakeshore. After the slightest of hesitations, he stepped out on to the ice and trotted towards her. His hands were thrust out, ready to hook his dirty claws under her skin. Clara thought how long Parsefall had lived in the shadow of this man. She felt a great swelling of love and rage, and her fear was as nothing. As long as Grisini chased her, she would run. If he caught her, she would fight. She would die before she let him have the stone. Her hands tightened around the ball of ice, and she pressed it against her heart.

The glassy shell of the opal cracked. Clara felt it: a tingling flash, the sensation of a bubble bursting against her fingers. Her hair stood on end. At the same instant, she heard a deep and hollow sound, like the vibration of a huge drum. The ice beneath her feet began to shake. Cacophony: a low booming, a nasal creaking, a series of snapping noises like gunshots. Clara opened her hands. The fragments of the fire opal looked like bits of sucked candy.

Grisini screamed. He swayed back and forth like a falling tree, his arms flailing. The ice beneath him shattered and gave way. There was a loud splash. Clara started forward. The ice groaned. She looked down and saw the cracks around her feet: crooked and angular, like the skeleton of a tree in winter. Dark water oozed up between them. Clara's slippers were wet. The water that would drown her was lapping at her feet.

'Lie down!' The voice was Lizzie Rose's. 'Lie down flat! We'll help you!'

Clara lowered herself on to her knees and stretched out on her stomach. The ice ceased to groan beneath her weight. But her sense of relief, though acute, was short-lived. Now that she was lying still, she felt the cold keenly. Her legs trembled, and she curled her toes and arched her back, trying to make herself smaller. Her teeth chattered. She hugged herself and squeezed her thighs together.

There was a faint creaking to her left. Clara twisted her head. Before her, walking barefoot over the starlit ice, was an angel. It wore a white robe and crept towards her with a queer mincing gait. Clara's blood ran cold. Was it Death, coming for her? Had she drowned or frozen without knowing it?

But the angel was wingless and had no halo. It made its way over the ice in an oddly haphazard manner, zigzagging around the larger cracks. And the white robe wasn't a robe but a nightshirt – and all at once Clara's face broke out in a smile of wonder, because surely this was the angel of her twin.

She raised herself up a little. Now that he had come, she remembered him with perfect clarity. She had not seen him for seven years, but she remembered how he looked in his nightshirt.

Every morning he left his bed to creep into hers, and the two of them played together before their nurse was awake. They made caves of their blankets and pretended to be bears. She remembered how his cheeks broadened when he giggled and how his eyes curled up at the outer edges. Her brother, her own dear twin, had come to comfort her while she lay dying –

But no: Charles Augustus had dark hair, like her own. Charles Augustus was a solid little boy, whereas the boy in the nightshirt was spindly and light haired and carried a coil of rope over his shoulder.

'P-Parsefall,' croaked Clara.

He halted, checking his balance. The ice squeaked and he got down on his belly, skittering towards her like some skilful insect. 'I got a rope,' he told her. 'Lizzie Rose uses it to tie up her bloody 'orrible dog. She thought I'd better bring it 'cos I'm lighter'n her.'

'Thank you,' Clara said with absurd formality. She stretched out her arms, and he uncoiled the rope and lashed it like a whip, so that the end was within reach. 'Is Grisini –?'

'Drownded,' answered Parsefall. He was shivering as hard as she was, but he didn't seem a bit sorry that his former master was dead. 'Bleedin' cold, ain't it? Don't move yet. I'm goin' to get back where the ice is thicker, and then I'll pull you.'

Clara rolled to one side, trying to slip the end of the rope under her sash. Her fingers shook. 'I broke the fire opal,' she said. She crossed one end of the rope under the other and pulled, making the first half of a double knot. She jerked her head at a small mound of snow. 'It's there.'

Parsefall reached down and scooped up the snow. He peered at the remains of the gemstone. Then he clapped the snowball back together and tossed it over his shoulder.

Clara heard a faint splash.

'I'll pull you,' Parsefall said. He was backing up. Already his voice sounded far away. 'Just 'old on. I'll pull you.'

Clara lay flat. She felt the tension of the rope as she began to move, the ridges in the ice scraping her skin. She heard her skirt tear. She thought, *Parsefall is pulling my strings,* and in spite of the danger and the piercing cold, she laughed.

# Chapter Forty-seven

# The Witch's Tears

Lizzie Rose stood at the edge of the lake and prayed. She heard the squeal and crackle of the ice, and she strained to see through the darkness to the place where Parsefall was trying to rescue Clara. The children had come to the lake just in time to witness Grisini's fall. It was Parsefall, with his cat-keen eyes, who spotted Clara; she was fifty-some paces further from the shore than Grisini had been. Lizzie Rose had been forced to think rapidly, to direct Clara to lie down, to remember the rope that served as Ruby's tether, to agree – too quickly – that Parsefall would be safer on the ice than she would. Now she held herself rigid and prayed that no one else would drown.

She heard footsteps behind her, crunching through the snow. She looked over her shoulder and saw two bundled-up shapes: Mrs Fettle and her son, Mark. Mrs Fettle was carrying a lantern. Lizzie Rose turned back to the lake and resumed her prayers.

She watched as Parsefall, bent like a plough horse, towed Clara across the jagged ice. He was swearing but almost cheerfully;

Lizzie Rose had heard him swear like that backstage. Clara half crawled, half skidded towards the shore.

Mark Fettle took off his coat and handed it to Lizzie Rose. 'Give my coat to the girl. I'll carry the boy.' He went to the lake's edge and held out his arms. 'Come here, lad. I'll carry you back to the house – save those bare feet of yours.'

Parsefall looked startled but did not protest. As soon as he came within arm's length, Mark Fettle swept him up, one arm around his shoulders and the other under his knees. Lizzie Rose went to Clara and draped Mark's coat over the girl's shoulders.

'Inside,' Mrs Fettle said curtly.

She lit their way up the path. Mark Fettle followed, carrying Parsefall, then Lizzie Rose and Clara, with the rope dragging behind her like a tail. They were halfway up the hill before they saw the house. Lizzie Rose halted, staring. She heard Mark Fettle say, 'God!'

'The tower,' said Parsefall.

'It's fallen,' gasped Mrs Fettle.

The shape of the house had changed. The great tower had collapsed. The remains resembled a hand with the three tallest fingers drawn together. There was a trio of uneven peaks where the tower wall adjoined the house. Near the bottom, where the hollow of the hand might be, was a great mound of rubble: stone, plaster, shingles and timber.

'I told Madama it was unsafe,' said Mrs Fettle. 'I warned her, but she wouldn't listen to me.'

'That must've been what we heard,' Mark Fettle said in wonder. 'We came out into the garden and I felt the ground shake. I thought it was an earthquake.'

'It was an earthquake,' declared Mrs Fettle. 'What else could make the tower fall and the ice crack? Someone might've been killed.' She rounded on the children. 'What were you doing out on the lake past midnight? And what was the meaning of all that screeching? And who's this girl, and what's she doing here?'

Lizzie Rose said imploringly, 'Oh, please, ma'am! It's dreadfully cold, and we haven't any proper clothes on! Mayn't we go inside?'

Mrs Fettle sniffed. 'You may and you will,' the housekeeper said grimly, 'but once you're inside, you're going to tell me the whole story.'

Lizzie Rose quailed at the prospect. She followed Mrs Fettle up the path, trying to think how to explain the events of the evening to a grown-up. Her mind was still blank when they reached the house.

The kitchen door was ajar. Clara hastened to the stove and knelt down, her teeth chattering. Parsefall squatted an arm's length away. Lizzie Rose took the poker and stirred the coals, clouding the air with smoke and coal ash. 'Might we have a basin of cold water, Mrs Fettle? I'm afraid of frostbite – Parsefall hasn't any shoes on and Clara's slippers are wet.'

Mrs Fettle filled a basin with water and banged it down before Parsefall. 'There. Stand in that and let your feet thaw.'

Parsefall dipped one foot in the water and jerked it back again. 'It's bloody 'ot!' he said, outraged.

'It isn't,' snapped Mrs Fettle. 'It's cold water; it only feels hot because you're half frozen. And I'll thank you not to use that language in this house.' She darted a sharp look at Clara. 'I'd like to know who you are and what you're doing here. Where did you come from?'

Clara sidestepped the first two questions, fastening on the third. 'From London, ma'am.'

Mrs Fettle's eyebrows rose. 'If you live in London, why are you here? When did you come, and where are your parents? Why were you out on the lake in the middle of the night, without any coat on?'

Clara hesitated. She fumbled with the buttons on the borrowed coat, playing for time.

Lizzie Rose spoke up. 'Grisini was chasing her.'

'Chasing her!' exclaimed Mrs Fettle. 'Mr Grisini's down at the gatehouse. He's too weak to chase anyone. Why on earth –?'

Parsefall interrupted her. 'He ain't down the gatehouse. He's dead. 'E fell in the lake.'

'Do you mean just now?' Mrs Fettle stared at him as if he had lost his mind. 'Tonight? Do you mean he's out there –?' She turned to her son. 'Mark,' she said urgently.

Mark Fettle shook his head, dumbfounded.

Parsefall stopped chafing his toes. 'He drownded,' he explained. 'I saw it. The ice cracked and 'e slid down between the pieces. His 'ands was snatching at the edge, but he couldn't catch 'old, 'cos the ice broke off. Then he sank, an' he never come back up. We both saw, didn't we, Lizzie Rose? And Clara too.'

Lizzie Rose looked pleadingly at Mrs Fettle. 'We couldn't help it, Mrs Fettle, indeed we couldn't. There wasn't time.'

'You might have told me,' Mrs Fettle said resentfully. She picked up the kettle as if to refill it, then set it down again. 'We'll have to send for the doctor –'

''E's *dead*,' Parsefall insisted.

Mrs Fettle frowned at the ceiling, calculating. 'There'll have to be a death certificate. And the constable had better come. You'll have to go, Mark.'

'Aye, I'll go.' Mark Fettle looked uncertainly at Clara. She stood up and took off his coat, holding it out to him. He touched the rim of his cap. 'Thank you, miss.'

'Thank you,' Clara said courteously, and he shrugged himself into his coat and went outdoors.

The jangling of a bell made them all jump. 'Dear heavens!' breathed Mrs Fettle. 'Madama.' She raked her fingers through her hair and rushed out of the kitchen.

Once she was gone, Lizzie Rose breathed a sigh of relief. For a little while at least, there would be no more questions. She felt a sudden weakness in her knees and realised she was trembling. So much had happened: the attempted escape, the torture of Grisini, Parsefall's nightmare, Grisini's death . . . and Clara. Lizzie Rose stared at Clara as if she was a ghost.

Clara seemed to understand. She smiled and patted the floor, inviting Lizzie Rose to sit by her.

Lizzie Rose sank down on her knees between Clara and Parsefall. Clara snuggled against her, burying her head in Lizzie Rose's shoulder. The two girls clung together, rocking a little. Parsefall rolled his eyes and rubbed his toes.

No one spoke. Shoulder to shoulder, the three children sat before the kitchen fire, gazing into the flames. They inhaled the dense smoke, watching it billow and change shape. Lizzie Rose stared at the orange-red coals until the backs of her eyes smarted.

Clara said wonderingly, 'I'm hungry. I'd almost forgotten what that was like. Puppets don't get hungry.'

'I still can't believe it,' Lizzie Rose said in a low voice. 'Parsefall said you were a puppet – and I saw you – I *knew* it was you – but there were times when I couldn't believe it. How can a person be a puppet? And how did you change back again?'

'It was the stone,' Clara answered. 'The witch cast a spell on me, so that I could come back to life. Only in order for the spell to work, I had to be willing to steal the fire opal. And I was afraid to steal it, because it's evil. Then tonight – when Parsefall –' She left the sentence unfinished. 'I *had* to steal the stone, because I was afraid Parsefall would steal it –'

'I would've stole it,' broke in Parsefall. 'I woz going to use it to torture Grisini.' He pointed at Lizzie Rose. 'Only, she wouldn't let me –'

Lizzie Rose took up the thread. 'I held on to him –'

'Then we 'eard you screaming like a stuck pig –'

'And we followed you down to the lake –'

'And both of you saved my life,' Clara said softly, finishing the story. She did not elaborate but gazed into Parsefall's eyes. He reddened and smirked, ducking his head.

'He was very brave, wasn't he?' Lizzie Rose said proudly. She cupped her hand over Parsefall's toes. 'That's better. You're almost warm.'

Parsefall disagreed. '*Almost* ain't warm.'

Somewhere upstairs a door slammed. There was a high-pitched sound, like the mournful cry of the wind. Lizzie Rose lifted her head. 'That must be Ruby. I never heard her howl before.' She leaped to her feet. 'I'd better see what's wrong.'

She hastened out of the room, almost running. Clara and Parsefall followed at her heels, up two long flights of stairs and down the passage. Just outside Madama's room, they saw the triangular shape of the sitting dog. Ruby tipped back her head and howled again.

'Why's she 'owling?' demanded Parsefall. He sounded cross: a sign that he was frightened.

Lizzie Rose felt her skin prickle with goose flesh. She recalled a ghost story her father once told her, a deliciously frightening story that she now wished she hadn't heard. 'They say when someone dies –'

She stopped but too late. Clara was as white as her frock.

'I killed her,' gasped Clara. 'I took the fire opal, and it killed her.'

She looked as if she might faint. Lizzie Rose put an arm around her. But Parsefall said crossly, 'No, you didn't. Listen to 'er.'

He was right. Beyond the doors, someone was sobbing bitterly. 'Of course,' Lizzie Rose said, relieved. 'That's why Ruby's howling. She always has to be with anyone who's miserable.' She opened the double doors and let the dog into the witch's room.

Ruby bounded over the carpet and leaped on to the bed. Cassandra Sagredo caught her to her breast, squeezing so tightly that the animal yelped.

The children stared. The witch was as red faced as a newborn child. She sat on a stripped bed; the bedclothes lay in heaps on the carpet. 'Fettle took the dog away,' she wailed. Her voice was ragged from sobbing. 'She took her. I hate Fettle. I wet the bed. So I wanted Fettle to put dry sheets on it, but she made a prim face at me, and I slapped her and told to get out. And then she took the dog.' She pressed her face against Ruby's coat. 'The dog was the only good thing. The only good thing.'

The three children looked away, embarrassed. The old woman's nightdress had risen to her knees, showing her mottled legs. Cassandra fastened her eyes on Clara. 'It's gone, isn't it? You broke it.'

'Yes, it's gone.' Clara clasped her hands, her fingers curved as if she was holding a ball. 'I took it to the lake, and it cracked into little pieces. It's gone.'

Cassandra pointed at the looking glass. 'The other witch is

gone too. Look! She's not there any more.' She spoke so commandingly that all three children faced the mirror.

There was nothing to see. The glass reflected nothing but their faces and the objects in the room. Lizzie Rose sniffed cautiously. The hot-wire smell was gone.

'She's gone,' Cassandra said hoarsely. 'And the fire opal is broken. It was my power – and my beauty – and you killed it.' She glared through her tears at Clara. 'It was all I had. And yet it gave me no happiness, none at all.' All at once a look of naked fury distorted her features. She released the dog, curled her hands into fists and struck at the mattress so violently that Ruby leaped off the bed.

'It was a sham!' she shrieked. 'It was all a sham – a cheat and a torment! I could make people do what I wanted – I could see into their very souls – but it gave me no joy – not one moment's happiness! None of it – *none* of it – was any g –'

She stopped in mid-word. Her eyes blazed. 'There's something else, isn't there? Something you haven't told me.'

Parsefall began 'The tower's fallen –'

'I know that,' snapped Cassandra. 'I heard it fall. It's been rotten for years. What's the other thing?'

Lizzie Rose closed her eyes for a moment. Tentatively she said, 'Mr Grisini –'

'He's dead,' concluded Parsefall. ''E drownded in the lake.'

Cassandra threw back her head and laughed. All at once she looked years younger, and she chortled like a spiteful young girl. 'I'm glad. I'm glad he's dead! God grant he burns in hell!' She inhaled so sharply that the breath sang at the back of her throat. 'I was forty-six when I met Grisini. Forty-six, a fine age for a woman to make a fool of herself. And he was twenty-three! Twenty-three! Imagine what a fool – to think that he could love me! He couldn't love anyone – and no one could ever love me, ever –' She dragged her wrist under her nose. 'All the others – the men in the cabinet – I enchanted them. But then Grisini came along, and I thought – I *believed*! But it was my magic he desired, not my love. He stole the fire opal – but I took it back. Oh! How I punished him! I made him bleed, I did, I did! I was the stronger one. I could make *men* do what I wished; he could only jerk the strings of puppets!' She glowered at Clara. 'He changed you – but that wasn't my fault. And you.' Her face changed as she looked at Parsefall; for a brief moment, her eyes were profoundly sad. 'He took your finger. I wouldn't have done that. He was worse than me.'

Then all trace of sadness vanished. She laughed aloud and threw up her hands. 'Ah, but he was handsome when he was twenty-three! That young, young face – all sharp angles, and that queer cruel smile – and the graceful way he bowed and kissed my hand! I was a fool, but it's all right now, because I can enjoy him being dead.' She sniffed violently. 'But my head hurts. Why didn't Fettle brush out my hair? I can't undo the pin, and it frets me! No, I remember; I threw the hairbrush at her. And later on I slapped her and told her to get out, and she took away the dog. And now she'll go away – all my servants will leave, now that my power is broken.' Her face was sober. 'I shan't have anyone to wait on me. I shall die all alone. I'll *die*. I didn't think I would have to – not really.'

She raised her arms, fumbling with the pin in her hair. The snarl of hair around it defeated her, and after a moment, she let her hands fall and began to cry again. Lizzie Rose stooped by the bed and started to gather up the blankets. The witch's head came up sharply.

'Don't you pity me,' she said, 'Little milk-and-water miss!

Little Goody Two-Shoes! I won't have you staring at me – I don't want you. The three of you have taken everything and told me my last love is dead – and I won't have you watching me die – get out, get *out*!'

Parsefall was already at the door. Clara shadowed him, and Lizzie Rose laid down the bedclothes and prepared to follow. But Ruby shot forward and leaped on to the bed, sniffing and licking the old woman's face. Cassandra wailed, stopping only to gasp for breath.

Lizzie Rose said, 'She's crying.' It was not a thing that required pointing out. The two other children looked at Lizzie Rose with wonder. Nevertheless, Lizzie Rose repeated the words. 'She's crying.'

'She's wicked,' Parsefall countered. He thought a moment. 'She ain't as wicked as Grisini,' he said, conceding a point.

'Grisini's dead,' Clara reminded him.

Lizzie Rose bent down and gathered up the blankets, beginning to tuck them around the weeping woman. After a second, Clara went to the other side of the bed and helped her.

'Just 'cos she's crying don't mean she ain't wicked,' Parsefall said. He drew up the stool from the dressing table and straddled it.

Lizzie Rose sat sideways on the bed. Gently she finger-combed the old woman's hair, loosening the knot that trapped the jewelled pin.

# Chapter Forty-eight

# In Which We Encounter
# an Old Acquaintance

On the afternoon before Grisini's death, Dr Wintermute sat in his library with a medical journal in his lap. He spent half an hour reading the first page of an article, only to realise that he had understood nothing. He fell into a sort of gloomy daydream and did not hear the opening of the library door. The voice of his butler made him jump.

'Sir, there is a person who wishes to speak to you.'

Dr Wintermute lifted his head. His usual patients were not persons but ladies and gentlemen. 'Did the person give a name?'

'Yes, sir,' answered Bartlett. 'She says her name is Mrs Pinchbeck.' He sounded dubious. 'I told her you were not to be disturbed, but she assured me you would wish to see her.'

Dr Wintermute laid aside the medical journal and stood up. His heart was pounding. 'She is quite right. Please show her in.' After a moment's thought, he added, 'It will not be necessary to inform Mrs Wintermute that we have a caller.'

'No, sir,' agreed Bartlett. His tone of voice was neutral, but Dr Wintermute fancied he saw a flash of sympathy in his butler's eyes.

Left alone, Dr Wintermute tried to prepare himself for what Mrs Pinchbeck might say. He had asked her to call on him if she discovered any clue as to Clara's whereabouts. Desperately, he tried not to hope. Mrs Pinchbeck was not respectable, and she undoubtedly drank; when he last saw her, he had rashly given her a sovereign. No doubt she had come for more money. He resolved to weigh her words carefully and keep his head, but he felt his stomach churn with excitement.

He had not long to wait. Mrs Pinchbeck swept past the butler and paused in the centre of the room. She stood with her head up and her shoulders flung back, as if she was about to take a curtain call. The pose allowed Dr Wintermute an opportunity to take in the details of her dress.

He felt a hysterical urge to laugh. The first time he had seen the woman, she had received him in a soiled robe and curl papers. Now she had taken pains with her appearance, and the effect was electrifying. She wore a pansy-yellow gown, suitable for a girl of sixteen, and a short jacket that would not button over her bosom. Both garments were much ornamented with cheap trimming. Dr Wintermute beheld Mrs Pinchbeck befeathered, beribboned, crinolined, corseted, frizzled and festooned, though not washed. With some effort, he maintained a grave face. 'Please be seated, ma'am.'

Mrs Pinchbeck chose a soft chair before the fire. 'That man of yours tried to tell me you wasn't at 'ome. Spoke to me as if I was common, but I said he'd better show me in. I told 'im as how you gave me a sovereign last time, and if you gave me a sovereign when I 'adn't anything to tell you, you'll be bound to see me when I 'ave.' She held up her hand. 'Here, now! I didn't say I know where your daughter is, because I don't. On the other 'and, the last time we met, you was asking me about little Lizzie Rose. What I brought might lead straight to *her*. Or even Mr Grisini, if it comes to that.'

Dr Wintermute slipped his hand into his pocket. Mrs Pinchbeck drew herself up, tossing her head like a horse refusing the bridle. 'Ah, sir, you insult me! Don't think I come in search of sovereigns! No! If I knew where your daughter was, I would tell you and never take a shilling! Nor even a farthing! Not if I was starving! I may be a poor woman, sir, but I am not without heart!' She heaved herself to her feet, gazed rapturously towards the far side of the room and laid one hand over her swelling bosom.

Dr Wintermute blinked. He had not attended the theatre for many years and did not realise that he was looking at a Picture. He said apologetically, 'I beg your pardon, ma'am. Please be seated.'

Mrs Pinchbeck sat. She looked a little cross. Dr Wintermute saw that he had somehow fallen short of what she might have expected of him.

'You had something to tell me,' Dr Wintermute prompted her.

'I do, sir.' Mrs Pinchbeck reached into her bosom and drew out a rectangle of crumpled paper. 'You said if I was to find out anything about Lizzie Rose or the boy, I was to tell you, and you'd give me another sovereign. Which isn't why I come, sir, but it was what you said.'

Dr Wintermute held out his hand. It took all his self-control not to snatch the paper away from her. 'You have a letter –?'

'Not a letter, sir. A n'envelope. Addressed to Gaspare Grisini.' She smoothed it out, turning it so that he could read the letters. 'From a place called Strachan's Ghyll, Windermere, up north. I

343

didn't think anything of it when I first saw it. I wasn't feeling meself, and I was looking for the – the medicine bottle, sir, and I saw that one of the dogs 'ad been naughty under the sofa, so I took up one of Lizzie Rose's old aprons to wipe up the mess. And I felt there was something stiff in the pocket, and it was this envelope. I didn't think anything of it, because there was the dogs to see to – they miss her, sir, no doubt about that, and the house is in such a state as you'd never credit –'

Dr Wintermute could restrain himself no longer. He nipped the envelope out of her hands and examined the postmark. 'This was sent to Professor Grisini after he disappeared.'

'I noticed that too, sir,' agreed Mrs Pinchbeck. 'But somebody opened it – and it must've been Lizzie Rose, because it wasn't me, and the boy can't read. But it was what the pawnbroker said that started me thinking – for there's no denying I've fallen on 'ard times, sir, with my lodgers gone and Mr Vogelsang behind with the rent. And as I was sayin', Mr Grimes, the pawnbroker, told me as how Lizzie Rose come in just before Christmas and pawned a gold watch. He said it was a fine gold watch, and he thought it might've belonged to Mr Pinchbeck, my poor departed 'usband. But Mr Pinchbeck never 'ad a gold watch, so the watch had to 'ave been Grisini's. He 'ad some very nice pieces of property, Grisini did – jewellery and ladies' things. I've an idea he once knew better days, poor Grisini, and I sometimes wondered if he might've been saved by the love of a good woman.' She pressed her palms together and rolled her eyes heavenward.

Dr Wintermute was not keenly attuned to Mrs Pinchbeck's theatrics, but he was aware that in her he beheld the aspect of a Good Woman. He murmured, 'Admirable,' and wondered what he meant by it.

Mrs Pinchbeck averted her head and made a little circle with one wrist, as if waving away a tray of sweets. 'I often thought Mr Grisini admired *me*,' she confided. 'Only, I could never fancy any man except Mr Pinchbeck, sir. He was the only man I ever loved.' She shook her head regretfully. 'Struck down by an omnibus in 'is prime. I never got over it, and I never *shall* get over it. Lord love you, sir, I know how the faithful 'eart grieves! Which is why I come, sir.'

Dr Wintermute said, 'I'm much obliged, ma'am.' He tried to think of some words of sympathy for the fate of the late Mr Pinchbeck but found himself unable to concentrate. 'You were telling me about the pawnbroker, ma'am?'

'Why, I just *said*,' Mrs Pinchbeck said irritably, rubbing her nose. 'Mr Grimes said as 'ow Lizzie Rose pawned that gold watch, and he asked me how I'd spent the ten quid so quick. "Ten quid!" I said to him. And he said yes, he'd given ten quid. And I said as 'ow Lizzie Rose 'ad run away, and how it broke my heart, living without her, and the dogs being as bad as dogs can be, sir – which is considerable. And he said as how the girl 'ad been asking about trains to the north country, to this Windermere that's on the envelope. So I thought to meself, that's where she went – her and the boy – and who knows but what Grisini might be there too?'

Dr Wintermute gazed at the envelope in his hands. It was quivering like a live thing. He forced himself to speak calmly. 'It may mean nothing. The whereabouts of the other two children may have nothing to do with Clara.'

'That's so,' Mrs Pinchbeck conceded with a lucidity that floored him. 'But it might mean everything. It's a mystery where your daughter's gone, and a mystery where the other two've gone, and maybe it's one mystery instead of two. Whatever you might say, there 'asn't been any bodies found, and where there's life, there's 'ope. Now, when Mr Pinchbeck was struck down by the omnibus, he was killed right away.' She gesticulated and made a noise, giving a vigorous and surprisingly vivid impression of wheels rolling over a man's body. 'Crushed the breath out of 'im! There wasn't any 'ope then, I can tell you. But with your daughter, sir, there isn't any omnibus, and when there's no omnibus, there's 'ope. An' if I was you, sir, I'd go to this Windermere and start asking questions.'

Dr Wintermute folded the envelope and put it in his breast pocket. 'I shall do so. I'm very much obliged to you, ma'am.' He put his hand back into his pocket. 'Pray allow me –'

Mrs Pinchbeck became coy. The conversation that followed took longer than Dr Wintermute could have dreamed. Mrs Pinchbeck insisted that she would not take money from him, all the while pointing out that any other woman as hard up as she was might have felt it her duty to accept a sovereign. Naively Dr Wintermute assumed that the interview was over, but Mrs Pinchbeck seemed in no hurry to go away. It was some time before it dawned on Dr Wintermute that she was waiting for him to force the money upon her. He was quite willing to part with a sovereign or two, but he was even more eager to part with the woman, and it maddened him that she could not be rushed. He argued, coaxed and sympathised; he emptied his pockets of a five-pound note – and still she would not leave. At last he rang for Bartlett and instructed him to find Mrs Pinchbeck a hansom cab. By the time Bartlett ushered the woman out, Dr Wintermute felt that he had been through a long and shattering ordeal. He dropped into the chair before the fire and took out the envelope to study it.

The door opened. Dr Wintermute raised his head, dreading the reappearance of Mrs Pinchbeck, but the woman in the doorway was his wife.

'Thomas, who was that very singular woman in the front hall?'

Dr Wintermute said heavily, 'Her name is Mrs Pinchbeck.'

'Is she – a patient?'

'No. No, my dear, she is not a patient.'

'Why was she here?

Dr Wintermute could think of no answer but the true one. 'She was landlady to Professor Grisini. I questioned her a week or so ago. I encouraged her to come to me if there was any chance – if she thought of anything that might shed light –' He smoothed the envelope between his fingers. 'She knows nothing about Clara. I am convinced of that. But it seems that the other two children have also disappeared, and I wanted to question them again. Mrs Pinchbeck thinks they may have gone north. She gave me an envelope with an address on it. I don't suppose there's any real hope –' He tried to speak levelly, but his voice was husky. 'All the same, I should like to question them again. I must go to Windermere and see if I can find them.'

Ada crossed the carpet and stood before his chair. She put out her hand for the envelope. He gave it to her, and she took it as if it was precious. 'It's a lady's handwriting.'

'That struck me too.' He spoke very calmly, afraid of any word that might cause her to distance herself from him. He was tempted to reach for her hand but held back.

But it was she who reached for him. She knelt down and placed her hands on the arm of his chair. 'Thomas, let me come with you.'

He shook his head. 'My dear, the journey is a long one, and you haven't been well. If only – if I could – there is nothing I wouldn't do if –' He found himself unable to finish his sentence. He knew that he was about to weep and closed his eyes. A drop of warm liquid seeped between his eyelids. All at once, he felt his wife's touch. She brushed the tear aside, spreading its moisture across the surface of his cheek. Ashamed of his weakness, he opened his eyes.

Ada looked more alive than she had for months. Her mouth was trembling, but her eyes were resolute.

'I'm coming with you,' said Ada, and when he attempted to dissuade her, she pressed her fingers against his lips and would not let him speak.

# Chapter Forty-nine

# The Confession Resumed

Cassandra wept. It was the night of the stone's destruction, and she couldn't stop crying long enough to fall asleep. She was chilled to the bone, and she couldn't get warm. She tried to explain this to the strangers that stood around her bed, but her voice was ragged from crying, and the syllables came out in the wrong order. Two girls left the room and came back with their arms full of blankets. An untidy-looking boy put coal on the fire, stimulating it to a mighty roar. It occurred to the witch that the strangers were children, and that was odd: surely her sickbed was no place for children? She looked for the bell cord so that she could ring for the servants.

Her eyes became fixed with terror. Suspended over her head was a yellow monkey. He was shinnying up a golden cord and leering at her cruelly. Cassandra pointed at him and tried to tell the children he should not be there. He was a fiend; he would drag her into hell, where there was no mercy for sinners. But the strangers only looked at her with wonder and pity, and she despaired of making them understand.

She fell into a dream. The monkey was beside her, gibbering and hissing. There was a lake of fire, and a puppet named Grisini danced on the rim of the shore. Marguerite was there, weeping because someone had strangled her little dog. Cassandra opened her eyes, and there was the spaniel, snoring peacefully. She pointed to it and tried to tell Marguerite that all was well. But Marguerite had gone away, and the yellow monkey was smiling at her. Cassandra shifted her gaze to the rope that passed through its body. Traitors were hanged, and she was a traitor. She pawed at her throat, trying to loosen the rope around her neck.

One of the children seized her hands. Cassandra bit her. Then she wept, because the child had beautiful hands, petal soft and clean and strong. Her half circle of ragged teeth marks was an obscenity. But she could not apologise. The children's faces blurred and went dim, and she was asleep again, weeping still.

When she woke up, the dark-haired girl was standing on a chair beside her bed. The child was using her teeth to loosen the knot in the silk cord. When the knot gave way, the girl pulled the brass monkey over the kinks in the cord.

'What if she misses it?' asked the red-haired girl. 'She's used to having it to open and shut the bed curtains.'

'She won't miss it,' the other girl said firmly. 'It's giving her nightmares. Anyway, she'll still have the rope.' She handed the brass statue to the boy. 'Take it out of the room, Parse.'

The boy weighed the object in his hands. 'It's int'resting,' he said. 'Might be worth two, three shillings.'

350

'It's horrid. Take it out,' commanded the dark-haired girl. The boy wrinkled his nose at her, but he took the monkey out of the room. He came back empty-handed.

Cassandra gave a great sigh of relief. She rolled over so that she could pet the red dog. Stroking it, she fell back to sleep.

When Cassandra awakened, one nostril had cleared, and she could breathe through her nose. The inside of her mouth was as dry as wool. Her neck hurt; she had scratched it raw. Dizzily she lifted her head.

The candles had burned out, but the room was not dark, only dim. It was dawn outside and the children were asleep. Cassandra looked from one to the other, recalling their names. The boy sleeping before the fire was Parsefall. The dark-haired girl in the armchair was Clara. The girl sleeping at the foot of her bed was Lizzie Rose, and the red spaniel belonged to her, not to Marguerite.

Cassandra shifted. The dog stirred and yawned. Lizzie Rose awoke and pushed herself up on one elbow. 'Are you more comfortable, ma'am?'

Cassandra consulted the child's worried face. 'Yes.'

Lizzie Rose stretched towards her, laying one hand on Cassandra's brow. 'We'll send for the doctor today. He'll make you feel better.'

Cassandra took the girl's hand, examining it for teeth marks. 'I thought I bit you.'

'That was Clara.'

'I can leave you Strachan's Ghyll, you know.'

Lizzie Rose looked embarrassed. 'You needn't if you don't want to.'

Cassandra frowned. 'If someone offers you something you want, you should take it.' She swallowed, running her tongue over her lips. 'I want a glass of wine. Will you get it?'

Lizzie Rose slid off the bed. She tiptoed barefoot across the room. Cassandra watched her with an aching heart. Dear God, but the girl was young: to be able to move so easily, after being up all night! Cassandra accepted the wine, gulping it so that it spilled down her front.

Lizzie Rose took the glass and refilled it with water from the washstand. She moistened a handkerchief and mopped the sticky patch on Cassandra's chin. Cassandra spoke impatiently: 'For God's sake, child! What good have I ever done you that you should serve me thus?'

Lizzie Rose's forehead knotted. Cassandra could see her trying in vain to remember one good deed.

'There isn't anything,' Cassandra said testily. 'Mind you, I'll leave you the house – you and the boy – that'll be worth something. But first I want to tell you – I must tell someone – what I stole from Marguerite.'

Lizzie Rose sat cross-legged on the bed. 'It was the stone, wasn't it? The fire opal.'

'Yes,' Cassandra said. 'It was the stone.'


'It happened more than seventy years ago. It was Marguerite's birthday, and mine; I was thirteen and she was twelve. It was Carnival time in Venice, and Marguerite's father persuaded the nuns to have a birthday party at the convent. Marguerite was allowed to invite her six dearest friends. We were all dearest friends – Marguerite was very given to endearments – but I was her dearest, *dearest* friend. Fool that she was, she loved me best.

'It was my birthday too. I beg you to remember that. Marguerite gave me an ivory fan painted with peasants or nymphs or some such dainty nonsense. It was the only gift I had that day. Before my mother ran away, I always had birthday presents, but my mother didn't know where I was. I knew there was no chance of a letter from her. I was afraid that my father would forget me too, so I wrote to remind him of the date. Every day I waited. I even prayed. He sent nothing: no letter, no gift.

'The sixth of November came, the day of Marguerite's party. Monsieur Tremblay came, and we received him in the nuns' parlour. There were little cakes and confetti and chocolate to drink. We sat and watched Marguerite open her birthday presents.

'She was giddy with excitement and cooed over her gifts in a way that tried my affection sorely. Her doting papa brought her a large and costly doll – she was still fond of dolls – an Indian shawl and a leopard-skin muff, which grieved her a little, because, she said, she pitied the poor leopard! I am sure that no leopard ever felt more pitiless than I did at that moment. I wanted to claw her eyes out.

'But I pinned a smile to my face; I gushed and simpered with the rest. Marguerite's last and best gift was a rosewood box full of pearls. Her father told her that now that she was twelve, she was old enough to have her mother's jewels. She squeaked with joy and began to adorn herself.

'We all envied her; it wasn't only me. There were so many pearls. Cream coloured and silvery, bracelets and earrings and rings . . . Marguerite loved pearls. I didn't. I thought they were insipid. But these were so soft looking, so translucent, that they seemed to have no edge. Marguerite passed the jewels around so that we could all try them on. The other girls made peacocks of themselves, trying to see their reflections in the windows – there was no mirror in the nuns' parlour. But I had my eye on the rosewood box. It was not quite empty. There was a small pasteboard carton left inside. I asked Marguerite what it held, and she told me to open it and see. That was the beginning of my doom, though of course I didn't know it.

'I opened the box and saw the fire opal. It had a different setting in those days; it was a simple pendant. The colours so dazzled me that I gasped, and the other girls flocked around me, asking me to let them see. I felt as if the necklace were mine. All of us were astonished by its beauty; none of us had ever seen anything like it. But Marguerite showed no desire to try it on.

'We passed the jewel from hand to hand. I fancied that it smarted and stung my palm – a feverish tingle that I found first painful and then agreeable. I tried not to let anyone see how much I longed for it to be mine.

'That night I could not sleep. The image of the fire opal so teased me that I slipped out of bed and crept on tiptoe to Marguerite's cubicle. Leaving our beds at night was strictly forbidden, but the dormitory partitions were only curtains, made of rough cloth. There were no locks to pick, no doors to rattle, and in fact Marguerite and I often crept into each other's beds after dark. So I went to her cubicle and asked in a whisper if she was awake.

'She lifted her blanket so that I could slide into bed with her. She said she had been unable to sleep, thinking of me. She asked me if I hated her for having so many presents when I had only her ivory fan. I lied, of course. I said I loved her dearly. She believed me. Then I asked her about the stone.

'She said she had a horror of it. She knew it was foolish of her, but the jewel was a fire opal, and her mamma had died by fire. Madame Tremblay had been oddly superstitious about the gem, even obsessed with it. She used to call it her wishing stone.

'A wishing stone! How those words excited me! I thought of all the things I wished for: that my mother might return; that my father might love me; that I might shrink and become delicate and fairylike, as Marguerite was. I wanted to marry a nobleman; I wanted to live in a palazzo . . . But of course I confided none of these things to Marguerite. I changed the subject and we talked about the party. Then Marguerite fell asleep – she could fall asleep quite suddenly and deeply, like a child – and I slid out from under the blankets and crept to the trunk at the foot of her bed.

'The moon was full that night. When I opened the trunk, I could see the pale colour of Marguerite's birthday shawl. Underneath was the pasteboard carton. A subtle warmth seemed to come from it. I opened it and found the stone. I gripped it in my fist and wished that my father would remember my birthday. I think when I opened the trunk, I meant only to wish on the stone, not to take it. But of course I did take it. That night I hid it under my mattress. The next day, I sewed a tiny pocket for it in the bodice of my chemise. I wore it there like a second heart – hotter and stronger than my own.

'My father's birthday parcel arrived within the week. It contained a workbox for my sewing – I detested sewing – and a book of essays, entitled *Christian Thoughts*. I looked for a letter, but there was only a single sheet of paper with the hastily scrawled inscription: *To Cassandra, for her twelfth birthday*. I read it and began to cry. There was nothing in the parcel that showed that my father had any acquaintance with me. He had forgotten my age, he had given me the kind of book I most disliked, and his letter could not have been less affectionate. Since that day, I have had better reasons to weep. I have known betrayal; I have known cruelty. But nothing has broken my heart more than the package my father sent for my thirteenth birthday.

'It was nine weeks before Marguerite found out that something was missing from her trunk. She was perfectly bewildered, because only the six of us – her dearest friends – had seen the necklace. No thief had broken into the convent. Her precious pearls were untouched. But her mother's favourite necklace was missing, and that meant that one of her friends had betrayed her. Of course we were searched – our trunks, our cubicles. Sister Beata took me into an empty room and told me to remove my clothes.

'I was horribly embarrassed. I was ashamed of my figure, which was too well developed for a girl my age. I pressed my hand against my second heart and wished that I might be spared the search. I shall never forget the queer look that came over Sister Beata's face. "Of course it was not you," she said. "You are Marguerite's dearest friend. You have said that you are innocent and I believe you. You may return to your room."'

'So my secret was never discovered. As for Marguerite, she was heartbroken. One of her dearest friends had proved an enemy, and she didn't know which one. "The only thing I know for certain," she used to say, "is that it wasn't you." I couldn't imagine how she could be so stupid. Had she forgotten the night of her birthday, when she told me it was a wishing stone? Why didn't she remember? I think perhaps it was sheer obstinacy. She was determined to trust me in the very teeth of the evidence. Indeed, she treated me with greater affection than before. Sometimes when she brushed my hair, I had to leave the room, so that I could be sick – but I couldn't vomit up the lie. There were times when I almost confessed – except I knew that if I told the truth, I would have to give back the stone. I couldn't give it up.

'So I kept my secret, and in time Marguerite went back to New France. For years she wrote to me. I never answered. Before she died, she sent me the little portrait that you found in the library. *In remembrance.* She wrote that on the back. I've wondered what she meant by it. Perhaps, years later, she came to understand that I was the thief; perhaps she wanted to remind me how I'd wronged her. Or perhaps it was a token of forgiveness. I'll never know. That she should hate me, that she should forgive me: either one is a torment. For seventy years, she has haunted me.'

'You loved her,' said Lizzie Rose.

'Did I?' asked Cassandra. 'I don't know. She loved me. She was the last person who ever loved me. I never had another friend. I had admirers, of course; with the power of the fire opal, I could make men fawn on me. But their affection was neither lasting nor true, and I quickly tired of them. It's queer, isn't it? When I look back over my long life, there were only two people who mattered. One was Gaspare and the other was Marguerite. He betrayed me and I betrayed her.' She moved restlessly. 'You look as if you pity me. Don't. Remember, I brought you to Strachan's Ghyll to steal the fire opal. Any of you might have inherited its curse: you or your brother or Clara, if she hadn't been so strong. I knew what I was passing on. A wasted life, a fiery death. I didn't care. I'm telling you the truth: *I didn't care.*'

Cassandra's voice did not falter. She risked a glance at Lizzie Rose and read the shock in the young girl's eyes. Cassandra twisted away from her, dragging the bedclothes over her shoulder to signal that she was too tired to talk any more.

Ruby gave a little grunt of irritation. She got up, stretched, and made her way to Cassandra's pillow. Carefully, systematically, she began to lick the tears from the witch's face.

# Chapter Fifty

# A Reunion

When Parsefall opened his eyes, he was in Madama's room. He sat up and used his fingernails to scrape the grit from his eyelids. Then he kicked off the blankets and reached for his clothes, only to recall that he had left them in the White Room.

A ray of sunshine streamed through the crimson curtains. It was full daylight. Lizzie Rose was not there, and neither was Ruby; they must have gone for their morning walk. Parsefall wondered why none of the servants had come in with breakfast. At the thought, his stomach growled, and he got to his feet.

He had forgotten Clara. She was asleep in the chair, curled as tight as a fist. To an adult, she might have appeared small. To her former puppet master, she looked enormous. Parsefall felt a pang of regret. She was no longer his. He recalled the thrill of making her dance and the queer un-loneliness he felt when he cradled her in his lap. Now she was separate from him, a thing he had lost.

She stirred and her eyes opened. One cheek was red from the arm of the chair. 'Is there any hot water?'

Parsefall shrugged. He had a vague knowledge that the servants at Strachan's Ghyll brought water for washing every morning, but the matter had never much interested him. It occurred to him that Clara was probably going to be like Lizzie Rose, always wanting to clean herself. She tiptoed to the washstand, dipped her fingers into the water pitcher and frowned. Then she came back and picked up her slippers. He followed her into the hallway.

She spoke in a low voice. 'I'm hungry. Do you suppose there'll be anything to eat?'

'There usually is,' Parsefall said. He sniffed hopefully, but he lacked Lizzie Rose's acute sense of smell, and he could pick up no scent of bacon or frying ham. 'Let's go and see.'

They fell into step. When they came to the staircase, Clara sat down on the top stair to put on her slippers. It reminded Parsefall that he was still in his nightshirt. 'Wait 'ere,' he directed her, and went back to the White Room to change. He threw on his clothes, shoved his feet into his boots and clomped back down the hall to Clara.

He found her waiting with her hands in her lap. In his absence, she had tidied herself, reknotting her sash and finger-combing her hair. It hadn't done much good. Her curls were snarled, and the skirt of her dress was torn. 'Do you suppose Mrs Fettle will be at breakfast?' she asked.

He shrugged. Then he understood. 'She's going to start askin' you questions, in't she? Wot are you goin' to tell 'er?'

'I don't know.' Clara clasped her knees. 'I suppose I shall have to say that Mr Grisini kidnapped me and held me prisoner. It's what happened, after all. Only as soon as I say *kidnapped*, everyone will want to know where I've been, and I can't tell the truth, because no one will believe me. I suppose I might describe an empty building – I'm sure there *are* empty buildings about, shepherd's huts and so forth – but I've never been in a shepherd's hut and I don't know what it's like.' She pinched her skirt between her fingers and added petulantly, 'I'm ever so tired of this dress.'

Parsefall sat down next to her. He didn't care about dresses, but he was always interested in the construction of a plausible lie. 'Tell 'em it woz dark. Tell 'em it woz so dark you can't say what it looked like. Then one night, you found a rusty nail and pried open a loose board and crawled outside, and come 'ere. And then Grisini come after you.'

Clara gazed at him admiringly. 'That's a good story.' She bent her head, hugging her knees tighter. 'But whatever story I tell, someone will send a telegram to London, so my parents will know I'm safe. And then I shall have to go home.'

'Why?' demanded Parsefall.

'Because I must. I *want* to go home,' she corrected herself. She got to her feet and started down the stairs.

Parsefall trailed after her. He saw that her back looked stiff and that she moved like a clockwork figure. He supposed that was what thinking about her family did to her. 'Wot if you don't go back?'

Clara turned to face him. 'I must.'

'You don't want to.'

Clara shook her head in unconscious agreement. 'I know Papa and Mamma have been dreadfully worried,' she said, her forehead puckering. 'It makes me ache, to think of the pain I've caused. Of course, it isn't all my fault; I didn't ask Grisini to kidnap me. Our home isn't a very happy one, but that isn't why I mind going. It's leaving you and Lizzie Rose. I never had friends before. I never met anyone –' She stopped to compose herself. 'I never met anyone like you in my life.'

Parsefall was immensely flattered. He wondered if 'you' meant just himself or himself and Lizzie Rose. He hoped it meant only him. But Clara was still speaking. 'I wish we needn't part. I could bear it if we could go on being friends. But of course, I *will* bear it. It's only that I shall miss you. That's all.'

Parsefall shoved his hands in his pockets. 'It ain't as if we're going to stay 'ere forever. Lizzie Rose'll want to stay till the old lady dies, 'cos she feels sorry for 'er. She's always feelin' sorry for people,' he added resentfully. 'But after the old lady dies, we'll go back to London.'

Clara shook her head. 'Madama's going to give you Strachan's Ghyll. I heard her say so this morning. I was half asleep, but I heard quite clearly. She's leaving the house to both of you.'

'I don't want the blinkin' 'ouse,' Parsefall said testily. He swept his hand through the air, dismissing the carved staircase, the gold-framed portraits, the melancholy stags with their branching antlers. 'It's 'andsome enough, but I can't make a livin' 'ere. There ain't no audience. Once the old lady dies, I'll come back to London an' live at Mrs Pinchbeck's. Only thing is, the coppers is after me.'

'Why?'

'Because I prigged a photograph of your bruvver in 'is coffin.'

'What do you mean – prigged?'

Parsefall wrinkled his nose. 'Stole,' he said, as if experimenting with the word. 'The frame woz silver. Lizzie Rose wouldn't let me hock it at the pawnshop, an' your father went to see Lizzie Rose and saw it on the mantelpiece.'

'Oh,' said Clara. 'Well, never mind. I'll tell Papa you saved my life, and he'll make the coppers leave you alone.'

Parsefall had forgotten that he had saved Clara's life. Now that he was reminded of it, it occurred to him that his conduct had been heroic. He had crossed the breaking ice without fear and on bare feet. Under the circumstances, Clara ought to admire him more. 'Ain't you going to thank me?'

Clara considered this. Something flashed in her eyes, and Parsefall recalled that she'd stolen the fire opal in order to keep it from falling into his hands. The corners of her mouth lifted in a smile. 'One day.'

It was a curious answer, but it suited Parsefall. Lizzie Rose sometimes wept when she felt grateful or tried to clasp him around the neck. Now that Clara was human again, he didn't want to get too close to her. She seemed to feel the same way and kept him at arm's length.

They went on downstairs and descended to the cellars. To their disappointment, the kitchen was empty. The fire was burning, but there was no smell of food, no dishes in the sink, nothing to suggest that a meal had been served or would ever be served. Parsefall had begun to explore the pantry when the door opened and Lizzie Rose came in with Ruby.

Lizzie Rose's cheeks glowed with cold, but her eyes looked troubled. She knelt down, removed the leash from Ruby's collar, and said, 'There, now! Run upstairs to Madama!' She looked accusingly at Parsefall and Clara. 'Did you leave Madama's door open?'

'Dunno,' Parsefall began, but Clara answered, 'Yes.' She went to Lizzie Rose and took her hands. 'What's the matter?'

Lizzie Rose said, 'The servants are gone. And Grisini –'

'Ain't he dead?' gasped Parsefall.

'No, no, he's dead,' Lizzie Rose said quickly, 'but, oh, it was so dreadful! I took Ruby out and she headed for the lake – it's ice again; it must have frozen overnight. You can see where the cracks were – but Grisini's there, under the ice, dark with the cracks all round him, like a spider in its web –' She shuddered. 'Someone will have to break the ice and get the body out – but the servants are gone, all of them.' She pointed to a sheet of paper on the kitchen table. 'I came down this morning and found that letter. Mrs Fettle wrote that she paid everyone's wages out of the housekeeping money because they all decided to leave. Everyone at once. *We've come to our senses and at last we're free* – that's what the letter says. I suppose they were under a spell, and now it's broken. But I don't know if Mr Fettle ever went for the constable, and Madama ought to see a doctor, and now there's Grisini and his horrid, *horrid* corpse.' Her eyes brimmed with tears. Parsefall felt the familiar knot in his stomach.

Clara drew out a chair and pushed Lizzie Rose into it. 'You've been up all night, and you've had a shock,' she said evenly. 'Parsefall, put the kettle on. Lizzie Rose ought to have a cup of tea. And look in the pantry for some sugar. Papa says sugar is good for shock.'

Somewhat to his surprise, Parsefall complied. He hoisted the kettle and found it full, placed it on the stove and began to search the kitchen shelves for a tin of tea. He wondered if he was going to like Clara now that she could speak. It was plain to him that she was going to be even more domineering than Lizzie Rose.

'We shall have to keep the fires burning,' Clara said, tallying her ideas on her fingers. 'That can't be so very difficult; one puts on coal. There's likely to be food in the pantry, and I suppose someone could fetch a doctor, if there's a horse in the stable

– only I shouldn't know how to put on the harness. Have either of you ever harnessed a horse?'

Parsefall looked blank. Lizzie Rose only sobbed.

'I suppose not,' Clara said, answering her own question. She patted Lizzie Rose's shoulder. 'Never mind, dearest, we'll manage. There must be a road somewhere, and we can ask . . .' Her voice trailed away, as if she, too, felt daunted by the problems ahead. She turned to Parsefall. 'Have you found any sugar for your sister's tea?'

Parsefall began mechanically, 'She ain't my true sister –'

Clara slapped his face.

The slap shocked all three of them. Parsefall stepped back with his hand to his cheek. Lizzie Rose cried, 'How dare you?' and leaped to her feet, ready to fly at Clara.

Clara spoke up fiercely. 'He oughtn't to say that,' she said. 'Parsefall, you mustn't, do you hear me?' Her voice softened. 'He doesn't mean to be unkind,' she told Lizzie Rose. 'It's just that he had another sister, who died in the workhouse. Her name was Eppie.'

'Eppie?' echoed Lizzie Rose.

'That was her name, wasn't it?' Clara asked Parsefall. 'Eppie was his true sister, and she was very good to him. Parsefall's loyal. He doesn't want to forget her – but you mustn't say that any more, Parsefall, because Lizzie Rose *is* your true sister. I've seen her fight for you and share her food and hold your head when you're sick. There isn't anything truer than that.'

Parsefall cast a hangdog look at Lizzie Rose. Lizzie Rose knew this for the apology it was and forgave him at once. 'Oh, Parsefall!' she cried – but all at once, they heard a bell ringing, and Ruby began to bark.

'It's Madama,' Lizzie Rose said breathlessly, but the placard under the ringing bell read FRONT DOOR. 'Perhaps it's Mrs Fettle coming back. Or even the doctor –' She snatched up her skirts and ran.

Parsefall and Clara trailed after her. Neither of them cared to admit it, but the idea that an adult had come to the house was reassuring. An adult would know where the village was and what to do about Madama.

'Clara!' shrieked Lizzie Rose. 'Your papa! Oh, Clara, *Clara*!'

Clara was a little behind Parsefall. Now she flashed past him like a falling star. She flew up the stairs and through the rooms and across the tiles of the Great Hall. She flung herself at her father, and he lifted her and spun her in circles. There was a great confusion of sound: shouting and sobbing and Ruby barking, accompanied by sympathetic noises from Lizzie Rose. The front door stood open, and a cold draught roared in.

Parsefall shivered. He wished someone would shut the door. He considered doing it himself but held back; in order to get to the door, he would have to pass through what seemed a great crowd of weeping, rejoicing people. He remained in the shadow of the stone columns, watching the scene with his hands in his pockets.

'Mrs Wintermute, ma'am! Oh, Dr Wintermute, help me!' Lizzie Rose ran to support Clara's mother. 'Oh, please, sir – she's quite faint!'

Clara broke away from her father and rushed to her mother's side. Dr Wintermute caught his wife before she fell and dragged her to the staircase. He ordered her to sit with her head between her knees. 'Oh, poor Mamma,' breathed Clara while her mother wailed, 'Oh, Clara, my dearest, why did you run away? How could you be so cruel?'

Clara was speechless. Parsefall stepped out from behind the

column. 'She didn't run away,' he said coolly. 'She woz kidnapped and locked in the tower.'

Clara flashed him a look of intense gratitude.

'In the tower that fell down last night.' Parsefall pointed in the direction of the ruin. 'Grisini kidnapped 'er and locked 'er up all right and tight. And the tower woz fallin' down, an' everyone said not to go near it. Didn't they, Lizzie Rose?'

Lizzie Rose picked up her cue. 'Oh, yes, they did!'

'I didn't know where I was,' Clara said, taking up the thread of the tale. 'All I knew was that I couldn't get out. But Lizzie Rose and Parsefall were suspicious of Grisini, and they came to Strachan's Ghyll to find me.'

Parsefall grinned, appreciating the fact that he had just been promoted to the role of rescuer. 'So then we come.' He crossed to the door and slammed it shut, enjoying the bang. 'We 'ad our suspicions, didn't we, Lizzie Rose? We followed Grisini up 'ere, and we looked for Clara, but we didn't go into the tower, 'cos it was too dangerous and might fall down.'

'But I escaped,' explained Clara. 'There was a loose board and I pried it open with a rusty nail. Then Grisini came after me – and it was dark, and I was running away from the house, and he chased me out on to the frozen lake. It was only last night,' she said, amazed that it had all happened so recently.

'And there was an earthquake,' Lizzie Rose put in. 'It made the ice break and the tower fall –'

'And Grisini fell through the ice – and I should have fallen too, only Lizzie Rose called out to me and told me to lie flat. And Parsefall brought me a rope – he walked across the ice as it was cracking into pieces. He saved my life!'

Clara drew herself out of her mother's embrace and stood erect. She stretched out her hands, and the other two children stepped forward, as if the three of them were playing a scene they had rehearsed.

'Papa, Mamma,' said Clara, clinging to Lizzie Rose's hand, 'this is my sister. And Parsefall is my brother.' She extended her other hand, and Parsefall gripped it tightly. 'They set me free and they saved my life. They're my brother and sister, now and forever. They must come back with us and live with us in Chester Square.'

Dr Wintermute looked bewildered. Mrs Wintermute stopped in mid-sob.

'Only, Papa, dear Papa, you mustn't send Parsefall to school or make him be a gentleman,' Clara went on. 'He doesn't want to be a doctor, do you, Parsefall? He wants to be an apprentice with the Royal Marionettes. You could arrange that, couldn't you, Papa? And then one day he'll have his own theatre.'

Parsefall nodded emphatically, squeezing her fingers.

'But Lizzie Rose can be a lady,' Clara said coaxingly, 'because she's going to inherit Strachan's Ghyll. Madama – the woman who lives here – is going to leave her estate to Parsefall and Lizzie Rose. So Lizzie Rose will be an heiress, and we can have lessons together from Miss Cameron. And Parsefall will work during the day, but he'll come home every evening, so we can be together.'

Her parents continued to look stupefied. Lizzie Rose intervened. 'Clara,' she said, 'I don't think this is the time –'

'There is no other time.' Clara's face was implacable. 'Please, Mamma, say you agree! Please say that Parsefall and Lizzie Rose may come and live with us! I want them so – oh, Mamma, please!'

Mrs Wintermute began to weep again. It didn't seem to Parsefall that this was any kind of an answer, but it seemed to satisfy Clara. She flew at her mother and kissed her rapturously.

'Oh, Mamma, dear Mamma! Oh, thank you! Oh, we're going to be so happy!'

Mrs Wintermute's face was a study. She was smiling tremulously, but her face was pale. She touched the tips of her fingers to her forehead and gasped for breath.

'Clara,' said Lizzie Rose reproachfully, 'we ought to give your mamma a glass of wine. There's some in Madama's room – oh!' She turned to Dr Wintermute, clasping her hands. 'Oh, Dr Wintermute, please, won't you come upstairs and see Madama? She lives here and she's very ill, and it wasn't her fault Grisini kidnapped Clara, and the servants have all left. We've been so worried! But thank goodness, you're a doctor, so if you would just come and examine her –'

Dr Wintermute's face changed. It lost none of its happiness but became alert and purposeful. 'I will certainly see to Madama,' he promised, and, as yet unable to part with Clara, he took his daughter's hand and followed Lizzie Rose up the stairs.

# Chapter Fifty-one

# Last Rites

There was a Thing on the ceiling. In the last days of her life, Cassandra felt it brooding over her: a Thing that hovered, waiting. She couldn't see it, because the canopy of the bed blocked her vision; when she was in her right mind, she told herself it wasn't there. Nevertheless, the fancy persisted. She felt its presence most powerfully when her eyes were closed and she heard the rush of air beneath its wings. Once she dreamed that she floated up on the ceiling and hung beside it, gazing down at her swollen body. Then she tumbled down again, into that body and on to the bed.

The house had changed. There was mercy in it now. The servants who tended her were strangers who didn't know her and therefore did not hate her. They treated her as if she was deserving of pity and respect. There was a new doctor, an imposing man with a deep voice and deft hands. He spoke to her kindly, and his drugs eased her pain. In her moments of clarity, she understood that the doctor was Clara's father. Then the fever returned, and he became a hobgoblin, an impostor. Cassandra shrieked at him, demanding to know where he came from and why he didn't cure her.

He couldn't cure her. Even as she clung to life, Cassandra understood that. Her body was failing. At intervals, her old nightmares returned to mock her. She cowered inside a ring of flames: scarlet and yellow and green and blue. She screamed and thrashed with terror until the doctor came and held her, murmuring nonsense, as if she was a sick child.

When the fever broke, her mind was knife sharp. She was wide-awake when the lawyer came and she dictated her will, leaving Strachan's Ghyll to Elizabeth Rose Fawr and Parsefall Hooke. The gatehouse went to Clara, along with any jewels that Parsefall had missed. Cassandra also instructed the lawyer to arrange for Grisini's burial in the Strachan family cemetery. Grisini was a monster, but she would not deny him the hospitality of a grave.

There came a night when her fever reached its pitch and the pain was harrowing. A priest appeared at her bedside. She saw that her dressing table had been covered with a white cloth and set with a crucifix and candles. *'Asperges me, Domine, hyssopo, et mundabor; lavabis me et super nivem dealbabor.'* Her father had taught her Latin when she was small, but she no longer understood the words of the psalm. She had forgotten most of the faith of her childhood but not all; when she realised that the priest had come to administer the last rites, she opened her lips and began to confess.

Afterwards she had no idea what she said. Her sins were too numerous to name, and halfway through the telling of one, she thought of another. Often she broke off to explain that she had been tempted beyond her strength; what she had done wasn't entirely her fault. She told how she had stolen the jewel from Marguerite and sobbed with anguish for her lost friend. She tried to recount the spells she had cast, but the priest shook his head in bewilderment, and she knew he didn't believe her. She could not tell if what she felt was remorse or only sorrow, but she went on confessing until her voice gave out. As she drifted into sleep, she felt the soothing touch of holy oil on her eyelids. She thought, *Now the Angel of Death will come down from the ceiling and carry me away.* But she was wrong. The next day she was better, and the doctor said she had rallied.

The dog, Ruby, seldom left her bed. Even when Cassandra was too weak to raise her head, she heard the spaniel snoring and was comforted by its animal presence. The aroma of food sickened her, but she enjoyed the smell of the dog: a rank and earthy odour, like Stilton cheese. Having the dog on her bed helped to keep the Thing at bay.

Often when she awakened, the children were in the room. Lizzie Rose visited her faithfully, and so did Clara. Parsefall came seldom and never alone. Cassandra thought that he was more intuitive than the others; he sensed the presence of the Thing on the ceiling, and he didn't like it. Unlike the girls, he didn't know how to behave in the sickroom: he paced, fidgeted and swore, forgetting to lower his voice. 'P'raps she'd like to see the puppets,' he suggested one afternoon.

Cassandra had been half asleep, but his words brought her out of her stupor. She blinked and concentrated until the room came into focus. The children were lounging before the fire. They were warmly and handsomely dressed. Cassandra supposed that the new clothes, like the servants, had been sent up from London.

Parsefall persisted. 'She 'asn't anyfink to do,' he pointed out, 'and it's dull for 'er, just lyin' there. She might like to see the puppets.'

Cassandra sucked the saliva in her mouth, running her tongue over her gums. 'The puppets,' she said hoarsely. 'They dance, don't they? I want to see them dance.'

Parsefall scrambled to his feet. 'There, di'n't I tell you? She wants 'em. There's an 'ornpipe, and a skeleton dance, and a ballet –' He stopped. ''Cept there's no ballet, 'cos I don't 'ave the puppet for it. But we could give you the 'ornpipe or the Magnetic Skeleton. Which do you want? The skeleton's better.'

Lizzie Rose demurred. 'I don't think the skeleton dance –'

'But the skeleton dance *is* better than the 'ornpipe,' Parsefall insisted. 'She won't mind a graveyard and a few bones.'

'Bones,' echoed Cassandra. 'I don't mind bones.' She shut her eyes and sleep overwhelmed her. The children's voices seemed to swell in volume and then diminish. She slept.

When she opened her eyes, she saw that the children had erected a stage opposite the bed. There was a backdrop painted with tombstones, and Lizzie Rose was tuning the strings of a small violin. Parsefall pointed to Cassandra. 'See? She's awake. She woz just resting 'er eyes.'

'She won't be able to see lying down,' said Clara. 'We'll have to prop her up.'

Cassandra moaned in anticipation. It hurt her to be moved, especially by the children, who lacked the strength to lift her easily. But neither Clara nor Lizzie Rose understood that the groan was a protest. They yanked and shoved her into a sitting position, wedging a mountain of pillows behind her back.

The children took their places. Lizzie Rose slipped her fiddle under her chin and lifted the bow. Parsefall ducked behind the canvas. The Magnetic Skeleton capered on to the stage: a grotesque little figure with an insinuating grin. Cassandra found herself grinning back. It tickled her that the boy dared to make fun of the Thing on the ceiling. When the skeleton's legs broke away from the torso and began to jig alone, her grin broadened; when the skull munched the air, she clacked her teeth in sympathy. As the dance came to an end, she cried, 'Encore!' but before the dance began again, her attention shifted to Clara.

The girl was clapping enthusiastically. Her back was straight, and there was a smile on her lips. Nevertheless, she was miserable: Cassandra had not the slightest doubt of that. She snapped, 'What's the matter with you?'

Clara gave a little jump. She responded, 'Nothing, ma'am,' but Cassandra contradicted her.

'You're envious – that's what ails you.' She felt a childish triumph in being able to pinpoint the problem. 'I know envy when I see it! You miss being part of the show. I remember now; you want to be a dancer. Lud, child, if that's what you want, don't sit with your hands in your lap! Go and dance for me!'

'I can't.' A flush of mortification rose to Clara's cheeks. 'I could only dance when I was a puppet. I never had lessons – we were always in mourning. Mamma said it wouldn't be proper.'

Cassandra mimicked her. '"Mamma said it wouldn't be proper!" Lud, child, your mother's so glad to have you back, she'd let you dance naked if you chose. Don't hide your face in your mother's skirts! And for God's sake, don't blush!' Her voice sharpened. 'You're not a mouse! A mouse wouldn't have shattered my fire opal. Go and dance!'

'I'm clumsy,' faltered Clara. 'You know I am – you said so yourself, that night in the tower –'

Cassandra cast her mind back to that night. She recalled the puppet-child darting from mirror to mirror like a white moth. 'You're not clumsy.' Her eyes narrowed. 'You're ashamed. That's why you can't dance; that's what trips you up! You're holding on to a secret, aren't you, Clara Wintermute? I almost saw it when you walked the labyrinth. Then you stopped me. There's something you did – something that shuts you up and turns your limbs to lead. What was it?'

Lizzie Rose put down her fiddle. Parsefall came from behind the stage, still holding the Magnetic Skeleton. They moved towards Clara, one on either side. But Clara didn't seem to know they were there. She stared at Cassandra: a bird hypnotised by a snake.

'What is it?' Cassandra repeated. 'Whatever it is, you ought to tell me.' Her mouth twisted in an upside-down smile. 'In fact, there's no one better you could tell. Whatever you've done, I've done worse. Out with it!'

Clara opened her mouth, but no sound came out. Her pupils were dilated.

'Did you tell a lie? Steal something? Murder anyone?'

'I took my brother's life.'

Cassandra let out her breath. She knew that she must be careful what she said next. She racked her brains for something wise and kind. But the words that escaped her were callous. 'That's a clever trick, if you can manage it. How did you take his life?'

The room was utterly silent. Clara blinked the tears out of her eyes. 'It was in the watercress. The cholera. I didn't know that, of course. I only knew that I hated eating green things. And Agnes said that if I didn't eat the watercress, I shouldn't have any pudding. There was chestnut pudding that day, and I wanted some dreadfully.'

'Go on.'

'There were five of us children. So there were two trays at nursery tea, and Agnes had to help the maid carry the trays back to the kitchen. That meant we children were alone for a few minutes. I still had my plate in front of me, because I was supposed to eat the watercress, and Addie and Selina were playing with the doll's house. So I asked Charles Augustus – he was my twin – if he'd eat the watercress for me, so that I could have pudding. And he did. He never minded what he ate.'

'Go on.'

'But the sickness was in the watercress.' The words spilled out faster now. Clara was trembling. 'I heard Papa talking about it. Not right after they died but years later, when I was old enough to understand. He said there was a doctor who had studied – who had *proved* – that cholera came from filthy water. The watercress must have grown by a dirty stream. But of course, I didn't eat any of it. Charles Augustus ate it for me.'

Cassandra waited to make sure that Clara had finished. Then, deliberately, she opened her mouth and laughed. She cackled until the bed shook and the walls echoed.

Clara got to her feet. She looked as if she wanted to run away but could not make up her mind to do so. She pressed her fingers over her mouth.

'Is that all?' retorted Cassandra. 'Is that the secret you've been clutching to your heart all these years? That you wanted a dish of chestnut pudding? God save you, you poor, innocent little fool – everyone wants his share of chestnut pudding –'

'You don't understand,' Clara said desperately. 'He ate the watercress for me – I killed him –'

'Cholera killed him,' Cassandra said sharply. 'You stupid, stupid girl! Don't you know that killing is a decision? You never chose to poison your brother. You chose chestnut pudding over watercress. By the by, when the pudding came, did you eat his share? Did you steal his pudding, you naughty girl?'

'No,' Clara answered indignantly. A little colour came into her cheeks; against this charge she could defend herself.

'Neither did you steal his life,' Cassandra said. She beckoned with one limp hand. 'My dear stupid child, you must set aside your gloomy conscience. You killed no one. You survived. If you'd eaten the watercress, your parents would have lost five children instead of four – did you ever think of that? I tell you, leave it alone. And now you must dance. I am on my deathbed, and I command you.' Cassandra twisted towards Lizzie Rose. 'Play your fiddle, girl. I want to see her dance.'

Lizzie Rose looked uncertain. But Parsefall nodded, so she lifted her bow and placed the violin under her chin. Clara opened her mouth to protest. Cassandra felt a great fatigue – the laughter she had forced out of her body had drained her to the dregs. But she rapped out one last syllable, *'Dance!'* and Clara raised herself on half-pointe in order to begin.


It was silly to dance in a wool frock and cashmere stockings. Clara knew that she was doomed to make a fool of herself. She remembered the steps of the ballet – she had rehearsed them a hundred times – but she couldn't dance, not really. Madama was going to laugh at her, and so would Parsefall. Even Lizzie Rose would laugh, though she would try not to.

The voice of the fiddle was meltingly sweet. Clara brought her arms together, crossing her wrists. She shifted her weight to her right leg and swung her left foot forward, toes pointed so hard they hurt. She arched her back, following the movement of her hand with her eyes – her hand, which had no string passing through it. Her hand was her own, to move as she liked. Whether to dance or not was her choice.

And she chose to dance. It was harder than it had been when she was a puppet. Gravity fought against her, and her muscles were tight. But she was dancing, not being danced, and at that thought, she glided forward, not one stride but three. As a puppet, she had been forced to stay within the compass of Parsefall's arm. Now she could skip and spin over every inch of the room.

She quickened her steps and tried a *cabriole*, remembering how it felt to soar through the air. No one laughed, so she tried another, her arms opening as if to embrace the room. She glided and swayed, leaped and spun, until she was breathless.

The dance concluded with an *arabesque*. Clara concentrated, pulling herself into stillness. She couldn't raise her leg as high as she had when she was a puppet. But she kept her balance, sustaining the pose by sheer willpower, following the music – *one, two, three, off!* As she dropped into a curtsy, Lizzie Rose and Parsefall applauded, smacking their hands together with all their might.

Cassandra wanted to applaud too. She tried to move her right hand, but it stayed where it was, limp against the bedclothes. She endeavoured to speak. 'That was one good –' Her words were slurred. She wanted to tell the children that at her eleventh hour, she had done one good thing; she had released Clara from her secret, and set her free to dance. But all at once, there were no words. The sound that came from her was fearsome and strangled. It made the children rush to her side.

They looked dreadfully frightened. Clara shouted at Parsefall to fetch her father, but he stayed where he was, frozen and aghast. Ruby was barking, her hackles raised. Lizzie Rose caught hold of Cassandra's right hand, and Clara seized the left. Cassandra would have liked to grip their fingers in gratitude, but there was no strength left in her. She felt herself jerk as if some great beast were shaking her between its jaws. The world darkened, and the Thing swooped down. There was a moment of frantic struggle before she understood that the Thing was holy. Then the thread that fastened her soul to her body was broken, and she died before the children let go of her hands.

# Epilogue

The funeral was endless. Parsefall stood in the Strachan family cemetery, mentally cursing the priest. He scuffed the melting snow with the toe of his boots, watching the white crystals turn pewter grey. It astonished him how waterproof his new boots were; with wool socks and good boots, he could wade through the slush with warm, dry feet.

He looked over his shoulder at Lizzie Rose, the only person at the funeral who was teary eyed. She stood arm in arm with Clara's mother. Mrs Wintermute reached into her muff and brought out a lace-trimmed handkerchief for Lizzie Rose. *Thick as thieves* was Parsefall's summing up of the situation. Mrs Wintermute had not expected to have two strange children thrust upon her, but it had taken her less than a fortnight to grow fond of Lizzie Rose. Parsefall fancied that Clara was a little jealous, but he didn't pity her. From now on, Clara would have him and Lizzie Rose. She would be all right.

It was Lizzie Rose who had insisted that the whole family should attend the funeral, defying the custom that ladies should stay at home. 'We *must* go,' Lizzie Rose had said resolutely, 'or Madama won't have anyone but the doctor and the priest.' Her certainty had carried the day, and the three females had followed Cassandra's casket to the graveside.

The cemetery lay in a hollow near the crest of a hill. From its vantage point, one could see Lake Windermere. Parsefall cared little for scenery unless it was onstage, but the landscape before him compelled his attention. The day of Cassandra's funeral was windy and perversely bright. The ice on the lake had thawed, and the water reflected the colours of the winter sky. When the wind blew, it was as if a handful of diamonds had been cast over the waves. Parsefall raised his eyes to the sky. Lizzie Rose had once told him that the world was round like an orange and spun in a circle every day. He had thought that she was hoaxing him, but now he wasn't so sure; as he watched the cloud shadows move over the fells, he felt the earth moving.

'*Illuminare his qui in tenebris et in umbra mortis sedent*' – the priest raised his voice, trying to recall the attention of his audience – '*ad dirigendos pedes nostros in viam paci –*'

Parsefall yawned. Until Cassandra's funeral, he had never heard Latin, and he thought it was insane that anyone should preach in a language no one understood. It seemed to him that the priest had a malicious desire to prolong the service as much as possible. The old man had prayed and chanted and paid innumerable attentions to the casket. He had lit candles around it and splashed it with water and fumigated it with smoke from a little teakettle on a chain. Now that the body was at the graveside, he seemed inclined to start all over again, sprinkling more water on the grave and beginning another round of prayers. There was no telling when he would stop. Parsefall tried to catch Clara's eye, but she was on her best behaviour. She stood erect and still, with her hands clasped in front of her. Parsefall was tempted to pick up a handful of slush and slip it down the collar of her dress.

He shifted his weight and sighed heavily. Dr Wintermute caught his glance. During the church service, Parsefall had tried to amuse himself by rhythmically cracking the spine of his hymnbook. Dr Wintermute had gazed at him steadily and laid a gentle hand on his shoulder. It was a form of rebuke unlike anything Parsefall had encountered, and he hadn't yet learned how to fight against it. He turned sideways, avoiding the doctor's eyes. Old Wintermute had said he would have to learn to read. Parsefall wasn't looking forward to that, but Clara and Lizzie Rose had promised him that it wasn't hard and that it would help him to run his theatre one day.

His theatre. At that thought, the priest's voice receded, and Parsefall fell into a daydream. The thing he had dreamed of was going to come true. One day he'd have his own theatre – proscenium and backstage and bridge – and in the meantime, Clara had proposed that they should erect a theatre in the nursery. As soon as the Wintermutes returned to London, he would go back to Mrs Pinchbeck's and lay claim to Grisini's old rig-up. Clara was going to stitch the curtains, and he was going to teach her how to work the *fantoccini*. They could begin right away, and in a little while he would be apprenticed to the Royal Marionettes.

If only the funeral would end! He scraped the slush with his toe, admiring the vivid green of the moss underneath. Nothing could be done; no new life could begin, until the priest shut up. His eyes passed from the patch of moss to Grisini's recently dug grave. He smiled.

Grisini's tombstone was a small one, ordered in haste and engraved only with his name. There was nothing else to write: Grisini had been no one's beloved husband or father or brother, and the question of where he would spend the afterlife was best not raised. One did not describe a puppet master's skill on his tombstone. Nevertheless, Parsefall had a nagging feeling that something was missing. Quite suddenly, he knew what it was, and he sniggered, earning a sharp look from Dr Wintermute.

He would bring Madama's brass monkey to the grave and let it perch on Grisini's tombstone. He had known that monkey would come in useful sooner or later. What better than to have it leering over Grisini? It had bent legs; he was fairly certain it would stay in place atop the stone. If not, he could prop it up with rocks.

He wanted to tell Lizzie Rose. He edged closer and whispered into her ear, 'The monkey. Let's bring the monkey 'ere and put it on Grisini's grave.'

She looked startled.

'On the stone,' he hissed. 'Wiv its legs 'angin' over the edge.'

He saw her consider the idea. After a moment, she whispered, 'I suppose he'd like that.'

Parsefall rolled his eyes in exasperation. He wasn't trying to please Grisini; he was trying to desecrate his tomb. All the same, Lizzie Rose had a point. Grisini's sense of humour had been unholy; he might like that cruel-faced monkey squatting over his corpse. Parsefall's forehead knotted and then cleared. The thing was artistically right. He wondered what Clara would think of the idea.

She was still obstinately behaving herself. He stared at her back, frustrated. He remembered when she was a puppet. In those days, all he would have had to do was hook a finger under the string that screwed into her temple, and she would have turned her head –

Her shoulder twitched. After a moment, she twisted around to frown at him.

Parsefall whispered, 'I got summink to tell you.'

Clara nodded very slightly. She mouthed the word *later* and jerked her head towards the casket. The priest was making the sign of the cross. The pallbearers came forward to grip the handles of the casket. It seemed that at long last, Cassandra's body was about to be lowered into the grave.

Parsefall was tempted to fling his cap in the air. It was almost over. There was going to be roast beef and Yorkshire pudding for dinner, and afterwards the grown-ups would go off with their newspapers and embroidery. He saw Clara bow her head to hide a smile, and he turned back to wink at Lizzie Rose. They were waiting, all three of them, for the moment when they could be alone again and free to laugh together.

## ACKNOWLEDGEMENTS

Special thanks to Carol Mason, who helped me with British diction and dialect and inspired me with her impersonations of Parsefall Hooke and Mrs Pinchbeck. Special thanks also to Barry Smith, of the Friends of Kensal Green Cemetery, who shared his encyclopedic knowledge of Victorian burial customs and sent me photographs of catafalques, coffins and mausoleums.

I could not have consulted two more generous experts. And any mistakes in the manuscript are my own.